Rob Ryan was born in Liverpool in 1951, although his inability to master either the tricky accent or the legendary scouse wit eventually saw him exiled to the south, specifically London, where he ended up taking a Masters degree in Environmental Pollution Science at Brunel University. He subsequently lectured until the mid-1980s, when he stumbled into a bar in Soho and decided that he, too, would join the media. His first articles were published in *The Face*, *Arena*, American *GQ* and *The Sunday Times*. He joined the staff of the latter in 1990 as Deputy Travel Editor. In 1997 he left to help launch *Conde Nast Traveller*, before deciding that what he really wanted to do in life was finish *Underdogs*. He is now a freelance writer and lives in London with his wife and three children, one of whom has the uncanny ability to speak in a scouse accent.

underdogs

ROB RYAN

First published in Great Britain in 1999
by HEADLINE BOOK PUBLISHING

10 9 8 7 6 5 4 3 2 1

ISBN 0 7472 6119 9

Typeset by Avon Dataset Ltd, Bidford-on-Avon, Warks

Printed and bound in Great Britain by
Mackays of Chatham plc, Chatham, Kent

HEADLINE BOOK PUBLISHING
A division of Hodder Headline PLC
338 Euston Road
London NW1 3BH

To Deborah, for a thousand reasons and a reason

Our imagination, and our dreams, are forever invading our memories; and since we are all apt to believe in the reality of our fantasies, we end up transforming our lies into truths. Of course fantasy and reality are equally personal, and equally felt, so their confusion is a matter of only relative importance.

– Luis Bunuel.

PROLOGUE

The Ben Moc (Big Mac) Woods, north of Cu Chi Town, Vietnam. 1969.

He sensed the patrol even before he heard them, picked up the vibrations of the Armoured Personnel Carrier that disgorged the soldiers onto his patch, heard the wind carry their nervous, jokey exchanges. Crouching in his pit, surrounded by fetid, crumbling earth and the severed stumps of tree roots, Tran Van Giang was attuned to the surrounding soil. His entire body, after thousands of hours' moving through the blackness, had evolved, mole-like, into an organic receiver and amplifier of movement. From the heavy fall of enormous feet encased in GI boots to the softest multi-limbed scrapings of the giant centipedes that roamed the burrows, he perceived every intrusion into his world, above and below ground.

He tried not to think too much about the creatures that shared his crepuscular domain, about the mites that his wife had painfully picked out from his arms and legs with a heated needle just ten days before. Already, in the forty-eight hours since his return underground, he could feel new invaders slipping effortlessly under his skin, raising tiny tracks as they made their random progress around his limbs. His wife had been right: as far as the land was concerned, he must be like one of the mites, burrowing and digging and worming his way just below the surface. It wasn't, she said, natural. It was no way to treat the country, the planet, living in it like some lurking parasite, when he should be in the sunlight, farming and raising cattle and children.

He felt the APC rumble off, probably to a pre-arranged pick-up point. There had been a time when helicopters would have provided aerial surveillance and back-up, but their losses to shoulder-launched rockets had proved too grievous even for the Yankees. The soldiers, meanwhile, would be sweeping forward, looking for his underground hiding place. Well, not his, but any evidence of tunnels like his in the vicinity. He was glad and grateful that he had carefully re-planted the lid of the trapdoor just before dawn, meticulously arranging fresh green shoots into random patterns, and dumping the old decaying camouflage branches many metres away. He had deliberately taken his time so as to linger long enough to feel the first rays of sunlight on his skin, the beams that brought the Americans out of their camps and into the countryside, where, if all went well, he would kill them.

Now he could hear the patrol coming, probably line abreast, each one swivelling his head, frantically scanning the ground for Charlie, gooks, slopes, zips, VCs, slants, and all the other terms they used to dehumanise the elusive enemy. The element of surprise to Tran's assault was long gone: these days the GIs knew all about the pop-up soldiers and their trapdoors. Yet, despite that, every time they seemed genuinely shocked, like a little child with a spring-loaded toy, repeatedly wondering how it could possibly work, marvelling at how an entire army could operate underground almost without trace. And without cold drinks, too.

Tran played the old game, mentally gambling with himself as to just how many Americans there would be when he stood and lifted the lid. At stake, of course, was his life. If he misjudged this he, like too many of his comrades over the last five years, would be blown apart by M-16 fire before he had a chance to so much as aim. They would be taking him home in a couple of rice sacks if that happened. He realised he was holding his breath at the prospect of his wife explaining to their daughter, years in the future, how her father had died a hero. In a filthy hole in the ground. He must remember to breathe.

The air was the worst part of tunnel life. Going back to his village for a week's precious leave for the first time in over a year made him realise that. Not that he was complaining. He was lucky to have had it at all – the cadre had been uncharacteristically generous; the Northerners never got to return; the Ho Chi Minh trail was one-way for them.

But coming up and walking and cooking and eating above ground, seeing colours and the sky and even, away from this bomb-blasted, chemically scoured zone, trees and birds, perhaps it had been a mistake. He was ashamed to admit to himself, so ashamed he felt like blurting it out at the next self-criticism session, that the very last night he had dared to dream of not coming back, of not lowering himself into the miles of tunnels once again for . . . for how long? They had been at war for twenty-five years or more. Japanese, French, ARVN, and then Americans. It could be another twenty-five years.

Except he knew, when he heard the GI crying in the night after a punji had passed clean through the man's boot and out the top, that something had changed. When he had listened to the big black man wailing and sobbing like Tran's three-month-old daughter, the daughter he got to see for seven short days before coming back to his underworld, he knew that what the cadres had been saying since the Tet Offensive was right – the spirit of these large, hairy foreigners was indeed running low. Perhaps they were all crying like that inside, crying for their daddy to pick them up and take them home. Tran Van Giang, and his companions who made up his fighting cell, they or their friends or their sons and daughters could last another quarter of a century, even breathing this disgusting air. At least, he liked to think so. The Americans must be tiring of losing their feet, their limbs, their lives for nothing at all. Tran should have killed the sobbing soldier that night. Instead, he slipped back into the forest. He couldn't take the life of anything that had reminded him of his daughter. He sucked through his teeth once more.

At the core of that small packet of inhaled air was the scent of soil, the odour of the red clay, overlaid with a musty tang of ripe vegetation and the damp of mildew and fungal growths. But overriding all that were the corruptions added by human life under here – the sweat and shit, the smoke from the underground kitchens, the aroma of a hastily lit Compatriot cigarette, the nauseous stench of rotten rice. Added to this diabolical recipe was the acid sharpness of rat or bat droppings, and worst of all, the unmistakable odour of stale blood from discarded, decomposing bandages. The final ingredients of this olfactory soup issued from hastily buried limbs from even hastier amputations, and, ironically, the dead who had to be kept down here in makeshift graves, until they could be buried in less haste, with due ceremony.

As the casualties mounted, though, sometimes nobody was left who could remember where all the bodies were stored, so digging a new side tunnel occasionally unearthed forgotten heroes of the NLF or the People's Army of North Vietnam. And even those they never found, Tran occasionally felt their ghosts move by him in the tunnel, the breath of their unhappy souls hot on his cheeks. He had built a shrine at home to the dead comrades, charging his wife to tend it well, in case, he too, joined the list. He let himself embrace the feeling he had for his wife, relished the bitter-sweet pain. He missed her.

A rustle made him jump. Someone was sweeping the undergrowth very near his trapdoor. For once there were no booby traps up there, no tripwires, no punji stakes, no exploding Coca-Cola cans or Zippos, no Bouncing Bettys to leap up to groin level and fill American manhood with ball-bearings and steel splinters, nothing to warn them and put them on their guard that there was someone like Tran lurking in the blackness.

For a minute or more he had been aware of the scraping of a human form through the earth below, but from the speed of the movements he knew this was no clumsy, frightened American. There was an earth fall below and behind him, and the softest of grunts, although down here it sounded louder than a water buffalo fart. Nguyen, his face lit by a tiny bamboo shoot/nut oil lamp, appeared at the main tunnel entrance, a metre below. Tran quickly put his finger to his lips, a move he knew was probably unnecessary in Nguyen's case, but even the best of them made mistakes in their excitement. One word could float free of the earth and catch the ear of the Americans, particularly those who had started coming down after them. They, too, had begun to develop odd, inhuman instincts, although not as strong as the Vietnamese. They, after all, still went back to their luxurious bases at night, feeding, he had heard, on steaks almost bigger than Tran himself – perhaps that was where their distinctive greasy meat smell came from – and drinking beer and whisky and even washing in water that had been specially flown in for them, while Tran and the others choked on their cooking smoke or, if it was too dangerous to cook, feasted on what was left of their single rice-ball ration. The only advantage was that being below permanently kept the senses sharp.

Nguyen, who had been spying on the patrol from the far trapdoor, raised his fingers. Eight of them. He slashed the air. Walking in a straight line. He indicated with a pointed crooked finger. Just passing overhead. Tran acknowledged the information and Nguyen slipped away, taking his meagre light with him, leaving Tran back in the darkness. He didn't want to be blinded when he went up: any second now he would flick on the lighter he had retrieved from a dead American and stare at the flame long enough to constrict his pupils a little. Too many times he had popped up and wasted valuable seconds blinking away the scalding tears from eyes unused to the harsh glare of natural light.

The sweeping sounds had stopped. He heard the soldiers shout to each other excitedly, and the thump of running boots. They were too near to have discovered the other trapdoor, and, even though he understood not a word of what they said, he quickly sensed the despondency and disappointment (or was it forced, phony bravado he detected?) as they unearthed nothing but a false alarm. The search resumed.

Soon, then. He checked the carbine by touch. By now Tran could do everything in the dark, anything he was capable of in the light, even fieldstrip this weapon. It wasn't a proper carbine, of course, but one of the hundreds of copies turned out in the subterranean weaponries south of his position, in the Fil Hol garrison. A few metres down the main tunnel, resting in Tran's alcove, was a far superior Chinese AK-47. But that had such a strong signature when fired, GIs instinctively flattened. The carbine sounded like the US weapon that was its distant ancestor, the one that had been captured, stripped and copied and cast from sand moulds in the underground forges, and he knew that for a few moments the soldiers would freeze and check to see what their friends were firing at. Those few moments were all he needed.

Now. He flicked the lighter on and watched the details of his burrow grow dim as the flame danced before him, painfully searing his retina.

Crouched on his narrow ledge, all he had to do was stand and the lid flipped open. The movements were smooth and well practised. Stand, shoulder weapon, fire. Ignore the sky and the surroundings – not that the chemicals and napalm had left much beauty here to distract him – ignore the half a dozen sweet, sweet breaths he would get of real air. Just drop the enemy and disappear.

There were eight all right, six facing forward and two

behind. He was unlucky that day. One of the rear observers saw him immediately and almost got a warning shout out before Tran's carbine bullet took him and spun him backwards. Neck wound. Probably be dead when the medevac helicopters got here. The next two he hit in the back before they had a chance to turn, one in the shoulder-blade, the other in the top of the leg, punching out an arc of shockingly red blood, which seemed to hang there in the early-morning air. An artery, he thought happily. That was a spray of death if ever he saw one. The first rattle of an M-16 sent leaves and twigs dancing to his left. He had allowed himself to be distracted after all. One more shot and back down.

Now, he thought, as the trapdoor slammed shut on the overworld, the game really begins.

PART ONE

At 2.45 pm on June 6, 1889 an overturned glue pot at a workshop on Madison Street began the great fire of Seattle, which destroyed most of the old downtown, an area of more than sixty blocks. When it came to rebuilding it was decided to raise the floor level one storey, to help eliminate the drainage and sewage problems the city faced, especially at high tide. Many of the shops remained open at below street level (accessed by ladders) until early this century, when the sealing in of the original first floor of the city was completed.

These days Seattle, Washington is a city of 516,259 people. It covers 84 square miles of land, 8 square miles of water. It is bounded on one side by Elliott Bay, the other by Lake Washington, with the smaller Lake Union to the North. It has 35 inches of rain per annum, thanks to being in the rain shadow of the Olympic Mountains to the west. The top five companies in town are Boeing, Costco, the Weyerhaeuser timber company, Microsoft and the truck producer Paccar. The city has 1,260 sworn police officers, including 42 lieutenants, 138 sergeants, 224 detectives and 834 officers. There are 648 civilians employed by the Police Department. Seattle has an average of 40 murders per year, 260 rapes, 1,025 armed robberies, 7,695 burglaries and 6,944 incidents of auto-theft. The most popular cars to steal are older Volkswagens and Hondas. The police receive 2,429 911 calls on an average day.

ONE

The Paul Allen Athletic Club, Seattle, Washington. October. Friday 7.10 pm. Now.

Lewis had often complained about the public address system. Why, in the midst of a game of racquetball, should he have to listen to the fact that a lost child was at the reception desk, that tickets for the Mariners or the Seahawks were on special at reception, that Microsoft was proud to sponsor this year's Fringe Theater Festival?

Most of the time he managed to block it out, ignore the mundanities echoing around the court walls. Now he was two strides and a backhand away from victory when he heard the name. He had not been aware of the run-up to it, nor did the roar in his ears allow him to catch much of the second part of the sentence. All he really heard was 'Mr Dodo'.

Then the court lights seemed to dim, and he had to clench hard – then harder – his anal sphincter and his buttocks to prevent him soiling the polished wooden floor. The pucker effect they used to call it – some weird muscle that contracted and tried to pull your asshole inside-out. For a second he thought he was going to faint, but then the lights came up again. His forehead prickled as if his body was pumping pure hydrochloric acid out of its pores.

'Ha-ha'. While Lewis struggled to keep his bearings, Tenniel leapt in – or perhaps merely fell – scooped up the missed ball and hammered it against the wall with all the ferocity a fat cop can manage. They both watched it dribble feebly into the back corner. But it was Tenniel's point. He beamed with the pleasure of a man who can tell his wife how well the new fitness regime was going.

Lewis lost that one and managed another perfunctory game, sweating a quantity of fluid completely out of proportion to his exertion, before accepting defeat. 'What's the matter?' asked Tenniel. 'You're playing like you need a crap or something.'

'Sorry, John. You just outplayed me, I guess. Haven't got the stamina.' He managed a weak best-man-won smile.

Tenniel flashed his teeth back, ignoring for once the grating that he felt when Lewis's prissy New England vowels strangled stamina into stemina. 'Well, it had to happen sometime. You sure you're OK?'

Lewis knew that Tenniel was waiting for something to take the edge off the victory, such as Lewis revealing he had a hernia operation three hours earlier and it had blunted his speed, but he didn't have the heart. Or the excuse. He had been playing the cop for three, four months now, and the strain of trying to keep at least a pretence of equality in the scores was getting to him. But not tonight. 'Absolutely fine.'

As they ambled back to the changing room, Tenniel puffing a happy wheeze from his overheated alveoli, Lewis thought about Mr Dodo. A coincidence? Maybe unlike the bird, the surname never died out. But something made him sure this was a message for him, something in the way his left hand suddenly ached for the first time in three, four years. Something in the pucker effect.

In the changing room he batted off Tenniel's insistence on a drink. The cop had some time to kill before his shift, and was mildly pissed at Lewis: he wanted to celebrate the great victory over the fitter man (he would conveniently forget that Lewis was also a little older, shorter and that technically it had been a draw – to Tenniel this would go down as The Night Lewis Played As If He Needed A Crap). Lewis showered so fast it was a disgrace to the notion of personal hygiene and was out the door before Tenniel had squeezed into his bad suit. He just raised a hand as the policeman said with renewed enthusiasm: 'Same time next week?'

In the entrance hall he leant over the reception desk. 'Tammy, what was that message for—' he cleared his throat, frightened it would come out as a squeak – 'Mr Dodo?'

'Hold on, Mr Lewis.' He noticed that Tammy used everybody else's first name – it would no doubt be 'Goodnight, John' when the portly Tenniel swept by – but had trouble with his. Well, she wouldn't be the first to be phased by a white man hurtling towards fifty called Carl Lewis. The other one had kind of cornered the market in the title. Which was a little unfair, because he had had it first.

'It said: "Mr Rivers will meet Mr Dodo in the parking lot." We don't have a Mr Dodo as a member, Mr Lewis, or one signed in as a guest, but the man insisted on the announcement.'

Lewis nodded. 'Yeah, I . . .' Unsure of how to explain his interest he blurted: 'Can you book us the same time next week?'

Tammy looked puzzled. He and Tenniel had a rolling

slot; there was no need to reconfirm. 'Sure, Mr Lewis, it's already down.'

Another rainshower had started, this one a welcome-to-the-weekend drizzle. Lewis stood framed in the doorway, unsure of whether to sprint to his car and get out of there and not look back, or wait for developments. But if Mr Rivers could track him down to his health club . . . He stepped out and scanned the scene around him. It would be dark soon. Floodlights already illuminated the great walls of the bulk of the stadium behind him, the workers now hammering day and night to get it completed before they moved into the penalty period. Well, at least they got the sports club opened. Ahead of him, over the roofs of the parked cars, was a second freshly minted complex, the Mariners' new home, sitting smug and pretty, finished well ahead of schedule.

Headlights flashed from across the lot. A quick blink aimed at him, he had no doubt. Lewis took a deep breath and walked across, reluctantly passing his own car, onto the Mercury that had given him the come-on. The passenger door swung open, and he tossed his bag over the back and slid into the seat. The interior light stayed on long enough for him to get a good look at Mr Rivers, and analyse what a quarter of century down the line had done to him. He knew Rivera – his real name – was doing the same.

The light clicked off. Lewis could smell the driver, the scent of rain on a new woollen coat, an almost feline odour. But the cat in question was distinctly alley-bred.

'Mr Dodo. Howyadoin'?'

He thought he detected sarcasm and superiority co-existing in the words, but Lewis took the hand anyway.

It seemed churlish not to. Actually, what seemed entirely reasonable right now would be to grab this man by his throat, bang his head against the wheel a dozen times, put him in the trunk and dump him out near the Everett Field. That might just – just – convey how unwelcome he was.

Instead, all he said was: 'Willie.'

'You look good.'

'You smell like shit. Where did you get that coat from?'

'Still got the nose, huh? I been in town three days, I get wet every time I step onto a sidewalk, the coat hasn't had a chance to dry out. I swear, it's rotting on my back.'

'It's Seattle, Willie. Haven't you heard the jokes? Haven't you ever watched Frasier? A raincoat is what you need. Not a skunk-skin overcoat.'

There was an awkward pause. Willie started first. 'Shall we . . . ?'

'How did you find me?'

'Well . . . I saw one of your pictures in a magazine. Great shot up a mountain it was, real Ansel whatsit.'

'Adams.' This was not the time to tell him he despised Ansel Adams, and hated being compared to him.

'Anyways, it had a list of contributors and these pictures and fuck me if I didn't see right away it was my old friend . . .' He swivelled to face him. 'Carl Lewis. So I called your agent.'

'And he said, hey, he plays racquetball every Friday with a cop called Tenniel at the Athletic Club. Yeah, very professional.' Come to think of it, he realised, that did sound like the sort of thing his agent Michael would do – never let a client or a potential client slip away, nail them there and then.

'No, well, not exactly. Look, it wasn't hard, OK? I called your wife—'

'She's not my wife.'

'Well she sounded like your wife. She wasn't the maid, I figured that much. Anyway, I said I had special delivery UPS you had to sign for. She told me where you were. It's not like you've got anything to hide, is it? It's not racquetball with a big blonde, is it? No. Look, you wanna go for a drink? I checked a bar out while I was waiting. Just down the street.'

At that moment they both picked up the once-familiar whine of a starter motor pushing reluctant helicopter blades into making the first tentative swipes in the air. They listened as the pitch increased, and the turbine kicked in, and a deeper note, a whup, whup sound came into the mix as they fired up and the blades whisked and thickened the air beneath them. The fittings on the Mercury vibrated in sympathy, like teeth rattling in loose sockets, and the rear-view mirror started slowly to turn itself out of alignment.

From the roof of a former cold storage plant across the street on Occidental two mechanical locusts lifted into the air, illuminating the stadium complex parking lot with their nose lights. They wafted straight up to a hundred, a hundred and fifty feet, two hundred feet, then assumed the familiar slightly nose-down forward motion. Lewis could just make out men in fatigues and caps through one open hatchway, clutching their weapons; he knew that the new rapid reaction force – they had some acronym he could never remember – for the entire greater Seattle area was billeted next to the new Seahawks' football development. But what kind of incident needed two fully loaded slicks?

The Mercury rocked spasmodically as the double rotor wash hit them, and then the noise quickly diminished, fading to a low whistle as the pair turned east and disappeared behind the elevated concrete freeways of the I-5 interchange.

There was nothing to be said, but Willie said it anyway: 'Takes you back, huh?'

Lewis thought they would be heading for the cavernous F X McRory's, but Willie had the good sense to have picked out Chipper's opposite the main gate of the near-complete Seahawks' venue. It was reasonably full, although nothing like as if the Mariners had been playing ball down the road. The thirty-five TV screens were showing re-runs of the '97 season, when the guys could do no wrong. Nothing had seemed to click once they moved into the new space across Brougham Way. This last season, just finishing, had sucked. Nice stadium, shame about the team everyone said. Their last motto: 'You gotta love these guys' seemed a little hollow right now. Sports fans don't have to love anyone who isn't winning.

Lewis led them upstairs, where the screens were playing to just half a dozen people, and slotted them into a table well away from the others.

Now he could see Willie Rivera properly. The years hadn't been too bad to him. He was still small, wiry, although now with a little loose skin around his jowls and throat. Those bright-as-a-button eyes hadn't clouded too much. His Puerto Rican skin was still unmarked and smooth for the most part, except for a small scar at the corner of his mouth, which looked to be of relatively recent vintage.

Yes, the bits were intact, but there was some odd translucence to him, as if he was somehow less substantial than when Lewis knew him as a buddy. Time was making the man transparent, ethereal. He wondered if he looked like that. Maybe they all looked like that. Christ, they were almost old men now. Soon they'd be dribbling in wheelchairs, trying to get someone to listen to their great adventure, like World War Two Marines.

'You put on some bulk, man,' Willie said, as if to quash the notion.

Lewis shrugged. He had gained some muscle – and fat – since he had been a skinny young man serving with Willie. He liked it that way.

'How's the hand?' Lewis was suddenly aware he was fingering the scar on his palm, which was itching intensely. 'Sorry about that. Did I ever say sorry?'

Lewis raised his hands in a conciliatory gesture. No worries. Saved a life. A little scar was nothing. They ordered drinks, a seven and seven for Willie, an Amber Ale for Lewis. 'Hungry?' asked Lewis.

Willie wobbled his head in a so-so manner. 'How's the chili?' The nod convinced him and he added a bowl of red to the order. Then they sparred for five minutes or so, until Willie found the perfect way to bring the subject up. The movies.

'Yeah – and did you see Apocalypse Now? The Horror, the Horror? I mean, fuck, we seen a better quality of horror than that, didn't we? And what about the Russian roulette in The Deerhunter? I never heard of anything like that.'

Lewis snorted. 'What about opening a trapdoor to see if anyone is waiting on the other side to blow your head off?'

'I guess. Yeah, maybe. I can see that.'

'Willie. Why are we sitting in some asshole bar talking about Vietnam movies?' What he really meant was: what the fuck are you doing here in my life, calling up my agent, my non-wife and ruining my fucking game of racquetball? He noticed that even his mental language was quickly slipping back to army doggerel – every sentence doubled in length because of the weight of profanities it supported, but, thanks to the limited choice available, the repetition lending it a staccato rhythm.

Willie leant forward. 'Yeah, I was forgetting, Mr Dodo, huh? Straight to the point, eh?'

The stupid nickname made him flinch.

'You OK?'

Lewis shook his head. 'What have you been doing, Willie?'

'After I got back? I joined a band.' Ah, yes, Willie had been a trumpet player. 'Still do it now and then. Weddings, dances. We got to play SOBs, once. You know it?'

'Sons of Bitches? What's that, a punk club?'

Willie laughed. 'You know what it is. Sounds of Brazil. You been to New York yet? Well, we supported Gato Barbieri. You heard of him, at least?'

'Last Tango in Paris?'

'Right, yeah, Last Tango in Paris.'

'So you make a living out of playing?'

'A living? A living . . . no. Some money. I sold cars for my brother – he's a timbales player, but he knows cars. The Mercury is one of his. I still do that, too. Let's see, I got married.' He grinned. 'Three times now. I'll get it right soon.'

'And now you're looking up your old buddies?'

'Well, I tell you, Mr Do—'

'Don't call me that. Don't.'

'Sorry. Been a long time, and . . . the truth is, there ain't many of us left. Out of the eight, there is me, you and the Bat. And I tell you, the Bat is bats these days.'

'You've seen him?'

'He lives with his mother in Queens. She says he just don't go out any more. Stays in his room with the drapes closed. Wouldn't let me see him. Said it would upset him.'

'You're upsetting *me*, Willie. That didn't stop you coming here.' Lewis ordered another round of drinks. It was past eight; he would have to leave soon. The soundtrack changed to Miles. It was the Laswell remixes, bassier and spacier, more reverb than the original he remembered, but at the core was still that haunting, half-blown sound, the acoustic trumpet lonely and stranded in a wash of electronics. They're playing our song, Lewis thought involuntarily. Odd, he had never heard anything but En Vogue and Madonna in here before.

The bowl of chili arrived and Willie tucked in, fanning his mouth appreciatively. 'Good. Anyhow, the others? Wayland was killed in an auto smash. Joey Averne, killed himself. Yeah, I know. Cut his wrists. Couldn't use a knife in 'Nam to save his life. Managed to find the knack to end it, though. I couldn't trace Arnold. Went to South Carolina and everything. They said he just never came back after his discharge.

Hobbs? Last seen in '71 throwing his medals onto the White House lawn. Had become a Black Muslim. Well, we saw that comin', huh?'

Lewis counted. Someone was missing. Oh yeah.

'Why bother with them all, Willie? Why bother with me? It was a long time ago.'

'Look, I need some money.' Willie could see what he was thinking. You *had* money. 'Three ex-wives eat into your savings pretty damn quick.'

So all this was a simple hit? Trailing him around town to hustle some cash? That didn't add up. 'Well, you must have spent enough on gas chasing after me to feed you for a month. New York to Seattle . . . how many miles is that?'

'Not gas-money money. Stake-money money. Like ten grand. I got some of my own, mind, I got four. Well, when I sell the Mercury I will have four.' Willie mopped a trickle of chili from his chin with the napkin and signalled for another drink.

Lewis started gulping the beer. He didn't want to hear much more. Somehow a Willie strapped for cash with just a battered Mercury and a Cohn B flat to his name worried him. Lots of things about this worried him . . . he found he had been staring at the bank of television monitors, watching the play without registering.

'Put the moose on the table, Willie, for Chrissake.'

'I wanna go back.' For the first time in a long time Lewis felt that once-familiar dropping sensation, as if the earth was going to open up and claim him as its own. And there was a faint, ill-focused rattling in his ears. Getting louder. It wasn't a rattle. It was the bark of a Swedish K.

Willie stared, nodding, as if he could smell it and hear it and feel it too, echoing down the years. 'That's right. I want to go back to Vietnam.'

TWO

Special Weapons and Operations, Puget Sound (SWOPS) HQ. Occidental Avenue South, Seattle. Friday 7.46 pm

Major Michael Milliner had lost count of how many helicopter take-offs he had experienced over the years. From the early days of crouching in the doorway of a Huey, his helmet under his ass, to now, sitting up front, cradling the flight plan and the orders, it must be what – a thousand? Two thousand? No, not two. But certainly four figures by now.

But whatever the score, a lift never failed to release a little trickle of adrenalin from his kidneys, an excitement that spread, not from his stomach, but up his back, a creeping warm glow, like a fifty-dollar massage. And if anything the glow was even stronger these days, now he was the one whose voice crackled over the airwaves.

'Bravo Two?'

'Ready, Major Milliner.'

'OK. Let's go.'

He nodded to the pilot and Alpha Six stood on its tiptoes as the blades tilted, then gingerly let go of the roof of what had been the Permafrost Cold Storage building, inching its way upwards, a straight vertical ascent that slowly revealed the inside of the near-complete stadium across the road, its bonus-rich workers scurrying at double speed.

The ship rotated slightly and he found himself looking at the cluster of skyscrapers that made up downtown, to the blinking light atop the Space Needle and across to Lake Union, where the last Kenmore Air float plane was making a dash for home base before dusk turned to dark.

Across the harbour he could see the lights of the green and white Bainbridge ferry, smeared into starbursts by the rain on the Plexiglass, loaded with good citizens looking forward to their weekend out of the city. Milliner's attention was caught by some flashes on the highway to the north, must be on HWY-5. No, Aurora, to the left of it, but by the time he stared to look at them, they had gone. He got that sometimes, little lights in his peripheral vision, dancing like tracers, a kind of retinal battle scar.

Now he could see beyond Queen Anne Hill and Union across the Sound and towards Whidbey, the very name of which still caused him to shudder. Whidbey. They were all here, one way or another, because of Whidbey. Well, this trip could be the last of that.

Up and up, the two helicopters rose like glass and steel marionettes, each one packed with well-trained, well-armed men. His men. Milliner felt proud and not a little excited. He knew how much it must have galled Eastern Washington to call on his expertise but the FBI had insisted. And the FBI knew good SWAT teams – by any other name – when they saw them. And how could he refuse this assignment, of all of them? The finishing touches to the event that had made this force what it was today.

The helicopters turned once more, facing east this time, where the darkening sky just silhouetted the

Cascades, although, as usual, Mount Rainier, far down to the south, was lost to the clouds. The concrete knots of the freeway exits disappeared beneath them as the pilot picked up the tail lights of the cars crawling across the Mercer Island floating bridge, and began to follow them east towards Spokane. Lake Washington was criss-crossed as usual by the dying wakes of boats, but a little cluster of them were churning rings towards the Eastern shore as they circled like aquatic vultures: the last of the day's sightseers come to waste time trying to peer into the Gates compound.

Milliner ripped open the documents wallet and spread the contents on his lap. There was a city map of Spokane, a series of authorisations and the requests for assistance, plus an intricate, hand-drawn family tree. He switched on the overhead light to try and decipher this, but even then the cross-connections and hook-ups were almost too complex to follow.

It began with Whidbey and Father William and his link to the organisation that called itself the Alliance for Government-Free America. From there the spidery black lines ran out to other links, some physical, some merely electronic – shared websites and databases. All lines led to a motley amalgamation of various loggers, trappers and gun lobbyists, what he knew were called 'wise use' groups. These had names like Committee for Sustainable Use of the Planet. The lines made a geographical leap now, deserting the US and connecting to a clutch of Japanese whaling supporters, the more radical Inuit groups, and representatives of pressure groups from Norway, the Faroes, as well as African safari and hunting associations.

At the time of Whidbey he had thought they were dealing with yet another messianic cult. Well it was, but connected with all of the above, and maybe some others. The Aryan Nation, the White League, the Armed Republic, they would all feel happy in this company. A motley ragbag for sure, but shit, these guys didn't care who they got into bed with – they all just had the same aim: get the Federal government off their backs. Relax logging quotas, let us shoot our wildlife, fish the seas, bring back heads as trophies, collect our heavy-firepower weapons, no questions asked. And from somewhere out of this morass of self-interest the threats had come – let the Whidbey guys go. They didn't do the actual shooting. Put them on trial and wherever you move it to, you will feel our wrath. Well, Father William so traumatised Seattle – Boeing reckoned it cost them one and a half 777s in lost production time – that the lawyers had no trouble moving the trial to Spokane: every jury in Seattle would be a hanging jury, for sure. So, presumably, Spokane was going to feel the wrath.

Below them the highway traffic was thinning, speeding up as it unsnarled, sending off tributaries towards the commuter towns of Bellevue and Kirkland. Ahead were the Snoqualmie Falls and North Bend, marking the point of their climb into the mountains and the Snoqualmie Pass that would lead them through to Spokane, where, God willing, he would help lock up the men who had killed so many innocent kids, whose only crime was terminal gullibility.

Major Milliner refolded the various documents and settled down for the flight. Feel their wrath in Spokane? They'd have to get past him first.

THREE

Public Safety Building, 610 Third Avenue, Downtown Seattle. 8.47 pm

Basking in his healthy afterglow, Sergeant John Tenniel could not believe the silence on the third floor of the PSB. True, he was fifty minutes late for the usual chaos of shift change, having parked his young protégé Harry March in a safe place, but even so, this was like a morgue. He peeked over one of the shoulder-height blue-grey office dividers that were used to create the individual officer's workstations. He could see a still-steaming cup of latte. No, it was more like that ship, the Marie Celestial or whatever.

True, the phones were ringing, a shifting symphony of bells, tones and warbles, but like all cops some kind of neural filter kept that from his higher consciousness. Only the ring of his own receiver would penetrate through to his frontal lobes, like a penguin picking out the cry of its own offspring amid the chatter of a thousand others.

He stepped into his cubicle and took off his coat before returning to the outside and flipping the name plate. Knight always forgot to do it. Too keen to get out and into the safety of his home. Knight would be taking the pension cheque as soon as it was dangled, that was for sure. And he knew the new Chief was keen to see short-timers like Knight out the door, so the dangling wouldn't be too long now. Tenniel just hoped he wasn't included in the first sweep. He didn't want to have to face that decision just yet.

He heard footsteps and peered over the partition. It was the elegantly swan-necked Lucy Lutwidge, the Administrative Specialist One for their unit, as usual turned out in the crispest of outfits. 'Hey Luce, where is everyone?' he asked.

'Oh, around and about. Check your DIR. That'll give you a clue.'

'Yeah, thanks.' It was the first thing you were meant to do, check the Daily Incident Reports when you came on shift, so you knew what was happening in each of the four Seattle precincts. Was he being reprimanded by an AS1 now?

Tenniel was about to walk to the notice board down by the coffee machine, when he remembered he didn't have to do that any more. One of the Chief's other plans – the paperless office by 2001. He sat down and logged on, searching for the drive that contained the constantly updated DIR.

He jumped when a head appeared over the wall behind him and started talking. It was Girdlestone, another of the detectives in the Burglary/Theft Unit. He was whispering. 'You see that Lucy?' Tenniel nodded. 'See what she had on? Yeah? Well I got a question.' Girdlestone gripped the top of the partition, his tuft of black hair and long nose making him look for all the world like some piece of peek-a-boo graffiti. 'These women, they wear see-through blouses, yeah? So you can see their bra? And it looks great. But you know what annoys me? That little label they always leave sticking out at the back. With the size on or whatever. I mean, why don't they cut it out? Or do they want you to *know* what friggin' size they are?'

Another familiar head – one with even tuftier hair, this time a mousy brown – popped up alongside Girdlestone and winked at Tenniel, who felt himself squirm uncomfortably. 'The labels are for people like you, Girdlestone,' said Detective Isa Bowman softly. 'They always say: If You Can Read This, You Are Too Close.'

Girdlestone snorted and disappeared, and Tenniel heard the rustle of a newspaper. He hoped Bowman wouldn't come into his space, but she did. He couldn't get used to her in civilian clothes. Not that she didn't suit them, exactly, but her well-worked physique seemed to belong in uniform-blue – what she was wearing when he first met her six years ago when she was an SO – rather than the red T-shirt, black skirt and vest she was wearing. She had certainly jumped around a lot since Student Officer days, her ten card now listed assignments to Violent Crimes, Fraud, Media Relations, then a spell with North Precinct Operations, onto Property Crimes, and now the Chief had transferred her to Burglary/Theft in West, with him. Which was nice. Maybe.

'You're getting fat, John.'

He thought about recounting his thrashing of Lewis, but stopped. 'So my wife tells me.' Now why did he say that?

'She's right.'

'So it's unanimous then. It was why I transferred out of uniform. Remember?' They both knew it was a lie.

Well, a partial lie. There was no fitness test for patrol officers other than the two-month firearm review, but the unwritten cop code demands that when you think you are becoming a danger to your partner, then you get out. And not being able to run at your best, that put your partner in the firing line. Except in Tenniel's case the perceived danger – perceived mainly by Mrs Tenniel – came *from* the partner.

An invisible Girdlestone shouted over: 'Hey, John, you see the Sonics last night?'

'Nah.' Tenniel had a guilty secret. He didn't give a flying fuck about the Sonics or the Seahawks or the Mariners. He was that rare and lonely specimen – the American Male Who Did Not Like Sports. Sure, he kept up with the basics, because it was an important social lubricant: 'What about those Hawks?' had all but replaced 'hello' in this city. But what he wanted to talk about was when he could afford to do that time-share on a boat out of Anacortes or Friday Harbor and go and catch him some salmon or halibut. Or, that even bigger secret, sit on an island and do some painting. Water-colours. It wasn't something they would understand in the squad room.

'Fuckin' A,' came Girldlestone's voice, 'I'll save you the sports section.'

Bowman said loudly, 'Hey, and be sure to pass it onto me, John.' She knew.

'You shouldn't be so hard on him,' said Tenniel in a low voice. 'He's OK. And he might end up being your partner in this big shuffle.'

She wrinkled her lip. 'Yeah. But comments like that bra thing I don't need. You know when I went to Cheque

Fraud, those assholes wouldn't tell me anything? I mean, I could read up on the cases, but the procedure . . . forget about it. They just wanted me to fuck up. It was like they had all the cards, and wouldn't even tell me what game we was playing. You know what saved me? People like Lucy. We had a daily meeting in the rest room, all the secretaries and me, going over what to to do next. I tell you – the admin staff know more about police work than we do. Those guys couldn't figure out how I was doing it. So I don't like jokes about civilian staff.'

'Yeah, well, they were Neanderthals back then. Things change.'

'Yeah, they've evolved to, what, Iron-Age man, now?'

'We got a woman Chief. What more do you want? No, shit, sorry, I didn't mean that.' He did that thing of pinching the bridge of his nose, the little ritual that sometimes made him relax. Being near Bowman made his temples throb.

'You OK?' Bowman asked. 'Where's your pint-sized partner?' It was her turn to curb her mouth. 'Sorry, what's his name? March?' She reddened at the insensitivity of what she had said, given all the memos about locker-room ribbing of officers of 'below average stature'.

'It's OK, young Harry the Action Man is cooling his heels on the wine warehouse stake-out on Henry. Nice and safe and easy. All he has to do is call in.'

She sat on the edge of his desk. He wished she wouldn't. Two weeks she had been in the unit, and this was the first exchange of more than three sentences they had managed. Now Moggs was on vacation a few days earlier than him, so here he was without a partner. And, funnily enough, so was she. Unless you counted exchange detective Harry March from Vancouver, who was being bounced to whoever would have him.

'How is he? Really?' He noticed when the vest flapped open she still kept a .38, like him. The whole department had gone over to Glocks, but a few sentimental old fools had been allowed to keep their old-style revolvers.

'Harry? Yeah, OK. Bit of a hot-head. You know the type? Pulls his weapon when a car backfires. All that two-handed Special Forces crap.'

'Well, I remember that feeling. You just want to hold it, you know that, just to remind you what you are. A cop. Or is that too long ago for you to recall?'

What was Bowman? She must be pushing thirty. March was a few years shy of that yet, though he looked as if he hadn't even started shaving. They both made him feel old, as if he had been in the job forever, like some of those ghosts you saw drifting in for the 4am shift, unable to let go, taking all the assignments nobody else could hack, just to stay with the force. These were the guys the female officers were traditionally teamed up with. Not any more, he suspected. He could see Isa streaking past him soon, shooting-star style.

He looked up at her and smiled. She smiled back. In three weeks she would transfer to South Precinct, when they split the unit into residential and non-residential. He would stay working David and Mary sectors of West Precinct, the non-residential burglary hot-spot, while she would be in Robert and Sam of South, down towards Georgetown, where it was homes at most risk. This, he thought, would probably be a good thing.

'You need drive D,' she said, pointing to the menu.

He grunted his thanks and pulled up the list. He already knew about the top one, flashing red. The First Lady staying at the Four Seasons with a $1,000 a-head dinner tonight at the Rainier Club. Lots of Secret Service and lots of Seattle's own SERTs. He began to scroll, and was only a dozen incidents into the catalogue when he started whistling. 'Shit, do you think this is the day we pay for Sleepless in Seattle?'

'What do you mean?'

'A drive-by on Aurora: car with the victims inside goes out of control, ploughs into two others, one of which bursts into flames. Meanwhile the victims hit four prostitutes looking for johns, killing one and seriously injuring the others. The guy in the flaming car, his sneaker melts to the gas pedal and the fireboys can't get him out. OK, our curious citizens slow down on the other side to watch the show – four more accidents, including a fuel oil tanker, which spills. The shooters – believed to be, get this, La Eme – hightail it to Capitol Hill and are currently holed up in in a bed and breakfast off Broadway, threatening the owners. What is left of the Seattle Emergency Response Team has them surrounded. Throw in a dozen car thefts, seven aggravated assaults, oh, yeah, and a couple of rapes. Sound like a normal Friday night to you?'

She shrugged as if to say: shit happens.

He was slightly surprised that, at the very least, she wasn't taken aback by the notoriously ramshackle Mexican Mafia coming to Seattle for target practice. 'OK, then. Look here. Three fatal shootings in South Seattle, and it's what, nine o'clock? Four in one night. We only had thirty-seven murders the whole of last year.

Next: two vagrants assaulted down on Second Avenue, at Pike. Just round the corner from Harry's stake. One might croak. We had a near-riot on the anti-abortion demo at Cobb Clinic up on Fourth. The one next to United Airlines? Now half the uniforms in the city are at Planet Hollywood, because five thousand people have turned up for the anniversary party, hoping to see the parade of the two-bit stars from the Sheraton. You know that thing Star 101.5 does with the red carpet down the street? Fuck, the radio station should pick up the tab for policing that.' And, he wondered, where was Major Milliner and his all-star big-budget team in all this? Not a single mention of SWOPS in any of the dispatches. Too busy buffing up their new insignia maybe.

The list went on. Commotion at SeaTac because the new Airbus A3XX came in on a display flight for American, and Boeing staff were not happy about seeing a rival strutting for business in their backyard. Trouble at a housing project in West Madrona: residents had taken a suspected child molester hostage and were refusing to hand him over. Fears were that someone, sometime, was going to suggest a little local surgery before the authorities got to him. The strangeness count continued to mount. 'Jesus, what's this? A complaint of branding? Treated as assault on a minor?'

Bowman ran her fingers through her hair – or what was left of it after that scalp butcher had got through. He had made her look like a dyke. 'Branding. It's what you go to after you haven't got any fleshy bits left to pierce. They do it up on that club on East Pike, Sizzle. You gotta be twenty-one, though. Otherwise they get done for assault.'

Tenniel thought about his daughter, now eighteen and slowly taking out some of the rings from her eyebrows and – the one he had wanted to see go most – that bolt through her tongue. He reckoned the day she set off the airport metal detector was probably the turning point (or, an internal voice chimed in, was that a joke he was too old to have recognised?). But she could pass for twenty-one easy. He just hoped she had grown out of self-mutilation enough to resist turning up like some steer out of Rawhide. The rose tattoo that peaked over her lower cut T-shirts was bad enough.

'Doesn't it hurt?'

'They have a trained paramedic. Applies anaesthetic and bandages.'

Tenniel continued to scroll through the list, occasionally muttering to himself. All the people who knew Seattle from soppy luvvy-duvvy movies would get a shock to find it could be just like any other big city when the mood took it. And tonight it had a big snit on. Usually detectives were the second string of attack, leaving their desks when there were bones to be picked over; the empty squad room suggested they had moved up to the front line. Which meant the Burglary Unit was bound to get a call-out soon. In which case he might have to take Harry off the stake-out.

'Told your wife?' Bowman asked suddenly.

'About what?'

'HEY TENNIEL.' It was Girdlestone, who excitedly came rushing into the small space, waving the Seattle PI. 'Seventeen. Into double figures.'

'Seventeen? You sure?'

'Seventeen, man. Look.' He held up the classifieds for

them to see the red ticks he had put next to certain ads.

'How many was it yesterday?'

'Nine.'

'And in '97?'

'Fourteen. We're getting there, John.'

Bowman looked from one to the other, wondering what the hell they were jabbering about. 'Seventeen what, Girdlestone?'

Tenniel answered for him. 'Seventeen missing dogs.'

'Is that bad?'

'Oh yes that's bad. That's very, very bad.'

She wanted to ask why, he obviously wanted her to ask why, but at that moment the first wave broke. There was a crashing of doors at the far end near the holding tanks as detectives and uniforms shuffled in the suspects. Some moved to their desk as they recognised their own phone, and others started to try and make up the deficiencies inherited from the last shift. A cut-and-paste of half a dozen conversations reached Tenniel's cubicles.

'Anyone got a tape for this goddamn machine?'

'Has this guy been Miranda'd? Whadayamean he came voluntarily? Who cuffed him then?'

'I need someone who speaks Spanish. Where's the duty translator?'

'Dodgson got shot? How bad is he?'

'Take the goddamn cuffs off, it's a no-bust.'

'What are they doing over there? Mexican what?'

'Well, which hospital is he in?'

'HEY TENNIEL, YOU SPEAK SPANISH? WELL, WHO DOES?'

'HAS ANYONE GOT A BLANK TAPE? HOW

CAN I DO AN INTERVIEW WITH NO TAPE IN THE MACHINE?'

The room started to fill up with more bodies, the usual cacophony seemingly cranked at a higher pitch tonight, tempers on shorter fuses, suspects treated a little more brusquely. Tenniel looked at Bowman and back at the screen. He rebooted and saw the list of incidents had already grown by a dozen since he first logged on.

'What about the dog—' she started, but amid the gathering swell of noise he heard his extension ring and reached out to pick it up. It would be the dispatcher. He was on.

FOUR

Bella Vista Apartments, West Highland Drive, Queen Anne District, Seattle, Washington. 9.27 pm

Lewis pulled to a stop by little Lookout Park, the patch of green a few hundred yards away from his apartment building, just close enough to keep an eye on the garage door and the front entrance in case she decided to call a cab. After all, she wouldn't want to drive because she'd be drinking. Not much. Just a glass or two of wine. Always did when she was mad at him. And she would be mad. He'd promised he would be back in time. Promised.

He hunkered down in the seat and ripped the wrapping off the pack of cigarettes, shucked a tube out and put it in his mouth, filter end first. He sucked. Harder. He flipped it so that the untipped end was next to his tongue, felt the little shreds of tobacco break off, imagined them flamed and burning, tasted the tar and the nicotine and hydrocarbons.

He couldn't light it. She'd smell it, taste it, and he knew she was still trying to quit. And knew she was at that Battle of the Bulge stage when the nicotine Nazis in her brain were trying one last push. But he pulled on the dry tube anyway, a virtual hit running around his brain. Been a while.

The rain had stopped at last – the last few days had been unusually heavy for Seattle, which, contrary to the national image, suffered from perpetual drizzle rather than great deluges – and he watched the residual waters in the gutter running towards the sewer gratings, the thin streams meeting and intertwining into a bright, fluid herringbone effect. He stared at pint after pint, gallon after gallon slip over the grilles into the darkness, felt the pull, as if he could ride the rivulets like some kid's paper boat, swept away from all this. It was then that he realised the reason for his immobility. For the first time in the three years he had lived with her, Lewis did not want to see Dinah.

The city seemed to be glaring at him in disgust, the hundreds of windows still ablaze in the shiny towers piercing his eyes. He stared at the Columbia Seafirst Center, the tallest of the crop of glass and steel that grew out of the business district. Funny how his eyes were drawn not to the illuminated squares, but to the frames that surrounded them, as if he wanted to make a negative of the city, to look at the darkness, not the light.

He panned to the right, past the Space Needle – after years as an anachronism, now looking remarkably chic and modern in an Astounding Tales kind of way – across Puget Sound to the Olympic mountains, where the long departed sun had left a streak of afterglow linking their peaks like a dot-to-dot puzzle.

He pulled back onto downtown, and the distant light coming from the two new stadiums, just visible between the Needle and downtown. He knew they had seemed a good idea at the time, but he kind of missed the ugly concrete clam that had been the Kingdome.

He loved this city, loved this view. Probably loved the woman who was waiting for him right now. But was this it he wondered: the time to move on? He had never quite clocked the moment it began. Took two years, maybe a bit more. And he was overdue now. So overdue he was almost certain it was over. Banished. Or maybe just matured away, the cracks and strains in his soul softened by time. But he couldn't be sure. Not now that Willie had turned up. Thin, see-through Willie, a man fading away, trying to find something solid to hold onto. Him. Vietnam twenty-odd years ago. Anything.

He looked at his watch. They had a fundraiser to go to. She would give him another ten, maybe fifteen minutes and then leave. Punctuality. It was a big thing with her. She would despair of him arriving, and jump the cab alone. Better that than let down the Foundation.

He waited forty minutes before it hit him he was wrong and she wasn't coming out. She was obviously building to blow. A mini Mount St Helens, ready to pour molten vitriol all over him. No point in putting it off. He stepped out of the car for a moment and tossed the smokes across one of the obsessively clipped lawns towards a shadow he could discern in the doorway of an electricity sub-station, a shadow that suddenly grew an arm and snatched them from the air. He knew who was there. Solly, someone else whose life hadn't quite gone according to plan. Queen Anne's only bum, like far too many of the vagrants in the North West a Native American, tolerated here if he kept a solitary existence and didn't bring any friends up, as long as he kept to the shadows. Old Solly – despite his name – claimed to be a Duwamish, a vestigial member of Seattle's original tribe. For all Lewis knew he might be telling the truth.

He took the car into the garage, noting that her Audi

was still in the bay. He looked at the elevator, an elevator he had never taken. Not in all the time he had lived with her. He had been figuring on trying it soon. Not tonight, eh?

He took the twenty flights of stairs to their apartment (well, her apartment) much more slowly than usual, no two-at-a-time run. He normally reckoned he could beat the elevator on a good night: now he heard it squeak past three of four times before he reached apartment 14. He pulled out his key and paused.

She opened the door even before he engaged the lock. The eyes said it all, that and the hardened lines around her wide mouth – new lipstick, an oddly observant part of his brain noted, makes her mouth look even wider. All the better to chew his ear off with. He also noted the new suit, bought for this cheque-gathering party. Highly tailored navy jacket, skirt with two small splits. Very fetching, but not the time to mention it. She stepped back to let him in, and he fastened his mental seatbelt.

FIVE

Central Seattle. 11.50 pm

Hilton saw the red wash of brake lights ahead on I-5, hit the brakes and pulled off onto Seneca, heading for downtown. It wasn't where he wanted to be. He wanted to be across in Chinatown, in the lot just by Kobe Park. He would have to go along Fifth. He almost made the turn when he realised he wasn't the first to think of that, and he carried on west. Traffic was just shit tonight.

In the seat beside him Duck carried on trying to count under the strobe effect of the street lights. Hilton knew he had enough trouble counting straight and in the light, and he didn't have either of those going for him, having insisted on a joint before they left.

'Turn on the navigation light. No there. THERE, you fuckwit. Don't you even get to know the cars you steal? This is a Ford, so they use the same lay-out on all their models. Overhead lights always here, Lincoln Town Car or a Contour, always the same. And I asked for a BMW or a Mercedes. Foreign, I said. Italian would have done. Alfa Romeo. Classy, so Annie will think, well yes, it's only four grand this time, but these boys have some kind of FUCKIN' STYLE. Now they are going to think: two low-rents on the make, barely got four grand between them, hope to turn it into eight. Hey, big time. They look like their main ambition in life is to steal a FUCKING

FORD. Even a HONDA or a RABBIT would have been better.' He grabbed the cheap cigarette lighter – indicative of the class of the previous owner he felt – from the dash, lit up and pocketed it.

Duck glanced over at Hilton. His two false front teeth always rattled when he shouted, but it didn't do to laugh. Hilton had some Swedish ancestry somewhere, out of Minnesota, which made him kind of beefy, but he claimed his folks were English. Well, way back. Back before someone in the family met the Indian you got in you there, maybe? Duck always felt like asking. But it wasn't safe, it certainly wasn't safe, to mention that. Maybe the high cheekbones explained why he had had such a tough time in Walla Walla.

Hilton was depending a lot on this deal, he knew. They had met when Hilton had had enough of humping sacks for farmers and started doing beauty parlours, robbing them on Friday nights when rich bitches had their hair done. Always lots of jewellery, sometimes cash. Worked well until one lot had fought back. You'd be surprised, there were a lot of lethal weapons in a salon. Hydrogen peroxide, hair spray, all sorts of permanent colourings. It was a miracle either of them could still see. Hilton had decided they would switch to some dope dealing, on account of you met a better class of person and it was far less dangerous.

Duck carried on counting best he could with shaking fingers. Three thousand and one, three thousand and two. He moved the bills across from one knee to the other, straightening them out and stroking them, as he went. Every so often he came across one with a possible hint of powder on it and, while Hilton looked in his mirror or over his shoulder, he licked it. Nothing yet, though, and the buzz from the grass was starting to subside.

'L-l-listen, Hilton, you try and get into one of those foreign cars. They all got real sophisticated alarms, I mean real sophisticated. You get in and fart and off it goes.'

'What, you think they put gas sensors in there? Hey, any perp coming in bound to break wind: let's put a methane meter in?'

'No, Hilton, you know what I mean . . . heat, movement, punching in the wrong security codes, those beemers got it all.'

'Did you even try a Mercedes? Did you?'

'If the beemers got it . . .'

'One day I am going to deep-fry your southern ass. You know? Like crispy fried duck, with pancakes and some of that sauce, 'cause there are days when you would be more use to me as calories than a partner.'

Duck kept quiet. He got his name because he knew when to shut up and, even better, when to get out of sight. And right now he didn't want to rile his partner. Hilton wasn't the easiest of guys to work with, but he wasn't – no matter what he said – the meanest. All he was trying to do was find a dishonest living that didn't entail much risk. And Duck was with him there. Three thousand, eight hundred. Uh-ooh.

Duck swallowed hard and started frantically to recount.

'Well?' asked Hilton as they came out of the tunnel.

'I lost count. Don't harangue me no more.'

'Just make sure we not givin' her too much.'

Duck skimmed through the bills double quick, watching one pile grow and the other diminish, at the same time peering into the footwell, hoping to see the stray notes.

When he had finished, Hilton looked at Duck. And Duck looked at Hilton. Duck managed to say: 'Three eight.'

Hilton hit the brakes so hard that Duck slammed into the windscreen, sending the money fluttering round his feet. As he ricocheted back against the seat, Hilton's right hand found his throat. 'Three eight. THREE EIGHT? There was four there yesterday, you said. There was four there this morning. There was four when we left Tacoma. Why is there only three eight now? Empty your pockets. Come on, come on.'

Duck was used to Hilton slapping him around, but there was real anger in the pokes to the ribs now. 'OK, OK.' He raised himself out of the seat so he could squeeze a hand down his Levis, and pulled out five dollars and twenty-seven cents. He offered it to Hilton. 'I . . . I don't get it.'

Hilton patted his own pockets, and managed to find a twenty and change. His large hands punched the dash three times, leaving a deep dent in the plastic. He took a slow breath. 'Count it all again. Look under the seats, make sure you have it all. Count it again.'

Five minutes passed as Duck, shaking, reassembled the notes into a neat stack, with Hilton's twenty and his own pathetic five crowning the pile. 'Three eight and twenty-five.'

'AAAAAHHHHHHHHHHHHHHH.'

Duck winced as his eardrum whiplashed under the

assault of Hilton's yell. Then there was a loud silence. A blue and white police cruiser came by and they both stiffened, but it was intent on something ahead. They didn't even get a glance.

Hilton flicked his cigarette butt at Duck, who felt it bounce off his cheek with a quick jab of pain. He stamped a foot on it. It was one of Hilton's party tricks, flicking butts at people.

'OK,' said Hilton. 'What with the Ford and being short on the money . . . but Annie, she's cool, Ricky said she'd be fine, she will understand it is an accountancy hitch.'

Duck wasn't so sure. What he had heard about Ricky's old lady suggested she didn't understand anything except full C.O.D. The first guy who had tried to short-change her because of the fact she was only Ricky's dep – and a bitch at that – had lost a kneecap for his trouble. So they said. But Hilton had met her once or twice, so maybe he was the best judge. Always a first time. Hilton pulled his Nokia out of his top pocket and, after a pause to recall the number, dialled.

Duck asked: 'Is this a good idea?'

Annie Haart sat down on the settee and smoothed her skirt down, eyes never leaving the man opposite, ignoring where his eyes kept flicking to. She ran a hand across the glass coffee table in front of them, over the samples, as if to say, this is what you should be looking at, you snatch-hound.

Leo Griffin, on the other hand, was rather enjoying the view. Doing business with a woman tickled him. He could tell from the sterility of this apartment that it wasn't her own, just some front for the likes of him to come to, probably rented for a month, then disposed of for another exactly the same. They hadn't even finished building this pier-side block, so short-term deals were probably easy to come by. Great look-out across the waterfront to Anthony's though, his favourite fish restaurant. But anyway, here they were, both on strange, unfamiliar ground.

Annie stood up, and walked to the drinks tray. 'I really do not want to talk price until you have tried one of the products . . . Leo.' She poured herself a small shot of Baker's 107 bourbon. How old was she? Leo wondered. There were dark lines under her eyes, and even darker roots were showing through the blonde. Tired. Hard business to be in, man or woman, especially if you're thrown in at the deep end. So . . . freshen her up and you'd have early thirties. And a fit early thirties. And now her old man was up the river for a hefty duration . . .

She turned to face him.

'Can I get you anything?'

She was hurrying him. She obviously had something else on. Let them wait. He smiled his most charming smile, all too aware that, over the years, his charm muscles had atrophied. His credit cards usually did the seducing.

Then the phone rang. 'Excuse me.'

'Annie?'

Leo was staring at her, not relishing the interruption cutting off his response. 'Who is this?' she asked tersely.

'It's Hilton. You know, we have an appointment.'

Annie looked at her watch. 'Not yet.' In fact it was just ten minutes to the meet. And it took fifteen minutes to drive it.

'Yeah, well we have a little accountancy problem I'd like to talk over—'

She heard a siren wail by on the other end of the line. 'Are you on a cellphone?' She was about to chew him out when she caught sight of Griffin looking at her, so she answered the question for herself. 'No, well that's good. Land lines are good.'

'What's good? No, it's bad, Annie. We are a couple of hundred short, but we wondered if, you know, we could, like, owe you.'

'No, I'm sorry. Not tonight.'

'Look, Annie, you know me, I used to deal with Ricky. And Ricky said you'd be cool.'

Ricky, Ricky, Ricky. All of a sudden everyone had been Ricky's best pal. 'I am. The deal was four. I'm not taking welfare stamps or IOUs for the rest.'

Hilton heard the edge, the finality in her voice. 'We'll be a little late. There in twenty.'

'With it all?'

'Yeah, the whole package.'

'OK. I'll wait ten minutes.'

She put the phone down and looked at Griffin. 'Trouble?' he asked.

'Just people who have no concept of what time-keeping or book-keeping means. I have to go out. You can stay here, I'll be fifteen, twenty minutes at most.' He yawned, so she added: 'Or we can continue tomorrow.'

Griffin reached out and picked up an immaculately rolled joint, put it to his ear like it was a fine Cohiba cigar and, with as much ceremony as lighting a vintage Cuban, he put a flame to it and sucked. The smoke came out of his nostrils ninety seconds later, twin streams like exhaust jets. He smiled. A real one this time, as if the stuff had unfrozen him. But then it could melt the polar ice-caps, this little number. Super Skunk No 3 crossed with George Washington High, with a few fancy genes from a couple of European strains. And none of that sudden loss of hybrid vigour. This one grew and grew.

'Can I get you anything?' she repeated once more.

A mischievous version of the grin came over his face. 'Pussy,' he said slowly, drawing the word out. And his eyes flicked to her hair. He let the word roll out like the smoke: 'Blooonde.'

She picked up the Yellow Pages and threw them on the empty space next to him. 'I'll Be Your Fantasy.'

'Huh?'

'I'll Be Your Fantasy. It's an agency run by a friend of mine. Under Escorts. A blonde will be waiting in your hotel room when you get back if you call now. A *real* blonde. And friends enjoy a substantial discount.'

But he had another lungful on the go, and just nodded. Annie knew that by the time she got back the high-hybrid in that joint would have paralysed him from the neck down, and put his brain onto medium-fried. And then he would talk price.

On her way out she opened the bedroom door. 'Pepper.'

And from the darkness out loped Pepper, her little insurance policy, six-foot-five of lean black man. He walked over and took up Annie's position on the sofa. She checked her handbag for the Para-Ord P10 Sub-Compact. She didn't need Pepper to deal with Hilton, not with a .45 that was barely bigger than her hand but would punch the buttwipe through the windscreen if need be; but bringing him out would make Griffin realise she wasn't stupid enough to overlook extra back-up for their negotiations. Word would get around. It was either that or do a few more kneecaps, just to keep the rumour factory primed.

Griffin's eyes just widened at the sight of Pepper, and then he let out a long, coughing laugh. 'I'll still be here, Mrs Haart. I think we can do some business on –' he puffed and emitted the last word as a squeak – 'this.'

Hilton clicked the phone off and jammed it in his top pocket. Duck almost daren't ask. 'Well?'

'Well, we're on if we can get two hundred in the next twenty minutes.'

'One seventy-five,' corrected Duck. 'Where you gonna get that from?'

Hilton started the engine. There was a suitable store not a couple of blocks away, he knew. 'I'm going to make a withdrawal.'

SIX

'You want to know about Lewis? I suppose you gotta know about the rest of us then. How many altogether? Seven . . . eight if you count Lewis. This was . . . when? It must have been '69 or '70 . . . shit, thirty years ago now. So don't be surprised if there's some gaps. Do the best I can. So there was eight of us, all brought together by Lewis, he was the, y'know, like focal point, the driving force of the whole idea. He pulled us in from all over, sweet-talked or browbeat our commanders to let us come. Six months only, he said, and we'd be out. So let me see . . . There was Hobbs, the only black guy in the unit, read a lot, keen to know, to understand, what he was doing there. History, y'know. Knew all about the way the Brits re-armed the Japs and let the French come back in. Dien Bien Phu, all that shit. What *we* was doing there. I mean, fuck, he'd tell you why we had come, and at the end of it you was no wiser really. Still boiled down to you getting your ass shot off a long way from home for something you didn't really care about. Hobbs was a hard-stripe sergeant, so, I s'pose, technically senior rank. But things like that don't mean shit once you are operational. You obey the guy you think is gonna get you out of there alive. That man is your commanding officer and, Hobbs wouldn't mind me saying this, it wasn't always him. You sure you haven't got a Coke or anythin'? OK, no problem. Anyways . . . there was Ed Bart, also known as the Bat, 'cause he liked to keep his sunglasses on, even at night. And because he was good in the dark. Wayland, you had to have respect for Wayland, he invented the C-8-shaped charge. It was something you blew tunnels with. Joey Averne, he was Cuban, but OK with it, really. And Arnold, the only one of us of any size. He had to be five ten, eleven, but I tell you, he was like a fuckin' rubber band, you could thread a needle with that guy. How many is that? Then me, an' Lewis and Fix. Line us up and say pick out the odd one, it wouldn't be Arnold, even though he was taller'n all, it'd be Fix. The rest of us were dog soldiers, y'know, been there too long. No, no, he *was* one of us. Well, eventually. Shit, he gave us our name. That made him, like . . . lucky. A talisman, that's what Fix was. Fix? Fix . . . it was short for Felix. Felix Chessyre was his name. Got called Fix because he used to repair and hone surfboards on the beach – did I say he was Australian? He was Australian. Young. Nineteen. Maybe even eighteen. Terrible jokes, just all the time, man. All the time. Like what? Ghost walks into a bar, asks for a bourbon, the bar tender says, sorry we don't serve spirits. Bad? That was one of the diamonds. So what was Chessyre doin' there? Lewis has picked him up at Aberdeen. No, not the one in Scotland. The one in Maryland. I'll tell you about it later . . . look, I gotta get a drink, my throat is something else. There's a vending machine over there. All this talkin'. Aberdeen, Aberdeen. Where was I? Yeah, the boy Fix. He was on some sort of exchange scheme at the Proving Grounds, he was with the LWL. I'll tell you in a minute, once I have a drink. Well very quickly – he'd designed and developed a couple of bits of equipment. So he came over on a NETTS. It means New Equipment Testing and Training. He was there to see if his babies worked under field conditions. Lewis was kinda supervising him – he wanted to see if we could use them. You know, if the stuff was worth putting into production. What was it they was testing? Can I get that Coke now? Great. Some night-sight goggles. A probe for trapdoors. And one thing they were both real excited by . . . I'll be right back. You need anythin'? OK, OK, I'll tell you. Chrissake. Then I gotta get a drink. Y'see, the fuckin' kid had gone and invented a gun.'

SEVEN

Riverfront Park, Spokane, Eastern Washington State. 11.52 pm

The landing zone had been laid out in part of the converted Expo '74 grounds, a big white square visible on the grass as the two helicopters came in along the river. When his slick banked for over the opera house for its approach, Milliner caught a glimpse of the courthouse across the way. A bizarre attempt to make a municipal building mimic a French chateau, even from this distance it looked like an elaborate ants' nest there were so many men crawling over it. He felt a stab as he wondered if his team would get lost in the mêlée.

He could see another helicopter – a TV one – hovering over the city. Damned parasites. They should have put a media black-out in place. They might not tell them what they were doing, but any fool – and the people at AGFA might be fanatics, but they weren't stupid – could guess what was going on.

As soon as his helicopters touched down, his men were out in seconds, fast and neat, he noted with pride, forming up into two respective five-man squads. He stepped out and, as always, ducked. In fact, you would have to be a Lakers' defender in high heels to catch one of the slowing blades on one of these new models, but old habits died hard.

There was a lot to do. A lot to unload. The Bomb

people in the second chopper had sniffer devices, a robot and those fantastically bulky Bristol blast-proof suits. Then there were the chemical suits to worry about. Ever since the New York anthrax scare there was the sneaking suspicion that bombs were outmoded. Sarin, plague, VX, this was the modern way, released into a subway or confined space for maximum damage . . .

Spokane doesn't have a subway system, the voice in his head said.

He was listening for the next line when the reception committee, a lieutenant from the Spokane Emergency Response Team, collared him. As soon as Milliner was clear of the spinning disk he strode forward and held out his hand. 'Major Milliner? I'm Tom Flood. We would like to thank you for coming. We have billeted you across the bridge there.' He pointed south towards the Convention centre, still jagged from the effects of the explosion that had been AGFA's idea of a warning shot. 'Tents, I am afraid. Town is somewhat fuller than usual. FBI. Secret Service. ATF.'

Milliner nodded. It was a long time since he had been under canvas – not since Vietnam, probably – but he guessed finding motels for his type of unit was out of the question. He pointed at the news helicopter slowly heading their way, its finger-beam searchlight currently playing on the famous clock tower, in case viewers weren't sure where they were. The station was probably playing some Bing Crosby, too, just to ram it home. 'Can't you do anything about them?'

'What do you suggest? Shoot them down?'

'It would be a start,' said Milliner grimly. 'Aren't they going to give the whole ball game away?'

'We have told them that this is part exercise and part to give us time for a thorough sweep before the sentencing on Monday.'

'And you think these AGFA guys will go for that?'

'I hope so, Major.'

Milliner's Sergeant Marzo interrupted them, and pointed to the line of the SWOPS men, and the more relaxed clump of the bomb team. 'We are unloaded and ready, sir.'

Milliner acknowledged him with a nod, and, thinking again of the blood spilled on the sandy soil of Whidbey, said to Flood: 'I hope so, too, Lieutenant. I really hope so.'

. . . *but Seattle does*, the voice in his head finally finished.

EIGHT

Bella Vista Apartments, West Highland Drive, Queen Anne, Seattle. 11.59 pm

Human beings are full of surprises, Lewis thought. There he was expecting some kind of roasting of his *cojones*, maybe a lashing with that long tongue, a few choice phrases unknown outside of Raleigh, North Carolina, followed by a monumental sulk. Instead, Lewis found himself leaning up on one elbow and looking out through the rain-streaked window, down towards the lazily winking Needle, trying not to let the feeling, the warm glow of post-coital near-contentment, drain away. He wasn't sure of the exact progression from row to romance – it involved her being more worried about him than angry – but he was glad it went that way.

'What shall I tell Dennis?' came the regretful voice behind him. He looked over at her, lying on rumpled sheets, deftly completing the removal of her underwear. He wondered if she knew that he had faked it. Not that it took a Meg Ryan to fake the usual grunt and small exclamation of delight. She kept telling him to be more demonstrative in his sexual enjoyment, but he always felt silly, like he was in some bad porno. Perhaps it was a generational thing. Perhaps he just didn't like to let go. Scared to let go.

'Tell him . . . tell him your damaged-goods boyfriend needed some TLC for a change.'

She snorted. 'T and A more like. No really . . . I should have gone. Those kids . . .'

'You do enough for those kids as it is. It was a fundraising show. Three hundred people come along and look at paintings done by the kids who stole the stereo out of their car last year and put big bucks on the table and stash the painting in their loft. They know the fuckin' score, you know the fuckin' score, Dennis knows it. You weren't needed.'

'Hey, hey, what's with the language? Anyway . . . that's crap and you know it. The patrons love to hear me tell how some kid progressed from tagging Metro buses to being the new Keith Haring. That's what makes them buy it. Not altruism, just the thought that they might own the next big-bucks Basquiat.'

He pointed at a framed spray-painting. 'Well, one day we'll be rich –' The phone rang, cutting him off.

He hoped it wouldn't be Dennis, calling up with that weary-but-understanding tone that would suggest that if Dinah had been there they would have raised ten grand more.

'Uh . . . Carl?'

Sex had almost driven everything out of his mind, but somewhere behind his cerebral lobes there had been a pernicious nagging, the uncomfortable feeling that, even while he was immersed in Dinah, there was something wrong, something he should be sick to the guts about, a little rasping sound in his head that had kept him from committing himself fully to the whole business. Now he remembered.

'Willie. It's late. Where are you?' After a tale of damp rooms and greasy food, Lewis had lent him fifty dollars –

all he had on him – for his 'emergency fund' until the timbale-playing brother got to Western Union. He had kind of hoped it would keep him off his back for longer than four hours.

'I'm in the . . .' he could hear him fumbling with the hotel stationery '. . . it's the Sorrento.'

'The Sorrento? You can't stay at the Sorrento on fifty bucks, Willie.' He had pointed Willie at one of the near flop-houses down on First and Second at Pike. Not up the hill to the Sorrento. 'This phone call is probably costing you that. And don't open the minibar.'

'Sssallright.' Shit, too late. 'I borrowed a credit card before I left New York. But I just had it swiped. When my brother gets me the money, I'll settle in cash.'

'Look, Willie, if your brother doesn't come through, call me, huh? I'll settle for you. I don't want you banged up for credit-card fraud.' Damn – now where did that bit of ex-buddy magnanimity come from? Or was there something more selfish at work?

Behind him Dinah started to whisper about just how much a night at the Sorrento might be. A figure close to a month's rent was mentioned.

'Was there something else, Willie, or were you just calling up to tell me how soft the sheets are in swanky hotels?'

'He's still there, y'know . . .'

'Willie, we went through that . . .'

'Still down there. If they had found the body, it would be in the army records. It isn't. He is still listed as MIA.'

Lewis felt his ears start to redden. He knew Dinah was up and listening and puzzled now. He had to be careful what he said. 'Look, if some farmer had ploughed him up, say, what do you think they would have done? Reported it?'

'Yes. Yesss. There is a reward for any US Service bodies called in. A lot of dollars for some gook farmer, Carl. Sure they would have called it in. Anyways, they would need a fuckin' big plough.' He was shouting now, something Lewis was sure the Sorrento weren't used to.

'Calm down, Willie. I haven't said no.'

'I know, I know. And you will get a full third share.'

Lewis couldn't help himself. 'Third?'

'Bats. Bats is entitled to something, isn't he?'

'Yes, you're right, Bats should get his share.' Well, there goes a third of nothing, anyway. Was it worth reminding Willie that, after twenty-five years, the obstacles to cashing in were still exactly the same? Probably not now.

'Look, keep thinking about it. I'll call you tomorrow, huh?'

'Yes, Willie, I doubt if I'll have anything else on my mind for the next few hours.'

When he hung up he let out a huge sigh, and for a moment they sat there, illuminated solely by the glow from the bathroom, the only sound their carefully measured breathing and the tapping of the rain squalls on the windows.

'Willie?' she finally asked. 'I've never heard you mention a Willie. What kind of Willies stay at the Sorrento?'

'The kind that do it on other people's credit cards. He's an old friend.'

'An *old* friend? An *old friend*? You don't have old friends, Carl. Not once have you mentioned old college buddies, old army friends, girlfriends . . . and now suddenly we have Willie, who just happens to be a credit-card scam merchant.'

It was true. When he moved on from a city, he left them all behind, as if lovers, friends and acquaintances were an entity, a unit, a capsule you could discard. That part of my life is over, he would think. Time to move on. Los Angeles, New Orleans, Houston, New York, Chicago, San Francisco . . . two, three years or so, and time to move on. 'Well, one of them finally caught up with me.' And what a doozy he turned out to be, he wanted to add.

'Did you see him earlier? Because you have been very, very strange since you came in. I mean, something screwed up your orgasm, didn't it?'

He snorted in what he hoped was a non-committal way.

'Want to tell me about it?' she asked. 'After all, it will be me picking up the Sorrento tab tomorrow, won't it? Not unless grubby little Michael has come up with some more work for you.'

Grubby little Michael had not come up with more work, and the usual bone thrown by the Seattle cops when they needed a real photographer had been in little evidence these past months. Although maybe being beaten by Tenniel was a good move in that department. The Lewis coffers were low, but then again he should be grateful that Dinah only used the disparities in their incomes – her small trust fund made it possible for her to live beyond an art therapist's means – as a weapon when she was feeling snitty.

So here is the choice, he thought. Three years with

this woman, a pretty well-balanced, caring kind of person who uses her (self-confessed) modest talents in painting and drawing to capture the stunted imagination of kids the courts are just about to give up on. He goes along to shoot the works of these proto-Pollocks and finds the teacher is also interested in photography. Or maybe – just maybe – the photographer.

She doesn't worry that he obviously only just gets by in his chosen field, that he seems incapable of putting down roots, that he has a well-watered bunch of idiosyncrasies: always takes the stairs, not the elevator, even though she lives on the fifth floor, that, like a baby, he prefers to sleep with a nightlight on, and that he is happiest when he is up a mountain taking panoramic shots of some godforsaken wilderness without a machiata for miles and miles. Doesn't worry, until now, that he comes without friends, family or hangers-on. Just makes a new set and gets on with it.

This is the woman who helped tighten the bolts and spin the combination lock on the place where he keeps all his past spooled up.

Except someone like Willie doesn't even need the combination, he just comes in and plants a few thermite charges: I'm going back to Vietnam – boom – It is still there – boom – He is still MIA – double boom. Hi, I'm those dreams you hoped never to see again. And now he could hear that sound again, the one that always caused the lurch in the stomach, the spin of the head. The sound of a soft, soft kiss.

He shook his head clear. So what do you do, he asked himself, with the woman who picked you up, dusted you down, who doesn't mind calling off a visit to an important show for Chinese take-out and slightly unsatisfactory sex, the woman who knows that you love her even though you keep forgetting to mention it these days? Do you tell the truth or lie? He did the only thing possible. He lied.

NINE

Second Floor, 88 Henry Street, Seattle.
Saturday. 12.05 am

Harry March took another look through the camera, his tenth in the last two minutes. Still the loading bay at the rear of the wine store on the opposite block was shuttered and dark. He looked at his watch. The Sergeant had said – he stopped himself. He sounded like a schoolkid. 'But Sergeant, you said a two-hour stake-out max. They would be there by nine at the latest, loading up the cases of Silver Lake and St Michelle.' Four hours later and Harry felt like he was turning into a cyclops, he had been squinting through the Nikon for so long. Not even a peek out by the nightwatch guy, the one they had fingered for the disappearing stock.

He risked groping his way across to the bathroom – the glass coffee table had impaled his leg three times so far – and lit a cigarette. As he pulled the lengthening ash towards the filter, willed it backwards with each inhalation, he let rip with a little therapeutic self-pity. Surely he had been given this shitty stake-out because he was an outsider, a secondee, a Canook at that. And to cap it all, a Californian by birth, the lowest of the low as far as most Seattlalites were concerned.

So, just to punish him for his birthplace and his adopted town, he gets this no-hope survey. And how no-hope? They couldn't even spare a stake-out van to park in the street. No budget, Tenniel says, you want budget you have to join the SWOPS, they have all the greenbacks this year. No, no need to tie up all that manpower, Harry, call it in, man, and we'll come running.

He would bet a month's wages the rookie who had swapped with him was having a better time, swanning round the Gaslight district, helping the odd cute tourist find their way to a decent bar, riding shotgun on a couple of busts. And here he was, in the city of the Green River Killer, Ted Bundy and the South Hill rapist, waiting to see who is lifting some store's pinot noir.

He imagined his future father-in-law laughing at his discomfort. Didn't want his daughter marrying some cop. Didn't want his daughter marrying some white boy either, but that was a secondary concern. 'Why you want to be a cop anyway?' he asked. 'T J Hooker?' And he laughed that scary, gurgling laugh where you could hear the fluid rattling in his tubes. Scary, that was the word for the tough, little wizened guy. How did he manage to produce such a beautiful, delicate daughter?

He turned the bath tap onto the cigarette stub, hissing it out. Back to the lens. What really worried Harry, what really threw him was when the cantankerous old bastard became Mr Reasonable and asked him, straight out, why he really became a cop. And not a lawyer. Or even an accountant. Harry was a bit frightened of the answer to that. Frightened of the ridicule. It was safer to cite William Shatner. Best stop thinking for a while, he was winding himself up.

Time for another cigarette? Shit, only four minutes since the last one. He moved the tripod and started to pan down the street. Midnight, Friday night. This area was a weird mix. High-class clothes and food and wine shops, like the one opposite, nestled cheek-by-jowl-by-tittie with places like the Showbar, slogan: Fifty Beautiful Girls and a Couple of Ugly Ones. He was looking at one specimen now, the Skin Arcade at the very end of the street on the corner, where a group of conventioneers nervously debated whether they should go into its beating-off booths, secretly scared that someone would break the out-of-town amnesty oath and tell their wife. A girl in a white shift dress – and probably nothing else – appeared at the entrance to the arcade and they suddenly scattered like frightened rabbits, confronted by the sordid truth. Tenniel had told them about that joint's sales pitch. 'Wanna see my pussy?' was probably just too direct for those guys.

He panned back again. Henry was one of the few two-way streets left downtown, which made it difficult to keep track of the traffic flow. He found himself trying to spot good-looking girls through the blur of passing windshields.

Damn, if Tenniel didn't relieve him soon, all they would find was a babbling wreck in the morning. He gave the suspect store another pull. Nothing. Back to the road. Nope, all he got there was a big Winnebago, someone off to Snoqualmie to live the life of the backwoodsman for a weekend. Pacific Rimmers, they loved that outdoor-life schtick.

He wished Tenniel would call, even if he did have to suffer his hysterical Surfer Boy call-sign routine. Real professional, Sergeant. He wished he'd never told him he used to surf, that he had wanted to turn pro. Keep checking, Harry. Loading bay? Nothing. Winnebago?

Slowing up for the 7-Eleven. Or was it? Perhaps looking like Dudley Deer Hunter was the best cover a lifter of fine wines could have. You could get a lot of merlots in the back of one of those. He kept the lens on the camper as it rolled to a halt.

TEN

1st Avenue, Seattle. 12.01 am

Bitch. Bitch. Bitch, bitch, bitch. Ed Deane looked over at the curled-up form next to him, her long blonde hair dangling off the seat to almost touch the floor of the Winnebago. Fucking bitch. How could she do that? She must have left that school report lying round so he could see it, so his weekend could start with a big fat poke in the eye with a very sharp stick.

Deane. What was wrong with Deane? She thought it was a perfectly fine name when she swapped one nobody could spell for something real straightforward. 'Deane with an e' was all you had to say. Bitch.

He glanced over at her as she stirred, and he felt a sudden pang of pure love hit him in the solar plexus. It was so strong it almost took his breath away, that ridiculous feeling of wanting to wake your child up to tell them that they are safe and that you love them and they can go back to sleep now. And all you got in return was a heavy-lidded look that said 'but I *was* asleep until you woke me up'.

So now his sleeping daughter was Ali Pleasaunce, his bitch ex-wife's maiden name. Sometime over the next few days he would have to ask Ali – quietly, subtly, when his rage had subsided – just what she felt about the change in identity, to having eight years as a Deane wiped out, to begin again as someone completely different. The Pleasaunces were from some no-hope town in Iowa, so small even the one horse had got bored and left. He guessed, though, that a kid like Ali would think it cute that where her mom grew up the nearest thing they had to a metropolis was somewhere called Pocahontas. And shit, if ever a family had been misnamed, it was those ballbreakers. But the Deanes, they came from San Francisco, a real town, where his dad still . . . oh, damn, damn, damn.

In the heat of the whispered and spat argument he had left a carrier bag of supplies on the table, stormed out with Ali and hit the road without even looking in it. All he knew was that all her favourite treats – the little foodie bribes that would stop a sulk dead in its tracks – were in there. He didn't reckon he could get through a camping, communing-with-nature and, more crucially, TV-less weekend without some such back-up. And because she was reluctantly skipping soccer training to come with him, he had promised her double rations.

He skipped the turn for 99. He knew there was a 24-hour 7-Eleven a few blocks ahead (why did they still call them 7-Elevens when they stayed open round the clock?), and he started to slow up the great oil tanker of a machine. He was going to have to wake Ali up and let her choose the necessary stock. He passed the great hammering man outside the Seattle Art Museum on his right, crossed Union, Pike and made the turn into Henry, pulled into the kerb and hit the footbrake.

He didn't wake her for a moment. He had told her they wouldn't get where they were going until the very early hours – or later, now that the firefight with her mother had eaten up so much of the night – and, excited as she was, she dutifully curled up like some small mammal and went to sleep.

He leant over and sniffed. Asleep she gave off a comforting aroma, some primitive essence, a protective pheromone that made him want to wrap his arms around her and rock her, kiss her head, yet at the same time left him feeling terrified and bereft, because he knew he could never protect her from everything in this world – not even that name-changing bitch – and that one day, perhaps, the roles would be reversed, and he would be an old man in her arms. Hey – he should live that long.

'Ali.' Deane shook her shoulder gently. 'Ali, sorry, we gotta make a supply run.'

She stirred, stretched, blinked and managed a smile, the brave girl.

ELEVEN

Bella Vista Apartments, West Highland Drive, Queen Anne, Seattle. 12.38 am

It wasn't so much a pack of lies as a Frankenstein monster of the truth, bolted together from a combination of his history, Willie's story, a couple of movie incidents, and a bit of pure fabrication, and, to Lewis's amazement, it got up and tottered round the room relatively convincingly. He could see the holes in it, the dangling wires, the bad joints and the way the ears didn't match, but either Dinah wasn't paying attention or she was too tired to notice or care.

But, as he sat on the edge of the bed, he realised he was shaking, just a mild tremor really, mainly because the torso of the beast was, after all, the truth, a major chunk of reality that he had told – how many people about? Well, most recently, a shrink in New York, who at least gave it a name – or a set of initials: DFS. And then Judy, his last ex, the one who had flipped out totally, and, most stupidly, John Tenniel, his fat racquetball partner, and sometime employer, who looked at him funny when he had finished and quickly changed the subject. And, as far as he recalled, Lewis had told him even less than he had given to Di.

Maybe, just maybe, that was how it began. He let his mind backtrack, to other places, other girls, other friends. Other takes on the truth. Messy, all of them.

And now, Di. Well, of all of them, she deserved his best shot.

She was now sprawled diagonally across the big mahogany sleigh-bed – a present from her mom, her half-a-rainforest she sometimes called it in moments of guilt – and, apart from the bedside table with phone and multi-band radio, the only substantial piece of furniture in the room.

Lewis reached over and put a hand on her ribs, feeling the rhythm of her breathing. There was something oddly asymmetrical about the rise and fall of her thorax, as if one lung inflated fractionally more than the other. He had mentioned this to her once, and she had claimed it was spooky. She had broken three ribs as a kid while riding, but as far as she knew it made no difference to her breathing. He ran his fingertips across the top of her solar plexus and felt, or sensed, it again. He still had the touch. Fat use it was to him now.

He slid off the bed and tiptoed to the kitchen for a coffee. And maybe a brandy.

Dinah felt the mattress move as his weight came off it. She had detected the quivering of his body, and his fingers on the ribs, too, but had decided not to respond. He probably didn't want to know that her mind was spinning into the red zone at what he had told her. At what he obviously hadn't told her.

But then, she could hardly complain now. One thing – one of the things – she liked about him was the way he never let nine months in South East Asia become the defining moment of his life. No Vet associations, no camping trips with the old buddies, no obvious souvenirs around the place – not ones he knew she knew about anyway. It was just something that had happened to him, the same way she had done Europe at that age. Lewis wasn't like Oliver Stone who kept a claymore mine on his desk as a talisman. Or was that John Milius? One of those film-makers blessed with a surfeit of testosterone anyway.

But now she wondered whether, in fact, it was that healthy an option. Maybe he was in denial about it all, maybe he should have talked it out over some Robert Bly sessions deep in the woods. Maybe she should have got him to paint some stuff, try and see what was in there. Well, perhaps it wasn't too late to start.

She heard the coffee-maker hiss. 'Me, too.'

He put his head round the door. 'Sorry, I couldn't sleep.'

'And you think a quick blast of caffeine will do the trick?'

'You want de-caff?' It came out as de-ceff, as usual, but, post-coitally at least, she even liked the odd things he did to vowels.

'Can I move straight to the brandy?'

He fussed around for three more minutes and appeared with two large bowls, the bottom apparently merely smeared with best vintage Armagnac. Given the volume of the glasses, however, she knew it represented a generous nightcap. And there was a chocolate wafer. Now, that's the other reason he was easy to love: he never underestimated the role of chocolate in a woman's life.

'You know Elder's work?' she asked.

'Elder Sanchez? The car thief?'

'The stuff you described as looking like "gazpacho vomit", yes.'

'I meant it affectionately. I'm a fan of gazpacho.'

'You know how he does that stuff?'

'He's another spinning-wheel merchant, isn't he?'

'He uses a modified industrial centrifuge.'

'Isn't that just a very powerful spinning wheel?'

'Whatever. But he has got this theory that he knows what is going to come out. Well, it isn't his theory, it's a belief. He says that the final patterns are never a surprise, that random isn't a word he ever uses or accepts. There comes a point in the cycle, different for each work, when he knows to hit the brake and let the paint fly onto the stretched canvas. A frozen moment he calls it.' She took a slug and relished the burn. 'Kid's going to be a star, you know. We already got one piece sold to the new branch of Wild Ginger.'

'Yeah well, he will be with that bullshit about patterns. All the makings.'

'He did it for me once. He drew out the pattern that would be generated, before he had even put the paint in the machine. The colours, their location, the texture. Everything. He loaded it up, let it spin, and sat there in a kind of trance, listening, listening. Then he opened his eyes and hit the brake. The paint flew out of the pots, onto the canvas, and then he pulled it out of the machine. It was just like the drawing.'

'Di, all his paintings look the same.'

'No they don't. They don't. I have seen enough of them. I can tell you what year, what month he did them.'

'Yeah, well, he always dates them.'

'Carl, I am trying to make a point here.' She glugged

back the remaining Armagnac in frustration and gave a shudder and a cough. Too much.

'Sorry. You know, somehow I can't get Willie Rivera and conceptual art – even conceptual art by reformed auto thieves – to inhabit the same thought. The same brain, even.'

'Well, this is kind of about that. Elder believes there is this . . . moment when the pattern forms, that the mole-cules are in a particular time and space, some kind of synchronicity, and if he hits the button at precisely the right moment they will come out in the pattern he predicts. Because he knows where all the paint is, because he can sense when the time is right, I don't know. You know how thick his accent is.'

'He's from Wisconsin.'

'He's from Chiapas, via Wisconsin.'

Lewis drained his glass, and slid under the sheets next to her. What she was trying to do, he was sure, was blind him with art, take his mind off tunnel-dwelling Puerto Ricans. And Mr Dodo.

'I just wonder if, you know, Willie turning up, you telling me all that stuff – God why didn't you tell me before? You said you were in engineering?'

'I was. Technically. And you never really wanted to hear any of it before now.'

Fair point. 'I just wondered if that – this – was exactly the right time, when, you know, like Elder's frozen moments, what with Willie and all, when you get it out for good.'

He gave a hollow-sounding laugh. 'You want me to scribble you out a quick doodle so you can analyse it?'

She ignored the jibe. 'Oh come on, be serious . . . and don't belittle my work.'

The room gave a half-spin, just to let him know he wasn't going to get out of it that easy. Not now. Not after all this time. 'I am sorry. Jeez-us, but jumping in here.' He tapped his head. 'That's the dumbest idea I've heard all night. Go to sleep.'

TWELVE

Second Floor, 88 Henry Street, Seattle. 12.35 am

Damn it, Harry was going to give it ten more minutes, no five, five more minutes, or until ten more cars had passed, whichever was the sooner, and then he was going to call the Sergeant and tell him this was a big joke. The Winnebago had turned out to be a major disappointment: Dudley Deer Hunter was some regular guy with his little girl.

Although what, he thought primly, was a little girl doing up at this hour? And they were lucky it had stopped raining – the girl didn't even have a coat on. She couldn't have been more than ten or eleven. No, given the size of kids these days, probably seven or eight, artificially fattened and lengthened on fast foods. 'More junkety-junk-junk' as his father-in-law – putative father-in-law – put it. Where were all the fresh vegetables? the guy often asked, seemingly oblivious to the walls of plump, shining technicolour marvels that lined the entrance to the local Safeway. Well, perhaps he meant homegrown, not flown in from Zambia or Mexico.

God, the old boy was a difficult fucker. If he didn't want his daughter to meet Americans, why did he come to America? Well, Canada, then. But surely he didn't distinguish between . . . could it be that? Could it be that because the Canadians stayed neutral, that is why he settled there, and why he treated Harry with such disdain? Fuck, he hadn't thought of that. If he had just said he was born and brought up in Vancouver, the old man might've taken to him after all.

He was so mad at himself that he almost missed the Ford as it slowed down opposite the 7-Eleven, and when he did clock it he paid little attention, flicking back to the warehouse lot opposite, finding it, natch, still in darkness, then pulling back to the Ford to check it wasn't a sidewalk crawler. And he got a view finder full of some big dude hitching up his trousers and adjusting the .45 auto in his belt.

He hit the button and the motordrive gave him six shots straight off, from the trouser hitch, the repositioning of the gun, the buttoning of the jacket, the half-turn to walk across the street.

Harry froze. Action. He could hardly believe it. He could hardly believe it so much that the guy was halfway across to the store before he came to. He lunged for the ROVER communication unit on the coffee table, catching the corner again and hearing his Dockers rip. He pulled up the walkie-talkie and blurted out: 'The 7-Eleven on Henry. Officer needs back-up. Officer in plainclothes. Repeat, officer in plainclothes . . .' He remembered what they said in the academy: use the code. '10-1, 10-1.' Now what was the code they used in this town for armed robbery? Damn it. Then he remembered, it was the most straightforward code of all. English. Seattle didn't use any numericals at all. 'Armed robbery in progress. 7-Eleven on Henry Street. Just get me back-up.' Harry didn't wait to hear back from the dispatcher, he just sprinted for the door, cracking his shin one last time for good measure.

* * *

Hilton pulled up and looked over at the bright window of the 7-Eleven. Part of it was obscured by a big camper van, and about a third of it was opaque with decals and special-offers announcements and Lotto prize details, but from what he could see, the place was empty.

'The glove box,' he said to Duck with a snap of the fingers.

Duck pressed the catch and looked in at the two guns, a rather battered .38 and a shiny silver AMT .45 auto. He selected the latter and offered it over.

'Hilton, we could get two hundred for that, easy.'

Hilton looked appalled. This was his gun. He loved it, really liked the name – the AMT Hardballer. He thought it summed him up perfectly – you deal with Hilton, you have to play hardball. To Duck he just said: 'It's my gun, asshole. You go to a drug score, they expect you to be armed, you know, the way they expect you to have your pants on.' He waved the gun under Duck's nose. 'Look, he sees this, any shop clerk gonna think one-seventy-five is getting off light.'

Hilton stepped out of the car and slid the gun into his belt. He turned away from oncoming traffic and adjusted it. Walking with over a kilo of gun sticking in your dick was never easy. He buttoned the jacket, pulled out the woollen facemask from the pocket and turned. In, out, away. No more than thirty dollars in till, that is what the sign on the door always said. But he knew the kids who worked there didn't always fill the floor safe. And if all else failed, he could make someone empty the ATM machine they all had installed in the store. Just get the money. Don't get distracted.

As soon as he had gone, Duck did what came naturally. He ducked.

Harry emerged from the apartment entrance about thirty metres or so from the Ford, on the same side of the road. He peered at it for a few seconds. Despite the residue of rain that obscured his view of the interior, he was fairly sure the big guy who had just walked into the store had no company in the car. How long for back-up? The Sergeant had said they would be with him within five minutes when they dropped him off. But that was before the traffic downtown snarled up. He could still hear the horns drifting through the night air. He just hoped Tenniel realised he needed a siren right now.

But, he thought, let's be honest here. *This* is what you joined for, he said to himself, as he eased the Glock out of his shoulder holster. This was why he wasn't a lawyer or an accountant. This was the closest he got to that feeling when a big wave was bearing down on you, ready to pulverize you, crush your ribs, suck the air from your body and replace it with seawater. If you let it. This was the same kind of thrill. Exactly the same. So why did he feel so shaky? Four deep breaths, get some oxygen into the lungs, and go. Ride it, Harry, ride it.

Gun held down at his side, he walked straight across the street, before turning to approach the store, hugging the wall. The Winnebago was still there. Shit, that meant the little girl was inside the store. Let's hope nobody does anything real stupid. Just give him the money and Harry would get him on the way out. He knew the scenario. It went 'Stop' – bang – 'Armed police' – bang – 'Halt or we fire.' Bang, bang. At this range he wasn't going to wait for the opening salvo to come from someone desperate enough to rob a 7-Eleven. Must be a brain-addled junkie; everybody else knew that convenience stores rarely held more than thirty or fifty bucks at any one time these days.

He reached the edge of the store window, and pulled up the gun, hoping no passing car decided to stop and gawk. To add to the rip in his Dockers, the bottoms were now soaked from the great puddles of surface water slowly draining away. His Eddie Bauer pigskin loafers were acting like blotting paper, darkening as the tide slowly rose. Did the Seattle PD have an allowance for clothes ruined on the job, he wondered.

Duck risked a look over the edge of the door-sill, and snapped back down again. Fuck, who was that? The little guy looked like he meant to drop Hilton, that was for sure. Duck glanced at the glove box in front of him. The moment he reached and flipped it open to get the S&W, its interior light would come on. Now, Mr Well-Armed Cop – he had to be a cop – over there might not notice, but then again . . .

He heard the hiss of an approaching car, throwing up spumes of water. Duck waited until it was level, hit the button, grabbed the gun and slammed the compartment shut. There was so much light bouncing off the wet surfaces from headlights that the little guy couldn't possibly have picked it out from the surrounding glare. But just in case, he kept down. Then, almost in slo-mo, he reached across and turned the ignition key to spark up the electrics. One click, that's all – if he accidentally engaged the starter, the cop would be right onto him. He tried another peek. Nope, he wasn't looking his way. He hit the button for the side window. With the barest squeak, the window pulled free of its rubber seal and came down. And they badmouth Fords, he thought.

Hilton noted the guy and the little girl at the counter, but the father didn't look to be any trouble. All the guy wanted in life right now was the pile of candies and sodas in front of him and he'd be on his way. Hilton had pulled the mask down before entering the shop: don't worry about the cameras, he kept saying to himself, don't even look up to check how you are doing on the TV screen. Be calm. Be reasonable.

'OK, folks, you know what this is.' He had the glinting form of the Hardballer straight ahead of him, swivelling from head to head, clerk to customer. The customer put his arms on the girl and stepped back, leaving him a clear path. Ignore him. Hilton levelled at the clerk. Eighteen, nineteen, wide-eyed, thinking about the alarm. 'I need one hundred and seventy-five dollars. That's all. No more. Don't die for that, kid. I mean, when you gotta go, go for four figures or more, huh? I know what it says on the door, but either from the till or that—' He nodded at the slab of the cash dispenser. 'Don't worry me.'

The clerk nodded. Without a word he opened the till and counted out one eighty in tens and twenties. Lovely.

Hilton reached and grabbed the pile, shoved it into his jacket, had taken the first tentative step backwards, when the shop exploded over all their heads.

Duck had him lined up. Head shot? Too small a target

they always said in the gun mags. Go for the body. But the argument then was, you ought to have something with real stopping power. A long-barrelled Magnum, or a heavy slug like the .45 that Hilton had. Not a junked Detective's Special, bought off some cops who were meant to be melting them down.

The pocket-sized policeman flattened against the wall, putting his whole body side on. Easy. The big target; well, as big as it was going to get with this guy. And even with a relatively low muzzle velocity, a bullet to the heart was going to slow this sucker down.

Duck squeezed the trigger and waited for the thud and twitch of impact. Instead, he watched the 7-Eleven sign on the window shudder and shimmy for the merest fraction of a second, as if the glass was simply a film of soapy liquid, before it self-destructed into a thousand shards.

Harry heard the shot before the glass went, and buried his face in the wall. Then came the brittle cascade. A nugget of glass punched a jagged semi-circle out of his left ear, and he felt a trickle down his neck. Blood on my shirt now, he thought: it'll be a new wardrobe before the night was out.

For one second Harry believed the bullet must have come out of the store, but he saw most of the glass had showered inwards. He glanced across at the Ford again. Empty. But the window was down. And wasn't that a tuft of hair peeking above the parapet? He opened his mouth to shout 'Stop—' but realised this one wasn't going anywhere. It didn't take long to resolve the dilemma of how to play it. The Glock bucked as he punched two closely grouped holes through the door. He reckoned that would keep his sniper down.

The stray bullet smashed into the gum and cigarette display on the counter, sending up a shower of Wrigleys and Virginia Slims. The clerk was gone, prone, probably pumping that floor alarm for all he was worth. Next move, Hilton? Then he heard two heavier, closer gunshots.

He stepped across and grabbed the girl's arm. The father looked at him, not realising the situation for a minute, and then seemed to explode with fury. Hilton took one blow on the chin, and felt a stab in the eye. Still holding onto the girl he took a step back and lashed out with the .45, making contact with something.

His left eye started to water, and the right's vision was blurred. Fuck, fuck, fuck. This wasn't going according to the Convenience Store Robbers' Yearbook at all.

Deane could only see red rage, a great crimson tide that had swept across his retina as the blood boiled in his brain. Everyone wanted to take his little girl away from him. Well, not this cocksucker. He tried a punch, but it felt feeble, softened and absorbed by the woollen mask. What else? What else had they taught him in self-defence classes? He jabbed a finger into one of the man's wide eyes, at the same time as making a grab for Ali's arm, when something cracked in his cheekbone.

There was a stand-off for a few seconds, one man blinking, the other trying to keep his balance and stop from vomiting with pain. Deane broke it by sweeping a bottle off the counter and, aiming it at Hilton's head, launched himself forward. Before it had finished the arc,

Hilton fired, smacking his attacker across the aisle and into the shelving. In a shower of beans and soups and salsas, Deane slid to the floor, bursting the tortilla chip packets with a loud pop.

The impact of the round had made Deane lose his grip on the bottle, which continued its path and made contact with Hilton. Another pause as Hilton, braced for impact, felt it spring off the wool next to his forehead and watched it fall to the floor and bounce, the contents frothing up as it rolled towards the prostrate Deane, now leaking fresh red blood to join the multi-coloured mix smearing the floor around him. Plastic. A plastic bottle.

It was only then, with the roar of the gunshot fading in his ears, that Hilton realised the girl had been screaming all along. He cuffed her, harder than he intended, and the screams turned to body-shaking sobs. Better.

Harry had positioned himself at the edge of the now empty window-frame. He looked around quickly. The street was suddenly empty. No conventioneers, no bums. He risked a glance around the window-edge and glimpsed snatches of the tussle between the two men, a short, sharp spat, in the spaces between the aisles, but the girl was always in the fray. Harry was a good shot, but he couldn't adjust the course of bullets once they left that gun, and, in all the interplay, she was as likely to be in the line of fire as the big guy when the slug reached them.

He flinched at the boom of the gunshot, heavy and sickening, and the crash of shelving and cans. In the distance he could hear a siren. Come on, boys, I can no longer feel the bottom here, I am treading water. He knew his nerve was going, but at the same time there was a tingling warmth in his belly, that old excitement. Why you wanna be a cop? asked the old man. For this, was the answer, for this. Keep it together.

'STOP.' His voice sounded firmer, deeper than he thought it would. 'POLICE. RELEASE THE GIRL AND—'

The second boom sent him spinning back around the corner, flattening against the brick again. No way could Mr Masked Man have got a good sighting on him. Must have been a wild warning shot. Still, it worked. Harry heard the crunch of glass under large feet.

'I'm coming out. You know I've got the girl. I don't think you want her to see her daddy again quite so soon.'

Harry didn't move, except to raise the Glock to shoulder level. A few feet away, Hilton stepped into the street, his arm clamped around the girl's waist. Harry panned the gun-sight to follow the black-wrapped head. The girl had gone into some kind of shock, hiccupping more than breathing, and he was holding her high enough that for Harry to try a shot to his head was far too risky.

This was, they both knew, a classic cornered-rat situation. The man in the ketchup in there might just live, Hilton figured, if the shot to the side hadn't taken out too much collateral. Like a major artery. But killing – even shooting – a cop rapidly reduced his chances of getting away. 'Eathy,' Hilton said, trying to keep his tongue behind his wayward teeth. He didn't want to look nervous here. The guy was short, but in his experience the short ones were the worst. Little ones and women, both had a lot to prove.

Hilton risked a glance at the car, to see if Duck was ready to roll. No sign. Fuckwit was either sprinting halfway to the Cascade Mountains by now, or cowering on the floor. He looked again, and saw the two holes in the door. God alone knew what it looked like on the other side.

'I think your friend is out of it,' said Harry, noting the weeping eye. Dad got one in after all.

Hilton tightened his grip on the girl. Getting into the car, shifting Duck, keeping the cop covered . . . too much. All around him the sirens were growing louder. No more than a block away. He had been lucky there hadn't been a unit parked in one of the alleys. Maybe the luck would hold. He gave the cop a quick appraisal. His eyes were suspect, blinking and twitching, but the end of the gun aimed at him was rock-steady. Glock 23. Chambered for the S&W .40 round, rather than the lighter 9mm that Glocks usually had. No safety on those suckers either, you squeezed the trigger and you were in business. Serious shit. Yup, he reckoned the pint-size'd do it if he had to.

So Hilton did the only thing he could. He put the AMT .45 to the girl's head and pulled the trigger.

THIRTEEN

Central Seattle. 12.40 am

Tenniel jostled the two conversations at once. In his right ear the uniform was telling him that it was a case of all hands needed on deck right now, if he could just come and finish the interview with the suspect and in his left the first-floor dispatcher was repeating that 'his boy' was in trouble. Pushing aside the uniform and elbowing through the chaos of the squad room, he had grabbed his coat off the rack and ran, taking the stairs to the second-floor garage, hardly noticing that Isa Bowman was almost up his ass until she shouted, 'Let's take mine,' and jumped into her Chrysler.

It had stopped raining, but the streets were Vaseline-shiny and slippy, and Bowman fishtailed off the Public Safety Building garage ramp and onto Third Avenue. Tenniel reached under the dash and put the magnetic light on the roof. He needn't have bothered. Within two blocks they were snarled up on Third, one of the temperamental Italian buses designed to run in the bus tunnels below them having stalled. He didn't know why they closed the damned tunnels after dark – too scared of the homeless colonising them he supposed. 'Come on, come on.'

Bowman hit another squawk of the siren and the car in front pulled over enough to let them through.

'So. Have you told your wife?' asked Bowman as she negotiated the gap, clipping the guy's outside mirror and holding up a hand in apology. She saw the finger flash up in the mirror, but they didn't have time to worry about some asshole suing the city for the subsequent stress of driving home with cracked glass.

'What's to tell?'

'You know. Me.'

He was more likely to tell his wife he was patrolling with Officer Dibble than that Bowman was on the scene. A few years back, after they had paired up, he was told: transfer away from that woman or we are history. It was unfair. If Bowman had been a guy nothing would have been said about stopping for coffee at Avalon, a martini at Oliver's, a beer at McCormack's now and then. But because it was a woman . . . the old police wives' syndrome: they are going to take our men. As if someone like Bowman fancied a round or two with him.

Still he came off street patrol and back into the polyester once more, and Bowman had always hated him for breaking up the team. Well, resented might be nearer the mark. But she was right: they had complemented each other well. But now she was enjoying making him squirm.

'So that is a no, then? Well, she probably won't find out in the next three weeks. Before I go, I mean. That we are working together again. Well, at least in the same department. Not from me anyway. No sirree—'

'Isa—'

She finally swerved round the limping bus and hit the full siren. Two blocks to go. 'Only kiddin', John, only kiddin'. Look, I wouldn't want to be on your wife's shitlist—'

'Her name is Catherine.'

'Yeah, well. I heard what she used to call me, so forgive me if I can't bear not to gag when I say it.' They had never even met. Catherine had just observed the pair one evening when she had turned up to meet him at the end of the shift. It was just fooling around, high spirits, but apparently it looked bad.

As she flung the car round the corner into Henry, Tenniel suddenly felt it was going to be a long three weeks.

They turned in to see the white and red Medic One vans coming in the opposite direction. Christ, he thought, he'd got the kid killed, all for a few bottles of hocked hooch. Bowman pulled them to a halt outside the store behind a big Winnebago and they were out before the car stopped rocking on its suspension. After all these years, Tenniel couldn't help using his brain like a camera at a SOC, freezing and storing the images for future reference. Snap. Late model Ford; two holes in door. Snap. Winnebago. Snap. No glass in store window, splinters spewed across pavement, sitting like ice in the puddles.

He stopped doing it when he looked inside the 7-Eleven. One man lay in a mélange of smashed and dented convenience foods and spilled snacks, as if he had been the victim of a macabre shopping trolley hit-and-run. Another man – a boy, really – knelt over him, frantically trying to mop up the blood. Whether he was worried about the punctured John Doe or the state of the floor wasn't too clear. But the stiff wasn't Harry, he realised with guilty relief.

It was a moment before he spotted March down the

street, beyond the RV, pressed flat against the wall outside a metal-shuttered office supplies store. He was glancing his way, and beckoning.

Tenniel delayed long enough to make sure the paramedics were going to see to the carnage within – and that the uniforms who had arrived felt sure they could handle it without calling in a Scene of Crime technician – and loped – running was out of the question given his current girth – down the sidewalk to Harry. The kid looked pale. His put-me-in-the-line-of-fire cockiness was leaking badly, but as far as Tenniel could tell that was all that had drained out of his body, apart from a few drops out of a scratch on his ear.

'Little surfer boy—'

'Quiet,' Harry snapped back. He was pointing down an alley that started three feet beyond his left shoulder. His voice was a rasp. 'He's down there. With a kid. Little girl.'

'Who is, Detective?' Business-like now. Tenniel did not like to be silenced by his juniors. He was aware that Bowman was over his shoulder, pressing against him. He took a step forward.

'I don't know. Big.' Then he remembered that most people were big compared to him. 'Big-ish – six one, two. Got a facemask on. The girl's seven or eight, maybe older.' The voice was shaky. Forgive him the tetchiness, Tenniel thought. The first hostage situation is always a brain-mincer.

Bowman asked: 'Any of them related to the party in the Campbell soup display?'

'Daughter, I would guess. They came out of that Winnebago together.'

'Well,' said Tenniel, 'there goes his weekend.'

'Sergeant,' Harry barked impatiently. 'This guy is a psycho. He put the gun to the kid's head and pulled the trigger. Caught the hammer with his thumb. If he'd slipped—'

'You'd have shot him,' suggested Bowman.

March looked at her properly for the first time. She was telling him he would have done the right thing. 'Yeah. Maybe. Anyways, he didn't slip, but I couldn't shoot him without letting the hammer fall and killing the girl. He backed up here and ducked down the alley.'

Tenniel looked up to the opposite side of the five-foot opening. High on the wall was an old street sign, of the kind the city hadn't used in four decades or more. Liddell Row. It was odd it even had a name. And most alleys simply cut through to the next block. From what he could figure this one was a dead-end that butted up to the three-storey building next door in Pine. Must be the only cul-de-sac downtown. Odd he had never noticed it before.

'I stuck my head round and he took a shot at it. So he's still down there.'

At that moment they heard the boom of another heavy round, the sound zigzagging up the alley and bursting out into the street, fleeing up the wide avenues to die. Tenniel turned to the uniformed officer behind him. 'You got a pump in the trunk of that patrol unit? Get it.'

Hilton eased the hammer down as he turned from the street into the alley. It was slippy and smeary underfoot, a mash of rain-sodden newspapers and bits of blanket and old curtains used by the bums who often slept there.

The acrid smell of their bathroom arrangements mixed with the odour of the stuffed-to-bursting green dumpster hit his nostrils. The girl whimpered in disgust. 'Keep it down, this won't last long,' he said. Even as the words came out, they sounded like wishful thinking.

It was hard to estimate the length of the alley. His eyes were getting used to the gloom, and as far as he could see, it went nowhere. So much for luck. He loosened his grip on the girl, set her down, and started to drag her forward by the upper arm, glancing over his shoulder. The further he progressed, the slimier underfoot it became, the old garbage rotting to some mildewed compost. Twice she lost her footing, and he had to jerk her back to her feet, the last time eliciting a little scream as her shoulder joint popped. He found himself apologising.

He wished he had brought a spare clip of ammo. Three rounds gone, was that it? He counted, then made sure one was in the breech. No, two so far. Ahead the greyness softened to reveal concrete steps and, above them, faded graffiti on a doorway. Dead-fucking-end.

He sat down on the top step, felt the damp creep across his ass. He pulled the girl towards him, and down onto his feet. He didn't want her getting pneumonia just because he and Duck couldn't even turn over a 7-Eleven without it turning into Looney Tunes.

The illumination in the alley was all blown, but the entrance was perfectly lit by the street lights, framed like a cinema screen turned on its side. There was a blinding flash from a passing ambulance, wheels smoking as it braked hard to pull up in front of the shattered store. And then he saw the cop's head, sneaking round for a peek, screen right. Without any great attempt at aiming he raised and fired, making the girl jerk spasmodically as her ears roared. The slug hit the wall many feet short, sending up a spray of brick dust which hung in the light. The head disappeared.

Hilton looked up. No fire escapes. Shit. He touched the downpipes of the chaotic drainage system that sprawled all over the wall, and felt the slime under his fingers. Anti-climb paint. The nearest window was maybe fifteen feet from him. Too much to jump. And it was barred. He could dump the girl and try and scrabble up the brickwork. But for the moment she was all that stopped them lobbing CS down the alley and waiting for him to come out with his eyeballs bleeding.

'What's your name?'

She shrugged. Her ears still hurt.

'Come on. I'm less likely to shoot you if I know your name, didn't anyone teach you that?'

She turned to look at his face, still clothed in the mask. Right, as if she took advanced hostage classes. 'Ali,' she finally offered.

'Ali. Great. Cute. Ali in the alley, huh?' Blank stare. 'OK. Have it your way. My name is Hilton, OK? Hilton. All I want you to do is stand over here in case there is a ricochet – splinters, you know? – while I have a pop at this lock. I don't want you to think about running, cause I can catch you before you're halfway down there, understand?'

He lifted her and pressed her face against the side wall, then returned to the door and pushed the muzzle against the crack between the doors, level with the lock metalwork. He spun his face away and squeezed and wood and metal blew apart with a shriek.

* * *

Jolted by the gunshot, Harry's memory, clouded with the sight of a little girl a hammerfall away from having her brains in the sidewalk puddles, slowly started functioning. 'There's a shot, several shots on the camera.'

Tenniel didn't get it at first. He assumed March meant the store video, which would just show a masked man.

'The stake-out apartment. The camera has some shots of this shithead in it.'

As the uniform handed Tenniel the Remington pump-action shotgun, he sent him to get the film from the Nikon. 'That arts freesheet, The Rosebud, it has a darkroom in its offices. University and Fourth. Owner lives above the shop. Tell him I want prints in fifteen minutes. We don't care if they are still wet.'

Bowman looked at him quizzically. 'Can you develop a film in fifteen minutes?'

'Who knows? We'll find out.'

Bowman noticed a small dog limp out of the alley opposite, take a look and slink back in. She wondered if it was one of those in the ads. But they had more than missing mutts to worry about here.

Tenniel pulled the under-barrel slide on the shotgun and hefted it onto his shoulder, as if he was skeet shooting. The street lights here were old, elaborate numbers, with big round globes at maybe eight feet, and, growing out of them, an elegant curved neck that always reminded Tenniel of the probosci of the alien saucers in the old War of the Worlds movie. He blew out the globes first, exploding eight one after another in a shower of hot gas and glass. Reckon on three hundred dollars apiece, he thought. Still, it looked like it was going to be an expensive night for the city all round. Then he moved onto the higher-level bulbs, four of them detonating one after the other, each a small supernova, like military starshells brightening the street into near daylight, then fading, leaving the sidewalk a shade greyer each time. After he had finished, the dark of the alley bled out into the street.

'Now all we have to decide is who's gonna be the first to test my little theory of silhouetting.'

Hilton kicked the door, and the right-hand side swung open. The other was bolted, top and bottom. Ali was still at the wall, frozen, her fingers in her ears, lost in the eardrum hum from the previous round. With a bit of luck, Hilton thought, this building should lead them through to another street, and he could be gone before the cops realised they should have staked out the next block as well.

The first of the shotgun blasts sent him to his knees, gun straight out, but all he could see were falling yellow sparks, like something from the Fourth of July. He watched the oblong at the end of the alley grow darker. Shooting out the lights. Coming soon, then. He heard the distant clatter of a helicopter. Blind him from above, that would be the plan. He peeled the girl off the wall. 'Time to go, kiddo.'

The atmosphere beyond the doors was chill, several degrees below the street. Hilton groped left and right for the light switch. He remembered to close the door behind him before flicking it. Waste of time. Nothing. No power. Angrily he rattled the rocker up and down several times, willing it to be a bad connection.

With Ali held in his left hand he shuffled forward, feeling his way, as if he was in danger of standing on a stingray. Nothing on the floor. It was only then he recalled the disposable Marlboro lighter he had taken from the Ford. He fumbled in his pocket for it, flicked it, and kept the little lever pressed down. His thumb quickly went from warm through hot to second-degree burns, but he ignored it. The lighter gave off a feeble, jaundiced glow, just enough to convince him that the room was empty. It smelt vaguely of spices and of sacking and damp sawdust, but that was just an olfactory echo. But there was something else, something less pleasant he couldn't quite place. Something more degenerate.

But more to the point, there was no door out.

The metal collar of the lighter finally became unbearably hot and he let it go, pushing them back into darkness. He could hear the helicopter overhead. They were going to know the alley was empty soon. So it was that Alamo moment again. The Big Showdown. But there must be a door.

He strode across to the far wall, girl in tow, pocketed the lighter into his jeans and began stroking the damp plasterwork, feeling for evidence of a covered-over door jamb, or even a thin bit of partition he could tear down. He moved sideways, cursing as he picked up slivers of metal and fibres in his hands. He realised the bad smell was getting worse. It was when he felt the floorboards turn oddly spongy and bouncy under his feet, that he instantly knew what the smell must be. He tried to step backwards, but it was too late. His bulk broke through the bowing boards, tearing out a jagged square of floor, throwing up a choking mix of wood dust and fungal spores as he and Ali disappeared from the room, their screams almost masked by the loud splintering of rotten wood.

PART TWO

The Aberdeen Proving Ground (APG) is located in Hartford County, Maryland. The base is home to the US Army Test and Evaluation Command, US Army Ordnance Center and School, US Army Technical Escort Unit, US Army Garrison Aberdeen Proving Ground, US Army Chemical and Biological Defense Command, US Army Research Laboratory, US Army Aberdeen Test Center, US Army Environmental Center, US Army Material Systems Analysis Activity, US Army Center for Health and Promotion and Preventative Medicine, Maryland Army National Guard, US Army Medical Research Institute of Chemical Defense, and Kirk US Army Health Clinic. It covers 72,516 acres, has 16,000 phone lines, three golf courses, two airstrips, three swimming pools and twenty bowling lanes. During the Vietnam war, it also housed the Limited Warfare Laboratory and the Land Warfare Laboratory, both of which were charged with the development of weapons and techniques to allow the war to reach a successful conclusion.

FOURTEEN

'I said the same thing. God, that's better. Wanna slug? I'd've got you one if you'd said. So, no, I said the exact same thing – what is a kid doing inventing a gun? He said to me that Kalashnikov was ten when he produced his first pistol, and Samuel Colt was, I dunno, twenty-one when he got his first patent. It was what he was good at, y'know – mechanical things. Treated them like they was alive. He said that Lewis gave him a test when he first met him – at Aberdeen, before he came over, before we all got together – handed him a .45 and asked him what he thought. Fix said it'd work a lot better if he put some bullets in it. Could tell by the weight, y'see? Lewis would have liked that. He wanted him on board, even though he was a bit . . . well, he wasn't really a soldier, Fix, he was going to be . . . what did he call it . . . sapper. Sapper. Lewis, now Lewis liked a bit of discipline. Man wore uniforms that could go off and march by themselves, real neat, real stiff. Had tastes that the rest of us didn't really share. Knew about art. Yeah, sure. Took pictures, had a Leica, some great shots of the war. And opera, he liked opera. Rest of us were jazz and soul and Hendrix. Big on Verdi was Lewis. He was what we called strak – real straight. Didn't smoke. Didn't drink. Didn't . . . well, he didn't really indulge in certain things like a lot of officers. Kept telling Fix to keep his pecker in his pants once he got over – or it'd go back in its own pine box, even if *he* lived. Went fuckin' crazy when . . . well, Fix was like everybody else. You wouldn't have believed some of the things . . . I mean, we were old hands. Hobbs, Wayland and me had done two tours, we didn't see it any more. But Fix, Saigon, y'know, all those whores, he had never seen anything like it.

'So Lewis . . . yeah, even though he was strak, he liked people with what he called peculiar talents. It was what we all had. Shit, I *liked* the job. That was real peculiar. Liked the . . . contest. Me and them, kinda . . . equal for once. Two go in, only one comes out. I boxed a bit when I was young, and it was exactly the same. Gladiatorial. Is that the word? Only there it was fuckin' real. So that is what Fix had – a peculiar talent. The gun? Why was it special? It was based on an old OSS design from the Second World War Fix told me. Damnedest thing. Ugly, but light, and when you fired it . . . Shit, no recoil and this sound . . . it's hard to describe, just a little pop or plop, but it always . . . well, this sounds crazy, but to me it always sounded like someone blowing a kiss.'

FIFTEEN

Riverfront Park, Spokane, Eastern Washington, 1.27 am

Milliner was having a coffee with Flood in the mess tent, trying to ignore the voice in his head, when the call came. His men were catching some sleep before the dawn operation, although the Bomb boys had decided to work through until sunrise, sweeping with their molecular sniffers. Flood was explaining the thinking behind the night's operation, and suggesting the area that Milliner could take, on the east side of the courthouse. And all the time, Milliner was thinking, I have no proof that Spokane isn't the target, nobody has said a word, but it makes sense. It makes horrible sense. We're all here, who's left minding the store back home?

'As far as everyone is concerned, sentencing will be as normal on Monday,' continued Flood. 'But as you know, the prisoners will be here at oh-seven-hundred hours tomorrow. At oh-six-hundred we will gather up all the court officials, everyone we need for the whole shebang. Judge Royal is spending the night inside. So by eight we should have a few hundred years of jail time bestowed upon these two assholes and have them battened down en route for Walla Walla penitentiary.'

Milliner nodded. But he knew this wouldn't be the end of the story. 'The rest of their team will be mighty angry. Furious, even.'

'I know. We will have to keep a tight lid on this town for a few weeks at least.'

'I am afraid—'

'I know Major, you've got your own job to do.' He took a slug of the espresso. He wouldn't be doing much sleeping tonight anyway. 'And who is to say they will hit Spokane anyway? It could be Seattle, could be Olympia, Tacoma . . . we'd better all stay sharp, Major.'

This might be the time to voice his fears, to suggest they might be looking in the wrong place right now, never mind in a couple of weeks, but he was stopped short when Marzo appeared with the GS handset and interrupted them. He had known Marzo since the last days of Vietnam. In theory, both of them should be out to pasture by now. He was too fine a 2-i-c, though, especially now he had calmed down. He had been someone to reckon with in his youth. The original wild and crazy guy.

'Major Milliner? Sir? Sorry to interrupt, but there is call for you. From Seattle. Police.'

'Excuse me,' he said to Flood, and instinctively took the rig outside, out of earshot. Could this be it? He looked up in irritation at the amount of noise and saw that damned news chopper was still up there.

'Milliner here.'

'Major? It's John Tenniel. Sergeant John Tenniel, Seattle PD. What the hell are you doing in the East?'

The line was crackly, and Milliner shouted, assuming it would be the same the other end. 'Oh, the usual – trying to save democracy as we know it. What about you?'

Tenniel snorted: 'Trying to keep the streets safe for

honest, decent folk to walk at night.'

'All the honest and decent folk are fast asleep in Laurelhurst, John, you know that. Anybody downtown at this time of night is up to no good.' Polite, distant. He knew what Seattle cops thought of his outfit. 'What can I do for you?'

Tenniel took a deep breath. 'I want permission to use some of the men you didn't take with you.'

'For . . . ?'

'We got a possible psycho with a little girl. We need to get him out. Actually, we need to get her out. He would be a bonus.'

'Isn't kidnapping FBI, John?'

Tenniel sighed inwardly. The fragmentation of responsibility and spheres of influence was the Achilles' heel of this job, but he supposed it had been since the days when outlaws only had to make it to the state line to be home free. But at least that was simple then. And Milliner, with his little bit of empire building, had muddied the waters even further. Actually he had done more than that, he had silted up the whole works. SWOPS had been built at the expense of regular forces as far as Tenniel was concerned. He shouldn't be begging, crawling to use units that should have been his to call upon. Should have been in goddamned Seattle, not Spokane. He tried to keep his voice level.

'Under the last Segregation of Responsibilities Review Hostage-Takings-R-US, Colonel, you know that. This isn't kidnapping, he was surprised by one of my . . . detectives, and grabbed what collateral he could. Anyway, how long do you think it would take FBI Hostage-Rescue to get from Quantico, Virginia?'

'What about SERT?'

The Seattle Emergency Response Team. Tenniel looked at the computer screen on Bowman's dash and pressed on the SERTs' Call-Out Responses icon. An NS – new situation – bulletin flashed up. A fifty-year-old ex-employee at a software company had gone back to his workplace with a satchel of explosives and a bunch of pipe bombs. He had a sawn-off shotgun, a S&W. 59 auto and one of those nasty Calico M950s with the 100-round helical feed magazine. Lethal. And classed as a pistol rather than the mini-assault gun it actually was. Oh yes, he also had eight of his least favourite former co-workers tied together in pairs with bailing wire, with one pipe bomb per couple taped to their bodies. His beef? He should have been with Microsoft all these years, not with some rinky-dinky two-bit outfit who fired him to take on a couple of geeks. He would let them all go for $1m in shares of Microsoft.

So the black lycra and velcro boys, all ninja stealth and big dicks, were a little preoccupied, this being their third COR this evening, and, thanks to Milliner, now down to eighteen men, they were a little stretched. Anyway, Tenniel always thought all of them – SWOPS included – too keen to show off their Steven Seagal routines. 'SERT got their hands full with the First Lady, a situation up in Capitol Hill and a siege over at Micro-Core. And before you ask, Rescue are out in Magnolia.'

'Magnolia?'

'Mudslide after the rain. Took a dozen million-dollar homes for a paddle in the bay.' Actually it wasn't funny – people were still trapped inside there.

'Sounds like a busy night.'

'Remind me to fill you in some time.' He hoped Milliner didn't notice he was chewing his lip with impatience.

'Where has this guy got her?'

Tenniel looked through the windscreen of the Bowman car, watching the debris of the store being swept up, boards put on the window, the accomplice – still alive – being eased out of the Ford with two of Harry's large holes in him, and the father – also still breathing, but only just – being wheeled to the Medic One. Forced entry was being made into the Winnebago to try and ascertain exactly who the unhappy shopper was, and the items Tenniel had ordered were being carried down the alley. All this, for, so the clerk had said, one hundred and seventy-five dollars. If only he'd kept slotting it into the night safe, he kept repeating. Yeah, if only. If only Tenniel had booked a vacation starting today, not tomorrow, this would be someone else's mess.

'It's a long story . . .' he began wearily.

Bowman walked over from the Ford and tossed a bundle into the car next to him. A hefty stack of scruffy mixed bills, looking like they had been collected out of garbage cans. Curious and curiouser.

'John?'

'Yeah, sorry. You are shouting, Colonel. I got a good connection this end.'

'Sorry. Where are they? Which building?'

'Colonel, this is just a courtesy call. I just want some of the men you didn't pull out to Spokane. You must have some left down on Occidental.' Guys that rightfully belonged to SERT before you asset-stripped them with your deep-pocket sponsorship and made up your own little paramilitary force, he thought. 'It's not a lot to ask.'

'If I didn't bring them here, there is a damned good reason for that, and I want to know what they are getting into. The best are here with me, Sergeant. You must appreciate that. Some of those left behind haven't even done the Phil Singleton Dynamic Entry School yet. And that really is a prerequisite to a hostage situation, as you know.'

Tenniel's flesh crawled at the reasonable tone. 'Well, it looks like the pair of them fell through into that space beneath downtown. You know, the Underworld? Moran's Basement as it used to be called?'

It was Milliner's turn to be silent. Was this a coincidence? Or a sign? Superstition, he knew, but all soldiers were superstitious, all believed in the little hints that fate dropped now and then. Ignore at your peril.

'Major?'

'You want to go into the underground city?'

'Well, part of it.'

'Permission denied—'

'Major, don't be—' He stifled the word asshole. Mustn't show disrespect, he needed him. '—Difficult. Please. All I need is for you to turn three or four of your troopers to my command. Just for tonight. There is an eight- or nine-year-old we got here—'

'Sergeant, permission denied until I get back there. I want to supervise this personally. My operation. It's part of my brief.'

'What? Why? How far away are you?' Tenniel felt his blood pressure pushing a column of mercury into the danger zone. A pain started behind his eyes. At one time the Special Deployment units had been all theirs, directly under police control. A call to his Captain was all he would have needed then. But these SWOPS were something different. What a pisser.

Milliner was busy guessing: 'Two hours' flying time, maybe one and a half if we push it. I'll have to check with the pilot. You try your hostage negotiating I'm-your-only-pal-in-the-world routine, and I will be there before you have finished. I've got it all worked out, so don't worry.'

'What worked out?'

'I submitted a plan almost ten years ago – ten years – for a search-and-destroy to clean up the filth down there—'

Filth? What filth? Tenniel had done the tourist tour of the Underworld, had even got into some of the areas not open to the public. He'd heard all the fanciful tales of opium dens and bootleggers. Didn't believe the half of it. Surely Milliner didn't fall for that moonshine? 'Colonel, that's ancient history—'

'Clean out the filth and seal it forever. That's what I said at the time. Make good the work that should have been done a hundred years ago, and seal it. Waste of time, they said. Tunnels already over budget, near bankrupting the city. Over-reaction they said. Reinforce where necessary, then seal. Well, we can do both now, can't we? Save your little girl, I mean. And sanitise the shithole while we are at it. I will call you en route, with an ETA. And thank you, John.'

Milliner broke contact and put the handset down and felt himself hyperventilating. His hands were clammy. Why did it all happen at once? He willed his pulse and breathing rate down. He tried to rationalise his motives. He had a gut instinct about an attack on Seattle. Well, yes. And there was a little girl to be rescued. Check. But if he examined his soul he would find he still burned with embarrassment from the day the first dual-power vehicle had emerged out of the tunnels, and the cover had been pulled off in front of everyone – the mayor, the civil engineers, the visiting Japanese, the president of Boeing, the Italian bus builders, not to mention the TV networks.

He still recalled the great shroud, stencilled with the Metro logo, slowly billowing off the bus, inching back, revealing first the burnished metal of the vehicle, and then the obscene, degrading scrawls underneath, all designed to mock him, accuse him, to show that, as consultant to the tunnel security, he couldn't stop them, couldn't catch them. And it was there, all on film, all in the archives for anyone to call up and replay.

'Marzo?'

'Yessir?'

'I want you to pull off five of the best – the very best men – right now and prepare to return to Seattle on Alpha Six. Five, plus yourself. Now.' He had lied about the Phil Singelton Dynamic Entry Course – the best system for penetrating and clearing a hostile room he knew – all his men had to have passed that plus the FBI Chemical Agent and Sniper schools and gone through hell at Fort Bragg's Special Operations Training Facility (SOT) with the men of 1st Special Forces Operational detachment – better known as Delta. It was tough and time-consuming, why it took so long to train them from scratch, why he had filched some personnel from other

Special Operations units, and why SERT was still understrength. So the men he had left behind on Occidental could easily have formed a Crisis Entry Team. But they weren't going to. Not without him.

As he sprinted across to the large GP tents, Marzo knew better than to question the Colonel, or to tell him that the Secret Service, the FBI and, especially, Flood were going to be mad, mad, mad at losing any men. But then again, from what he heard, it sounded more fun than picking through trashcans all night, wondering which one was going to detonate.

Five men. Let's see. Bayne, Liddon, Faussett . . . no, not Bayne, he beat him at poker the other night, so Marzo owed him a hundred and fifty bucks, Whiting, maybe . . . no, Collyns was a better bet in a tight corner. Collyns had gone through the SODS killing house like a chainsaw, not a single civilian hit, every bad guy blown away. Let's hope he could do it when the opposition could fire back.

In fact it was Bayne he saw first, looking up at the stars, catching a last cigarette. What the hell. 'OK, trooper, we got to pull out—'

'Hey, we're just about ready to turn in—'

'Bayne, you are done here. It's an RTB. I need a hand to rouse some of the others. Hey, Collyns. C'm here. It's Milliner Time again.'

Back at the mess tent, Milliner hesitated before pushing the flap aside. He knew Flood and his superiors would be furious at him, but even if he was wrong about the flying times, he could explain that if he supervised the initial entry into the Underworld, then left Marzo to do the final clean-up, he could still be back in Spokane by seven-thirty, eight, in time for the grand finale. Best tell Flood now though, and best if he hammed it up. Not lone psycho . . . something more . . . city in danger, absolute priority he return. Gas in the subway. Yes, threat of gas through the bus tunnels. Crazy coincidence. Almost impossible to believe. Mad psycho with bomb has little girl in underground city. Strange days, though. Strange days. Nerve gas. Wipe out Saturday-morning shoppers into the bargain. Flood would go for that. And, just in case the voice in his head was right, he would give those tunnels a once-over for himself. Just like the old days. And who knew what – or who – he might find down there?

John Tenniel spent a long time staring through the car windscreen when the radio link was broken, eyes focused somewhere off over the invisible Cascades, oblivious to the fresh rain spotting the screen, to the patrolman knocking on the window, holding up the still glistening ten-by-eight photographs, trying to ignore the increasingly frantic figure of Harry March crouched at the entrance to the alley, beckoning him once more. He knew the SWOPS Major was going to come back with his own agenda, an agenda that had 'Get Little Girl Out Alive' pencilled in at the bottom. Faintly.

And he had just remembered what they used to call Milliner for the first few months after he got the Seattle/SWOPS command, something carried over from his previous assignment that slowly fell into disuse as he proved himself to be a hard-working, no-nonsense commander. It came back to him, fuzzy as the windscreen. Milliner had been something to do with tunnel security. Had been charged with flushing out the bums who had made Third Avenue their home. Or at least the subterranean portion of it. And they had got their very public revenge when the new Italian bus rolled out. Spray-painted down one side in lurid glittery pink – still wet and streaky, so it had been done after the covers had gone on – were the words: Seattle. Beware The Mad Milliner. Murdering Milliner, it had said on the other side.

Well, nothing had ever been proved officially, but he knew the story. That Milliner had felt the tunnels were breeding grounds for disease, that the nests the vagrants built needed sanitising before he could allow his men to touch them. When one of the patrolmen was bitten by a rat it seemed to confirm his theory. So he had used flamethrowers to burn out the sections where the bums had built shelters of cardboard and rags, newspapers and plastic sheeting. Except in one of them they hadn't cleared it out properly. Tucked in the corner was a sleeping vagrant. Shit, easy mistake to make – some of them looked like walking garbage dumps. Even so, horrible way to go, incinerated without warning.

After the bus incident came the poster campaign, with names and dates, and that journo from the Post-Intelligencer had started making noises. Milliner left the city rather quickly, and it all died down. Ancient history now. And it didn't affect Milliner's subsequent appointment at SWOPS. Maybe because everyone knew that unconventional soldiers and policemen were needed to run Special Forces. Hadn't he read that the guy who set up the Brits' SAS had been a failed gambler who would burst into tears at heavy losses? And that, despite losing almost a third of his force on his first mission, they had let him go ahead and keep the unit anyway. And he knew for a fact that one of the senior figures of US Special Forces had introduced a strenuous swimming routine to the qualifying test in the belief that it would 'keep them goddamn niggers out'. Nice.

Strange how he had not recalled the Milliner incident before, though. Like everybody else, maybe at the back of his mind he had thought, well, it was just a bum, after all. No big deal. Not compared to Whidbey, or losing a large chunk of your men because you insist on parachuting in high winds, or even institutionalised racism.

He looked at his watch. Two hours, maybe sooner until Milliner got back, old grudge and all. That was the last thing he needed – a team of heavily armed sub-humans led by a close-to-retirement Major with some scores to settle. Tenniel shivered and stepped out into the rain. He stood there for a few seconds, still ignoring those clamouring for his attention, then slid back into the car, picking up the handset once more.

Isa Bowman climbed in at almost the same time. He froze. 'Detective?'

'Isa. Remember. John, stop acting like you got a stick up your ass. Please?'

'OK. Sorry. It's just . . . tense. I'm a little tense. Last night before the vacation, and look at it.' He pointed at the dash laptop, which had streamed out a new set of incident reports, including that mudslide in Magnolia. None of those houses insured, either. Hell of a lot to pay for a great view in a nice neighbourhood. He imagined the tangle of timber and concrete as the sludge pushed the homes aside, twisting them into grotesque shapes, streaming through windows and doors, fouling carpets and furniture. Maybe even engulfing the occupants. Death by liquefied mud. Uh. He pinched his nose again. Didn't seem to be working tonight, couldn't shift the throbbing.

A new symbol appeared on the computer screen, a flashing megaphone. Call in and be reassigned. Nice things about symbols, they were easy to ignore. Anyway, he had his assignment.

'Please call in. Please call in. Please—' He switched off the back-up voice prompt. 'The computer must've gone down, sir,' had become the standard PD excuse for everything from sneaking a quick coffee to ignoring response calls altogether. Only a matter of time before the radios came back as first-line, he knew.

He ran Bowman through the Milliner conversation, and as he wrapped it up, a thought came to him. 'You done the FT hostage programme?'

She shook her head. 'Not the Field Training unit. FBI short course. Portland, and a refresher at HRT.'

'Even better. But at the moment we got no way to talk to this guy, agree? And talking is all we really got. If we are to get the girl out.'

She nodded. It wasn't covered by the books, this one. You normally had the hostage-taker locked down in a fixed setting, with family, friends or strangers being threatened. You knew who they were and how to talk to them. Nobody was going anywhere, no matter how it came out. A situation in an underground maze? That was novel.

'Listen, you are going to think I am crazy, but I've got an idea. I know how to make contact with someone who might just have the experience we need.'

'If you tell me our best shot is if I dress up like Minnie Mouse and go after him, I'd listen.'

'I'll call him.' But he didn't move.

'Really, John, go with your instincts.' She arched an eyebrow to let him know what she was thinking. 'Just for this once, eh?'

He punched the number. She was right. Tonight, anything was worth a try.

SIXTEEN

The Ben Moc (Big Mac) Woods, north of Cu Chi Town, Vietnam. 1969.

Crouched, eyes closed, Tran sprinted as best as he could, away from the trapdoor and the screams of the dying, scuttling through the earth, kicking up a choking dust, trying to make the alcove. Even above the scratching and scraping of his running, above the snorted breaths, he could hear the shouts of the Americans, roaring, careless, angry, all their precautions forgotten, wild animals now.

What would they use? Gas? Grenades? If it was gas then he would have scant time to make the water trap, the filthy stinking cesspool that he would have to dive into, dragging himself along the rope through the narrowing chamber, his shoulders barely scraping through, waiting until his lungs started to burn and screech, until they told him to give up, to take a mouthful of the stagnant liquid, before, finally, he could surface and gasp and spit while the gas rolled through the chamber he had just left. No American, weighed down by equipment and fattened and broadened by their over-rich food, no Yankee could ever hope to follow. But he prayed it wasn't gas, because one day, he knew, he would pay heed to the little voice that told him one lungful would end all this, would leave his wife a hero's widow and his son and daughter a hero's offspring.

Well, perhaps – the idea of being fêted by his neighbours in either life or death seemed a little less likely since his last leave, when they made it clear that as a regroupee, trained in the north, with a fresh, harsh accent and northern puritanism, he was no longer quite as integral to village life as before he left. Thanks, friends.

He reached the small alcove, and flung himself in, curling up like a strange, emaciated religious icon. He swapped the carbine for the AK-47, pulled it to his body as he turned his face to the wall and stuffed the rags in his ears.

The first whump drove the breath from his body, pressing his face into the earth, filling his nostrils and eyes with the red crumbs. At the second he felt something pop in his ear, and a terrible humming take the place of real sound. He pushed the dirt from his nose, just in time for the third grenade to fling him back again, twisting his neck so hard he screamed. But he couldn't hear it, just feel the sensation through his skull bones.

It was bad this time. He had been deaf for two, three days before, but this time the concussion had ripped something inside at least one of his ears. He gingerly felt for the trickle of blood, but could find nothing. He sucked air over and over again. Grenades rarely did damage to the fabric of the tunnel – the clay was too hard – but they consumed oxygen. His lungs ached, but he knew there was enough left for him. He had survived on less when the heat of the day became unbearable, and you had to lie close to the floor to pick up the last, vile dregs of breathable air. Tran wondered if there was enough oxygen to support a candle to inspect his wounds, but realised he mustn't worry about that now.

There was work to do. He took the rags from his ears. The pitch of the internal thrumming did not change.

Slowly he groped his way out of the niche and back down towards the trapdoor. Through the smoke and dirt he could see a yellowish light. As he had expected the tunnel had absorbed the grenade blasts, channelling it to the far end and up the ventilation shafts. There had been minimal earthfall. Now the trapdoor lid was off, and daylight was penetrating this underworld.

Tran knew the next bit. Either he had miscalculated and would be taken by the fourth grenade, or they would be coming down to get him. He could just about hear – or at least, feel – them shouting. The light disappeared, blocked as, in all likelihood, one of them poked their head down. He went forward a few more metres. The light returned, sickly with coiled smoke, as if a thousand lungfuls of cigarettes had been exhaled at once. He tried to listen beyond and above the buzzing of his tortured cochleae. Silence. A decision had been made. He covered the last section of the tunnel just as the lower half of the American came through, dangling and kicking for a foothold, looking like some bizarre topsy-turvy version of two earthworms. Always the same. They always came in feet first. Stupid, stupid.

He raised the AK-47 and let rip, the normal thudding strangely muted to him, half-turning his head as the bullets perforated the groin and yet more Yankee blood squirted from veins and arteries and capillaries as they were cruelly ripped apart. A short burst was all that was needed. Don't kill him. Leave him there, so his comrades have to pull him up. They would always tend to their wounded first.

He turned to make for the escape passages, dimly aware of a high, pain-filled wailing sound above the dynamo hum in his ears. He wished he could hear Nguyen and the others, who would have crawled from the other trapdoor and were now scything down the men struggling to pull their dying friend from the hole.

Another patrol that wouldn't be coming to get him tomorrow.

SEVENTEEN

Underworld. Seattle.

It was the pain in the side Hilton noticed first, stabbing between his ribs with each breath. Not that he could actually breathe that much: a great weight seemed to be bearing down on his chest, forcing the air out of him as fast as he could draw it in. He tried one big gulp and the rusty knives ripped up his side to his armpit. He had read that this was the sign of a heart attack. Maybe he was dying.

And to put the final big kisser on it, he had gone completely blind.

He knew his eyes were open, he could feel the blinking, the eyelids scraping over his eyeballs, but the eyes themselves, they registered nothing. Black, black and more black. The impact had obviously detached his retinas. Impact. As the word formed in his brain a hundred new pain sites – squibs to the Fourth of July display show currently marching up and down his left flank – started up. He was lying on a hard, cold and very wet floor. Well, kind of wet – the fluid under his fingers had the consistency of mucus – but definitely hard. Concrete? He pressed through the layer of moisture and felt something slide under his skin. A splinter. Wood. More planks, like the ones that had given way, but much wider.

And, he realised, he wasn't blind. There was just no light down here. He reached up to check the damage to his ribs and hit the reason for his trouble drawing breath. The girl was splayed across his ribcage. She squealed as he touched her, wriggled, and sent another fiery spasm on its way. 'Keep still for fuck's sake. Jesus. You OK?'

She didn't reply. With considerable difficulty he lifted her off and laid her on the floor next to him. She was OK, he had broken her fall. In fact, he remembered . . . no, why would he have done that? He probably grabbed her to try and break his fall, and got everything all ass-wise. Well, had it gone according to plan she would be pressed ham right now. And that wouldn't have been right somehow. But he reckoned he'd cracked a rib at best.

He'd had a lighter, he recalled. Had he dropped it? Had he pocketed it before the floor went? He realised one of the pains came from his rear pocket. He rolled over and eased the lighter out. He probably had a Marlboro symbol pressed onto his ass right now, but he would suffer permanent buttock damage in exchange for an undamaged lighter. He flicked. Nothing. Again. Nothing.

He used both hands to feel the bastard thing. The top was bent, but he couldn't tell whether it was leaking fluid – his hands were too slimy for that. One last go and it caught, its pathetic flame threatening to die if he so much as moved. He looked up at the ceiling, maybe fifteen feet above him, the light just illuminating the jagged ends of the boards where they had fallen through. How long ago? He looked at his watch, but it hadn't survived the impact. The face and one hand were missing. It was something after twelve. Great.

'Stay there.' Hilton gently got to his feet, holding the lighter at arm's length to avoid a stray exhalation snuffing the flame. The gun was there, five feet away. As he bent down to retrieve it he caught sight of the other guy. Or almost a guy, more a spectre. His heart thumped against his ribs so hard he gasped, grabbed the gun and—

'It's a mirror,' said the girl, far more coolly than he could have managed. 'It's you.'

He looked at his image in the cracked glass, a wild-haired silhouette, only the central section of his face illuminated, alternating deep shadows and skin with the sickly pallor of death. It was true, he looked like a dead man already.

He walked forward to try and convince himself this was an illusion and crashed into something solid. The mirror was behind a long counter, and it was a few seconds before he recognised it for what it was – a bar. This place was a tavern of some kind. The bar-top was warped and split and thick with something that looked like congealed soot – with a fresh topping of a lighter-coloured dust from their destruction of the ceiling. Shelves behind the bar still held the odd old advertising sign, for something called Yesler Brew, Speidel's Ale and the Maynard Safety Razor System. 'As used by . . .' the sign was too blackened to read the endorser. But there was nothing else of what was once the establishment's stock in trade – no glasses, no bottles, no spirits. The place had been picked to the bones a long time ago – there were ragged holes where even the old beer pumps had been wrenched free. Treading carefully so as not to slip, he walked behind the bar. 'You OK?' he called out.

'I guess,' said Ali.

'It's gonna go dark again for a while. Just stay put.' She didn't reply, so Hilton ducked down and pulled at the cupboards. It took him a moment to figure out they slid rather than swung. A couple of empty bottles, some tobacco display cards and . . . an oil lamp. Well some kind of lamp anyway. It had a brass base, a wick, but no glass. He carried on along the bar and found the missing part, at least the bulbous lower half of it. But it might do. He scoured the entire length of the underbar cupboards, hoping that something powered by Duracell might turn up, but a gross of toothpicks were his only haul. He piled some of them on the bar-top, tore up pieces of the card and put the lighter to it. As it caught into a damp, smoky mini-pyre, he finally put the lighter down and shook his roasted thumb.

'Where the hell are we?' he asked himself as he positioned the lamp next to his bonfire. Ali slithered towards him, edging into the light. He was relieved to see she looked as spooky as he had. 'Here,' he said handing her the toothpicks 'keep that going.'

'I think this is what was left when they rebuilt the city after the fire.'

'No shit? We're in the basement?'

She didn't answer. As far as she could remember this wasn't the basement, but the actual first floor. But the memory of the last hour hit her like a sledgehammer – she felt the blow in her brain, a sudden screeching neural overload. Her dad . . . her mom . . . this man . . . she felt her throat constrict and the sobs started again.

Hilton ignored her. He didn't blame her. Part of him

felt like crying, but another part – the bit of him that wanted to stay alive – knew he couldn't afford to lose it now. The wick on the lamp fizzled and burnt quickly – too quickly. It sparked a few times and went out.

'Dry . . .' said Ali between gulps.

'Eh?'

She sniffed what sounded to Hilton like a couple of inches of snot back into her throat, rallying now. 'Open it up and see if there is any oil in it, maybe.'

There was, but not much, but he resoaked the wick, and tried again. After the pinpricks of light generated so far the sudden burst from the lamp seemed like staring at the sun.

The room was about thirty feet square, Hilton estimated, wood-clad, although much of it had been stripped off at some point to reveal bricks and grey, rough plaster underneath. Apart from the mirror, there were no fixings or furniture – just four ornate cast-iron pillars running to the ceiling – and the floor was indeed covered in slime, and dirty black slime at that. He looked at Ali; she, too, was caked in it, hands and feet. She was also shivering – all she had on was a light sweater and some jeans. Worry about it later. He had more problems than that right now.

There were two sets of doors, one of which obviously went out back, the other that would have led to the street. Which meant the street was still out there. The street it would be – he was fairly sure that whoever had vacuumed this place clean of useful goods – one damaged lamp excepted, praise the Lord – would have done the store room as well. 'You OK?'

'Stop asking me if I am OK, you asshole.' He jumped

back and started the pain in his ribs again.

'Look, kid, I'm sorry you're here. I'm sorry I'm here. It's what we in the robbery business call an A-1 fuck-up. OK? I mean, you understand? It ain't anything to do with you or . . . or your old man. Just wrong place, wrong time. Bad luck, 'sall. Here.' He slid out of his jacket and reached it across the bar. He instantly felt the damp start penetrating his shirt. This place hadn't seen the light of day for— 'When was the fire?'

'About a hundred years ago. No, thanks, you keep the coat.'

'Nah, put it on. C'mon, I ain't cold. I got a T-shirt on under here,' he lied. Ali climbed into rather than put on the jacket, which came down to her knees and nearly went twice around her. But she felt better.

'Listen, kid, we gotta get going.'

'Aren't we waiting here? Can't you leave me here? Please?'

'I wish I could. Wish I could, kid.'

'Ali or Alice. Not kid.'

Jesus he couldn't figure this one. One minute crying, the next worrying about what he called her. And calling him an asshole. 'How old are you kid?'

'It's Ali—'

He banged the bar-top, sending up a shower of ember from the dying toothpicks and she leapt back. 'Don't get mouthy with me, huh? Look, I don't want to hurt you, but I don't want to be hurt either. Without you, Seattle's finest come in firing. Let's give it a name, huh? Without you, they kill me resisting arrest. With you, they think twice. So it doubles the odds.'

'But isn't kidnapping a . . .' Her voice tailed off. How

much more seriously was it than gunning down her dad?

'We gotta go, kid. I don't want to drag you, tie you up, gag you or anythin', you know what I mean? But I will. Believe me, 'cause at the end of the day, I gotta get out of here, one way or another. I will. How old are you?'

'Eight.'

'Yeah, well – do eight-year-olds still believe in promises?'

'Depends.'

He thought he heard a movement above. A footstep. Anyone could poke their head through the hole in the ceiling and pop him where he stood perfectly outlined by the lamp.

He continued to stare at where the floor had given way and saw what might have been the flash of a torch beam. He looked at Ali. 'Put your hands over your ears. Press harder.' He aimed at the dark shape of the hole and squeezed off one round. The sound hammered around the room, but above that he heard the cartridge case ching its way into the blackness. He waited for the last reverberations to die away. 'If a head shows in there,' he shouted, trying his best mean-son-of-a-bitch voice, 'I'll shoot it off. And then I'll shoot the girl.'

Maybe he was just being spooked. Maybe his eyes were playing tricks, and that was no torch beam. Even worse, maybe he had just wasted a precious bullet. And perhaps also this was not the time to start worrying about extracting oaths of allegiance from an eight-year-old. He took her elbow and started for the door. For the first time, he wondered how Duck was. Those holes in the door looked mighty big and well-placed and if Duck had been – as Hilton imagined he would be – busy sheltering . . . and then he put it together. It was Duck who had taken out the window and started all this. 'I hope the prickless cunt is dead,' he muttered.

He started to peel Ali's hands off her ears and tipped her chin up. 'OK, kid, listen, these are the breaks – we got to go exploring.' He grabbed her wrist, tight, held the lamp aloft, and marched towards what would once have been the outside world.

EIGHTEEN

Bella Vista Apartments, West Highland Drive, Queen Anne, Seattle. 1.39 am

The odd thing is that Lewis didn't dream. Well, not really. No visions, no ghosts, no bodies. But sounds. Soft sounds that invaded the periphery of his sleep, scuttling around the edges, flicking out of sight when his subconscious tried to get a handle on them. They wouldn't stand up and be counted, they couldn't – but his sleeping brain knew what they were; it compared them with the old, dog-eared memories and came up with IDs: spiders, centipedes, fire-ants, bats, and snakes, circling and sniffing, staying just out of sight, ready to strike.

And the smells, too. It was smells that always haunted him, that crept on him unawares, that lurked in the corners of cupboards, elevators, small rooms, in dark places. Of boiled meats, of decayed rice – an aroma that made him gag, even in his sleep – the metallic tang of freshly spilled blood, the evil stench of old, congealed wounds, the sweat of friends and enemies alike, both too close for comfort, and, of course, the mustiness of tainted earth, earth defiled by the bodies and bodily functions of humans.

But no vision. Not this time. Sometimes he saw it all framed in the harsh whiteness of flashlights, other times bathed in a green fuzz, others in the soft afterglow of dying embers, human shapes silhouetted black on red, but now there was nothing. All he had now was the sound and the smells of the soil.

He got the phone on the first ring, with a speed of reflex he could never find in racquetball. Even before he answered he realised he had been in the tunnel-collapse brace configuration: on his knees, ass up in the air, head down covered by arms, the tunnellers' equivalent of a foetal position.

His head was thick from the beers and Armagnac, and it took a while to register that calls at one-thirty in the morning weren't the done thing. Willie. Who else? 'Yeah?'

'Lewis?'

At least his brain was alert enough to register this wasn't Willie. 'Yeah?'

'John Tenniel. Sorry to call you at this time.'

''Sallright.' He clicked his tongue a few times. He had to sound sharper than that. Next to him Dinah lifted onto an elbow. She mouthed 'Willie?' he shook his head and waved her back down.

'Lewis, we got a situation down here, one you may be able to help us with. It's just a thought—'

'Where are you?'

'Henry and Liddell. Henry is between Pine and Pike. Know it? Liddell is a little alley, but you can't miss it – it's the one with all the Do Not Cross tape and the cop cars around it. Listen, the reason—'

'Liddell. I'll be there—' I need the cash, he said to himself.

'Lewis—'

'Ten minutes, OK? Fifteen at most.'

He cradled the receiver and sat up, felt his head spin

half a rotation then flick back. Shit. Now that, that was an early warning sign.

'Not Willie?' asked Dinah.

'No, surprise, surprise. Cops. John Tenniel wants me to do something.'

'What is it?'

'I don't know – waste of time asking them over the phone. Henry Street. It's always something the uniforms can't get with their Polaroids.' The officers did it all themselves now – fingerprints, photographs – at all but the most intricate scenes. So instead of keeping a group of snappers on the payroll, the city just called in the odd freelance like himself.

Lewis went to the walk-in closet next door, pulled on a thick sweater and an MA-1 and pulled out the cases from the back. The smell from his dreams hit him again when he saw the one with LWL stencilled on it. He snorted, as if to clear dirt from his nostrils. Willie, you meddling cocksucker. He pushed the case deeper into the dark of the closet and grabbed the ally flight case. Probably be a Nikon night, he figured.

The main light clicked on in the bedroom and Dinah appeared, a robe wrapped around her. 'Want me to come?'

He hesitated for a moment. 'Why?'

'Everything just feels a little weird right now.'

'You said it. But this is probably just someone whose luck ran out . . .' As he said it he felt the words turn bitter and coarse, as if he was describing himself. Again: what would Willie do if he didn't help him? What could he do after a quarter of a century? Surely there was a statute of limitations. His head gave another half-spin.

Stress, that's what did it. Stress-induced positional dysfunction, as a doc once told him, before he discovered what it really was. Fear.

'You all right?' Dinah watched as the last of the colour went from his cheeks.

'Yeah . . . just a touch of vertigo.'

'Vertigo? You suffer from vertigo? Claustrophobia and vertigo. Anything else?'

'What have you got?' He shook his head to clear it. 'It's not fear of heights you know—'

'Obviously. I have seen your pictures.' She pointed at one of a knife-edge ridge near Bryce Canyon that framed a sheer drop each side. She knew he had walked the ridge to get the shot. It was beautiful. Cold and precise and austere. She knew there were some who thought his pictures lacked soul, but she wasn't one of them. After the tortured inner demons she saw on the page day after day, a little coolness was a welcome relief.

'It's just dizziness. I used to get it when . . . when I got back. I think Willie is reminding me. I gotta go. You know the form. Two hours tops. Keep the bed warm.'

She didn't say anything as he left. Instead she wandered into the living room, and pressed play on the CD player. Great bass line. 'No matter how softly we touch, we seem to bruise . . .' Great voice. She found the case. Kip Hanrahan. Next up, Love is like a Cigarette. That was what she wanted. A cigarette. She wanted to stand on that balcony and blow smoke up Seattle's ass. Except someone would probably take her out with a hunting rifle and get away with justifiable homicide – blatant and unwarranted pollution of the city after midnight. Nope, cigarettes didn't go with doing business in this city, so she had dumped them. Dumb thing was, smoke a fashionable cigar and the same people would be fawning all over you. But she hated cigars. Which meant all she had to do to while away the two hours was fret or watch cable.

What was happening with Lewis? Was he coming apart at the seams? Maybe that Puerto Rican horn player was going to bring some sort of delayed post-traumatic stress syndrome to the party. Wasn't there a 24-hour Vets line you could ring to get help, like the Samaritans? Now, that would be crazy. He was hardly on the roof with a high-powered rifle just yet. 'Hi, an old army buddy of my man turned up and I think he's given him vertigo,' didn't sound too terrifying. 'Well, ma'am, at least he is unlikely to go on top of any tall buildings with a high-powered rifle.' 'No, you don't understand, vertigo is not fear of heights. It's probably Alfred Hitchcock's fault you think that . . .'

She stopped herself. Now who's going loopy? Maybe she should have talked it out of him, asked how it had been for him. But by the time she had hooked up with Lewis he had been through two or three or four other relationships, had purged all the night sweats and cultural dislocation out of his system. So he claimed.

They had a tacit agreement about the past, that it was a scab they wouldn't scratch. Once you have been through several relationships they seem to reach some kind of critical mass, big enough to sit there and brood, to make sure they destabilise any future involvements – the emotional baggage, the scars on the psyche and the soul, the latent toxins of jealousy and betrayal. But there was none of that with Carl. No walk-on parts for old flames who were better at sex, had a more refined taste in music, books, holidays. Who could cook.

And she had to admit, the last thing she needed after a day looking at the images that sprung forward from the kids' – and most of them were kids, no matter how big they were – brains, the last thing she needed was some deep shrink stuff with her man. She walked over and looked at the two pictures side by side. His was a view from the upper level of the Brooklyn Bridge, a shot he had taken of a motorbike parade. Hers was a pale blue square of paint with a thin red line across it. Innocuous enough, unless you knew what the artist liked to do with razor blades. This was her equivalent of a glass of cold water in the face. She couldn't bear to look at it too long, but it reminded her why she did what she did.

She walked back into the bedroom. He was normally so cool about everything. So controlled. His side of the bed had looked pretty much like a ploughed field tonight, though, and one assaulted by a blind tractor driver at that.

Maybe they should have scratched the scab after all. It wasn't as if she hadn't tried. No, that wasn't true. She hadn't really tried at all. Face it, what they had was resolutely superficial.

She remade the rumpled bed, picked up her now-crumpled suit and his clothes. This was partly because he hated coming back to mess but mainly to avoid what she knew she was putting off. She walked to the closet, rubbing her hands dry on the robe, pausing only to flick the heating on – she was suddenly cold.

Dinah pulled out the case marked LWL and took it into the bedroom. He never knew she knew he had this. Opening it felt like a violation of everything they had going. Sure, she had done it once before but that had been a mistake, she had been looking for some film for her camera. Shocked, she had slammed it shut without really taking it all in. That was accidental exposure. This time, she couldn't fool herself it was anything but intrusion.

Take your time, she thought; you have two hours to find out what this shit is. But her hands were shaking.

She flicked on the multi-band and began to scan the airwaves; perhaps she might come across some mention of whatever he had been called out on. She knew each portion of the city had its own police waveband, but Lewis always worked downtown, so she flicked to the West frequency.

'Drive-by . . .'

She heard the words as she flicked by the slot, and spun back quickly. A few crackles and then '. . . no kidding?' No kidding indeed. Seattle and drive-bys went together like Los Angeles and friendly neighbours. 'To top it all, there is a hostage situation down here, and they have called in some civilian expert on tunnels . . .'

Dinah gave an involuntary moan. Tunnels. He had called Willie a tunnel rat during his long improvisation on the truth. An underground fighter, literally. His own job, he said, had been to debrief them to contribute to the sum knowledge of the activities underground. Did that make him a tunnel expert? What was the name of the cop who had called? It had been Tenniel, hadn't it?

She thought of Elder Sanchez and his spinning

pictures. It was too much of a coincidence. He, Lewis, must be the one they were talking about. And he thought he was going to take photographs. She clipped up the catches on the LWL case, and went to the closet for some clothes. Liddell Street, wasn't it?

NINETEEN

Riverfront Park, Spokane, Eastern Washington. 1.45 am

Milliner counted them in, approving Marzo's choice of men to RTB. He could see the puzzled look in their eyes. Why return to base so soon? They had barely started here. The last fifteen minutes had been fraught, with Flood and a Secret Service man, Ragg, doing their best to dissuade him from going. He maintained that as his assistance had been requested, he was not at liberty to refuse. It was his home turf. Madman with little girl, not some theoretical threat like here.

He knew what they were both thinking. Who is the girl's family? Can she cause trouble, the sort of trouble they would get if security lapsed here? The truth was that no matter how emotive, the death of a little girl at the hands of a psycho was a couple of days' news, with no real fall-out. But they couldn't say that; they had to maintain the pretence that all were entitled to equal protection. And his addition of the fictitious poison-gas threat (*'If it is fictitious,'* said his internal voice) had silenced them. As a final flourish he said: 'With the state troopers, FBI, ATF and Secret Service people, you will have hundreds of men here tomorrow. I am taking six back to try and save one innocent little girl. Are you prepared to order me to stay?' Not that they could. Outflanked, and out of jurisdiction, they went so far as to wish him well.

Milliner climbed aboard the slick and strapped himself in. He nodded to the pilot and the whines started. They were bathed in the red glow of the instruments, and Milliner felt a thrill through his body. Back to the bus tunnels. He wondered if the guy, his tormentor, was still down there. What a wrap-up party that would be. The final expunging of his ignominious exit from Seattle last time around. Shit, he felt like he was getting a hard-on. He shifted in his seat and pulled on the intercom rig.

He turned to his men and signalled them to put on their headsets. He kept half-turned as he spoke, and was gratified to see them nodding, as if they agreed with his decision. In fact, he could tell them very little. He had checked locations with Seattle PD, and that was about it.

He tried to stay calm, detached from the subject, but he couldn't get the face out of his mind. After the paint-daubing incident they had watched the security camera tapes, over and over. And they had three seconds of a figure scurrying across University Station, three seconds with one furtive look straight at the camera, one rat-eyed glance up. And that grainy, over-enhanced image had stayed with him, that look of contempt for everything they had done, burnt into the video tape – and his synapses – forever. He still saw it everywhere – in an odd cloud formation scuttling across the sky, in abstract paintings, once, memorably, in a bowl of porridge. The cheeks and the hollow eyes, the barest hint of the physiognomy was all he needed to fill in the rest, to make it flesh.

He had been for going in to find this character, the

bus painter, but no. Too expensive, bad publicity. Then the posters and flyers started, the ones with more accusations. They didn't understand what it was like down there, he could taste it still, the air was thick with a sediment, of body odour and decay and bacteria and viruses and dessicated rat droppings. They had agreed quickly enough when he told them it was a war – Harassment and Interdiction – deny the enemy the terrain they need by superior firepower. So after the H&I you had to burn, it was an antiseptic, that was all, sterilisation, to make sure they couldn't recolonise, worm their way back into those vile nests they made down there. OK, so mistakes got made. They got made in every campaign.

Try telling that to the city, though. They had rerun the ceremony at a later date for the posterity files, after he had been told, with much embarrassment and undue haste, thank you, your job is done here. Well, it hadn't been. This was the real finale.

From his knowledge of the underground topography, he had a vague idea of useful entrance points in his mind, but had yet to formulate a full strategy. Every time he thought of that word his mind drifted to the kind of strategy he didn't want. The scenario he would never lead his men into, even though he wanted that bus painter real bad. Whidbey.

Some of his men had been there, some of them had seen their friends and fellow-SERT members killed. Milliner had watched it all, from his hotel room in Boston on Fox News, live from the armoured farmhouse. He clenched his jaw as he remembered the frustration. He had even tried to call the police in Seattle and King

County and Island County, the State Troopers, the FBI, anyone who could get him through to the operational commander.

The Riverfront Park below was shrinking, the tents, lit from inside with the glow of torches and cigarette butts, the men restless, unable to sleep, became canvas dots. The pilot picked up the thread of I-90 and banked them towards the passes through the mountains that would lead them home to Seattle.

Milliner had been in Boston for a security conference when Whidbey happened. The other delegates were out tying one on, but he had a paper to give the next day, on security techniques for protecting visiting dignitaries. So he fiddled with the presentation while he flicked channels for the latest bulletins on the farmhouse siege somewhere north of Seattle.

He had never lost the soft spot for the city, despite the multi-channel humiliation it had inflicted on him. He had watched, horrified, the storming of the farmhouse. They had used an armoured car, a military vehicle with a very large blade welded on the front, like an extra-wide bulldozer, behind which the foot soldiers of the SERTS, the SWATs, FBI and Alcohol, Tobacco and Firearms crouched. The machine reminded him of a scaled-down version of the 'hogjaws' – toughened bulldozers that the engineers had used for jungle clearance in 'Nam.

On the screen, as the TV news chopper pulled back, Milliner could see the movement to either side of the road to the farmhouse. Not much, it could easily be dismissed as the product of rotor wash, but he sensed from three thousand miles away it was trouble.

They shouldn't have gone in the first place – it was an

emotional decision, not an operational one. The brain-dead cultists inside had cut the throat of an ATF agent and thrown him out the door. It was another technique he knew from South East Asia. The VC had no illusion about how important body counts were to the US Army, how much they invested in recovering the bodies of fallen comrades, so they often hid the corpses to frustrate the Yankees, or taunted them by stringing up the dead, daring the soldiers to come and cut them down. The grunts would then either be caught in sniper fire, or maimed when the body, booby-trapped with a claymore, detonated, showering the jungle and the man's buddies with flesh and blood and bone.

The same hand was being played in Whidbey that night. For four days the charismatic leader 'Father William' had held off the law-enforcement agencies. Inside he had the usual mix of deranged disciples – young runaways, college drop-outs, the religious maniacs, a clutch of dim-but-beautiful girls under his spell and a very large collection of heavy-duty firepower. It was almost as if someone had published a blueprint for How To Organise A Cult And Have Women Eating Out Of Your Hand (And Sucking Your Cock), and every two or three years some messianic maniac implemented it. What this particular group believed in, exactly what the leader had formulated, was never clear – some sort of variation on the Armageddon down the road, time to arm up. Which is where the links with the far-right gun lobbyists and the whole AGFA thing came in. America's Most Looniest.

Hell, it was easy to be flip and cynical now, but that night he had yelled himself hoarse at the television, shouting and crying, causing people to rush to his room and bang on the door, the fellow guests and the staff all coming in to watch open-mouthed as the tragedy unfolded. Father William had stationed two units of armed disciples in a complex trench network running out from the farmhouse in two arms, each at forty-five degrees to the front of the house. Heavy machine guns had been set up at the apex of each one, with various other lighter weapons – because of the reduced range – being stationed at intervals back towards the headquarters.

Crazy they may have been, but the concealed cultists waited a long time, mainly because Father William was no hot-head kid, he had seen action – not real action, Grenada – but he knew a little about tactics. The large force of law-enforcement officers hiding behind the junior hogjaw were completely exposed to the guns that had out-flanked them.

The slaughter was fast and furious, the heavy-calibres puncturing the men's vests like they were made of the kind of cheap aluminium foil you'd wrap a Thanksgiving turkey in. In fact that's what it was – a turkey shoot. It even out-whacked Waco.

Four minutes and twenty-seven seconds the AAR, After-Action Report, claimed. Seventeen dead, nine wounded, and the farmhouse and those trenches intact.

To their credit the authorities recovered enough to CS-gas the trenches, neutralising the occupants. Then the firing within started. Father William lined them all up, asked them to kneel and hold hands, and shot them all. Them all. Afterwards he had calmly walked out, squelching blood from the soles of his boots, arms raised, to surrender, no weapon in sight, flanked by his two lieutenants. What would he get? Washington was one of the few states to still have death by hanging, but nobody was going to put the noose round that man's neck. Not when they found the people – the boys and the girls, really – who had knelt down and offered their necks to him in a bloody benediction. More than a few testaments short of a Bible was the only rational judgement.

Maybe the SERT man was thinking just that. Maybe he had just seen his buddy blown apart next to him. Maybe he, like Milliner, had been thinking of the parents who would have to identify the daughter they last heard of in Minnesota, or SoHo or heading for Los Angeles, the son who hadn't been able to take the pressure of medical school and had decided to spend a summer out west, the Kurt Cobain or Bruce Lee fan making the pilgrimage to their hero's final resting place.

In the reruns they would show in every news bulletin the officer looked too young to have a family of his own. So he probably wasn't thinking of his own kids when he stood up, shouldered his H&K PSG-1 sniper's rifle and smacked a round straight into Father William's forehead. In the cool light of day, you had to admit it was a hell of a shot. Hell of a shot. Win him all sorts of prizes at the FBI Sniper School. Too good – the prosecution had tried to argue that no man deranged by events would have been so cool and collected, that he would have fired randomly, a mad-minute frenzy. Would have shot the two cohorts as well, instead of leaving them to stand trial in Spokane a year down the line.

But the trooper's defence fund was swelled by the likes of Milliner – who sent a thousand dollars – and the lawyers argued that this man had been pushed over the limits by the incompetent operational approach which had seen the needless death of dozens of people. There wasn't a jury in the North-West who would convict. Just the way they had had to move the trial of the disciples to Spokane to have any hope of an unbiased jury.

But the reverberations went deeper than one trooper walking free. The City of Seattle convened a law-enforcement conference, trying to tackle the increase in crime which came with a new, burgeoning population. Milliner had got to speak, to present a paper, to argue with politicians from King, Island and Whitcom Counties about how the only way to take on the creeping chancre was co-operation, not fragmentation. And such was the horror of Whidbey, the little incident in the bus tunnels seemed like nothing at all. Collateral damage they would call it now.

So he got to organise this outfit, the Specials Weapons and Operations Puget Sound – SWOPS. Much to the disgust of the SERT – Seattle Emergency Response Team – of course, but that shot looked like poor discipline, and the unit was under a cloud. Didn't stop him taking some of their best men and recruiting from King County's Tac-30, South Snohomish SWAT, Everett's Tactical Team and Bellevue's Tactical Arms Group – all of whom had shown themselves brave and resourceful, all of whom he could point to for failures of inter-group communication. Let them still exist for local incidents, he argued successfully, but let's have a 'super rapid response' team. No more Whidbeys.

The city balked at the cost, but the president of MicroLine Systems had pledged $1.3m towards the operating budget. Milliner got a three-year contract, gave himself his old Vietnam rank – recently abolished by the Seattle PD in a rationalisation of command levels – and organised the new unit along military, not civilian police lines. And goddamn it, it worked. OK, next year the budget would be cut – when he had asked for three choppers he was sure they would whittle him down to one, but the city was so shocked by those TV images that he got two.

Now, of course, as the memory faded the politicians were griping about cost, the outlying counties were carping about what was in it for them, and the Seattle PD were lobbying to regain control. And the $1.3m was running out fast. Once it was gone, he could see SWOPS being a brave experiment in cross-regional response quietly put out to pasture. Along with its commander.

But no matter what happened to SWOPS, tonight might finish some things forever – back in Spokane Father William's two apostles should get life for their role in the Whidbey massacre, because the defence had mounted a credible they-were-under-the-influence-of-a-madman diminished-responsibility plea. And ahead, a chance to clean out the tunnels (*'And make sure I'm not right,'* said the voice), maybe find that face, the one that ran him out of town. That would wrap things up nicely.

He asked the pilot to raise SWOPS headquarters and spoke to the duty sergeant. 'What is happening in Seattle, Sergeant Krycek? Over.'

Krycek, who could access the DIR from the PD computer, started the litany, beginning with the First Lady's visit and moving onto multiple homicide and all points in between. Milliner let it wash over him, like a familiar, grubby, tainted downpour.

'Did you say drive-bys? Over.' He shouted into his mouthpiece.

'Yessir, that is what the regular cops are saying. Whole family. In a pick-up. Caused chaos along Aurora and I-5. Guys still holed up somewhere. Over.'

Milliner thought of those flashes he had seen on take-off. Son of a bitch. Not his visual impairment after all. Still, too late for whoever was at the other end of those muzzles. 'Any news on the incident at Henry Street? Over.'

There was a pause while Krycek searched for the docket that Seattle PD were obliged to file to SWOPS for actions assessment. 'Just that one perp and one girl are still unaccounted for, sir. Over.'

'Sergeant, I want some things ready for me when we get back. I want some Sure Fire lights, big ones, the sort we used in the sewer operation. Got that? Over.'

'Sir. Over.'

'And a set of night-sights, some body-heat sensors, flare pistols, full communications gear. A whistle for each man. And listen carefully, along Henry and Stewart and Third and Fourth, and maybe even Fifth, there are glass squares set in the sidewalk, close to the wall. Over.'

'Sorry, sir, that broke up. Grass squares? Over.'

'GLASS. G for Golf, L Lima. They are transparent, well, opaque. They look kind of purple from up top, but they are transparent. I want searchlights set up over them. Shining down. And over any grids that they can find. There is a movie being shot down by Pike Place Market – if you can't get some from the Fire Department, sequester the film company's. Tell them the city will pay. Over.'

'Yessir. Over.'

'Who's on point right now? Over.'

'Captain Robertson. Over.'

'Good, get him to organise the lights. One more thing, Sergeant. Over.'

'Yes, Major? Over.'

'Do you think you can get me some flame-throwers?'

TWENTY

Alaska Apartments, Pier 66, Seattle Waterfront. 2.20 am

Annie Haart slumped down on the sofa and eased off her shoes. She should get back to her own apartment, but she was just too dog-tired and her feet ached too much. Leo Griffin had been harder work than she anticipated. That strain of dope normally turned men into total numbnuts, literally paralysed their cock and balls. It even happened to Ricky who, God knows, had smoked enough high-grade shit in the last year ('Hey, we gotta check which are the best hybrids,' he had explained whenever she complained about his permanent stoned-age condition) that his body should have grown accustomed to it. But no, one small joint of Owl's Own Brand and his scrotal sac sagged liked a tired bowling bag.

Griffin, on the other hand, had passed through the blissed-out impotence stage in double-quick time and moved onto the dog-rubbing-itself-against-your-leg syndrome without passing Go-To-Sleep at all. Pepper was embarrassed by being around a man slavering so much, and had kept flashing his eyes in a 'can I go now?' signal, but she had kept shaking her head. She felt sure that the problem was with the wiring of Griffin's brain – he would exhaust his overstoked libido eventually. It happened twenty minutes ago, when finally the bulge in his slacks subsided, having come to terms with the fact that instant gratification wasn't on the cards.

She had quickly confirmed his order for the drugs – no schmuck was going to turn down that stuff after a hard-on that rivalled the Space Needle in terms of man-made achievement – and got Pepper to drive him back. And now she had a commitment to all she could supply for the next year.

Griffin had finally realised that Ricky's strain of dope – out of Holland, genetically interfered with by one of the top botanical engineers in England – needed nothing in the line of free cuddly toys to promote it. Griffin knew if he hadn't taken it any one of a dozen others would. Well, not that scum-sucking bottom-dweller Hilton, perhaps. Four lousy bills and he can't even get it together. She had waited in Kobe Park up on Seventh for fifteen minutes. By the end of it Annie was beginning to suspect she was being set up. She was glad she had dumped the stuff at a pick-up point rather than bring it in person, glad that the Para-Ord was a legit registered weapon.

But all that came her way was a drunken bum, too ugly and convincing ever to be a narc – unless they had developed a way of cosmetically eating away half the undercover cop's face – who slammed on the windscreen a few times. She was so shocked she had toyed with the idea of shooting him anyway, cop or no cop. Maybe she was getting too trigger-happy. Off with their kneecaps. She had done three now, and the word was getting around. Don't fuck with that lady, she's worse than Ricky. She laughed to herself. She was a *lot* worse than Ricky.

After admiring the view from the apartment window, watching the dinner-cruise ship ease itself into its berth and discharge its wobbling consignment of conventioneers, she poured herself a couple of fingers of the Baker's as a nightcap and stripped off down to her underwear, stopping to make a half-flattering appraisal of herself in the full-length mirror. Yeah, she could see Leo's point. Poor Ricky. The fabled one last job – one last heist to fund the next batch of daylight lamps and the shipment of seed plants. And it all went well, nobody hurt, clean getaway and he got to buy both light and the seed plants.

He did it by the book. Paid cash. Bought the lights at garden centres all over the state so no one big order went into one store. Changed the plates on the car when they picked up the order. Didn't drive straight to the growing site. Those garden guys, she wondered, what did they really think they wanted the big 1500-watt halides for? The mother of all lettuces? And why specify the sodium lights that mimicked the spectrum of sunlight in fall? Everyone knew what the end product was going to be. But you couldn't be too careful. Any one of the retailers could be a stake-out. So it took months to get it all together.

Then the idiot Ricky had chosen as his driver decides he has waited long enough and walks into a show room and puts a deposit on a new Ferrari. A yellow one. With a top-of-the-range Alpine stereo, please. Oh, and I'll pay with these bills that have been marked with a fluorescent u/v pen. Jesus, Ricky had told him to trade them in, he would get a 60 per cent deal, or to sit on it for two years or more. Or, like Ricky, get it laundered out of the country. Anywhere but Seattle.

So the driver gives Ricky up, but luckily for her Rick already has the dope plants, Pig, Pepper and their crew in place as minders, and The Owl (who claimed he named himself after some legendary drug mentor she had never heard of) in charge of production. All Annie had to do was get the short leather skirts out of the closet – plus the Para out of the shoebox – and start shifting. Respect was taking a little longer to come, but it was getting there.

Of course the cops are all over her looking for the cash, but it's long gone – and she can account for the BMW and the rest from her nail-extension business. You mean Ricky was a criminal? And all this time he told me he was independently wealthy. She knew that at least one of them hadn't swallowed it – the older, fatter one of the team had hung around for a few days. She wasn't sure whether he didn't go along with the act, or he had the hots for her, but even Seattle had enough going down elsewhere that the department couldn't afford a lovesick cop on permanent stake-out, and he had faded away. If only they knew it was all under their noses – or under their feet at least.

Taking her time, enjoying the solitude at last, Annie used some Clinique she had stashed in the apartment to take off her make-up, brushed the knots out of her hair – she must do those roots before her next visit with Ricky – and gasped as she slid into the cold sheets of a bed that hadn't been slept in for weeks. She was reaching for the light when the phone rang in her purse. She cursed and padded back into the living room. Was this Leo Griffin having second thoughts? Or up for a little phone sex?

It was Pepper. 'Annie? You asleep? You better get over here. There is some weird shit going down.'

TWENTY-ONE

Henry Street, Seattle. 2.15 am

Tenniel had this image of the city that night, one he couldn't shake. Towering over downtown was a giant figure, like something from a Ray Harryhausen movie, Jason and the Argonauts maybe, a big malevolent approximation of a Greek god. And it had its laurel leaf loincloth or whatever Zeus would wear, pulled down, and a God-sized dick plopped out and it was pissing all over central Seattle, a great hissing stream of vile effluent, clogging up the streets, burning eyes and noses and mouths with its stench and acridity. Here, take that, mudslide on Magnolia. Ha, let's douse these couple of vagrants. Let's see if we can terrorise some poor inn keepers up on Capitol. Everyone was being swept away in the ammoniacal downpour – cops, citizens, fire department – flumed along the streets and deposited in Elliott Bay. And then there were Girdlestone's dogs, the number rising day after day. He was beginning to think the idiot was on to something.

Best switch to de-caff for the rest of the night, he thought.

But whether it was the gods relieving themselves or not, it wasn't your average Friday night in Seattle. Shootings, muggings, fires, kidnappings, even assassination threats – we get them all, he thought, but normally with enough air between them so that you get to finish the paperwork on one before the next starts up.

Already he had had two requests and a near-firing from senior officers to leave the little girl to others and come and sort out this problem and that problem. He had resisted to the point of insubordination. 'Tenniel, this will go on your record,' they had said. That was the best threat they had? Everything else they offered involved dead bodies or post-crime trauma, he explained, and tragic as that may be, what was more important was that they had a real, live breathing person involved here, one that could be saved, maybe. Me and Detective Bowman, we've both done hostage courses. And the SWOPS are on the way if that fails. So fuck you and get me some more resources. Give us time, they said, we are a little stretched.

In truth the last thing they needed was more people. Especially we'll-take-it-from-here-Sergeant Feds. The room with the hole in the floor was already crowded, a position made worse by the fact that everyone took great care not to go near said hole since a bullet and a threat came flying out of it some time ago. Tenniel doubted the duo were still beneath them, but as he wasn't going to be the first to offer his head as a pumpkin, he couldn't really blame the others.

They managed to get a probe from the Technical Support Unit – basically a Cohu camera on a stick. It showed an empty room. God knows where he was at now.

The alley had been taped off, the few reporters who turned up mainly sold some yarn, although one who had managed to pick up a stray message that mentioned the

Underworld hostage situation was sticking around. Ever since the media saturation of Whidbey, when all and sundry got their balls fried live on Nationwide prime-time TV, media control and containment had been a Seattle obsession, to the point of distraction. Still, on this occasion he really did have enough trouble without nosy scribblers and cam crews.

Light had been restored to the old spice storage room, and he could see what years of neglect had done to it. The far wall was sodden with accumulated damp, the plaster had the consistency of foam rubber, and where it met the floor the constant trickle of water had turned it to pulp. It was there that the two had fallen through. It had been cold enough to freeze meat when they came in, but the bodies and activity had raised the temperature so that the men's breath no longer showed. What was it like underneath? He was really in no hurry to find out, not by falling through the floor anyway.

So Tenniel had set up the trestle tables well away from the rot, and now a mixture of uniforms, detectives, two fire-department representatives – who had promised their best search-and-rescue guys just as soon as they came free – Zeus pissing on him again – an electrician, a surveyor and the bleary-eyed Curator of the Museum of History and Industry tried not to bump into each other as they milled around. The latter they had christened The Man With The Plans, because he had unfurled a large-scale ground plan of Seattle circa 1890, and another of the new sewer system and a third of modern down-town. It was hard to see how the three related, but the MWTP seemed to understand.

Isa – Detective Bowman he reminded himself – was

in and out, calling to Rescue, Medic One, anyone who had any bright ideas. She was a real dynamo. But then she was fifteen years younger than him, about a third the weight, and had almost cost him his marriage when nothing had even happened. Sure, she had swum into his more lurid dreams now and then, but so had Madonna and Jennifer Tilly and that redhead from the shampoo commercials on occasion.

Right now, though, Harry was the one Tenniel was worried about. He was pacing the floor, moving ever closer to the hole, silent and withdrawn. He was going through the blaming-himself period, thinking he should have taken a chance and fired. Tenniel tried to reassure him but, like Harry, he had one big question: if Harry hadn't interfered, would the girl be down there now? Probably not. Would Tenniel have done the same? Definitely. Except he might have hesitated in shooting the guy in the Ford, and got killed for his trouble. He couldn't decide whether Harry had a great talent for self-preservation or was stupidly reckless and not likely to see thirty. If it was the latter, please God let it happen in Vancouver. Then he hated himself for the thought. Same old Tenniel – anything for the quiet life. Never raise your head above the parapet, never take the chancy option. Well, maybe this once, eh?

He went over to the Man With The Plans: 'What do you think?'

'Hard to tell. Do you know what happened down there?'

'Yeah, they had a fire, they filled it in and built over the top, then opened some of it by Pioneer Square as a tourist attraction.'

The MWTP said excitedly, 'Yes, but that is only part of it.' He had that wild this-is-my-moment enthusiasm that all specialists – the more arcane, the wilder the enthusiasm – had when they got to parade their expertise for a moment. Tenniel still remembered the joy of the taxidermist they had to consult when a body turned up that had been perfectly stuffed and put astride a carousel horse, Roy Rogers-style.

The MWTP cleared his throat. Tenniel knew he was going to be pinned to the wall. 'The fire started on Madison and spread mainly to the south. Where we are now was scorched a bit when they blew up some burning buildings, but not destroyed. But, like the rest of the city, it got buried when they raised the floor level. They filled a lot of it in with brick and with rubble and some soil and earth. Even sawdust in some places. The new sewers were often laid running down the old streets and avenues. But in the nineteen-twenties many of the underground streets were partially excavated again.' Tenniel nodded. He knew this. But the flow continued. 'The bootleggers brought in the booze from Canada, usually by boat across the Sound, then they were taken and stored underground somewhere up here.' He waved his hand over the north-west of them. 'They have never been explored properly, but there were at least two underground warehouses north of here. But at some point the Feds dynamited the entrances to prevent them being used again.'

'Big?'

'Thousand of barrels I've heard. But that's not all. To feed this city's speaks, the bootleggers tunnelled a network of passages through the soil and rubble, propping up where they had to, and ran the booze directly under the feet of the police.'

'So our man could be using the same tunnels?'

'He could. There is no light down there, of course, so it would be pretty difficult, I'd say.'

'Is there a choice of routes?'

The MWTP shrugged. 'I would guess.'

'And how big are the passageways?'

'They vary from large enough to pull a handcart through down to ones where you have to turn sideways to pass – it depends what they were meant for. There are even some sections of whole streets intact. There is another problem, though.'

'Which is?'

'What we have here –' he pointed to the old plans – 'is what Seattle was *meant* to look like. When it was surveyed for the bus tunnels, it was found the reality and this –' he stabbed the paper – 'didn't match.'

'How come?'

'This is what the city got the money to do. Drain the cesspools, fill them in and so on. It turns out that what we really got was a cheap'n'cheerful shoring-up job and a holiday in Vegas.' Tenniel raised an eyebrow. 'Well, whatever a holiday in Vegas equivalent was back then. Seems a man called MacDonald did the absolute minimum and siphoned off the rest. He was supposed to install a modern sewer system designed by a man called Williams from Chicago. Instead, he dug a huge cesspit and let it all run into there for twenty years or more. Nobody knew any better until it started flowing through Pike Place Market one morning.'

'So is it dangerous under there? I mean, might it collapse on them?'

'Not now. They braced much of it up when they did the bus tunnels in the eighties, but it is scheduled to be resurveyed and properly filled in, in about 2010. But it will be fine once you get down there. No chance of a collapse, I mean.'

Tenniel ignored the 'you' in the sentence and looked at his watch. Someone was going to have to go down soon. They had already had a call from the Mayor, one of those easy-to-act-on demands – do something, but make sure whatever you do doesn't harm the girl and get the city any more bad publicity. The First Lady mustn't share the front page with mudslides, drive-bys *and* a dead little girl.

'Anyone down there now, do you know?' asked Tenniel.

'I think most of them were swept out when the tunnels were built. You know what the rumour is, don't you?'

'What rumour?'

'That *he's* down there.'

Oh he was loving this. Humour him. 'Who, exactly?'

'The Green River Killer.'

Tenniel laughed. 'Yeah, right.'

'The one you couldn't get.'

'King County's beef, not mine.' The GRK got everywhere. He killed forty women one minute, eighty-six the next; he was that guy from Tacoma, a biker, an ex-Marine. Next he must have been a cop, maybe one who retired from King County in '84 when the killings stopped (although the copycats had never gone away). In fact the prime suspect had been a collector of police memorabilia. But once the police had voiced their suspicions, the guy had sued. It was a lucrative business, being accused of serial killing. And now this version – he was some subterranean boogeyman. Well, it was a new one on him.

Tenniel wondered how long before the SWOPS got there. He couldn't figure Milliner. He had got this gig on the strength of an ill-conceived action by SWATs, SDS and ATF. From the sound of him on the radio, he was going to make the same mistake. Milliner was rushing into the situation thinking he could make up for the fact that some bums with a can of paint and some posters humiliated him all those years ago. As if anyone else cared this far down the line. They gave him SWOPS, didn't they? How much more rehabilitation does a man need?

There was a commotion at the door and a civilian entered, escorted by Bowman. 'This guy is trying to take shots of the crime scene,' she said. 'And about to get himself whisked back to the PSB. I figured he was the guy you wanted.'

Tenniel nodded affirmation and stepped forward, offering Lewis his hand. 'You OK? Sorry for, y'know . . .'

'I wasn't sleeping so good anyway. Glad for the chance of some air.'

'I know, you were so goddamned keen, you never really gave me a chance to fill you in.'

'Well, I'm here now.' He set his camera case on the trestle table next to the plans. He took in the room, the hole in the floor, the lack of direction he could sense. 'Where do you want me to start?'

'Sergeant, the Lieutenant wants a word,' shouted a uniform. 'Now. Urgent.'

'Tell him I've got my head down the hole.' He put his arm on Lewis's shoulder and turned him away from the others. 'Possibly up my ass, depending on what you think. I don't want you to start anything yet. I want some advice. And maybe some help, I dunno. This is a long shot, to be frank.'

Tenniel filled him in as quickly as he could on the events of the night. Harry, hearing his name, came over to listen to how it sounded coming out of someone else's mouth. No better, he decided. He couldn't help noticing that the guy Tenniel was talking to was getting paler with each sentence. He looked sick, grey.

'So I remembered that night when you told me about . . . the war. And what you did. And how you were a member of this hot-shot unit. The bit that stuck in my mind – this is what you claimed – is that the team could operate in total darkness.'

Lewis's throat was dry. He kept looking at the hole, the soft grey line where the light stopped penetrating into whatever was down there. If he stared hard enough he could see lines in there, as if a vortex was spinning and forming, that old black magnetism, pulling at him already. Like a siren song. He cleared his head and managed to croak: 'I said that?'

'Kinda. We'd sucked back a few beers by then. But as I say, it stuck in my mind.'

'Jeez,' Lewis said, listening to his voice shake. 'I must've been drunk.' And downright fucking stupid. Why wasn't he over it yet? He turned his back on the torn aperture in the floor, but he could feel its presence between his shoulder-blades, like a horsehair poking through his shirt.

'The thing is we need to get a line to him somehow. A two-way thing so we can . . . you know, negotiate. We can't do it with a bullhorn. He'll want to give himself up, for sure. We just got to tell him how. Help him do it. We need someone to deliver the handset or whatever. This is the guy—' Tenniel gestured for Harry to fetch the blow-ups from the table. 'Funny thing is I know him. Busted him a couple times. Name's Hilton Badcock.'

'You're jokin'?' He did a double-take on Harry. Guy was small enough to be a tunnel fighter.

'No. He changes it to Babcock now and then, and he has a couple of street names, but it's really Badcock.'

'Why didn't his mother just call him Hilton Psychopath Mutherfucker and have done with it.'

'It's an old English name, so he claimed. The truth is, I don't think he is . . . I mean, this isn't Hilton. He's a lowlife scam artist, but this kid thing—'

'He held a gun to her head and pulled the trigger,' objected Harry tetchily, in case they were forgetting what had confronted him. 'That doesn't make him a Trainee Care Bear, does it?'

Lewis looked at Tenniel quizzically. 'Caught the hammer?'

'Yeah. Maybe.'

Lewis's guts were churning, hoping they weren't going to ask him what he knew was coming next. Deliver the line. In pitch darkness. To stall he said to Harry, 'There might not have been a slug in the chamber.'

'What?'

'If he had dropped the magazine and ejected the shell, there might not have been a bullet under that hammer. It was a bluff.'

'Oh, man . . . are you saying I was suckered?' Harry coloured up with a mixture of rage and chagrin.

Tenniel said quickly: 'It's a guess. All I'm saying is this is a jump of a league or two for Hilton. I don't believe he wants to kill the girl. Not unless we force him to by doing something reckless.'

'He killed the father,' insisted Harry.

'Shot. He shot the father. It might be a machine doin' the breathin', but he's still alive. An eight-year-old girl is kind of different. He just might have rigged a little pantomime for you, is all we're sayin',' said Tenniel with an appeasing shrug. He wasn't sure he believed it himself.

'Why don't we ask him?' suggested Lewis, with a sigh of relief.

'What? Ask who?'

'Your pal Hilton. Why don't we ask him if it had one up the spout.'

'You wanna shout down the hole?' Tenniel pointed at the floor. 'Go ahead.'

'Why don't you call him? Look.' Lewis flashed the picture to the two cops and tapped his finger at the blurred figure. They had been so mesmerised by the gun in his hand they had missed the other details. 'In his top pocket. That's a cellphone. It might still be working and it might be in range. Give him a call.'

TWENTY-TWO

'I don't know what the two of them – Lewis and Fix I mean – got up to in Saigon. Not really. Just bits. I only met them – well, I knew Lewis from before, when I was with him in The Big Red One – but this time round we flew into Ben Moc Fire Support Base, in Cu Chi, and Lewis and Fix were already there. Been in-country two, three days. They had built us a sweet little set-up, away from everybody else on the base. A coupla GPs – tents, they're big tents – and showers. One thing a tunnel fighter loves is showers, y'know? There was a bit of tension between them, I noticed that. Lewis was hard on the kid. I asked him, and he said he'd gotten out of line. Fix wouldn't say much – he'd hooked up with a bad crowd. Well, not bad, just partyin'. There were some Australians and a French guy, some kind of spook who hung out in this bar, the Dark Star. Lucky's we used to call it, after the miserable Cambodian who ran it. Hugo, that was the spook's name. I remember. God – it comes back doesn't it? Can't remember my mother's birthday . . . Spook – you know, spy. Some hangover from the fifties who was making a fortune selling US passports to Vietnam officials who knew the whole thing was going down the toilet. And the Aussies were bush fighters, in for some R&R, and they got Fix fucked up on some dope – they used to lace the dope with opium and . . . I think he went to a place called the Fruit Bowl. No, you don't want to know. Well, all the girls were named after . . . fruits – you know, strawberry, raspberry, mango. And I think Lewis caught Fix having what we called a fruit salad and dragged him out by his dick. They had left a trail across the city . . . shit, they weren't hard to find. One of the Aussies . . . I can probably get that as well. Hold on. Grogan, that's it. Grogan had got into a fight with some GIs over the ARVIN. This guy liked them, y'see, and the GIs were badmouthing them, so he broke a couple of noses. The ARVIN? Regular South Vietnam forces. I forget . . . you're too young for this shit, aren't you?

'Nah, Fix didn't fight. Fix wasn't like that. Problem was, with Fix, he just couldn't say no. If he thought it would upset you, he'd go right along with it. Shit, you should have seen him when Wayland told him his gun was crap, he went straight to Lewis and insisted, demanded that he be allowed to go down the tunnels real time, not just as an observer, but, you know, on patrol. Show them the damn thing worked if you treated it right. What did Lewis do? Well, Fix was all fired up. I remember hearing him, pacing up and down that little office Lewis had, yelling. There was this great photograph Lewis had taken . . . he took great pics, did I say that? Fantastic shot of his first tunnelling unit in Vietnam – I was in there – and Fix ripped it off the wall. 'I'm no younger than these guys,' he shouted. And he had a point. So he let him go down with us. Maybe that was his mistake. I never thought of it like that before. Maybe that was when it all went to shit.'

TWENTY-THREE

Underworld. Seattle.

Well, it might have been a street once. What Hilton and Alice stepped into was a circular brick chamber, the walls oily with grease and damp, the floor lumpy and uneven where clumps of rough mortar had fallen down. It smelt too, but Hilton couldn't place it. Singed mildew and a ripe earthy smell overlaid – well, just tinged – with a faint, faint sweetness.

He looked down at Alice. She was staring at the floor. She should sulk. She at least had the jacket, even it was covered in black slime. Already he could feel the goose-bumps up his arms, and he had to suppress any shivering reflex. When he shivered his two front teeth rattled, an effect so comic that any terror he held for this little girl would instantly evaporate. He probed his ribs and winced as he hit tenderness. But he was now pretty sure nothing was broken, just a couple of ripped muscles. He could live with that for the time being.

Both their breaths were coming in clouds, the way it billowed out of horses in the winners' enclosure. Two questions occupied him now – how much colder was it going to get, and how long would the lamp last?

He raised the light as slowly as he could, frightened of any sudden movement extinguishing the flame, which was exposed on one side by the broken glass. The room was around twelve feet high, the ceiling a mess of wooden and steel struts. At ground level there were five exits – just holes in the walls, really – to choose from. Two to the left, three to the right. He tried to figure out which way was north, and which west. His instinct told him he didn't want to head for the waterfront, that the recent development down there might block the tunnels, and anyway that direction guaranteed an end at the sea. If they could go north, north-east, all he had to do was find another room like the tavern, and hack his way to street level. Shit, there might even be a door somewhere.

But the passageways looked odd. They were very, very roughly hewn, almost as if someone had chewed them out. He had no idea which of the three to take.

'Whaddayathink, kid? Come on, work with me here.' He cleared his throat. 'Ali, we gotta move it. I don't want to be in these tunnels when this lamp goes out, and neither do you.'

Ali looked up and sniffed. Two big globules had formed on the lower lids of her eyes and slowly, ponderously they broke free and rolled over her cheeks. Hilton felt a squeeze around his heart. Then he thought about his nephews and nieces. They could turn the waterworks on when they wanted pretty good. Mind you, he didn't shoot their dads on any kind of regular basis. But shit, kids – the most manipulative species alive.

'Ali, we got to choose a way out. I think we go that way.' He waved at the three dark arches. 'But which of them, I dunno . . . can you help me out here?'

He heard a scuttling, a patter, and so did she. He couldn't see anything, but it was odds-on rats were down here. It had come from the left tunnel he was sure. So was Ali. 'That one,' she said sulkily, indicating the centre hole, and took to examining the shadows on the floor again.

Hilton had to stoop to clear the roof of the opening. He tentatively put his head inside, and felt tiny invisible threads brush his face, causing him to twitch in disgust. It was just like some old-time ghost train or house of horrors, only this time it was real. He took a step in, keeping his mouth tightly closed, pulling Ali after him. The crude corridor was too narrow for them to walk side by side, so he gripped her hand and yanked her along. She wasn't exactly resisting and dragging her feet, but she wasn't skipping either.

He looked back over her head. Darkness had returned to the round chamber. No police flashlights yet. If he could get some distance between them, round a bend or two so the pursuers couldn't see the light, then they would be faced with the same three-to-one odds he had had. But for the time being the tunnel ran straight, just like the streets above, the floor rising steadily, as if they were going uphill.

The wall came up sooner than he hoped. An almost shiny sheet of reinforced concrete, obscenely new and forbidding. He looked down at Ali, who had also spotted it. 'What's that?'

'Nordstrom's for all I know. It's someone's basement wall, that's what it is. We gotta turn back.'

He started to move, but she stood her ground. He nearly toppled them both over. 'Hey, move willya?'

'What about that?'

'What?'

'THAT.' She gave one of those petulant sighs that

suggested adults aren't so bright after all. The truth was that the aperture was too low down for Hilton to have noticed. It was around three feet high, and ran off to the left, parallel with the concrete.

'I ain't goin' down there. Christ, it's for midgets.'

'We can crawl.' Then, with a logic that he found irrefutable: 'All the tunnels back there might end up hitting this. We can make ourselves small enough to get through.' She was right; and he might have made a bad call coming this way, but there was an equally strong chance they were all bad calls.

Hilton stepped forward, stooped down and peered in. More blackness, although the walls seemed very smooth and well packed. But inviting it wasn't.

The cold was getting to him now. He couldn't hide the fact that his muscles were hammering away of their own accord. He tried to stop his rogue teeth from rattling. He found wedging his tongue behind them did the trick. But he was seriously chilly now all right. Great, survive armed robbery shoot-out, die of hypothermia because given up jacket to hostage. 'OK, you go first.'

She looked at him with disdain. 'I'm the kid here, remember?'

'And I've got the gun and I don't want to get my ass stuck halfway into that tunnel and hear you high-tailin' it back down here.'

Ali nodded at the understandable wisdom of this, and there was a bizarre *pas de deux* as they struggled to switch places and she went down on her hands and knees. She thought briefly about spiders, took a deep breath and started in.

Hilton scrambled to keep up, careful not to knock the

lamp. 'Hold up, kid,' he shouted, but she was away, with the ease of a beetle, while he, down to three limbs, found progress jerky and uncomfortable.

But concentrating on trying to give some kind of rhythm to his movement meant he could forget about exactly where they were. Each scratch and nick distracted him from the strange smells and tastes he was getting from the walls, from the darkness that closed behind them, from the shuffling of the girl in front of him, from the idea – the intolerable idea – that if they were to hit another concrete wall, they would have to reverse all the way.

Alice's crawling was dislodging more and more material. A fine dust was being generated that was starting to clog his eyes and nostrils. As he blinked he could feel the specks scratching under the lid. How much longer? The concrete to their right had disappeared, replaced by older bricks and then packed earth. He could sense that the route was curving a little, arcing away from that blocking basement. It was also going down again.

There was a yell in front as Ali's rump disappeared, to be replaced by the sight of her two legs. She was standing up. Hilton put the lamp down and pulled himself out, coughing the dust out of his throat before examining their arrival point.

He groaned as he retrieved the lamp. 'Fuck me.'

'What's wrong?'

'You ask for one door and you get three.'

This chamber was bristling with opportunity. To his right, a brick wall, then another dark entrance, then another blank façade, and to the left three wooden doors, their surfaces warped, split and blistered. Hilton held up the lamp. The doors had to be ten feet high. They ended just short of the concrete trusses that again festooned the ceiling.

Hilton reached over to the nearest door knob, which at least was at normal height.

'STOP.'

He jumped so hard he nearly dropped the lamp. 'Fucksake, kid. What? WHAT?'

'I . . . I don't know. Isn't this like . . . one door is right and the others . . .'

'The others . . . ?'

She took a deep breath: 'Have something horrible behind them?'

'Like, worse than what is on this side?' He waved an arm round the chamber. 'I don't think so.' But, a little uneasy voice asked, why would they be so tall? Half the size again of normal. 'OK, you choose.'

He watched as Ali mouthed some sort of counting game, a take on eeny, meeeny, but it started 'Killa, Digga, Ghost and Priest . . .' and then carried on with a selection of letters until she proclaimed: 'O . . . D . . . B.' The finger ended pointing to the middle one, so she did a quick mental recap and ran through the rhyme again, ending up with, he guessed, the one she felt most comfortable with. 'This one.' It was the door he had been going to try in the first place.

Fire, smoke, damp, and freezing cold had twisted and swelled and distorted the door, forcing it into the frame, buckling it where the wall wouldn't give to its advances. Hilton put his foot against the wall and pulled. He handed Ali the lamp, and heaved with both hands. There was a loud splitting sound and it tore from its jamb with a shower of dust.

Ali gave a little grunt as it swung back.

A framed grey expanse of concrete filled the entire aperture, like a brutal-art installation.

'Shit, shit, shit,' said Hilton. 'I guess they'll all be the same.'

'No they won't. Next.'

'Next? Hey, I nearly put my shoulder out on that. You wanna have a go?'

'It's a big door. And I am a little girl.'

Hilton wasn't so sure. He was beginning to think he had kidnapped a forty-year-old dwarf by mistake. The second came easier, just a mild hint of protest as it revealed its solid grey middle. Disappointment showed on Ali's shadow-filled face, but she didn't say anything. Hilton shrugged and, without being asked, went for the third. Why not collect the set?

As he pulled the door knob, the entire unit, including the frame, tore free with a shower of brick dust, arcing out of the wall, towards his head. Hilton raised his arms and braced himself, taking the weight of the ten-foot slab of three-inch thick wood, grunting and swearing as he managed to push it to one side. Even as he put his shoulder into heaving it upright, he registered there was something other than concrete there.

He retrieved the light from Ali and stepped forward, illuminating a large, lofty cupboard, with a strange plinth occupying its centre. It was a few seconds before he realised what the column was, or more to the point what was sitting atop the column.

'It's a john,' said Ali.

'I can see that.'

It was what was left of a john, the porcelain cracked and chipped, the wooden seat hanging askew, kept on by a precious looking slither of frayed rope and a collection of sagging cobwebs. It was sitting on a pedestal that had to be seven feet high. At its base were the remains of the ladder that must have been used to gain access – you'd've had to be John Holmes otherwise to use it, and women wouldn't have stood a chance. And anyone who suffered from vertigo had best get constipated real fast. 'I can see that,' he said again, 'but what the fuck is it doing up there?'

Ali said confidently: 'In the old days, when the tide came in, it used to rush up the sewers. If you were sitting on the can at the time –' she giggled – 'you got a free douche. That's what Mrs Cole told us in history.'

He picked up a faded piece of wood from the floor, and slanted it to catch the weakening rays of lamp light. 'Men: Lift The Seat' it admonished. He realised that, before someone built something on the other side, all the doors had led to a similar set-up. 'So there were three of them. Then these were like, the public, you know, crappers, for—?'

'I don't know. But I need to go,' said Alice.

'Yeah, so do I. The sooner we get out of here the better. Just hold on, willya?'

'To the bathroom.' She squirmed to make the point.

'Up there?'

'Anywhere.'

'Well, I don't think there is anyone around to object.'

'I can't . . . you know. While you are here.'

They settled on her crouching at the foot of the

pedestal – he didn't fancy lifting her up there to have her ass bitten by some sewer rat – while he shuffled the detached door across to block her from his view. Embarrassed by the sound of the stream hitting the floor, Hilton began to shout.

'About your dad. The whole thing . . . It was a kind of accident. Got out of hand.'

The sound stopped and she squeezed through the triangular gap between door and wall into the small circle of light, looking at the splashes on her shoes in disgust. She knelt down in front of him. 'You didn't have to kill him.'

'He might not be dead. I only shot him once.' Big bullet though. Up close.

She nodded. 'He'll be so disappointed.'

What, if he doesn't die? he thought.

'He was taking me camping.'

'In this weather? Kind of cold, isn't it?'

'Not in a tent, stoopid, in his RV.'

He remembered the Winnebago outside the store.

'You like that? The Great Outdoors and all that shit.'

'S'pose. It can be pretty cu-ool sometimes, though. Don't you think?'

He had had enough of the Great Outdoors in the small towns his parents dragged him around in the boondocks of Minnesota and Iowa and Wisconsin – first both his parents, then his mom only and finally his aunt – to last him a lifetime. Working in feed stores, humping sacks, pulling down fifty dollars a week if he was lucky. He was happy in cities these days. Though not this much 'in' them, that was for sure. 'I guess,' was all he said. 'So what do you do on these trips?'

'Oh, Dad tells stories and plays games –' Hilton winced at the use of the present tense – 'he won't let us have any TV or anything.'

'You like TV.'

'Sure.'

'What's your favourite?'

'Oh, Sweet Valley High. Buffy the Vampire Slayer, I think that's neat. Sabrina, that's cool, although I liked the girl in it better when she was Melissa.'

'Yeah?'

'And I like some UPN shows, which Mom thinks is a bit strange. Y'know – In the House, Good News. They're funny. But I still like Melrose Place and Friends and South Park, and The Simpsons.'

'Hey, I like The Simpsons. Did you see it last week? The one where Homer is backstage at a concert and kicks that box and out comes a giant inflatable pig and floats away and the roadie says: "There goes Peter Frampton's big finish."?' He chuckled at the memory.

'Yeah, I saw that one. Who's Peter Frampton anyway?'

'He's well . . . well he was a big rock star. When I was a kid.'

'Like The Beatles.'

'Well, no . . .' Actually, to an eight-year-old, the distinction between the sixties and seventies is going to be kind of minimal, he thought. 'Because there were four of them and only one of him.'

She nodded at this and said: 'But what I mostly do is play soccer.'

'Soccer?'

'Yes. Soccer. Like, I am a member of an invitation-only

Premier team. Mr King coaches us. He's real good. I keep goal.'

He knew girls played sports and got scholarships these days, but soccer? Ah well, he always thought it was a faggot's game anyway.

'Did your dad – does your dad like music?'

'Real old stuff. Real old. Talking Heads. The Clash. He used to play tapes when we were trying to sleep. I'd make him wear my Walkman but you could still here the tsst tsst, and he would sing 'London's Burning' in my ear. Although he got to like Nirvana 'cause they were from Seattle and his mother's name was Grohl, like the drummer.'

Hilton rubbed his eyes. They were almost clear. 'In your ear? This is, like, a small RV.'

'Nah, we would always bed down together. He said it saved on laundry and heating. He was kind of a tightwad, my dad, that's what Mom always said, that's why they split up. Well, one of the reasons. She said I would guess the others when I'm a bit older.'

Hilton stopped shivering. 'But, you know. Nothing happened.' She cocked her head and stared at him. 'I mean nothing weird happened. While you were in bed?'

'Listening to The Clash as a lullaby is pretty weird. And when he couldn't sleep he would make me . . .' She hesitated but he let the silence hang there in the dark just beyond their circle. 'Well, he had this strange way of making me stroke him. Said it relaxed him. Said I shouldn't tell Mom—'

Hilton felt a burning in his ears and a lurch in his stomach. He jumped up and paced quickly. The dipshit fuckin' cunt. Christ, he hoped he hadn't died so he could shoot him all over again. He thought of that time his uncle had made some kind of move on him. Remembered the whirlwind that descended on the house when he had screamed blue murder. Fuck, must happen all over the place. He made himself calm. Now was not the time to get all emotional. Just another tough break for the kid. And anyway, the guy wouldn't be doing that any more. And maybe the information would come in handy.

He made to ruffle her hair as he reached for the lamp but she twisted away. Ah well, time to move on anyway. Now the trio of doors had yielded nothing useful, there was only one fresh exit left. Another tunnel to the right of where they had entered. 'Let's go.'

The sudden trilling noise made both of them jump. Hilton threw himself against the wall and yanked the gun out of his waistband, waving it at each of the dark holes. A moment later they both realised it was coming from Ali. From her top pocket. Or rather, the top pocket of his jacket. 'Oh, just fuckin' A,' said Hilton. The phone was ringing.

Ali pulled it out between two fingers. 'Want me to get it?'

TWENTY-FOUR

Henry Street, Central Seattle. 2.45 am

Annie Haart dropped the BMW into a low gear and crawled along First Avenue. The city looked pretty, the wet sidewalks all glistening in the new, improved street lighting they had put in. Unfortunately, it also illuminated the doorways where the bums tended to stretch out so Seattle's homeless problem was now pinpointed in bright pools of yellowy light. And because the light kept them awake, the bums had built bigger, thicker cardboard canopies to shield themselves.

She even knew some of them well by now – you got to when your business took you into the city's darker places – the Indian family who bedded down on Seneca, the trio who appeared permanently glued to the bench at Pioneer Square, and old Laurence, the slightly crazy one who always hovered around the Elliott Bay Bookstore, whose proudest moment was when he got a couple of bucks from Norman Mailer, who was doing a reading.

She turned into Henry as Pepper had told her. The first scene he had described was up on the left. There was a flash from the store. The officers were taking Polaroids. A motley collection of uniforms and plain-clothes were at the door, with a few satellite groups milling around a Ford and an RV.

Beyond that was a dark spot where the street lights

were out. She glided on up the street, her view partially blocked by the Winnebago, but as she came level she could see the garish police tape and the barriers. There were no more than a dozen people, most of them uniformed cops, but down the alley she could see bright lights and more people milling.

She tried to look like just another gawker while taking in the scene. One of the uniforms had already spotted her and was thinking about waving her on when his coffee arrived. The all-night Cafe D'Arte around the block was doing good business.

The inquisitive one bent his knees to bring himself level with her and motioned his head sideways. Move on. Now. Nothing to see here. It's all over, folks. She nodded, blipped the throttle and moved on up the hill. Asshole.

Pepper was waiting on the corner at Fourth, eyes darting back and forth, looking for all the world like someone begging to be arrested. She slowed and opened the door, barely having to halt the car before he had folded himself in.

'What's happening?' she asked.

'Woo. Like I said—'

Too fast. 'From the top, Pep.'

'OK. Let's see. I dropped Leo off at the Inn on the Market – I mean, dropped, he damn' well fell outta the car – he went down that alley like he had legs made of rubber – and spun round here for some Winstons. Hang a left, I'll show you somethin'. I saw the shit you saw back there first, then I cut through to go to this other joint I know. Here, slow.'

She crawled around the corner at Pine at the Key Bank Tower. Pulled half onto the sidewalk between the trees outside the Bon Marché store was a truck, the kind they convert for Brinks-Mat or Wells Fargo armoured cars. Around it were six or seven men in fatigues, some with flak jackets, unloading what appeared to be lighting rigs. Further down the street, by the terracotta edifice of the old Doyle building, one of these units was assembled, a whole row of lights positioned on the sidewalk, their electrical umbilicals snaking off to a generator. They hadn't been turned on yet.

Annie drove on, flipped a left on Second and stopped. 'Where's your car?'

'Up a block on Pike.'

'OK, wait for me in it. I'll be five, ten minutes.'

When he had gone Annie pulled off her tights to leave bare legs and folded her blouse away out of sight. She used a wipe to take off the tiny bit of lipstick she had put on before leaving and mussed her hair. With her coat pulled around her with excessive overstatement someone might just believe she was naked under it. She got out and retraced the way they had driven.

The street echoed to the steely, brittle sounds of frames and casings colliding and being slotted together. The first SWOPS she came to was outside the steel shutters of the Metro Tunnel set into the storefront of the Bon Marché, screwing together what looked like theatrical lighting onto a wheeled base. A large scribbled note was dangling from it: Fourth and Olive/outside Mayflower. They were being deployed all over the area then.

'Sergeant,' she said politely, in the firmest voice she could manage with a dry throat.

'I'm just a private, ma'am.' He was just a boy really, a hick from out in the State. Had a hell of a zit on his chin.

These were the Special Forces? Looked more like the Oxy-Ten Patrol to her. The boy swallowed. 'How can I help?'

'I live in the apartments over there . . .' She nodded vaguely, acting as if she did not want to make any sudden hand movements. Up on the corner another SWOPS private had stopped to watch them. Lucky stiff, he was probably thinking, how come the flashers go and talk to that sluicehead. She stepped into the road so the van obscured the curious one's view. The private instinctively followed. 'And all this noise is keeping me awake. And if I am not mistaken that is a generator.'

'Yes, ma'am.'

'Which will be very noisy.'

'Well . . . yes, ma'am, to some degree, I'm afraid.' She could see he was worried, the normal excessive politeness hiding the fear that perhaps residents could sue the Department for lost sleep. 'But don't you have, like, extra soundproofing on account of the market traffic and all?'

Clever little jerk. 'Well, it seems to keep out traffic, but not the kind of noises you make. And you are shouting.'

'We are?'

Right on cue one of them yelled: 'Conrad, you moron, I need some more cable.'

'Blow it out your ass,' came the reply.

The exchange bounced down their way and the private nodded. 'I'll have a word with the Sergeant.'

'Look, I don't mind being disturbed if it is in my civil interests.'

'Oh, it is, ma'am, it is. Absolutely. Bona fide. One hundred per cent.'

'You're not just shooting some Bruce Willis movie?'

He looked at the lights and understood her

immediately. 'No, this is real, proper duty.'

'And you are shining lights through the grilles on either side of the street.'

'The grilles and the little glass things up yonder along Fourth. Like this one here . . . but this is over the Metro, so we don't need to.'

'And you mean to tell me that illuminating the sidewalk is in my interest?'

He laughed nervously. 'Not the sidewalk. What's under it.'

Her heart spasmed painfully against the inside of her ribs.

'You OK, ma'am?'

'Sorry, just feeling the chill. I should have . . . wrapped up a bit better.'

'I've got a flak jacket . . .'

'No, don't worry. Just tell me why on earth you are doing this, and I'll get back inside. I'm a lawyer and I have a busy day in court tomorrow . . . that is, today.' As she said it she almost bit her lip. It was Saturday. Would he realise that most courts don't sit on Saturday?

But he was still smarting from the sting of the word 'lawyer'. 'Look, ma'am, we don't rightly know. Honest. We are just grunts. But the word is – ' He looked around. 'As an officer of the law I can trust you not to repeat this?' She nodded a firm yes. 'That some piece of shit – pardon me, ma'am – has taken a little girl hostage into the kind of catacombs that are under here. Well, we're just shoving some light down there. So the Colonel can see better when he arrives to deal with the situation. But you did not hear that from me.'

'A little girl?'

'Kind of like a hostage, yes.'

'Thank you, Sergeant.'

'Private, ma'am.'

'Oh, I'm sure it's only a matter of time.'

'Yes, ma'am, thank you, ma'am. And good luck in court. We'll try and keep it down. The noise I mean.' She raised a hand as she turned, and he saw the coat flap open, showing, disappointingly, that she was clothed. And what was that she had whispered? No, he must have been hearing things.

Pepper's eyes were closing when Annie leapt in beside him, slamming the door with a vehemence that shocked him. 'Of all the . . .' She quivered for a moment before she screamed. 'Jesus fuckin' Christ, it isn't FAIR.' Pepper kept silent. Let it work itself out. 'How – who – aahhhhh.' And then she slumped, head against the dash. She was sobbing. Pepper cleared his throat. First he has to watch her play pussy-foot with that slimetrail Leo, and now she goes all female on him. He had promised Ricky he would be there for her, but it wasn't easy – you could never tell which side of her you was going to see. Pepper just kept quiet in case this was a momentary blip. He was attached to his kneecaps.

And then she snapped back into work mode. Cool, and controlled, the way he liked her. One sniff, a wipe of her eyes, and then business. 'That's not going to do us any good. A hayseed SWAT, or SWAP or whatever they are called now, reckons there is a kid down there. Below.'

Pepper lit two cigarettes – his last two – and handed her one. She took a drag and coughed a little. She hated the taste of Lites. 'A kid? Like some punk?'

'No, some kid like a little girl with some psycho

scumbag holding her hostage.'

'Whoaa.' On dangerous ground here. They were not even a couple of blocks away from their gear. Far too close for comfort. A quick solution to this would be in everybody's interests. He could guess what she was thinking. Two years' work, a few hundred thousand dollars and some shit-for-brains with a gun blows it all.

'We got to find them,' she said firmly.

'What?'

'Look, we know that place better than the cops, better than those TWATs. At least our part of it. If we find them, we can give them up or . . .' Her mind was racing. 'Look, we don't want to let Ricky down, do we? We've all got a lot wrapped up in this. And I ain't going back to nail extensions, and I'll be ass-fucked before I end up back at I'll Be Your Fantasy, slapping and burping some diaper-wrapped dildo of a Microsoft programmer. Some little kidnapped kid is going to drive me to that?'

'So what was the "Or" option?' Pepper asked coolly.

'Look, let's be flexible on this. If we can contain the situation, then fine.'

'And if we can't?'

She looked at Pepper for a long time. Him and Pig, they were Ricky's oldest people, been with him ten years, pulled some funny stunts. There had been a fourth once. Bill. Bill was a reptile, she had always thought, a cold fish. Played the horses, and played his friends like he played the horses, and tried to give up the other three once on a heist in Cleveland. It was mostly a dumb idea, turning over the Rock'n'Roll Hall of Fame, but it had its redeeming features. Bill wasn't one of them, and the snake had done a deal. Pepper had clocked him with his police snitch, confronted him and popped him all in five minutes. Not bad considering Bill was his brother-in-law. So maybe Pepper was game for it.

'This is a guess, OK? But I reckon the Mod Squad are going down after the scumbag, and that's it. Get the girl, end of story. They ain't going to stick around down there to party. If we have to we . . .' She couldn't say it. She could think it, easy as pie, but not put it into words. And then it came out in a rush. 'We kill the guy, and if we have to, only if we have to, if there is absolutely no alternative, we take the girl out and dump them where the GI Joes can find the two of them. We just sit tight 'til it blows over. It's not like they'll stumble across us. Not unless they are reduced to doing a real thorough search.'

She stared at him, letting the words sink in. They both knew she wasn't offering any hope of an alternative. Pepper pulled on his cigarette, watching the tip glow. He must get some more before they did whatever they had to do. Another SWOPS vehicle came by. More lights. 'Well right now, sitting in this car, I can't think of any other option.' He turned to face Annie. He could see from her eyes this wasn't theoretical. 'I mean, it's not like I believe in God or nothin'. That we get punished more if they're under-age. This kid is in the way, we gotta do what we gotta do to protect Ricky's investment. Our investment.'

'Pepper, you'll make the cover of Forbes yet. But listen – we got to get *our* lights out, 'cause if even a little bit shows through the wall, it will pull them in like moths to a flame. I'll see you at the entrance.'

She eased herself out of the car and headed for the BMW. They might just save the day. If they all stayed strong. If they found the guy. If they killed the girl.

TWENTY-FIVE

'OK, there were certain rules, and one of them was the three-shot rule. Why? 'Cause if you fired any more the other guy figgered you was low on ammo, and came atcha. So three shots, he knows you still got at least three left, enough for him and his buddies. They tended to work in threes, did I tell you that? Sorry, I'm . . . I'll try and put it in order. The gook tunnel fighters went in threes – they were farmers mostly, dressed in those black pyjamas. You saw them now and again – usually dead after we pumped CS gas into the tunnels and then greased them – although sometimes you came across NVA, the real army. Once we hit a patrol of NVA and we just froze. They shone their torch on us, we shone on them. No room to turn around, just starin', waiting for the other guy to fire. Hobbs was on point that day, but I could see over his shoulder, hear his breathin' . . . smell him, f'Chrissake, and them, everybody shit scared. So what happens? We back up. Both of us. I mean them and us. No firefight, nothin'. I dunno why. Just wasn't our turn to die, I guess, not us and not the NVA. Anyways, the three-shot rule. What Fix's gun did, they called it, uh, the Chess, I think, and some initials. Gone now. But it enabled us to fire seven – it took a six magazine with one in the spout – without the gooks knowin' how many we had left. They couldn't hear it, see. And it had a low velocity, low muzzle flash .22. Actually not very Geneva accords, 'cause it caused a lot of damage, but you know, they didn't seem to apply a whole lot down there. So that was the gun. OK, if it got dirt in it – too much dirt, I mean, it jammed. What did we do? Put them in plastic bags. They still worked. That's what a NETTS was for – solutions like that you'd never think of in a laboratory.

'No, no, the kid was good. The kid was fuckin' good. Old Fix, he could read those tunnel walls like they was a book. In the slick – the Huey – on the way back from his first time down, things changed. He was one of us. No, we had our name by then. It was superstition, you always had to have a name. Mole Patrol, Tunnel Rats, Dirty Diggers . . . every unit had a monicker. So we had a vote. And Fix came up with it. Just like that. Underdogs, he said. And we all nodded, 'cause that's what we were. These crazy little fuckers running round beneath the earth. So Underdogs it was.'

TWENTY-SIX

Underworld. Seattle.

'Rabbit?' the voice at the other end said.

Rabbit? Nobody had called him that in five years, since he got those two goofy front teeth knocked out of his mouth at Walla Walla. 'Who's dis?' Defensive now, edgy – his voice always went low, his vocabulary and diction truncated. Street Hard was the effect he wanted. But it often came out Retard.

'It's Sergeant John Tenniel. Seattle PD. Back when you was Rabbit, I pulled you on a possession charge. You were up for Grand Theft, Auto and managed to walk. You decided to celebrate by running some hot stuff in from Tacoma. Remember?'

He did remember. Cocksucker wasn't too bad for a cop. Kind of laid-back: Relax, let's get this out the way and we can all be friends again. It was an act, 'cause you don't get to be an old cop by being a real marshmallow head, but it kept the tension down.

Hilton glanced at the girl, who was huddled against a wall at the edge of the lamplight, coat pulled tight. He tried to stop his teeth chattering again as he said: 'Whaddayawant, Sergeant?'

'What do I want? What do you think I want? Whether you'll give me ten to one on the Sonics? A delivery of those Hitachis you used to push? I want the girl, Hilton.

I want her, and you, up here alive and smiling and warm. Before things turn ugly.'

Ugly? Things were pretty ugly right now, way he saw it. 'How'd you get this number? It's unlisted.'

'I know. It's probably a re-chipped scumbag job, right? Am I right? Yeah. Bought it off Tommy Talk I'll betcha.'

Tommy Talk, Hot Phones Cooled Quickly. He was right. 'Tommy wouldn't give up this number.'

'No, but your shit-for-brains partner would.'

'He's alive?' Hilton saw the girl look up with hope in her eyes.

'Yeah. Well he's got shit-for-guts to match his brains, but at least he was well enough to tell us the number.'

Hilton was surprised Duck could remember it. But he was kind of glad his partner wasn't a stiff after all. 'He gonna make it?'

'I guess so.'

'And the other guy?'

Tenniel tried to get the words out smooth and easy, but they were spiky, like some kind of cactus fruit, and snagged on his throat. It was the swallow, the hesitation, that did it. 'He'll be OK, too.'

'You're fuckin' lyin' t'me. He's dead, ain't he?' Hilton ignored the sob from the girl. 'Tell me straight. Now. Dead?'

'No.'

'Liar.'

'Hilton, he ain't dead. He isn't here playing Donald O'Connor up the walls, but he ain't dead, so you aren't on a murder rap yet.'

Well, they would say that, wouldn't they? And when

he got up top they'd say, well, look-ee here, poor guy stiffed it five minutes ago. Looks like it's Murder One after all.

'Fuck. He—' Hilton lowered his voice, but she was huddled up and crying, and couldn't hear anyway. 'He was – is – a fuckin' pervert, you know. Did things.'

'What you talkin' about?'

'You know. Things. She told me.'

'To his daughter?'

'No, his horse, you asshole. Yeah.'

'He sexually abused his daughter?'

'You got that right.' The thought of being hanged flashed through his mind. 'You think that'd help?'

Another silence. 'I got to level with you, Hilton. You didn't know what he was before you popped him, so you can hardly claim to be the Winged Avenger here. No, but listen, listen. At the moment, it's a kind of unfortunate fracas. Get some good representation and it's not going to be a death penalty thing. Hurt the girl, however . . .' He let it tail off.

Hilton heard the scream in the background, the sudden torrent of profanity, the demands. 'Who the fuck is that?'

There were muffled sounds and shouts and a strident female voice overriding them all. He heard the woman's voice shout: 'They're coming to shoot you like a dog—' before Tenniel yelled, 'GET HER OUT. NOW. F'r Chrissakes, one of the medics give her something.' He was breathless when he came back on: 'Hilton? Hilton? You still there?'

'Yup. Was that Mom?'

'Sorry about that.'

'Is that right, they coming in to get us?'

'No, no, she's just runnin' off at the mouth. It's cool. We'll work this out. Hilton, listen. We can work it out. Get everyone out nice and safe, talk to the DA about how this guy is a scumsucker—'

'No SWAT units arming up up there then.'

'No. Absolutely no way. Just you and me. Let's work it out. Must be gettin' cold down there—'

The tone of the voice was soft, friendly, and extremely irritating. And that woman, she sounded like someone who'd just seen her husband under a sheet. 'You a lyin' fuck, Sergeant.'

'No. If we can work this out . . . no SWATs, no police.'

'So you keep me on the phone while a bunch of assholes in flak jackets start stalkin' us. Is that right? Huh?'

'No, Hilton. I know you won't hurt her. The gun thing. Outside the store. It was a bluff, wasn't it?'

Hilton took three paces over to Alice and hoisted her to her feet. She sniffed and wiped her eyes, thinking she was going to talk to her mother. 'Yeah? You think so?'

The boom of the gun was deafening, masking the first part of the squeal from the girl, but they must have got the tail-end of it. She collapsed in a heap on the floor.

Hilton let the sound die away, down to a residual ringing. 'Flesh wound, Sergeant. Big chunk of meat from her arm. But she'll live. Now listen, I see one flashlight, see one SWAT motherfucker, hear you guys breathin' down here, she's dead. OK? Good representation? Hey – from the State? What you think my middle name is? Orange Juice? I ain't got the money to get a fair trial, that's the truth of it. And Sergeant?'

'Yeah?'

'Don't call me at work again—'

He flung the Nokia full force at the wall and heard it shatter and tinkle to the floor. It was then he realised that if the cop could get through he could've made a call out. Hell, who would he phone? 'Hey man, it's Hilton. Yeah, Hilton Babcock. Rabbit? Remember? Look, man, I'm trapped underground with a big-mouthed eight-year-old girl and a SWAT team up my ass. Any suggestions?'

He looked down at the girl and poked her with his foot. His ears were still buzzing from the shot. It must have been even louder to her. She was rubbing her arm where he had twisted it. Two long trails of snot were creeping to her top lip. He knelt down and used the sleeve of his jacket – her jacket – to wipe them. 'That hurt.'

'Get up, get up. Your ears'll be buzzin' is all. I had to make it seem genuine.'

'YOU HURT ME.'

'Yeah? Well the real thing would've hurt a damn sight more. Fuck, this is some mess.'

'He's dead?'

This was not the time for tantrums, he didn't want to have to be draggin' a sulking kid through this hellhole, so he said: 'My partner Duck, gave them the number and then croaked. Your old man's in a bad way, lost a lot of blood, but he's . . . steady. Real steady, they said.' He stared at her, waiting for something to register, some indication that she went for this. Nothing. Was she at an age where she believed whatever adults told her, or had the Santa Claus effect kicked in? 'Look, I'm thinking that, what I could do is leave you here. They'll find you eventually. I could be long gone. Suit both of us.'

'What about the light?'

He shook his head. 'That'll have to come with me.'

She sat up. 'I can't sit here on my own in the dark. There's rats and things.'

'You only got two choices. Come or stay.'

After a couple of silent minutes she struggled to her feet, still rubbing her arm. 'I'll come.'

They made good progress through the next tunnel, or at least it felt that way. It was warmer, and the air less rank. Occasionally Hilton heard cars and buses and trucks, and running water – sewers he assumed, although sometimes they seemed to be at the side, sometimes below – and there was the hiss of steam through invisible pipes, the city's old heating system rumbling on and on. It couldn't be seen, but they could feel it in delicious hot-spots that lasted a few welcome yards, before the cold crept back. They held hands now: Hilton with the lamp out in front with his left, his right holding onto Alice's left.

The floor was still sloping upwards slightly, which made him think he was heading in the right direction. They had several false hopes shattered – there were alcoves here and there, and even a door (DRY GOODS, was all it promised, but the wall behind was mockingly soaked in green slime), but they were all dead-ends. This part of the city had been well and truly sealed off.

'You OK?' he kept asking.

'Yup,' was all she would say in reply.

Still trudging uphill, the floor became powdery, dusty, and in the yellowy light Hilton could see it had an odd pearlescent glow. There was a faint crunching sound, as if he was walking on shells. He bent down and picked up one of the objects half-buried in the silty surface and rolled it in his palm.

'Tooth,' said Ali.

He threw it down. 'What kinda fuckin' tooth?'

It was her turn to fish around, and she retrieved a thin sliver of white material. 'Bone. And look.' She waved something under his nose.

'Get off. What's that?'

'A jawbone. Can I keep it?'

'Let me see, let me see.' She held it in front of his face. 'Is that human?'

'Naaaah,' she said. 'It's a cow, a baby cow, or a sheep. Can I keep it? It's clean. Can I?'

'I dunno.' Why should he care what souvenirs the kid took? 'Yeah, yeah.'

'Cool. I'll take it into biology. We got a whole skull there.' She levered it into his jacket pocket and grabbed his arm. 'C'mon then.'

The crunching and the glistening of gruesome relics – he supposed there must have been animals killed in this fire – continued for another twenty yards, and stopped abruptly when they came to the first door that looked really promising.

The Arthur Denny Theater said the peeling sign above the frame and below that: Fire Exit. But didn't theaters usually have more than one fire exit? Maybe one that led out of here? He grabbed the chain, unwilling to waste another round on more breaking and entering and yanked. The metal hoops it was threaded through broke free with the merest groan and fell to the floor.

The wood had gone rotten, the screws no longer had any purchase.

'Wanna see a show?' he asked.

She curled her lip at him and pushed the doors.

He stepped in and risked turning up the wick slightly. The auditorium was a large single room, low-ceilinged, and with no balcony. They had stepped straight onto a railed, raised platform which ran around three sides of it, with steps leading down to the stalls proper, where twenty rows of metal chairs faced the small stage which occupied the fourth wall directly in front, its boards framed by shredded drapes hanging forlornly from the proscenium arch. Hilton angled the light onto the walls, the gilt long gone, the once-fancy plasterwork dissolving like so much dandruff. He stepped towards the rails, now bent and twisted with many of the uprights missing, to survey the seating.

The chairs must have once been covered with cushions of red velvet, because hints of the material still hung from the odd one, but for the most part all that was left was the brown tangle of the horsehair stuffing. He walked along the raised section, obviously for those patrons unable to afford a seat, looking for the other door, the box office or foyer, but there was no evidence. One way in, one way out.

Except, perhaps, backstage.

He held Ali's hand and slowly descended the four steps that took him to the main stalls, testing each tread to make sure the slowly rotting wood could support his weight. They had barely taken a step down the centre aisle between the chairs when he heard a high-pitched noise, an almost inaudible squeaking. 'What was that?'

'What?'

He took another step forward and it became louder, a lower pitch now, with a kind of modulated whine built into it. The hairs on the back of his hands stood up. It sounded faintly like a baby crying, only a baby that had just swallowed some helium.

'Hilton – '

'Is it electrical?'

'Hilton – '

'Are you doing that, kid? Stop it.'

'Hilton, look at the seats.'

He stretched out his arm and the flame flickered on a pair of black eyes, then another, and another. He spun around and tried the seat behind. On that, too, little dark eyes, the light barely reflecting in the pupils, looked back at him. Nothing moved, but again the squeal cranked up a notch.

It wasn't horsehair. It looked like horsehair. But it was rats. A tangle of brown rats on each seat, intertwined, old and young, biding their time, staring, waiting, following their every move. And all the while, tiny threatening noises growing in their throats. Hilton took a step back to clear the aisle, ready to run. The squealing dropped a fraction. Twenty rows, with twenty-odd chairs in each. Four hundred chairs. A dozen rats on each – that was . . . er –

'Let's go, Hilton.'

They backed away slowly, hardly daring to breathe, wondering if the rodents were just waiting for the right moment to attack. But there was barely a movement as they made the steps up, then the broken door, and stepped back out into the old street.

Hilton slammed the entrance shut and they stood there panting for a moment, wondering if they hadn't imagined it. A theatre of rats.

'What time do you think the show starts?' asked Ali, just as the flame finally flickered and shimmered before stuttering out.

She didn't scream. He didn't say anything. They just stood there, listening to their breathing. He strained his ears, wondering if he would hear the rats moving now, now they were blind and defenceless, whether the brown stream would come tumbling and scrabbling through the doors, but all he got were the creakings and gushings of his own body. Eventually he managed: 'You OK?'

'Yup.' But she wasn't. It was nervy, shaky.

'OK, we got to feel our way along. This way. Take our time. We gotta hit something soon. Something without bones or rats.'

'What about the lighter?'

'I reckon we got to save that for an emergency.'

'This being . . . ?'

Christ, he couldn't figure this. One minute a whiny eight-year-old, the next right there with the sassy comeback. Kids.

Hilton reached out, touched the wall, and began inching along it, with Ali holding onto his belt. He realised he had lost all track of time. All he knew was that progress was painfully slow now – anyone with a flashlight could overtake them in minutes. The wall was a mixture of earth and what felt like flint. It cut his hands if he slid them along, so he had to tap at intervals. The darkness was complete, so complete he was back to thinking he had gone blind. He tried to keep a lid on his panic, for both their sakes. He could tell the thoroughfare was narrowing though, from the way sound was bouncing back at them.

'Talk to me,' she said suddenly, making him jump.

'Talk? I don't do talkin' much. What you want me to say?'

'Tell me what you are doing. What you were doing.'

'In the store?'

'Well, yes. Is that what you do? Rob stores?'

She made it sound so mundane, like working at a feed supplier, the only straight job he had really ever had. And all he ever got from that was a set of muscles from humping sacks all day.

'I was short some money for a deal, and . . . it seemed like a good idea. I guess it wasn't.'

'What was the deal?'

'You don't want to know—'

'Was it drugs?'

He laughed nervously.

'Coke? Heroin?'

'Hey, hey what you know about that stuff?'

'Was it?'

'No it was . . . you know, dope.'

'Marijuana? I tried that.'

He stopped and turned round in the dark, feeling for her face. 'You're shittin' me? I mean kiddin'.'

'No, there are some kids at school . . .'

'For Chrissake. Alice, look, you don't want to—'

'I didn't say I liked it. I only took one puff. It made me cough. Can we go on? I get cold when we stand still.' He took up her hand again.

'I was going to quit you know. Duck and I had another plan. Legit. Kinda.'

'What?'

'We got some car air-conditioning units from Mexico we was going to score and sell them. In the summer.'

'Air conditioning? You know what they put in those? CFCs. We did it in class. They erode the atmosphere, cause the greenhouse effect.'

'No they banned them. Even I know that.'

'Not for rip-off ones. They still make the stuff in Mexico. Put them in counterfeit air-conditioning units. Sell them for a hundred bucks or something. Is that right?'

'About a hundred a pop, yeah.'

'Full of CFCs.'

'Hey, kid, you'd rather we stayed in the dope game?'

She thought about this. 'Mrs Cole thinks it should be legalised. She got into trouble with the principal for saying so. So maybe. You could open a shop if they did.'

He gave up. There was a logic at work, but not one he recognised – don't try and make an almost honest buck, it'll fuck up the planet. And could he see himself as Johnny Joint, your friendly neighbourhood roach king? No, Mary Jane's, that would be a better name for the chain.

And, in that moment of silent fantasy, he heard the water loud and clear ahead of them and he stopped and put his foot out. It waggled in empty air.

'Hold it.' She bumped into his back and he swayed before he caught his balance.

'What is it?'

'A hole, I think. Collapsed water main maybe.' Hilton

fished around for the lighter and flicked. It wouldn't catch. After six times he gave up. He bent down and felt along the floor. There was a ragged edge right across their path, and nothing beyond it he could touch. Just space. He could feel the temperature change over it as the cold water streamed by. He tried to reach down to touch it, hoping it wasn't a turd-filled sewer, but his fingers just grabbed space. So he didn't know how deep or how wide it was. 'Any stones back there?'

He heard her scratch around and she pressed four pebbles into his hand. He flung one into the black and heard it hit solid ground. He tried a smaller arc, and he thought he heard it splash. He tried again. Solid. And then a deep, croaky voice from somewhere beyond said: 'Hell, it's only two, three feet across. You could jump it real easy.'

TWENTY-SEVEN

Henry Street, Central Seattle. 2.46 am

As the line went dead a stillness settled over the room. The motley assortment of medics, cops and city engineers held their breaths, whispered their exchanges, suddenly became very concerned about a hair floating on their coffee. The lights were heating up the room, and many were starting to sweat under the heavy protective clothing they had donned against the chill. Most were thinking the same thing: give it up, Sergeant. We know you have done the courses, and you handled that bank siege last year, but this is different.

He took Bowman outside and they stood inhaling the fetid air of the alley, delicately scented with the garbage from the dumpster. 'Not too good, eh?'

She shook her head. 'Beta minus, John. Time for that refresher course.'

'You could have done better?' It wasn't an accusation, but a genuine question.

Fred Flintstone probably could have done better, she thought, but she said: 'Well, women you know, better communication skills. The line dead?'

'Yeah, either he broke it or he moved off. I don't think he believes the father is still alive. He is still alive, isn't he?'

Bowman nodded. 'He was five minutes ago. And the shot?'

'More play-acting. He's not an MV.'

'Unless he sees the SWOPS or SERTs.'

'You think?'

'I ain't so confident as you, John. I'm with Harry on this. Major violator or not, you never can tell.'

'Yeah, but you know what happens with hostages and takers over fifty per cent of the time. If she was eight years older they'd come out engaged.'

'Yeah, that works with adults, maybe, but what if she is some *whiny* eight-year-old who gets on his nerves?'

He considered this for a moment. 'So?'

'So can your boy really see in the dark?'

Lewis was slumped on a fold-out chair, head in his hands, unable to believe what he had heard. He gets them the phone, the man on the other end, and they blow it. And now he couldn't stop thinking about the sound of that gunshot echoing over the airwaves, echoing across a quarter of a century it seemed. There were images now, coming unbidden: Willie, face streaked with bug juice and camouflage stripes, a battered Jones hat perched on his head. The Bat, emerging from his room wearing only a M1953 flak jacket and long johns, ready for patrol. Joey Averne rapping about great bets of his life – how he took odds on Apollo 13 not getting back, and how he cleaned up on Frasier-Ellis. It really had started now. No going back. Which city next? Vancouver? Calgary, maybe. Nice and close to the Rockies.

'Lewis.' It was Tenniel.

'Wasn't in the mood for talking, eh?'

'Well, no, that was . . . That was a fuck-up, Carl. That's what that was. And now I want you to get my ass out of the fire. That's about the size of it.'

Lewis smiled. 'We used to operate in holes that a cat couldn't get through. Now I can't even get in an elevator, man. Never even been to the top of the Space Needle.'

'Yeah, well the food ain't that great,' interjected Bowman, 'you only missed the view.' She stepped out of Lewis's sight and drew a finger across her throat. Forget this one, John. Next plan.

Tenniel shook his head a fraction. 'So that's a no?'

But Lewis was too busy thinking to respond. Thinking that they punch clean through you, punji stakes. Clean is the wrong word. The VC liked to smear shit on the points, to piss in the pits, anything to make sure the wounds festered. Make a terrible mess of a man. Terrible.

'Lewis. That's a no, then?'

'Wish I could help, here, really, really do. Little girl, I mean, fuck. But the darkness thing. It was the equipment. Well, not all of it. But it helps. I could do it if I had the gear. My gear. That is the key.'

Tenniel tried to interrupt but realised he wasn't hearing him anyway. Lewis was arguing with himself.

'I *could* get her out. I could. I had the moxie back then. But I need the stuff.'

He fell silent, staring off into the distance into the distant past, watching a slick blossom into shards, seeing the white phosphorous explode into beautiful white anemones over the forest, smelling the mix of shit and gasoline, feeling the rush of drugs. Ah well, now he had blown this it was probably goodbye to any more police assignments now. No more after-incident drinks. Maybe no more racquetball.

There was a commotion at the door. Two big guys in

coveralls shouldered their way through. They had utility belts strapped around them, ropes worn like bandoleers, and a sidearm each. The first was a big redhead, the second was nurturing a fine gut. They were carrying two field telephones and a drum of connecting wire. It was what the Sergeant wanted to see most.

'Tenniel?' asked the redhead, scanning the room.

'Here. Bruno?' The redhead nodded and pointed to his pal. 'Sylvic.'

'OK,' said Tenniel, 'This is what we have—'

Lewis looked at them, looked at Tenniel, could sense he was letting him down here. Just like, sooner or later, he let everybody down.

Tenniel fell silent as Lewis heaved himself out of the chair and walked over and began to eye up the new arrivals. Bruno said: 'What's your problem?' but Lewis ignored him.

'These guys going after her?' he asked, a sneer on his top lip.

'Go home, Lewis, you had your chance—'

'That girl? Ali? You send these two lunks down, you might as well bag and tag her now. This one –' he pointed at Bruno – 'I bet if you look at his boots. Nice boots, by the way. Look at the heels, and you will see the right heel worn down much more than the left. His right foot comes down like a steam hammer. Slim here. Well, Slim isn't really an ectomorph type, is he—'

Bruno said, 'Look, fuckface, we work the Metro tunnels every day of the week—'

'They'll be the nice big, bright –' he looked at Sylvic – 'wide ones, will they? Not the smelly, dark ones we have here at all.'

He spun round. 'If this is the best you got, I'll go down. I need to go back and get my gear, though.'

Tenniel hesitated, unnerved by the sudden emotional swing. 'We ain't got much time here, Carl. Can't wait for you to go and get shit. I can't be wonderin' if you are going to come back or not.'

Bruno went redder than his hair. 'Are you takin' this guy for real?'

Lewis was on a roll, fired up now, positive, and he ignored him. 'If he did shoot her—'

'*If* he did. I'm not convinced,' said Tenniel.

Bowman stepped forward again: 'If he did, then what?'

'If he did, she is likely bleeding to death. You don't get flesh wounds from a .45. You get half your meat taken away. Christ, you must've seen enough gunshot wounds. And if you're a kid with arms this big –' he held up a circled thumb and forefinger – 'you most likely lose it all. Now look, I know bullet wounds. I am fast and I am quiet. I can use those radios—' He pointed to the ROVER, the Remote Out of Vehicle Emergency Radios that would be linked to the big drum of communications wire to ensure a reliable signal. 'And I'm OK now. Really. It wasn't just the drink talking that night. We were real good, Sergeant.' He felt the old pride in the unit come back. Maybe he had been ducking all this too long. He grabbed the Sergeant's arm, and almost hissed: 'I was an *Underdog*.'

Tenniel pinched the bridge of his nose. And he still didn't wake up. And what, exactly, was an Underdog when it was pissing up a post? Lewis seemed to have oscillated wildly from fuck-up to fuck-you. But it was hard to argue with a confident man. There was a compromise here, he knew. 'You go down as pathfinder, with the radio, get it to within hailing distance of this guy. Detective Bowman here will talk him into picking it up. But once you put it down, your job is over. You run into trouble, you double-back. Get the handset to Hilton, Carl. Period. That's it. But what about the equipment you talked about—'

'He'll be needing this.'

There was a thud as Dinah swung the old LWL case onto the desk on top of the plans, elbowing aside their curator.

'Jesus,' said Tenniel. He took in the woman with her pulled-back hair, scarlet mouth and black clothes, all matter-of-fact and spunky. 'What is this? What are you – his personal trainer or fairy godmother?' Then he looked at Lewis's face and it clicked. Dinah. And Lewis obviously hadn't expected to see her. Or that case.

She didn't say anything, just flicked up the catches. The little group fell quiet at the sight of the gun, goggles and accessories.

Lewis walked up to her, close, and whispered something. She shrugged. 'It was on the radio. I put two and two together. What with the Willie story, it wasn't hard to second-guess what the detective here was thinking—'

Tenniel snorted. It was hard enough for him to figure out what *he* was thinking tonight. And blurting it over the radio? Idiots. No wonder they wanted to switch to e-mail. Old habits die hard, though.

'You think you'll be using that?' It was Harry. 'The gun, I mean.'

'If I have to, I guess.'

Tenniel was about to tell him he would be doing no such thing when Lewis said: 'Thing is, if I have to shoot the guy, he won't even hear it coming with this.'

Harry shook his head and said. 'Be murder.'

Tenniel nodded. He was right. Being an authorised police photographer does not give anyone permission to shoot felons and kidnappers. Not with anything other than a camera.

'Can't you deputise him?' asked Dinah.

'Yeah, like this is Gunsmoke,' said Bowman.

Dinah met the detective's eyes and curled her lip at this sarcasm. Bowman locked on and met the gaze. They held for a couple of seconds, enough to let them know they inhabited different planets for the time being.

It was Dinah who broke off. She was damned if she was going to start bonding with some crop-headed bitch cop, just because she happened to share the same sex. Yeah, well she could play tough, too. She turned and took the two steps over to Lewis. He was not distracted enough to notice she looked great. Black jeans, black poloneck. He thought she was going to kiss him, but she whispered in his ear, 'I want to come with you.'

'Are you nuts? *I* don't even want to go.' This explained her cat burglar outfit. He started to panic. The last thing he needed was her down there. She would just get in the way. Physically and otherwise. He wondered what she was trying to prove by even offering. But she was right about one thing – a partner would be nice. Back-up. Never go down a tunnel without back-up. Otherwise who's going to drag you out by the ankles if something goes wrong?

He looked around. What he had said about Bruno

and Sylvic was true. Too bulky, too clumsy. Too dumb, he suspected.

The solution surprised even Lewis. He had liked the way one guy had padded around, had looked the part. Obviously had good balance, co-ordination. Springy and little, just the way he liked them. Little was good down there. 'I'll take him. He's small, light on his feet, even got the right shoes on. And he can do the shooting. If there has to be any.'

They followed the finger. It was a few seconds before they all realised he was pointing at Harry.

TWENTY-EIGHT

'Lewis, Fix, Hobbs, the Bat, me, Joey Averne. Joey looked like Desi Arnaz, did I tell you that? Exactly the same. Same bad skin. And then Arnold and Wayland. The Underdogs. What it was, Lewis had this plan. We was his sort of research team, the best tunnel rats that was left in Vietnam. He was writing the manual, y'know, *the* book on tunnel fighting, and this he would hand over to the ARVIN when we pulled out. Everything we learned, every technique, how to flush these guys out, how they rigged the tunnels to blow, because Lewis thought the tunnels were the lynchpin, thought Tet wouldn't have worked without them. They could hide thousands of men down there. By this point, you see, the defoliates and bombs were being phased out. Well, even the ARVIN were saying we'd like something of the country left to win, please. Because by the time the Fly boys had destroyed a tunnel complex, they had pretty much fucked up everything else. So this was going to be Lewis's final thing before he went home to his wife and kids. Yeah, he had a family. Well, look, there is a story there, but I said I'd do it in order. What I didn't know was that Fix was taking some kind of speed. To get thinner, that's why. He was a bit bulky for the smaller tunnels, and it slowed us down, so he was burning up his metabolism. Of course Lewis knew. Lewis wanted the Underdogs to be the best fuckin' tunnellers ever, and if that meant the kid dumped a few pounds, so be it. No, it was Lewis who gave him the shit in the first place.

'We used to laager at a clearing about ten clicks from the Big Mac base. Rest up, y'know. There was a water-hole there, and the slick pilots could get some of the shit off the machines and we would swim. And every time we touched down these kids would appear. The croaka-crola kids we called them, selling us drinks, cigarettes. Couldn't see the village, but they always knew we were coming. Fix used to practise his Vietnamese on one of them. '*Chi tu đau đen?*' Where you from, that kind of thing. Everyone had some kid who would make a bee-line for you. His was called Mae, she was what, thirteen, fourteen? Probably cute under the rags and grime. I tried to buy her bracelet once. Real gold I reckon. Odd that she should be in rags and have something so . . . well, he wouldn't let me. Fix. Said it was probably her dowry or some such shit. I said she'd be turning tricks anyway inside a year, which got him real mad. And Lewis backed him up. Lewis said not everything in the country was for sale. He was wrong though. It all was. All of it.'

TWENTY-NINE

Underworld. Seattle.

The big MagLite had its lens covered in many layers of muslin cloth to diffuse the beam, but even so it still hurt Hilton's eyes when the man flicked it on and directed it at him.

'Hey, hey, shine that somewhere else.'

'Sorry.'

The soft light showed that they were in fact on the edge of a three-foot-wide gap – if he had had enough nerve he could have reached over and touched the other side in the dark. What he couldn't see too clearly was the figure in front of them, just a soft outline and a reflection of a grey beard. The girl, of course had no inhibitions about asking: 'Who are you?'

'Who am I? Who the hell are you? I've been hearing you stumbling about for hours.'

'We're lost,' she said.

The man hooted at this. 'Lost. I'll say. You coming across?'

Hilton stepped over the uncovered water main, and Ali jumped easily. Hilton could smell him now, a bitter-sweet aroma of dirt and decay. But he would know that uniform anywhere. The man was a cop.

He was a head shorter than Hilton, had long, matted hair, that beard, and lively, ferrety eyes, and the uniform was torn and dirty and shiny with wear, but the Seattle Police shield confirmed it. He was a cop. Must've been on the beat a hell of a time, though.

Hanging from his belt, next to a pair of handcuffs, was an army water bottle, which he knelt down and filled. 'Don't worry – it's not sewage.' Hilton must've been staring. 'Don't worry about the uniform, pal. I ain't going to turn you in to whoever you runnin' from. That's not what we do down here.'

In which case, Hilton decided. There wasn't much mileage in wasting pleasantries. 'Can you get us out of here?'

'Out?'

Hilton shivered. His bones were beginning to ache. Maybe he should just drop him and take the flashlight. 'Yes, out. Like, we don't want to stay down here, pops.'

'Out isn't as easy as getting in, Ace.' He looked at the girl. 'You want something to eat? A hot drink?'

'Are you a policeman?' she asked.

'A policeman? Well, once maybe. Kind of, now. Do you want that drink?'

She nodded.

'Let's go, then.'

'Hey, hold on—' Hilton had to get on top of the situation, and he automatically reached for the gun. The knife blade was at his throat before his fingers were round the handle. It wasn't long, four inches maybe, but it was damned sharp, and Hilton could feel the point penetrating the first few layers of skin at the side of his neck under a steady pressure.

'Want me to take that off you?' Hilton shook his head, very smoothly, very slowly. 'Good, 'cause it's no use to me really. Makes too much noise. I'm just going to offer you a drink and some advice is all. And then you can go on your way. Might even lend you a flashlight. But I will not have you disrespecting me. Clear?' A nod. 'Good.'

Everybody called him the Captain, he said – even though he had never been at that rank – so they could too. Hilton wondered exactly who 'everybody' would be down here, but thought better of mentioning it. When he pressed him again on exits, the Captain told him to shut up and just follow. The passageways he led them through were much bigger here, perhaps the old main streets of the original Seattle, not some alleyways or later borings through the earth. After ten minutes they turned down a narrower street, and eventually came to an alcove with an old floral-pattern curtain hanging over it. The Captain pulled it aside and ushered them in. Another, thicker blanket hung ceiling to floor and when he pulled that aside the old man said, 'Welcome to the Precinct.'

It was junk, of course, but junk from the last hundred years, from cases of proprietary medicine and stacks of brownish, glass-stoppered bottles to old Zenith TVs, antique cobblers' lasts to two half-drunk bottles of Jack Daniel's. Plus a showroom mannequin, a stuffed fox, a pile of old shellac records, half a dozen radios, scores of empty bottles and a bare lightbulb suspended over them all. There was also a small electric heater – run off wires which dangled from the ceiling – a two-ring cooker and a camp bed.

And then there were the Police Do Not Cross blue barriers, dozens of them stacked in one corner, and bundles of the yellow and black crime-scene tape, neatly re-rolled, but obviously recycled.

Two twisted chunks of metal suggested modern sculptors, but on close inspection they were old-fashioned barbers chairs. That explained the medicines, this was the equivalent of a pharmacy back when the fire happened.

The whole place smelt like the old man, only stronger, thicker. But after where they had been, it was positively cozy.

He sat them down on two packing cases – Hilton picked out 'Speidel's Hair Tonic and Restorative' on the side of his – and the Captain started fussing with the heating ring. 'Coffee? Good. None of that fancy stuff they have upstairs though. This is strictly Taster's Choice.' And he chortled.

Hilton eyed the whisky, but said nothing. He could feel some heat coming into his limbs from the small fire, and he didn't want to get rousted out at this point. And the old man still had a knife on him somewhere. He may not have been in the force, but the speed and positioning of the knife – even Hilton knew where the carotid artery was and what it meant – suggested he could handle himself. And he could still feel the points at which the fingers of his other hand had dug into his neck. Strong. Maybe he *was* a cop. Late for roll-call, though.

His eye caught a glint over in the far corner. Something gold. He stood up and moved over. Underneath a sheet of grubby polythene he could make out some braid. It was a formal police dress uniform, the kind worn on parades.

'Special occasions only,' said the Captain. 'Don't get much call for it these days.'

'So you were – are – a cop?'

The Captain turned to him and stared, as if what he was about to say made perfect sense: 'Some days I am. Some days I ain't. I usually decide when I wake up in the morning. Now this morning, I had the feeling I was going to be required. And I was right, wasn't I? The thing is, you get respect in a uniform. Doncha think?'

Hilton shrugged then looked across at the girl and she smiled weakly at him as if to agree that the old coot was obviously crazy. He wondered if he looked as awful as she did. Her hair was thick with dust and masonry chips, her face streaked with the dried slime from the tavern. The black grime had gathered under her high cheekbones, making her look gaunt, starved. He probably looked worse, he decided – at least you could still see she was cute underneath.

As he boiled up the water he had collected, the Captain asked: 'What you been up to?'

Ali bounced back: 'We robbed a 7-Eleven.' Then blushed.

'Did you.' He fixed Hilton with one eye. 'Kinda young to be playing Bonnie to your Clyde, isn't she?'

'He's my brother,' she continued. 'It's a family concern.'

'How much did you get?'

To Hilton's surprise she pulled out the dollars he had stuffed away from the bungled heist. 'Oh, enough.'

'What's that?' asked the Captain.

'What?'

'That in your pocket?'

'Oh, it's a jawbone. Cow I think.'

'Foal,' he corrected. 'You been by the abattoir and stables then?'

'It was just on the floor.'

He waved a hand, dismissing the bone. 'You see the theatre?'

Hilton interjected. 'The one with the rats?'

'You went in then?'

'Yeah. And we got out. Why?'

He shook his head. 'They know you are here then.'

'They didn't move. We backed out, and they just . . . sat there. It was weird.'

Distractedly the Captain said: 'Best get you out of here.'

Hilton snapped: 'Well hooray for that thought. Just tell us how.'

'Hold on. We gotta talk. We're OK here, nobody comes near the Precinct.'

Ali asked: 'You live down here?'

'For the moment.' He idly went to the wall and tore off a chunk of what looked like some kind of herb covered in white, greenish mould. If the kid was old enough to knock off convenience stores, she wasn't going to worry too much about this. He started to chew. 'I have been here off and on since . . . oh, a long time. As you can see, it's easy to get some power down from the overworld, so I'm quite self-sufficient. I suppose I first came down in the seventies and I was here off and on for a few years. Even tried it up top for a year or two. Didn't work. Trouble, trouble, trouble. I came back here before they built the tunnels, the bus tunnels, and getting between here and there was a lot easier then. But when they came in to drive the bores, they tried their damnedest to get me out. Couldn't.'

'Why?'

'Why did they want me out? Oh, one day I decided to take a look at the tunnels – there are access and emergency escape doors that open it to here – and some people saw me, and they decided I was some kind of threat. You know, crazy mole people threaten new transit system, I saw the headlines. Didn't have the uniform on, y'see. It was always easy when I wore my blues, a quick shave and I could move around no problem. Respect. You know, you can make people do almost anything you want. Anything. Like you're a different person. They don't see you, y'see, they just see the blues and the badge.

'Well, anyway, they came after me – us – but this part of the city, it's not like the tourist bit over at Pioneer, all high ceilings and walkways. Nope, there's a million places to hide here. That's why the bootleggers used it, even though they'll tell you different over at Doc Maynard's. Sorry, I've only got one mug – can you share? Anyway, there was a bunch of us back then – ten, twenty, forty depending on the time of year.'

The Captain parked himself on the camp bed while they shuttled the scalding tin cup back and forward, both burning their mouths, both welcoming the glow running down into their core. He sipped noisily, slopping some down the front of his tunic. Hilton could see how it got the shiny, brittle finish. 'At first it was just social workers. Offering coffee and meals. Then they got heavy. Threats. Then . . .' He took a large slurp and stopped.

'What?' asked Ali.

'They came in like . . . came in treating us like animals. Tried to burn us out. Burn. They got most of us in the end, one way or another. I had . . . a friend. Had several friends. There was me and Red and Sammy. Sammy

Napoleon Wilson his name was. Once promised me he would tell me where the Napoleon came from, but . . . well, he died. They burnt him where he slept. Cremated him. We sort of got our revenge, though.' He laughed as he remembered daubing the bus, and walking around, invincible in his uniform – it was clean back then – pasting up the flyers they had written.

He passed around some surprisingly fresh biscuits. 'So, desperadoes, eh?' he said between mouthfuls. 'Kill anyone?'

Hilton looked at Ali but she shook her head.

'So what was the firing I heard?'

'Warning shot.'

'They coming after you? The cops?'

'Uh-huh.'

'Well, keep them away from me.'

'I thought you *were* police,' said Ali in a puzzled voice.

'Not that sort. And I don't want welfare coming down with hot meals and Bible classes. I'm serious – no matter what happens, you never met me. OK? Or him.'

Hilton followed his arm to the bundle in the corner. Even squinting it was hard to make out as anything other than a pile of rags, but slowly he could pick out an arm, a foot, the shape of the head. 'Does he do anything?'

'Sleeps real well. Could win a Nobel Prize for it. Manages to hear every word I say, though. But you ain't seen us. OK?'

'OK.' This was just plain nuts, thought Hilton. Here I am taking coffee with a dipshit old subterranean hermit who could well be the original Dirty Harry, some sort of vagrant-in-a-coma, and a girl who has started playing Fantasy Island. Maybe she was after a spot on Oprah or

Ricki Lake – coming next, Pre-teens Who Rob. Hilton looked around the room once more. There were a few modern pieces of flotsam in the room, plus a stack of canned food with labels he recognised. 'You must get up to the top now and then.'

'I do, I do. But it's easy for me.' He got up and tore off another chunk of plant. 'But it's changed down here. First they built the tunnels. Then all the stores started opening up their basements, which closed off the best runs. And now—' He popped the plant into his mouth, revealing the fibrous globule he had formed from the other bud. 'This.'

'What?'

He spat on the floor, raising dust and leaving a green-brown circle. 'That.'

'What is it?' asked Ali.

'Well, it's kinda like chewing tobacco. Only a mite stronger, I can tell you.'

'Dope?'

'Got it in one, Ace. Here.'

He handed some over and Hilton sniffed. It was brittle and dry, but some kind of crystals stuck to his finger. He crushed them and sniffed. He recognised that aroma. It was Ricky's stuff. It was the dynamite they were trying to buy off Annie. His heart raced. They were saved. 'They grow this down here?'

'In two or three big rooms yonder.' He pointed over his shoulder. 'They blocked off all the ways into them except two. But, I opened up another hatch from this side they ain't found yet. But the only way to the surface is through those rooms.' He thought for a minute. 'Or under them, but I wouldn't recommend that.'

'Well, it's no prob – I know the guys doing this stuff.'

He looked dismayed. 'You do?'

'Yes, yes. Well it's a guy and his old lady. She'll see us to the top all right.'

'You sure?'

'Yeah. Why not?'

'I get the impression they don't like too many people knowing about what they do. There's rumours about what happened to . . . to people who got too close.' He remembered the body they had found by the wall, two bloody mangled patches where the knees should have been. Looked like he had managed to crawl a few yards before his strength gave out. Whether he had been shot anywhere else had been hard to see, not after the rats had finished with him.

'How can you grow plants underground?' asked Ali. 'In the dark?'

'You'll see,' said the Captain. 'I can point you in the right direction. If you're sure.'

Sure he was sure. In one way Annie got him into this. So Annie could get him out. And then a thought occurred to him. 'Why don't you smoke it? Instead of all that chewing?'

The Captain shrugged. 'Force of habit. It would be OK in here, apart from the fact they might smell it and come lookin' for me. But elsewhere, you gotta be careful.'

'Why?'

He pointed at the floor. 'Somewhere under here is the old sewage system. Well, that rather glorifies it. What it is, is basically a lake of shit that has been pumping out methane for a hundred years or more. You don't wanna go down there with a joint in your hand.'

'I thought you said they burned you out?'

'They don't know squat, do they? Anyway that was, what? Fifteen years ago? Wasn't so much of a problem then, but some of the sealing around the lake has gone . . . it's leaking out more and more now.'

Hilton thought of the naked flame of the oil lamp he had been charging around with. And suddenly now he badly wanted a cigarette. He wished he hadn't brought the subject up. 'So no smokes?'

'Not unless you want to get up top the quick way, Ace.' He made an exploding movement with his hands.

Hilton drained the last of the coffee. 'OK, we'll be on our way.'

'Why do you live here like this?'

The Captain looked at the girl. He wondered if she would understand that sometimes you find what makes you well, what keeps you out of the hospitals, or worse, from being thrown out of the hospitals and onto the streets, with just a card saying come back for medication every two weeks. Down here he didn't need any medication, except the odd chew on these plants. He smiled, showing his stumpy, broken teeth. Nor did people question who you were, not most of the time. You could be who you wanted. Out of harm's way. Out of temptation's way. 'I like it.' He tore off another strip of dope as if to make the point.

Hilton couldn't stand it. Now the topic of cigarettes had come up he wanted one real bad. 'Can I have some?' he asked.

The Captain nodded and handed him the length. 'Takes a bit of chewing to get anything.'

Hilton winced at the bitter taste, but shoved the

bundle in his mouth. He could do with relaxing a bit. It was all too much. 'You mentioned something about a flashlight.'

'Ah yes.' The Captain fished around for a few minutes in a pile of packing cases. He threw Hilton a cardigan, and the girl a large brown sweater that she put on under her jacket. 'Keep the coffee warmth in a bit longer.' Eventually he came up with a tiny keyring flashlight. 'Not much, but it's got a coupla hours in it. More than you need to find your friends.'

Hilton felt the first hint of spaciness, the words bouncing around his head and off the walls. 'Friends' seemed to hang in the air for a long time, reverberating and distorting, slowly shrinking and diminishing into the silence. Well, he thought, not *friends* exactly.

THIRTY

'Ladies and Gentlemen, allow me to introduce myself. My name is Major Michael Oxford Milliner, US Army, and I am here tonight to talk about the MFT-117, also known as the American Beauty, and its use in combat situations, with particular reference to H&I operations. That is Harassment and Interdiction, for those of you not familiar with the term. It is a phrase first coined in Vietnam, and refers to the use of artillery to deny the enemy a stable base to operate from. Now, we in the Texas Thunder division also used the term for the scorched-earth policy. This was a simple concept – in areas where the Viet Cong were obtaining succour – willingly or unwillingly – from local villagers, then we would relocate said locals and destroy the villages, thus denying the VC food and shelter.

'Now the version of this we used then, the MFT-101, was heavy and cumbersome. The tanks were aluminium, the rest steel. This new model is constructed mainly of Kevlar, ceramics and titanium. The tanks contain a viscous form of petroleum with an impacting agent, that is a chemical which makes the fine globules adhere to any surface, including human skin. Ignition is by a high-voltage electric spark, rather than the old Zippo-style lighter at the front nozzle. Now, the action of the stream, which can be propelled up to twenty-five metres, is two-fold. The very high temperatures, due to a phosphate compound intermixed with the petroleum, causes a crisping of the skin. This peels back, just like on a regular Chinese duck – to expose the subcutaneous fat. The "sticky" globules then actually ignite the fat, turning the victim, in effect, into a human candle or, more accurately, given the speed of immolation, a human flare. It is estimated death takes less than ten seconds, and that survival rates from a direct hit are less than one half of one per cent. Of course the MFT was designed to burn materials as well as people, but for tonight's demonstration we have selected one of the vagrants living under your streets. Over here we have a stop-watch, and, if I just hoist the MFT onto my back – very light, in spite of the liquids, you see, and do up this strap. Gentlemen, if you will just move aside I will demonstrate the effectiveness of the device on human beings –'

'Major. MAJOR.'

He jerked awake at the voice in his headset, and wiped the perspiration from his top lip. Long time since he had had that dream. A very long time. 'Yes?'

'Seattle, sir.'

He looked at the incandescent glow now visible on the other side of the mountains, a burning white light in the centre just like – he couldn't help it – a phosphorous bomb, trailing out to little cinders across the islands and finally darkness. And under the city itself, more darkness. And what else?

'Ten minutes, Major.'

THIRTY-ONE

Downtown Seattle. 2.51 am

Now Tenniel knew he was fucking crazy. There goes the pension, the reputation, the house, the wife, the dog, the bowling league and probably his mother. Time to move onto the islands, Orcas perhaps, and get some peace and quiet. Get away from making dumb decisions like this one.

Before him stood the two men he was entrusting with an operation to save a little girl's life, now both decked out in one-piece coveralls, with SPD stencilled across their back. Stupid People Downunder? Sociopathic Disasters? Anything but Seattle Police Department suggested itself.

Nobody would catch his eye for the moment. They were doubtless wondering every time they stepped on something whether it could be one of those marbles the Sergeant has obviously lost. But for the time being he was it – every other senior officer was out there trying to tell anyone who would listen that drive-by shootings did not happen in Seattle. And now according to the latest bulletin, there were three. In one night.

He could hear the Media Relations Unit even now. Sure, these *looked* like drive-by shootings, in that shots were fired from a car that was, well, driving by, killing an entire family in one case, a couple in another, and a young man in the third, and leaving a lot of wounded and distressed in their wake. No, we wouldn't call it a massacre. No, it probably wasn't the Eighteenth Street gang they would all be saying, or La Eme executive action, while at the same time praying it wasn't so.

All in all, it was Milliner's fault, he figured. That man had gutted the city's police elite like prime trout, and now he was coming back to screw up this operation.

Harry came over. 'It's gonna be OK, Sergeant. Honest.'

'Look,' he whispered, 'I have a kind of soft spot for Rabbit, for Hilton, I'll admit. But if he gets . . . You know, well, it kind of evens the score for the girl's dad. But do me a favour?'

'Sure.'

'If for any reason the girl gets hurt, shoot Lewis over there, then come out and do me before you turn your gun on yourself. Please.'

Harry waited for the smirk to come but it didn't. It was only partially a joke. 'Well, if your man's as good as he thinks he is . . .'

Lewis was playing with the gun, feeling its weight and balance after all these years, but caught the sentence. 'No worries here.' But the voice sounded odd, as if it no longer fitted him, like he had borrowed it for the night. There was some kind of conviction there, but he wasn't sure he – who he was now, so many years down the line – could back it up.

Harry picked up a flashlight and one of the Rover receivers. He transported the spool of communications wire over to the entrance hole, and checked it was running freely and plugged in the handset that would remain up top. 'How much of this is there?' he asked Bruno.

'About a thousand yards on that reel. But we can switch to extension reels if you spool out. They're in the van.'

'Get them,' said Tenniel. 'He's had time to put some distance between us and them.'

'If he's still down there.'

Tenniel nodded. It would be a blessing if he had found a way out. As long as he hadn't decided at that point that the girl was excess baggage. 'And Harry.'

'Yeah?'

'If the Green River Killer is down there, King County will be mighty grateful if you'd fetch him up.'

Harry checked. That was a joke. 'Yeah, well, I'll ask around.'

Lewis put his arm round Dinah and guided her into a quiet corner. He tried not to say too much. He knew it would probably be goodbye soon. Always was. 'Be fine.'

'You don't have to go. They got those two real experts.'

She pointed at Bruno and Sylvic.

Real experts? Real? He was the genuine article, not Ren and Stimpy over there. 'Yeah, but if anyone can get the girl—' He didn't know how to finish the sentence. He realised there was still a lot she didn't know. He softened his tones.

'I should come, too.'

He shook his head with as much conviction as he knew how. 'I used to do this. I know, I know I said I was the up-top guy, and I was that too. But I can deliver the phone. I could even get her out, if they'd let me. But I have to do it alone. Not with you to lean on.'

Dinah hated herself for the rush of relief she felt. She was no Sigourney Weaver after all. But she felt like she had to offer. 'Sure. I understand.' She laughed. 'It'd be nice to get the elevator up to the apartment. Just once.'

'Yeah?'

'Yeah. And they are big airy spaces down there. I did the tour at Pioneer. Not little at all.'

Yes, well, kill or cure, he thought, but refrained from saying it. He took her in his arms, his head buried in her throat. He could smell her, over and above all those other phantom odours, and he breathed deep. He knew he didn't want to let this one go. No Vancouver, no Calgary. No goodbyes. This is where you make your stand, he thought. No matter how scary it gets. This one can take it. It was whether he could that worried him. Time to strap in for the ride.

Tenniel looked at the piece of paper handed to him. Lieutenant says to wait until he gets there before committing any men. Just has to record a press statement about the drive-bys. Also Major Milliner expected within fifteen minutes. Cock-fucking-sucker, he thought, apologising to himself for his language. He screwed up the message into a ball and said: 'Get going, and good luck, and call in every five minutes, even if you just let us know you're OK. Make that three minutes, I can't stand waiting.'

Harry struggled into a Second Chance armour and offered one to Lewis, who shook his head. Too bulky. Underdogs never used them – slow you down, get you caught. The pair moved towards the PD aluminium ladder that disappeared into the blackness. Lewis held the light while Harry went down, gripping the communication handset and making sure the drum ran freely once more. When he had reached the bottom Lewis threw him the LWL case, a first-aid kit and then the light. He swung onto the ladder and held there for a minute, looking up at a dozen anxious faces. 'They'll probably be heading north-west, remember,' said the Man With The Plans. Lewis ignored him. He would know where they were going when he got down there. He raised an arm at Dinah and Tenniel and Bowman and slid down into the waiting darkness below.

The beam revealed they were in some kind of old tavern, just about recognisable from the bar and some old ad hoardings. A double door looked as if it led to the street. The slime on the floor had been streaked and skidded over, but Lewis could clearly see two sets of footprints, one large, one small. They left tracks heading for those doors.

Lewis opened the case and took out his flashlight, the goggles and the gun. He pushed an arm through the first-aid backpack, slid the gun into the belt he had threaded around the outside of the coveralls and slipped the goggles and their strapping system on. They looked to Harry like binoculars that fused down to a monocular. Lewis twiddled with the knob at the side and the world turned bright, painful green. The image intensifier still worked. 'Turn your flashlight out,' he said to Harry.

'You crazy? It'll be pitch-black out there.'

'You can hold onto my belt. He sees the beam of a normal torch . . . well, you heard what he said. That's why we're here. That's why I'm here.'

He let that hang there. They snapped into semi-darkness for a second, just the light from the hole above illuminating the room, before Lewis flicked on his light. He knew its IR beam wouldn't help Harry, but, with a few more goggle adjustments, now he could see – after a fashion. It was a very flat, fuzzy world, with little lateral vision, but it offered a good summary. Better even than some of the newer night-viewers, he thought proudly. He touched Harry, who jumped ten inches into the air. 'I can hardly see a thing.'

'You'll be OK. Follow me.'

'You can?'

'Yup. You got everything?'

Flashlight. Gun. Handset. 'Yeah. You wanna give me that pistol of yours? Just in case you get tempted?'

Lewis smiled to himself. 'No. You feel like trying to take it off me?'

I could, old man, he thought. But maybe they shouldn't start with a fight. 'Nah.'

He felt Harry's grip tighten on his belt, and they stepped through the door into the first room. The size of the chamber hit Lewis in the chest. This was no street, it was a grave. What happened to the big, airy spaces? This was in-fill. Small tunnels burrowed through in-fill. Harry felt him stiffen. 'You OK?'

No answer.

'Lewis. You OK?'

Lewis could smell them. He looked at all the apertures and instinctively knew which one they had taken, could feel them groping along the walls, could see where hands had tested the surfaces, had snagged the spiderwebs.

And then he realised he would have to follow and felt the pucker effect as his anus contracted. He fought off the panic, ignoring the tugging at his belt.

A second smell came in. The rice. The rice was always a giveaway. If it got damp it became high enough to gag a maggot. And now he had that acrid sharpness in his nose. That and the sweat and the odour of men who had been underground too long. Lewis suddenly felt calm. It was home turf. His baby. He'd screwed up before, that was true. Not this time. Please. He remembered that thought above ground. Let it come. Don't fight it. This time he was going to get out the other side.

Then he realised Harry was stage-whispering into his radio. 'Yeah, we down here, but we're kind of stuck. Lewis won't move. I don't know, Sergeant, he's your pal.'

Lewis swivelled to Harry and put his hand over the transmitter. 'I'll go point, mate. We'll switch every three trapdoors. Just stay sharp. OK? And watch for those fuckin' snakes.' He heard the words, and didn't believe them, like a dispassionate observer part of his brain knew this must sound crazy. *Let it come.*

Harry grunted as they shuffled forward. Trapdoors? Snakes? What the hell was he talking about? But it was too late, Lewis was off, and Harry felt the walls close around him as they entered some sort of corridor.

THIRTY-TWO

Underworld. Seattle.

Maybe the dope had been a bad idea, thought Hilton. He wasn't stoned exactly – well, just a little – but the edge had gone off the world, as if it had been softened, cushioned, encased in bubblewrap. He could hardly feel his feet touch the floor, for instance, which made stepping over the assorted debris on the floor very tricky. The Captain was leading the way, out of his narrow alley and into wider tunnels, boulevards by comparison, so wide the diffused torch that the old man used hardly reached the sides. They were streets, or what were once streets, high and mighty, and now leaking like rusty old hulks: drops of water detached themselves from the ceiling and went into freefall, fifteen, twenty feet, landing with a soft plop all around them. It was as if the earth was porous, bleeding down on them. There must have been businesses here: stores, hotels, smithies, stables, probably, but most were faded and twisted and torn, just the shells. In some places, maybe between buildings, there were great mounds of in-fill, some held in place by thick steel mesh.

And, it seemed to Hilton, there was a strange mixture of pillars supporting the overworld. Some were cast-iron, ornate, too elaborate to be hidden away like this. Others were rough-hewn timber, old, spongy, and then there were the brutal, rough concrete beams, like coarse-cast versions of the ones that supported the monorail, which must be overhead and to the . . . left, he figured.

The truth was that after several lefts and rights and what felt like a U-turn, Hilton had lost his sense of direction. The dope again. But hadn't they passed that hotel sign before? It was then he realised the old man was deliberately looping them round like some drunken garden snail, making sure they could never lead anybody to his little lair. As if Hilton ever wanted to see it again.

The Captain had dug around in the piles of sacking and boxes within his Precinct and brought out a battered police hat, which now perched precariously on top of his uncombed hair. Man was clearly a loony of the first order. And he was trusting him. What if the whole dope thing was crap, a ruse to get them . . . Relax, dope paranoia, is all, he thought. He could have killed him back at the water main. Unless he was a sadist . . . STOP IT.

As he shook his head to clear out the unwelcome fears, Ali clutched Hilton's hand tightly. She looked up and smiled. Smiled. The grubby little tyke was enjoying this, probably revelling in the little fantasy that she had helped knock over the 7-Eleven. Well, let her keep the one eighty anyway. It was the least she deserved. And if it was her way of coming to terms with the death of her father – possible death of her father he reminded himself: she still didn't know for sure – so be it. *He* didn't know for sure. Shit, yes he did. Dead. For sure. He grinned back, hoping he didn't look too stoned.

And then the street disappeared under their feet.

'What happened here?' asked Hilton.

'Collapsed.' The Captain flashed the beam around.

'This level fell into the next. There was a shallow basement. Look.' He shone his torch. 'Been a lot of excavation here over the years. The first bit of regrading they tried. Before they took out Denny and flattened it even.'

'Denny?'

'Belltown. It was on a hill once. Be sharp here, it's a bit rough underfoot, so watch your ankles. And you might want to hold your nose.'

They started forward scrambling down a slope where the ground floor had imploded into the old basements. This had once been a wooden sidewalk by the look of it. Now the timbers were scattered like discarded railway sleepers. Some showed signs of charring. Ali stumbled several times, squealing, until Hilton grabbed her and swung her onto his back. She weighed precious little. 'My Little Pony,' she whispered into his ear.

'Don't push your luck, kid.'

The smell hit them about halfway down. A choking concoction of shit and piss and ammonia and sulphur dioxide and several other vile chemicals. 'Jesus,' said Hilton involuntarily.

'It sort of clings to the floor,' said the Captain, 'so you won't suffocate.'

Great, but he might just puke. 'For God's sake – don't you get tired of this?'

'I got more tired of being up there, son. Look, it's only about four, five hundred yards. Watch your step, there.'

He flashed the beam at a circular hole, a missing manhole cover. There was a soft gurgling sound from underneath.

'That where this stink is coming from?'

'Yup. Lake Shit-i-ca-ca me and Sam used to call it. 'Scuse me,' he said to Ali, but she just giggled and repeated it. 'We ignited some once by mistake. Not here – over that way, just a small pocket, luckily. Weirdest thing you ever seen, blue flames dancing up the corridors and alleys like ghosts. Reminded me of—' He stopped.

'What?'

But he didn't reply, just moved the beam from side to side. Reminded him of watching people die when he was in the hospital all that time ago. What was it? Must be thirty years now. Some nights he thought he could see the souls of his fellow patients leave their bodies. And they didn't go willingly. They clung on by their spectral fingernails, fighting to stay with the flesh. But eventually the grip weakened, and one by one they drifted off. They were being killed with over-medication, he was sure. It was the next stop for him. Well, he had wanted to cling onto his blue flame a little longer. So he came underground.

'Was it like the X-Files?' offered Ali.

'What's that?' asked Hilton.

'You haven't seen the X-Files?' She was aghast.

'No, that.' He hadn't been talking to her.

The Captain steadied the thin light on a striped mattress, grown slimy with damp and mould, a huddle of brown blankets and what looked like the remains of a wooden sentry hut. All around it were bits of charred wood and piles of black ashes. This had once been a much larger structure.

'That? One of Sammy Napoleon Wilson's old places, when he used to lie low from the transit police. They wouldn't come down here after a while.'

'Really?' Hilton asked with mock incredulity.

'Sam reckoned after a week or two he couldn't smell it any more.'

'I bet they could smell him though.'

'Not well enough. They torched it while he was still in it.'

It was a second before this registered in Hilton's befuddled brain.

'Torch . . . you mean they killed him?'

'Burnt him where he slept.' He didn't add it was all his fault. He had got him killed. Not what he had intended at all. Trial without jury. Trial by fire, you might say. And thought of poor, scarred Red, who hadn't spoken to him since that day, who blamed him for the death and his own terrible burns. Ah well, they'd all been friends once. It was what happened when the outside world came visiting. And look what he was saddled with now. Trouble, that was what. 'Let's go.'

Occasionally Hilton flashed on his own light, to examine the ceiling, often concrete or steel, sometimes old, warped wood panelling. Up above, now hanging in mid-air, the ground tugged from under them, were the remnants of the old shop fronts – this time he could see a bank sign: Alki Allied & Mutual. He wondered what had happened to them.

The ground started to rise, and they had to thread their way through a small lawn of twisted metal spikes, some kind of reinforcing rods that had been exposed, left like rusted plant tendrils desperately seeking non-existent light.

'Not far now,' said the Captain, stopping to readjust his wayward hat.

Just how crazy is this guy? Hilton thought as he stepped around him. The red-hot needles that drove into his eyes seemed to answer him. The sockets went supernova, flaring into searing, excruciating pain. Desperately he clawed at them, but the burning got worse, he twisted around to try and get some bearings. There was a thin scream from Ali, as she was torn from his back. Released, he fell to his knees, gasping in agony, but managed to stumble up and flail, calling her name. The fucking mad bastard, what was he doing? What had he done to him? He tried to squint into darkness through streams of acidic tears, felt the blow under his chin lift him into the air, passed out before he hit the floor.

THIRTY-THREE

'I haven't really told you about the base. It was called Ben Moc, and it was on the edge of the Iron Triangle. It used to be an FSB, a Fire Support Base, but now it had grown into spookville. All the intelligence traffic, all the info from the ASDIDs – they were listening gizmos dropped by planes – all came through Ben Moc. So we knew a lot about where the tunnels were, and we would fly out and look at every new one. There was one . . . we got time for this? There was one, the first one, where we let Fix go point, with me behind him. Now, it's scary going up front, because you get to open the trapdoors. No, the tunnels went up and down on different levels, and sometimes you had doors, other times you had water traps to stop the gas. So you only got to do three doors before switching. Yeah, that was another rule. Everything in threes. Well, the strain was too great, you never knew what was on the other side, after three you got . . . jumpy. So Fix gets to be point. Lewis? Lewis was up top. Never came down much any more, but we knew he could. He had been Rat Six for the Big Red One. Top tunnel man. He didn't have nothing to prove. So Fix goes through the first door OK, and then we come to one that goes up. Fix pushes, it won't give. Then he realises. He puts his fingers on the door, and he can feel it. Someone is above. We start to back up and the trapdoor opens, and down comes a grenade. Big one. Brown. You could see it in the torchlight. Russian or Chinese. I tell you, everything stopped. Even one of those big centipedes that was coming out of its hole. Stopped dead. Four seconds. At most. But Fix. I dunno, maybe it was the speed he was on that gave him the edge. He picks up the grenade. One second. He tries the door. Fucker is sitting on it. Two seconds. He fires his gun through the wooden hatch. Strange noise, just the splinters and the thud of bullets going in. Not even a scream. Three seconds. He lifts the hatch with his shoulder, gets the grenade in, and wham. Four seconds. No, the blast goes along the tunnels, hardly affects us. What did he say? This is Fix, OK? He says: 'What do Australian girls put behind their ears to attract men? Their knees.'

THIRTY-FOUR

Downtown Seattle. 3.10 am

Someone was holding back the hands of her watch, thought Bowman. They should have at least called in a second time by now. But if time was slow up here, what must the perception of it be like down there? What was it like down there, period. Would there be spiders? Rats? And what was that crap about the Green River Killer? Anyone with internet access could get a list of prime suspects, and none of them featured a tunnel-dwelling freak with a taste for blue serge.

The waiting for the call wasn't helped by the fact that nobody in the room was talking, or breathing or making any sudden movements. Nobody had offered to go and get coffee either. She was suspicious that they all thought she should go. As the woman. Run along and take the order for two doubletall skinnies, three mochas, a granita and a Why Bother? (a de-caff latte with skimmed milk) for Tenniel.

She looked over at him, scratching his head, the great lunk. Excuse me, what's wrong with this picture? Well, everything. They had done it all fugazi, she knew that the moment she saw a rookie cop and a flaky Vet disappear down the hole. But the correct answer is . . . ? Well, she'd have to get back to herself on that one. If they did get the link-up with this Hilton guy, she knew she could get some positive transference underway, make him see reason. Do a better job than John, anyway.

She wasn't sure why she liked being with him. It just made her feel confident. She knew she had weaknesses, and so did he, but when they had been a team, they had seemed to cancel each other out. And he treated her properly from the off. It had all come a long way since the academy taught women how to get out of squad cars gracefully, but the old Boys' Club mentality was still there. They would trust you – not like you, necessarily, but trust you – only when they had seen you fight. 'Yeah, but can she punch?' she had heard more than once. Harry would have the same problem. Little guys – next to women, that was what the old timers hated. So the shorties had to be twice as hard, twice as reckless. Maybe like Harry, who should've waited for back-up.

Women or dwarfs, though, Tenniel, he just got on with it. Had even bawled out those two guys who had pulled the standard initiation joke – putting two silicone breast-implant sacs, recovered from the morgue, in her locker. Truth was, she probably could do with them. Didn't do any harm to let them think she was a flat-chested dyke, though. It usually shut up the police wives who always thought you were going to hump their three-hundred-pound gorilla husbands. Didn't work with Mrs T, though. John was having too much fun, getting through too much work. Must be bonin' that bitch in the back seat of the patrol car. He wasn't. But then he'd never asked.

He came over, his smile tense and stretched. 'I've been thinkin'.'

So had she, but she said: 'John, what was it with the dogs?'

'Later. I've been thinkin', we should maybe pull Hilton's file, see if we can come up with an angle.'

'I'll get it e-mailed over to the laptop.'

'Great. Oh, and Isa? Can you get me a Why Bother? while you're out there?'

She rolled her eyes. Would the surprises never stop?

THIRTY-FIVE

Underworld. Seattle.

'Pepper.'

Hilton heard the word, but he was too busy drowning to take much notice. Water was pouring into his throat and his nose, and trickling down into his airways, his bronchioles, his alveoli. He didn't care, at least it was cooling him, let him drown. Then the cough reflex kicked in, he expelled a jet of water from his throat with a splutter, rolled to one side and dry heaved.

'Stay on your back, son. Pepper, like I said,' came the voice and he was pulled over. 'And open your eyes.'

He tried, but the merest movement of his eyelids started the pain again. He yelped as streaks of pure agony appeared like comets across his darkened vision.

'Keep still and open your goddamn eyes.'

The sluice of liquid poured around his inflamed sockets, filling his ears and soaking his hair, but softening the edges of his pain. It subsided to a dull red glow.

'Out of water, Ace.' It was then he realised it was the Captain speaking. He sat up and scrabbled for his gun in his belt. It was gone.

'Lost it. And your partner.'

'What have you done with her, you fuckin' loony?'

The Captain stood up and brushed down his uniform. Hilton squinted at him, and in the beam of the MagLite he could see the bloodshot whites and the residual tear. 'Yeah, look at this. They got me too. I told you you shouldn't have gone in that theatre. Territory, that's what matters down here.'

'Yeah, you told us after we had been there. Give me a hand up. Fuck it hurts.'

'Pepper.'

'What?'

'A pepper spray. They stole it from me. It was one of my collection. 'Course the pepper's long gone, but they fill it with any irritant. You was lucky, they used to use battery acid. You'd've been able to pick your nose from the inside-out if they'd done that.'

Hilton gently touched his eyes. Whatever it was was wearing off fast; he could blink now without feeling he was ploughing his irises.

'Rats?' he asked. 'The rats use pepper sprays?'

'Maybe it's stronger than I think – done something to your brain, has it? Rats don't use pepper sprays, not even down here.'

OK, OK, put it together, he thought, one thing at a time. 'Where's Ali?'

'They've got her.'

'WHO THE FUCK HAVE GOT HER?'

'Well Myrtle, mostly, he's the one to worry about.'

'And he's got my gun?'

'No, I've got that.' He pulled it out from under the police tunic. 'I just didn't want you shooting until you knew who you should be shooting at. And it ain't me.'

Hilton took it and said: 'Thanks. Look, you want to run me through from A to Z on this?'

'Myrtle must have seen you at the theatre—'

'There's only one way in, and it was locked.'

'No, there are doors behind the stage. That way you don't have to go by the customers.'

'The rats?'

'Yup. Now Myrtle has a couple of friends, one red, one white. Red, he got caught down one of the tunnels when the patrols came with those flame-throwers. Burnt his face pretty bad. And hands. He was trying to pull Sammy out, you see. Blames me for it. Never thought the whole thing was a good idea in the first place. Breaking the code.'

'What code?'

'Oh, it's old news now. Old news. Whitey, well he looks like he was born under a rock. Pale as pale can be. The three of them move around together, but Myrtle, Myrtle is the leader.'

'And what's her story?'

'His story. He's one of those guys becoming a woman in easy instalments. Got the tits now, thanks to the hormones and a bit of surgery here and there, but still blessed with the rest.'

'A chick with a dick?'

'I guess. Don't like to look too close, truth be known.'

'And what are they going to do with her? With Ali?'

'One thing you should know. Two minutes from here are your friends with the dope. You can be out and away. I'll go and get Ali, don't you worry. It's my job.'

'What's your job?'

'To protect and serve.'

Hilton looked at the madman, his spittle-encrusted grey beard, stained brown at the corners from all that chewing of dope. To protect and serve. Great. 'You got any more of that shit? To numb the pain? Thanks.' He chomped for a bit. Time to move on. 'OK, if you are sure you can do it by yourself.'

'Leave it to me, son.'

Hilton checked he had the small flashlight and that it worked and shone it ahead, where it barely penetrated the darkness. Somewhere not too distant was a way out of this mess, finally. Too bad about the girl, really.

'Five, six hundred yards, you'll hit a big grey wall, look for a wooden panel near the base. It comes off. Your pals are on the other side. Don't spook them though. Make it clear who you are. They might be a tad jumpy, if you know what I mean.'

'Yeah, thanks. And good luck.' He turned to go. 'What will they do with her?'

The Captain shrugged. 'I don't know. We don't get that many cute eight-year-old blonde girls down here.'

Hilton's heartbeat had become a metallic sound, like a hammer striking an anvil, cold and hard and brutal. He even tasted it – a bitter, silvery taste as if he had been sucking nickels and dimes. It was the drugs, he knew, making him sound like a machine, a collection of pumps and valves and switches. He didn't care. He could feel, celebrate even, every vein, artery, capillary, marvel at the blood squeezing through the smallest of gaps in his tissues, the red cells contracting and distorting, each one snatching a minuscule load of oxygen from his lungs to deliver to his muscles. He rejoiced in every fibre contracting, that mechanical thud of his heart, felt every cell in his fingertips burning onto the butt of the gun. Despite everything that had happened he was alive, and he was ready to kill to prove it.

What will they do to her? That was what he really wanted to know. His mind ran through the scenarios, all of them horrible. He pictured her looking up into the face of a hideously burned monster, a pale, insect-like creature, or a grotesque transsexual as they did unspeakable things. He was glad he had changed his mind.

They had tried the doors to the theatre – the ones round the back he and Ali never found – but they had been bolted from the inside. The Captain then led him through a warren of narrow tunnels until they emerged at the bone-strewn soil. The doors to the theatre had been crudely re-chained, but the Captain dug out the hoops with his knife and laid them softly on the floor.

'Whatever you see, leave it to me,' he said. 'This is my beat, remember. My neighbourhood'.

The Captain clicked off the MagLite and Hilton felt the now-familiar panic, the stab of claustrophobia, as the darkness snapped in. The doors swung back, and the sound of laughter drifted towards them. From within his body Hilton heard the noise again, the industrial thump of his heart, the cold, cold heart. He wanted to pull back the slide on the gun, but he remembered what the man said. His call, this one.

The Captain tugged his cardigan sleeve to motion Hilton down, and he put the gun into his waistband and they both belly crawled onto the raised part of the auditorium, looking through the twisted remnants of the railings and down on the stalls, pulled forward by the glow coming from the stage. Splinters penetrated Hilton's elbows, scratched his knees, but he hardly noticed.

The light flickered from half a dozen candles suspended in front of aluminium sheeting above the stage. The yellowy reflection barely illuminated three feet at the lip of the boards, and threw virtually nothing across the seats, for which Hilton was grateful. He knew the rats were there, could hear the massed breathing of their tiny, ratty lungs, and that was enough.

Then his eyes finally adjusted properly and he realised what, exactly, he was looking at on stage.

Just at the edge of the darkness was Ali, or at least the silhouette of her, sitting cross-legged, head bowed. It must have been some trick of the interplay between the shadows and light, but she looked larger than he recalled, like some kind of Buddha figure, but at the same time defenceless, vulnerable. He swallowed hard. It wasn't just his body that had been stripped bare to his senses, his emotions were equally flayed, he knew. Stay calm.

He concentrated on the stage. Showtime. Flitting in and out of the darkness were two of the people the Captain had described. Red was, indeed, that colour, half his face criss-crossed with a fine network of paler scar tissue, like fungal threads on a background of lobster-red. Whitey, on the other hand, had skin that was was thin and ghostly, like parchment, a complexion better suited to some carpet-dwelling blind bug than a human.

Out of the shadows stepped the third, and Hilton almost gasped. Myrtle was big, perhaps six foot four, with black, black hair scraped back from a needle-pointed peak into a severe ponytail. She was built – and dressed – like a quarterback, apart from a pair of breasts that must have caused a world shortage of silicon for a month or two, a mockery of a bosom. He, she, it, was clad in a grubby Seattle Mariners' shirt and pants, finished off with a pair of heels that must have added another three inches and made touchdowns a might difficult. Myrtle was also blessed with skin that looked like rough asphalt on a summer's day. Make-up, he realised, an attempt to give a tan. But what was even weirder than this hybrid she-male was the staff Myrtle held in his hands, a hefty chunk of gnarled wood, topped by a skull. A cow's skull – or, given its small size – maybe a calf's would be Hilton's guess. Ali would know.

The trio were circling her, as if in some slow, formal dance, reaching out to touch her matted hair, although she wasn't reacting. Hilton felt his pulse rise – that metallic throbbing again – and the blood press behind his eyes as Myrtle halted for a few seconds, took a few clumps of her hair and played with them, separating the tangled mass into individual fine strands. Lobster-face and Whitey followed suit.

It was obscene and degrading; just watching made him feel like he was in a bath of maggots which were squirming over his skin. He could feel them, those little blind black-specked heads searching for the darkest corner of his body, burrowing away from the light . . . fuck, that dope again. Must stop it.

The movement on stage got faster and faster. Myrtle was tapping out a rhythm with his staff, keeping the beat going, the dance getting faster, the hands on her almost continually now. In the semi-darkness Hilton tried to read the Captain's face, to see if there were signs of revulsion or disgust there. Nothing. Just another night at the theatre for him maybe. Hilton rolled slightly and freed the gun. He had it level with his head when the Captain's hand took his wrist. The old fool was shaking his head. Why? He couldn't miss from here. Christ, he could hit them with a flicked cigarette butt.

The Captain squirmed closer and put his mouth to Hilton's ear, who tried not to recoil at the heat and smell of the rancid breath. 'The rats,' he whispered. 'They'll tear you to pieces if you use that.'

Hilton lifted his weight onto his elbows and raised a querying eyebrow, but the Captain nodded vigorously. He leant back in. 'My call, remember.'

The dance was continuing, circling, the touching growing more frequent, more prolonged, more lascivious. Hilton pointed with the barrel as if to say: 'Well do something soon, then—'

The Captain stood up, smoothly and quietly, but obviously not afraid to be seen, and approached the steps down. Hilton waited for the squealing to start from the rats as he made the aisle, but there was nothing.

'MYRTLE.'

It even made Hilton jump, such was the power of the voice. A ripple ran through the rats as they shifted position.

'Myrtle . . . ' he said again, softer.

The tableau froze in mid-step. 'Ah, *mon Capitan* . . . ' The voice was dark, treacly, almost seductive. 'Come to join the party?'

'She's mine.' He was down in the auditorium now, and Hilton waited for that noise to start. It didn't; the rats settled back down, passive observers once more. Why? Maybe the Captain smelt right to them.

'Since when?' hissed Lobster-face.

'You remember. Strangers. They have always been mine. Even when you were with me, Red. My partner. You remember.'

Red fell silent.

'Time for a change then,' twittered Whitey.

Myrtle didn't say anything at first, just reached out and stroked Ali's hair again. 'A trade, perhaps?'

'For?'

'Your hat.' He reached back into the dim rear of the stage and produced the battered cap that the Captain had lost in the scuffle.

'I got other hats.'

Myrtle put the cap on the skull, adjusting it so it was at a jaunty angle. 'A cruiser, then.'

'Cruiser?'

'A police cruiser. I know where there is one we can get our hands on. Saw it last time I went to get my pills. We could have it down here in hours. Old model of course, and there is perhaps only one road you could use it on but . . .' He turned the skull on the staff towards him and asked it: 'Sounds like a good deal to us, eh?'

Answer him, willed Hilton. Tell him to go fuck himself, to shove the skull up his ass. But the silence just grew.

'Well, Captain?' sneered Whitey, reaching out once more for a feel of that golden hair, running his long, translucent fingers over her face, searching for her mouth. They were the last words he said before the heavy ACP round smashed through his teeth and exited from the back of his skull in a shower of blood and bone.

Hilton didn't even remember standing up, let alone aiming (and aiming so well, he couldn't help thinking) and for a second looked at his gun disbelievingly. Christ, must be the dope, affecting my mem—

The squeals drowned out the rest. Small, writhing forms began to stream over the seatbacks nearest the stage and into the light, each one issuing a hideous squeak. The Captain sprinted to the stage and leapt on it, slashing out at the astounded Myrtle with his knife, sending him stumbling back into the darkness.

Hilton held his fire as the scene dissolved into animated chaos. The pale figure lying prone next to Ali was already all but covered in scurrying, furry forms. Red was desperately trying to pull them off, screaming as sharp incisors penetrated his skin. He lifted up his hand and brought three of the rodents with him, their jaws locked onto his flesh. Myrtle reappeared, tears streaming down his face and blood down his arm from the knife wound, banging at the rats with his staff, but still they kept coming onto the stage, like malevolent lemmings, wave after wave, crowding over the body three, four, five deep, jostling for some bare flesh, the excited shrillness now painful to hear.

In one movement the Captain scooped the limp form of Ali under his arm, jumped from the stage and raced through the stream of animals back towards Hilton. Myrtle was yelling: 'CAAAAPPPTAAAIIIIN', but he didn't stop or look back.

'You fucking idiot,' he shouted as he streaked past. Hilton ran after him, puzzled. Turned out rather well, he thought.

THIRTY-SIX

Downtown Seattle. 2.59 am

As the lighting rigs were completed, so the streets of the city were being blocked off, armed patrols turning back traffic so nobody snagged the power umbilicals now running like black intestines across Seattle's streets. They wasted twenty minutes trying to get to their entrance point. Pepper parked and joined Annie in the BMW, figuring it was easier to get one car through than two.

She used every trick in the book to try and get past the taciturn sergeant at the Do Not Cross barrier. 'No ma'am, no traffic up here, I am afraid.' When he repeated it for the fifth time Pepper was worried she might just pull out the Para from her purse and persuade him that way, but when it became obvious she was going to be a pain in the ass for as long as it took, he let them by.

The entrance was a garage off Henry, just above Fourth, a nondescript steel-shuttered doorway, set back at the side of the Cineplex. It looked like the delivery bay for one of the new restaurants. But it was a very expensive chuck of concrete flooring, leased by Ricky for two years.

Pepper jumped out to make sure there weren't any troopers lurking, nodded the all-clear and Annie flicked the remote and watched the steel shutter lazily groan into action, accelerating as it gained momentum. Pepper stepped inside, and Annie drove the BMW in as soon as there was headroom. She reversed the shutter before it had reached the top. There was a short squeal of protest and then the metal curtain started down again. She waited until it locked into place before hitting the lights. Pepper leant over and pulled a ring in the floor, levering up a six-foot section to reveal a shallow ramp running down to a passageway.

Rick had done a good job, here. Electric lights were slung along the underground alley for several hundred yards until they hit the first of the four rooms they called their own. The lights were already on, because Pig was down there on duty, which mainly consisted of watching television, and keeping an eye on the computer to make sure no condition-critical warning came up, in which case he was to call Owl.

Pepper opened a footlocker and brought out a compact Ingram M11 machine pistol and a trio of spare magazines. 'Hey – just in case.' Annie nodded and swapped her coat for a heavy blanket-lined REI number. It could get cold down there away from the plants. She asked Pepper, 'Where do you think they will go in? Henry?'

Pepper shook his head. 'I seen where they coming in. It's perfect – about two blocks from here on Fourth, near Virginia, but it drops down onto that big wide underground street. It's close to the Annex Theater. You know?'

She knew. It was far, far too close for comfort, sandwiching them between the SWOPS and the bus tunnels. She pulled out the Para Ord from her purse and shoved it into the pocket of the jacket. The anger had been growing inside her ever since she spoke to that soldier on the street, growing and feeding and eating, until it was now a strong, healthy thing, healthy enough for her to do whatever was necessary. She had to stop them taking down her operation, and if she had to take somebody down to stop them doing it, so be it. So be fucking it. She felt her stomach knot once more and smiled at Pepper. 'Ready?'

Milliner could pick out the familiar landmarks now. He looked for the Seattle Tower, an elegant Deco gem amidst all the garish steel, always his lodestone for the cityscape. A case of beer for the pilot, that was for sure; he had red-lined the machine all the way from Spokane. For a moment he thought of those times when he had been in a slick that had been hit, gone into autorotation, dropping at 1700 feet per minute, the pilot attempting to get some angle on a machine with the aerodynamics of a house brick. He had had some rough landings, survived them all.

Bad news about the flame-throwers, though, despite that odd dream, the one that came after he read the posters about the bum being burned to death. No longer government-approved issue. Even the National Guard drew a blank. Well, maybe just as well. Maybe the dream was a little warning. The flame-thrower had let him down last time – an honest mistake, sure, but they never let him finish his contract because of it.

He knew where they were going to enter this time. He had instructed Robertson to lift the big steel panel from the lot he had described on Fourth. Going to make a hell of noise, wake a few concerned citizens. What the hell.

He remembered the last few times he was in there, before the flame-thrower incident, the faces on the civic engineers as they discovered that the city was sitting on a rotten core, as if termites had undermined the entire downtown fabric. They had buttressed and supported and made safe, but sooner or later they were going to have to go in and do it properly.

Why not now? he had asked. 'Do you know how much these bus tunnels are costing the city?' one engineer had asked. 'You want Seattle to declare bankruptcy? It's lasted a hundred years, it'll do ten more.'

MacDonald, that was the guy's name. MacDonald and Williams, they had been responsible for the rebuilding after the fire. It was them who had siphoned the funds and signed off jobs that hadn't been done. And it was MacDonald who had squirrelled away a generation's worth of shit into one big underground sump, while billing the city for pipes and treatment. And we thought of graft and corruption and shoddy materials and fraudulent budgets as a modern disease.

'Coming in, Major Milliner,' said the pilot.

Fantastic. Time to remind Seattle how to conduct an H&I. Oh, and get the girl out. Mustn't forget the girl.

Pig looked up with a lazy eye when they entered. He had heard them coming five minutes before, and switched on the CCTV to check it was friends coming along the tunnel. He knew from the look on their faces it was trouble.

The control room was at the northern end of three large, interconnected rooms. Everything within those areas was controlled by a single computer – lighting, humidity, nutrients, heating, the air circulation in the smaller drying room beyond the two growing halls. The two big rooms – once the main storage for illicit booze in the north-west – were now full of miles of steel pipe and banks of very expensive lights – powerful high intensity discharge halides for the vegetative stage, softer sodium lights for when, as would happen in a few days' time, they switched to the twelve-hour on/off cycle that would initiate flowering in this area. In room two, separated from the first by heavy black-out curtains, that cycle had already begun. Soon it would be harvest time.

The hundreds of plants themselves, arranged in rows running away from the control room, sat clamped into a layer of wood fibre suspended over long stainless-steel troughs, with their roots submerged in a constantly changing nutrient broth.

A plant underground needs pretty much what a plant above ground needs. Sunlight, water, a source of nitrogen, a cocktail of essential minerals. The sunlight came from the complex array of lights. The slowly circulating soup was designed by Owl with a precision Mr Heinz would have envied. The roots were fed by aero-hydroponics, the tips of the network dangling in a dissolved mixture of chemical fertiliser, seaweed and gull guano, with needle nozzles bathing the rest of the root system in a fine mist of the chemical broth. The lights could also be raised to allow a nourishing spray of foliage feed (Owl No4, ingredients: classified) to be deposited on the leaves. It was complicated and it was expensive, but those plants, cossetted like rare orchids, would pump out THC until the cows came home.

The rooms were twelve feet high, capped by a modern

suspended ceiling. Above it was the source of the low hum – the air conditioning that was essential to dissipate the heat of the lights – these precious green monsters would fry without it.

And they were monsters: the healthiest plants were hitting seven or eight feet. And each one of these mutants gave a heavy, heavy yield of high quality grass and dope and oil. Ten – count 'em, four more than the best European skunk – crops a year. Most times Annie saw them she marvelled at their elegance, their beauty. Their very attitude suggested what they were capable of, the way they lolled in a kind of blissed out loose-leafed fashion. Even if you had never seen a dope plant before, you could guess what these mothers could do to your brain.

But for once she failed to notice their vegetative charms. 'We got trouble,' said Annie tersely.

'I figured,' said Pig. 'Cops?'

Pepper laughed. 'If only, bro', if only. We got the fuckin' National Guard coming in.'

Annie cut him off and explained the situation.

'This guy and the kid. They headin' our way?'

'Who knows?' said Annie ruefully. 'But when I find out who it is, I'm gonna shoot his balls off. One by one.'

Pig and Pepper exchanged glances. Bitch would an' all. It wasn't that much of a jump up from kneecaps.

Pig said, 'But the only way into this place is the way you just came. We sealed everything else.'

'Yeah?' said Pepper. 'They could easily spot the new cinderblock and decide to take a peek.' Ricky had rebuilt parts of the wall to hide the rooms from prying eyes, but his best attempts had failed to disguise that they were a mixture of recent and ancient vintage. It was possible that anyone who got too close might do some digging to see what was behind such endeavour.

'OK,' said Annie, stopping the discussion. 'There is only one thing we can do, short of shutting up shop. Get the guy and the girl and—'

She stopped when she heard her name. Was it her name? Whispering through the plants, blowing between the leaves. Was she cracking up? 'Annie?' Now the others heard it too. They exchanged puzzled glances, of the who-the-fuck variety.

Pepper cocked the Ingram, and the three of them felt the blast of hot air as they stepped in among the precious plants of room one.

PART THREE

The Seattle Metro underground bus tunnels were opened on September 15, 1990 (after an aborted ceremony on September 3). They run for 1.5 miles in an L-shape from Ninth Avenue, down beneath Pine Street, then along Third Avenue to the International District. There are five stations. The system cost $479 million, and involved the movement of 900,000 cubic yards of earth. The average depth of the tunnel is sixty feet below ground. The Italian buses are made to convert from diesel to electric upon entering the tunnel. They are extremely temperamental. Every station contains hanging silver spheres – 40 closed-circuit cameras. Pictures are fed to the Tunnel Control Center at the Metro HQ in the Exchange Building at 821 Second Avenue. From here, electricity can be switched off and on, stations monitored, and fires extinguished using the deluge system. Even though the tunnels close to buses at night, the desk is manned 24-hours a day. Security is provided in the tunnels by Metro's own force, mainly consisting of off-duty Seattle PD officers.

THIRTY-SEVEN

Big Mac FSB, Vietnam. 1970.

Tran slowly eased up the trapdoor and raised his head. Up above the last of the daylight was fading, and a cloudless sky was attempting to unveil its consignment of stars, but the lights from the camp's perimeter fence provided stiff competition.

Tran had hoped never to see this base again. He had moved on months ago, satisfied that it had been neutralised. Why waste time on an army too demoralised, too drug-infested, to even send out night patrols? For weeks he had listened to them enter the trees or even just the long grass and flop down to while away the hours smoking and joking. All it took was to kill one every now and then, or even to maim one with a trap, and they stayed in their base. His job done, he had switched his attention to some of the ARVIN bases fringing the Iron Triangle.

But things had changed. The last time he had popped up out of this trapdoor, it had been behind the grass and tree cover. Now it was almost in the open, such had been the extent of clearance. Refugees had been shipped in to machete the undergrowth, extending the base's size. Every day they went to work, their numbers shrunken by ones and twos from cutting accidents or bamboo viper bites. But every day they came back for a few pathetic piasters to hack and pick and pull for the Yankees. And then came the sappers, laying barbed wire and claymores and listening devices

He took out the Starlight scope he had liberated from an American patrol some weeks before and scanned the base. It had changed. There were freshly erected platoon tents – GPs the Americans called them – crammed with new troops. Not the desultory, enervated excuse for fighting men that he had left behind, but well motivated and led by all accounts. And some of them were old hands – Lurps, the long-range patrols who weren't frightened to take a walk in the dark. Plus fresh helicopters and pilots. And now it looked as if a major expansion was underway – the usual motley crew of Vietnamese hangers-on had appeared, liberally laced, of course, with informers, but even they knew little.

He scanned the compound to the sand-bagged building at the south of the helicopter landing ground and its satellite of GPs. Now there was a funny thing. These Joes never even got their hair cut by the regular barbers, and the barbers were his best source of information. The 'scuttlebutt' from the clippers was that the men in that hut were tunnel fighters, but little else was forthcoming.

He rotated the night-sight to focus it on the building, trying to pick out detail in the green screen. It was at the limit of its range, and confused by the light from the fence lamps, but he could make out a group of men sat outside their tents, relaxing as the heat of the day subsided, lazily swatting away mosquitoes. They were of small stature, so the information was probably right.

Even from this distance, he could hear them laughing, a relaxed, confident laugh. A bad, bad sign. Little happy men. When he had moved operations to the west, there was very little in the way of laughing going on, particularly at night.

He was startled by the sound of a helicopter starting up, a whine followed by a roar as the turbines caught. He watched it as the spinning rotor coned for maximum power, agitating the earth and sending up a flurry of dust and pushing itself free. It was one of those equipped with speakers – soon it would be flying over telling tales of unhappy ancestors and unfaithful wives.

Tran slid back down into the ground and repositioned the lid. He hunched on the ledge and ate a handful of his rice ration. He had to knock them back down again, these Americans, just like they were swatting the mosquitoes. And he knew how to do it. One particular blow had traumatised Cu Chi Base. The same would work for Ben Moc. But there was a lot of digging to be done.

THIRTY-EIGHT

Underworld. Seattle.

'What? What is it? I saved her goddamn life in there and you have blanked me ever since.'

The Captain stopped and hoisted Ali up further onto his shoulder. 'Because you, son, are a fucking idiot.'

'Why? Because of the Thin White Duke back there. Who is going to miss him?'

'Myrtle for a start.'

'Well I should've popped him, too.'

'And me as well?'

'I thought about it – you were taking so damn' long to make up your mind about the police cruiser—'

'HE MAKES THAT OFFER EVERY TIME, YOU MORON.'

Hilton didn't say anything. He realised they were passing Sammy Napoleon-whatever-his-name-was's place, close to back where the attack had taken place, and it made him jumpy. And he still wasn't sure about this phony cop. Maybe he was in on the weird set-up, and Hilton blew it, that was why he was pissed.

'The cruiser . . . it is his opening offer, the one he thinks he can hook me with. It's a game. OK, they play a little rough, but how long do you think we would last if we started killing each other? The rules are – you don't kill. Doesn't matter what you do up top – we're all down here because of something terrible up there. Some of us more terrible than others. But when you come into the Underworld, you don't kill each other. Not down here. Overlanders do that.'

'I'm an overlander.'

'YOU WERE WITH ME. With me. My responsibility. They will blame me.'

Hilton snorted: 'Well for cryin' out loud—'

'Stop it, stop it, stop it.' The Captain put Ali down with a start as he realised she was speaking. 'Stop it. Stop arguing. Please.' And she began to cry, little sobs that came as gasps mixed in with, 'Please stop. Please.'

The Captain looked at Hilton and shrugged. Hilton crouched and took her shoulders firmly, not creepily like those others were touching her. ''S OK, kid, home stretch. See the finishing line now. All over.'

She nodded and yawned. 'Thanks for coming . . . coming back. I didn't . . . didn't think you would.'

Never mind that she wouldn't have been there but for him. Thank God kids don't think things through too much. 'What? First rule of kidnapping. Never lose your hostage. Smacks of amateurism.'

He stood up. 'She OK?'

'I think they just gave her something to make her drowsy. I trade it with them now and then. Just a mild sedative. Is that right, sport?'

'Some medicine, yes. I spat most of it out. I am fine, now. Who were those men? And that woman with the strange voice?'

'Assholes,' said Hilton, 'ain't that right, Captain? Captain?' He lowered his voice. 'So I caused you trouble. I'm . . . I didn't know.'

'Don't worry, I'll make peace with Myrtle. He's still showing male pattern baldness. A case of hair tonic will make him forget Whitey.' But it didn't sound like he believed it. More than a dose of Regain was going to be needed to make this one right.

A petulant Ali said: 'Can we go? I'm getting cold now.'

It was a strange construction, the wall. Most of it was old masonry blocks, hastily but well built, but here and there it had been breached over the years and repaired with later materials, mostly bricks and cinder block. The most recent looked like steel panels. Hilton put his hand on it. It was vibrating. He thought he could hear a low hum from beyond.

'This was the site of the big bootlegger stand-off,' said the Captain. 'One hundred and fifty police kept busy by fourteen bootleggers. They'd built the wall, you see. Had left holes for defence. Jeez, the cops lost a lot of men.'

'And the bootleggers?'

'Seven wounded, two dead, rest escaped. Police and Feds sealed off as much as they could both here and street level after that.'

'When was that?' asked Ali.

'1931.'

'Wow.'

'Year I was born, little lady. Year I was born. Look, this will get you through.'

He walked up and traced the outline of a wooden square, about two foot across at ground level. 'Now, we could try crawling through this, or . . . well, we could go under.'

'Under?' Hilton dropped Ali down to the ground.

'Across Lake Shiticaca.' Ali giggled again. 'There is the remains of a walkway across it . . . but you got to be pretty good at holding your breath.'

'No, thanks. We'll be OK here.'

'No, hold up, hold up. Give me ten minutes to get away. I can't guarantee any friend of yours will be a friend to me.'

'Sure, OK.'

'I have your word on that.'

'I said, yeah.' Stupid old man. 'Ten minutes. And we never saw you.'

The Captain held out his hand. Hilton was about to take it when he realised it was pointing at Ali. 'Pleased to have met you. But I'd think of another career if I were you. Other than store robbing, I mean.'

'The pleasure was mine, sir,' said Ali in a well-rehearsed way. 'And I will.'

Hilton took the hand and felt the calluses and warts but forced himself to squeeze hard. 'Thanks. And, you know, the dead guy. Tell Myrtle . . . well . . .'

'Ten minutes.'

The Captain had barely gone five yards when he switched out his flashlight and the darkness wrapped around them. Just the merest hint of grey from above. Not enough to even make out shapes by. Hilton fumbled for his little keyring light and flicked it on. It was dry next to the wall and he hunkered down next to the panel. He'd give him two minutes. He tested the edges of the section with his fingers.

'Hey, what you doin'?'

'Just seeing how it opens.'

'You promised him ten minutes.'

'He doesn't need ten minutes. Guy's like a bat. Probably back in his little den already, hangin' from the beam.'

'Leave it.'

'Hey, shut the fuck up.'

'Leave it or I'll say you raped me.'

'What? For God's sake . . . Oh, come on. I haven't touched you. They won't fall for that. Those freaks never touched you there. They can do tests—' And then he remembered the father.

'By that time you'll have been roughed up pretty good, though. Cops don't like –' she pitched her voice at a sneer – 'Child molesters. Perverts. Sickos.'

'Hey, you're something else, you know that? This is some fuckin' weird shit.'

'Fuckin' weird,' she repeated.

'If I'd wanted a parrot I'da brought one along . . . OK, ten minutes. Ten minutes. Christ, you're a hard-nosed little bitch for an eight-year-old, aincha?'

'I do my best.' Jeez, whatever they had given her had worn off fast. They sat in silence for a few seconds. 'Ever see Gilligan's Island?'

'Gilligan's Island? You're too young to remember that.'

'It's on cable.'

'Right.' The eternal twilight zone of all television shows. Come to think of it, he was probably too young to remember it from the first time round. 'Bunch of people on an island, trying to get off.'

'I wonder if this is like that. We'll just keep coming back to the old man at the end of every show.'

'I seem to remember Gilligan's Island was funny. That

ain't funny.' And then he started to laugh. 'Yeah – well at least they had guest stars. Maybe we could have a few – Letterman. Seinfeld. Although how those guests got off and on the island always puzzled me. Know what I mean? And anyway, there was one big, important difference between that set-up and ours – those chicks were all grown up.'

'Thanks a bunch.'

'You know what I mean. Real women.' Shit, what was the redhead called? Tina something. He snapped the thought from his head, 'There was a sequel, you know.'

'Yeah? Return to Gilligan's Island? Gilligan Rides Again?'

'Nah, they remade it as Dusty's Trail. Same plot, same people, only they was cowboys. Lost wagon train going round in circles. Now that's more us. Wasn't funny, though.'

'Really.' Offhand now.

He gave up. He couldn't seem to pitch the conversation quite right. Or maybe she was upset by his insistence it would be better if she was a real woman. And now he couldn't get that stupid theme song from the start of the programme out of his head. Who'd brought up Gilligan anyway?

'Ten minutes yet?' he asked after a while.

'I guess.'

The panel came away easily, leading to a short passage, with a steel square at the far end. He hesitated and looked at Ali. She huffed. 'Like, I'm going to run off here and fall into Lake Shiticaca or run into Myrtle?'

Hilton dived in and scrabbled his way to the far end,

feeling the vibration in the air getting louder, and pushed the square back.

The light that came in nearly cauterised his retinas. He winced in pain as it flooded into the little tunnel, blooming in the inky streets behind them. He cursed as he pulled himself into the room, and felt the heat envelope him. It was delicious, but his eyes had closed up to tiny water-filled slits.

He felt Ali at his side, and knew from the way she groped for his hand she was experiencing the same blinding reaction. 'I can't see, Hilton.'

'Hold on, hold on, it'll pass.' He put an arm round her shoulder. He blinked and squeezed and felt a tear run down one cheek. As his vision unblurred he could hardly believe what he was seeing.

Tall plants swayed gently in the circulating air, flapping, and waving and nodding, wafting their scent – a mixture of sweet and sharp – towards them. Hundreds of them stretched in each direction it seemed, like a botanical army being bred for battle. And the atmosphere was vibrating, with the throb of air conditioning working overtime.

Ali looked up at him. 'Are these . . . ?'

He nodded. 'Sure are, kid. There must be . . . Jeez, I had no idea.'

About twenty feet in front of him the accumulated light from the rows of lights suspended from the ceiling created an impervious wall of luminescence beyond which he couldn't see. But he knew Annie had to be round here somewhere. He took the gun out of his waistband and shoved it down the back of his pants – no need to look intimidating. He grabbed Ali's hand and said quietly: 'Look, they may be a bit, you know, pissed at first. But it'll be OK.'

She smiled and nodded.

'Annie?' he asked tentatively, and felt his words sucked away into the undergrowth, and fade among the huge leaves. 'Annie?' He coughed a little to clear his throat. 'ANNIE.'

He heard a door slam. They'd be all right now.

THIRTY-NINE

'We was stood down for the weekend. Some of them had gone into Saigon, including the Kit Carsons. KCs? They were turned North Vietnamese, VCs who had had enough. They helped us find the tunnels. They could spot trapdoors we'd walk right over. So who was left? There was me and Fix, Hobbs, Arnold . . . I remember he was reading The Green Lantern. Hobbs is banging on about the battle of Dong Khe, about the French Foreign Legion versus the gooks, while Arnold is taking in 'By darkest day, by blackest night . . .' Remember that? Nah. Well, Lewis is writing up the book.

'I . . . yeah, this was funny, I was playing Fix some music. We was talking. I told him about this . . . my lucky charm. Del Cielo, my father's favourite fighting rooster. Yeah, that's what he does – what he did, he was a woodcarver. Anyway, I was playing some salsa – it was new back then, he'd never heard any – and trying to show him how to dance. I told him he danced like a fuckin' dodo. Well, it was his expression. Always saying dead as a dodo, I told him he moved like one of his dodos. I didn't know what a dodo was back then even . . . didn't have 'em in Puerto Rico. I mean, I know they don't have 'em anywhere . . . anyway, white boys can't do that shit, can't move their hips, haven't got the steps. I tried to show him, y'know, a dancing lesson, but I guess he thought it was faggoty. So I played him some Miles . . . new Miles, In A Silent Way, but he didn't like that either, so I asked him if he wanted to get off his face.

'Yeah, yeah, I know you heard all about the drugs in Vietnam. Let me tell you, Underdogs didn't do it. You didn't go down tunnels stoned, not if you wanted to come out. But the letter from my brother, when he sent the Miles over, that had some good high-grade acid on it. Not the fuckin' brain-Drano they sold around the bases, good and clean. And we had the weekend off. But Fix was worried. Worried about what happened in Saigon, y'know with the dope and the girls, and worried about Lewis. I told him the Major was going to see his family the next day, so we could recover in peace. And then . . . well, I shouldn't have told him. Fix said – he's going back to the US? And I said no, he's going to see his Viet family. It wasn't that unusual . . . he had the wife back home and another in Saigon, and a kid. I just . . . I just forgot how it might seem to an FNG like Fix. But you know, Lewis had been giving him all this moral stuff . . . well, Fix just grabbed that acid and gulped it down. Fuck it, he must have thought. I don't know if it was the speed or what, but he was there taxiing before I even got on the runway, big wide eyes, stupid grin. Got up and tried to dance. Still looked like a fuckin' dodo. Then the slick came in, the one that used to go out at dusk every night to broadcast to the gooks, telling them their wives were being poked by pig farmers while they were busy eating earth in the South. Can you imagine what it looked like?

A great streak of white in the sky from the nose lights, the faces of the pilots lit red by the controls, the noise from the rotors. Beautiful, we thought. I could see the look on Fix's face, the wonder, he said it was like an enormous flower opening. It wasn't until the blast hit us we realised it was blowing up.'

'What do you think happened? All hell broke loose. Lewis, Hobbs and Wayland came running. I took Fix round the back and made him sick. I put my goddamn fingers down his mouth, what do you think? No, I don't fuckin' know whether it was the right thing to do. It was all I could think of. Yeah, you're right, probably too late. Then the rest of the Hueys went up. Boom, boom, boom. The base was in flames, it looked like . . . it looked like hell. Lewis, though, he kept his head. He got a NOD – night observation device – and started looking for the mortar positions. Then he saw the guy, this thin scrawny gook with a rocket launcher on *our* side of the fence. They'd tunnelled in. The Vietnamese were inside the base. God, Lewis was mad. He watched the guy disappear and ordered us after him. Now this was crazy, you don't go down tunnels at night. And you don't do it in a hurry, if you know what I mean. But Lewis was . . . he was all fired up, not himself. He was stuttering, can you believe? Scared me. He didn't really notice how fucked up me and Fix were, he got us over to the perimeter fence, to the hole, and insisted on going point. He always used a Swedish K submachine gun, but he swapped with Fix for Fix's gun, and Fix looked all pleased and proud, until he realised what was happening. And then *he* got scared, too. I think me and Fix was both thinking the same thing – and it wasn't the residual acid, believe me – we both knew we weren't going to get out of that tunnel alive.'

FORTY

Underworld. Seattle.

'Annie?'

Hilton took a few tentative steps forward, heard his steps get lost in the lazy rustle of leaves stirred by the air-conditioning fans.

'ANNIE?'

'Keep your goddamn voice down.'

She stepped from a gap in the steel troughs that nourished and supported the plants. She was flanked by two big guys, both armed. Well, they had property to protect; how were they to know it was a friendly intrusion?

The trio just stood there, eyes flicking between the ill-clad, crap-caked pair in front of them, a mismatched couple if ever they had seen one. The little girl had nestled up close to the guy's leg, and he was stroking her hair, which looked more like something you would feed to horses. Annie narrowed her eyes and mentally wiped away the grime and the flecks of blood from scratches and the grimy stubble and matted out the halo of redness that encircled the eyes. She felt her shoulders slump. 'Hilton. I might have known.'

He grinned at that and took another pace forward. Pepper swung the Ingram up. 'Stay put.' He walked over and expertly patted Hilton down, finding the Hardballer inside five seconds. He stepped back.

'Annie, look . . . I'm sorry to jump in like this. I mean, I can see you got a sweet set-up here, but me and the kid, we got some trouble.'

'You got trouble?' she spluttered. 'You have brought half of Seattle's law-enforcement agencies down here, and you think YOU got trouble. Look at all this. LOOK AT IT. You think they gonna say – sorry, ma'am, but have you seen a psycho and a little girl? No, well just go about your business. Does this look like it's for personal consumption?'

Hilton could feel a stew of moisture forming under his clothes. The lights threw off a hefty belt of warmth, but he suspected it wasn't just that causing the sweat to start trickling. He could taste that familiar metallic tang in his mouth, the one that always told him he should be real scared about now. His tired, aching brain was finally catching up with Annie's.

He caught the look. Had seen it before. Whenever Ricky hesitated, Annie came in with that look: do what you have to do. Do what you have to do. The phrase echoed around his head. What you have to do. Have to do. Do.

It was a movement he got from a time of humping sacks at the feed suppliers, before he realised what a sucker's life that was. But it was in his muscles and skeleton like a pre-set sequence, just punch the button and go. He grabbed the collar of her jacket – his jacket – with his right hand, and swept up under her ass with the left, powering her on up.

Annie, Pig and Pepper stood open-mouthed as Ali took off, flying though the air, and disappeared over the top of the dope plants.

* * *

Milliner opened the rear doors and climbed into the Transaif Multi-Role Armoured Vehicle parked in the lot on Occidental below the SWOPS base, and waited impatiently as the others ducked under the slowing rotors and followed him down the metal staircase that led from the roof. He was keen to get downtown, get among them again. After all the pussyfooting over the years, here was the chance to finish unclosed business. Shit, it was almost genuine H&I – make the place uninhabitable for the enemy, deny them succour of any kind, push them to where you want them.

The driver said, 'Sergeant Robertson wants to know if they should hit the lights yet, sir.'

'Whenever he is ready. And tell them I want the entrance open and primed with a ladder. We'll be there in . . . eight minutes. We will be there in eight minutes, won't we?'

The driver gunned the Mercedes engine impatiently. 'Yes, sir.'

Ali felt the leaves brushing her face as she clipped the top of the plants. She wasn't spinning, it was a perfect trajectory, like a long, extended dive. Except it wasn't water she was going to hit, she realised, but concrete. Below her she was aware of the greenery and the steel, flashing by, and she reached out and began grabbing handfuls of vegetation and letting go, feeling it tear away in her hands, then reaching for some more. She was slowing, slowing, dropping now.

The big plant loomed up suddenly, right in her path and she reached out to embrace it, hugged it to herself, felt it bend under her weight, and slowly, gracefully, arc over and lower her to the floor between the troughs. She rolled, crashed into some pipework and lay still. She could hear shouting, abuse, running. They would be coming soon.

The Transaif was an Anglo-German design for Special Forces and Bomb squads, and Milliner had picked it up from Portland Police Special Emergency Reaction Team, which decided to stick with its Grumman van after evaluation. Milliner thought they were crazy – this was a freeway cruiser and armoured car all in one, able to withstand a high-velocity rifle shot at point-blank range. Designed to take fourteen, there was plenty of room for his small team to arm up en route, and he watched them with pride as they turned from silhouettes of men, into something bulkier, more business-like.

Starting from scratch he had been able to cherry-pick the best equipment from around the world, and he had been like a kid in a particularly deadly candy store. From the Israeli Ya'ma'm to the Brits' SAS he had plundered the anti-terrorist/covert operations subculture for appropriate outfitting.

The Nomex coveralls were British – light, tough and with great ease of movement. On top of that came the Kevlar body armour, by Armitron of the US, overlaid with the Eagle Industries TAC-4 assault vest, bristling with pockets, but highly modular, so each trooper could custom-build where he wanted his magazines, flashlights, gasmasks. The balaclava was SEAL Team 6 issue, the Orlite helmet Israeli. The throat mikes they were fitting were from David Industries of the UK, with lightweight ear defenders – designed to filter out gunshots and blast noise – housing the speaker system. A mike system was also included into the SF-11 Respirators they routinely carried. The grenades they were pocketing into their vests were plastic-cased Kilgore/Schermuly Mk V stun grenades, the safest models for use in hostage situations, all bang and bright light, but no fragments to make things messy.

Knives were the Tanto Razor, a Japanese blade used by the Belgian ESI, highly effective in close combat, and the SEAL's SOG SK2000. Like almost every other special force in the world, for sheer firepower he had opted for the Heckler and Koch MP5 submachine-gun system, with full add-on – flashlights, infra-red sighting, optional suppressors. Milliner himself used the Knight Armaments Company Modular Weapons System, based on the Colt RO927 carbine with the ITT Pocketscope and the Aimpoint 5000. The German guns may be better assault weapons, but when it came to something hefty, he preferred Made in America to be stamped on the breach.

Similarly the pistols they were strapping to their thighs were Sig-Sauer P228s, the finest handgun in the world (as created by those peace-loving Swiss). Based on the gun that was beaten into second place in US Army trials by the Beretta 92, its sole failing was that it was hideously expensive. The men loved them. Milliner himself, however, tended to mistrust the 9mm round, especially one with a reduced load like he had specified, because the lighter weight meant that you needed three, four shots to bring your assailant down. Up the charge and the bullet had a tendency to pass through the perp and hit innocent bystanders. So the gun he strapped onto his own thigh was the Colt Offensive Handgun Weapons System, which chambers ten rounds of the slow moving .45 ACP. When they found this little girl, he wanted to put a shot in that would stop the guy stone-dead.

Racked on the internal walls of the Transaif were the other additional tools of the trade – shotguns (Remington 870s and a Dragon 12×12, with the dozen 12-gauge cartridges housed in a circular magazine, like the old Thompson submachine guns), a Barnett Power Crossbow, An-M8 smoke grenades, M6A1 CN/DM tear/vomit-gas grenades, door-prying poles, battering rams, armoured shields, everything the Special Force operative could ever desire.

'You will need helmet lights,' Milliner announced as they neared the end of their preparation. 'In case the street overheads don't work – and they will not penetrate everywhere. And also, just in case, the NVGs.' – Pus-8s the very latest night-viewing goggles – 'Collins, take the crossbow. And I suggest suppressors on the H&Ks; it will get very noisy down there in a firefight.'

'Respirators, sir?'

'At the ready. Point man – make it Marzo – will mask up and activate the BioChem detector, the rest of us will keep our distance and deploy respirators if the audible alarm sounds. OK?'

The driver turned around and examined his cargo, who had changed from the men of a few minutes ago to strange barrel-chested, insect-like creatures, heavily exoskeletoned, bristling with odd-shaped protuberances. 'One minute, Major. Oh, and Sergeant Robertson said he loaded something special for you,' he shouted over his shoulder. 'Under the tarp.'

The Major smiled, reached over and pulled the sheet off. 'Ha. My little Beauty.'

The van pulled to a halt and there was a metallic chorus as gunslides were pulled and safeties checked and magazines piggy-backed together and suppressors slid home. Milliner picked up his surprise package, grabbed his CSS infra-red viewer/imager and Sure Fire tactical light, guaranteed to temporarily burn out the retinas of anyone who got in its way. Things were looking good.

Annie stood looking at Hilton for a good ten seconds, both in disbelief and a sort of admiration that a low-life like him should even think about someone else at a time like this. It was touching almost. She walked behind him, and with one vicious kick scythed his legs from behind, sending him flailing backwards. She watched with satisfaction as his head bounced off the rough concrete, sending his two front teeth out into the air and bouncing away under the nearest trough. She turned to Pig and Pepper and hissed: 'Find her.'

Pig headed for the wall where the duo had gained access to the rooms, in case she was retracing her steps, even though Hilton had thrown her in the opposite direction.

Pepper ran to the far corner to begin a methodical search. He felt the muscle in his lower back protesting as he scuttled, crab-like, occasionally dipping down as if he was performing push-ups, examining the underneath of each metal unit, squinting between the metallic guts that ran there, looking for a leg here, a hint of a body there, until he and Pig met head-on. They did the same for the plants, parting the stems and leaves, rustling them to make sure she wasn't clinging to a stem like a human greenfly.

It took them three minutes to realise she had gone completely.

'No sign,' said Pepper to Annie breathlessly, waiting for the torrent of abuse. 'Looks like she made it.'

FORTY-ONE

'Why are you so interested in the gun? Yes, I know it's strange, but people do invent things, you know. OK, well I got the full shit on this from Fix – so proud of the goddamn thing – so I do know about it. For a start I know you don't call them silencers. They only do that in the movies. They's called suppressors, 'cause that is what they do – they suppress the sound, rather than, y'know, remove it altogether. Now, having a quiet pistol wasn't new. The OSS had one in the Second World War, and – look, shouldn't we get going? I mean, time is moving on. All right, all right – we still had some of those Hi-Standards in Nam, had tried them down the tunnels, but they tended to clog up down there. Then there were the Hush Puppies. I think the SEALS called them that, cause what they wanted it for was shooting sentries and so on, but some of the top brass – those that hadn't quite got their heads around covert operations like Phoenix – thought that . . . what's the word . . . ungentlemanly. These guys are thinkin' it is the sort of war where people say things like: "Stop. Who goes there. Friend or foe?" Yeah, really. So the SEALS said, no, every time we approach a village the dogs bark and give our position away, so we need to take 'em out quietly. Hence, Hush Puppy. But they killed more than dogs with those things

I guess. Now Fix he told me how these things work – what you got to do is slow the bullet down to subsonic speed, 'cause it is the breaking of the sound barrier that causes the noise. Silen— suppressors have these plates in – washers, wipes, I think they were called, that the bullet goes through that reduces the velocity. No, you can't fire it slow – wouldn't come out of the barrel. You gotta fire it fast and *then* slow it down. What is this? The Guns and Ammo Helpline? OK, OK. You also got to get rid of the gases quietly. Well, what he did was build one of these things using surfboard technology. The bullet passed through some sort of honeycomb system that wiped away the speed, and the gases were released into this other, expanding foam stuff, and bled out through a series of holes along the barrel. I dunno, that's what he told me. He learnt it all from surfing. Anyways, it worked, because you could fire two hundred rounds through this thing before the suppressor unit needed replacing. It was twenty-four, I think, on the Hush Puppy. The other thing is you could select single shot or semi-auto. On semi-auto you still heard the slide action, on single it was real quiet. Even if you heard the noise it was hard to tell where it had come from. Yeah, it was clever. It had one big design fault, though – I don't think it was meant to be used to kill Americans, y'know what I mean?'

FORTY-TWO

Underworld. Seattle.

Ali could feel herself floating. Not like when she had been thrown, but an odd feeling, closer to the one she had had when those men, those things, had taken her and danced with her, round her. It was dark and suffocatingly warm, but oddly cosy, reassuring after those harsh lights. The strange smell filled her nostrils, like tendrils flowing up her nasal passages and caressing her brain. It was nice here. She lay down next to one of the warm pipes that ran beneath the steel troughs holding the plants. She could feel the slow gurgle of liquids pulsing through, echoing the flow of blood through her veins, could sense the slow, gentle rustling of the vegetation above, waving in the lazy circulating air, building up their strength, ready to burst forth. It was nice in here, she thought again. Maybe she could just curl up and wait and they would leave her alone. Maybe without her there wouldn't be any trouble. They would show Hilton the way out, and later, much later, she could go looking for her mom. Strange she hadn't thought about her. Or her dad. Not for quite some time. Time. What time was it? It was hard to tell, so much had happened, so much of it seemed like a dream. Had she really seen that man with the breasts? And those rats? She shuddered at the thought.

Would they figure it out that, instead of making for the wall where she and Hilton had come in, as they would expect, she had rolled into the next room, the dark room, and was hiding there? She had no idea how big it was, how many feet or even miles these tanks went on for, how high the ceiling was, how many plants there were. She suddenly felt very alone, as if she had been stranded in a giant nocturnal jungle. At least she hoped she was alone.

She heard the soft rustle, saw a brief flash of light, a soft step.

They'd realised.

But why hadn't they turned the lights on?

Because the plants need the dark, stupid, came the reply. They are trying to make them do something. Remember biology, periods of light and dark, growing seeds, et – et – etiolation, flowering. If they turned the lights on it would ruin the . . . what was it called? Photo—

The steps were three, maybe four rows away from her. She saw a quick flare of a beam slicing through the dark, running under the metalwork, shone at a right angle to the rows of plants, penetrating at floor level perhaps twenty feet away from her head.

Photoperiod, that was it.

Slowly she gripped the top of the trough and hooked one foot over the lip and pulled. She remembered the soccer training exercises, the arm and leg strengthening that Mr King made them do, a powerful goalkeeper, that's what he said he needed. She concentrated on contracting her thigh muscles to raise herself up. Then her foot slipped off the shiny surface and the buckle of her shoe made a faint scratching sound as it caught the metal.

The footsteps stopped.

She rehooked with the back of her ankle and pulled herself up off the ground, hearing Mr King's voice. 'Hold it, hold it, fifteen more seconds, don't give in . . .', dangling by her right arm and foot, closing the other limbs up close, making herself small, small, smaller, as little as she could be, like the hedgehog shape Mr King taught her to adopt whenever she dived in and grabbed the ball from the striker's feet, a perfect immune sphere. As she contracted she pulled up the tail of Hilton's jacket that was trailing on the floor, flattening her body against the side of the trough as the flashlight burst beneath where she had been lying a moment before. She clung on, her breathing frozen now, muscles twitching and spasming as the lactic acid built up, wondering what she had done to deserve this, what the little girl who woke up that morning looking forward to a camping trip had changed into. Some kind of frightened mouse, that's what.

The next beam flickered on and off, fifteen feet away from her feet. They had missed her.

Six more attempts to catch her and the footsteps receded. She heard the rubberized curtain rustle. Gone.

She lowered herself down, and shook her arm and leg, tingling now from the effort. Maybe they wouldn't be back.

'Ali.'

Oh no. She tried to block out the harsh grating voice coming from beyond the curtain, to hum a song, to sing. She couldn't think of a single tune, only nursery rhymes. 'The Queen of—'

But it was no good, even buried as it was under a mélange of childish chants, the meaning of the shouts still came through.

'Yankee Doodle—'

The image the voice was describing kept forming, solidifying, the edges becoming less fuzzy, the faces clearer.

'Humpty Dumpty—'

Hilton was on the floor. Annie had her foot on his throat.

'Old King Cole was a merry—'

The gun was pointed at his kneecap.

'Jack and Jill—'

The woman started counting, barking, the words grating and screeching like polystyrene on glass. In the mental picture the hammer was back on the pistol.

And now Ali couldn't remember another rhyme. The counting seemed to have stopped. The image moved on, she saw the blood and bone mix in with the dust from the floor, Hilton's face contort into agony, his back arch as he thrashed around. She waited for the boom of the gun. But it didn't come. It hadn't happened yet. The image was telling her, warning her. She saw the second knee dissolve into a tangled mass of tissue.

'All right,' Ali suddenly found herself yelling. 'I'm coming.'

FORTY-THREE

The Ready-Park 24-Hour Lot, Fourth Avenue and Virginia, Seattle. 3.05 am

It really hadn't been his fault. The thought flashed through Milliner's mind as they prepared to disembark the utility vehicle. Not his fault. They had worked in three-man teams – one flame-thrower, one firefighter to douse any stray flame, and an armed back-up. He had gone down to demonstrate the principle. There were rats everywhere, cocky, aggressive little bastards with attitude. Workmen, tunnel security, even a journalist had been bitten and had to have a butt full of jabs to stop them developing one disease or another. They had tried mass poisoning, but they were smart, too. He supposed you didn't get to be so ubiquitous by being stupid.

The shelter had been in the most fetid part of the whole area, one that had required respirators to stop yourself gagging. It was a real nest, a mad cobbling together of wood, plastic, straw, mud and timber. Security had already said it was cleaned when he had pulled the trigger on the American Beauty – it was a strange name for a flame-thrower, he had to admit, the designer must have been stoned watching the flames when he came up with it – and then the madman attacked him. He hadn't meant to burn him, he just turned to face him, and up he went. Well, the back-up had got the foam on him, put him out and they had tried to hold him for a medic to get to him, but he wriggled away. Must have died, with those burns, half his face gone.

And then the lettering on the bus. And the posters started the accusations. The nest hadn't been empty. Someone was in there. Couldn't have been. They'd checked. Unless he had gone inside the shelter in the fifteen minutes between the checking and the torching. But there were no screams, nothing. It wasn't his fault, he thought, as he shouldered the Beauty onto his shoulder. Collateral damage.

The one called Pig – it wasn't hard for Hilton to see how he acquired that monicker – went through the hole in the wall first, and covered them with his Police Special while Ali and then Hilton struggled through. Pepper brought up the rear. He had the machine pistol plus Hilton's .45 in his belt. Annie had stayed behind, she was going to shut down the halogens and turn off the air conditioning so as not to attract attention. The plants could take a couple of hours of silent, dark running, she had said. Nobody had said exactly what Pig and Pepper were meant to do, but then nobody had to. Even Ali had gone quiet, the cockiness replaced by a sad, doleful look.

Hilton rubbed his jaw, still aching from the earlier blow, as was the back of his head where it had cracked the concrete after Annie took his legs out. He wasn't sure his skull could take much more. Still, at least he'd got his teeth back. And, for the moment, both kneecaps were intact.

He wondered if Ali fully realised that they were dead meat. Her coming out hadn't changed anything. Probably made it a bit less painful for him, for which he was grateful, but the plan still stood. They would shoot Ali and make it look like the scumsucking kidnapper had done it and hope the police would happily say case closed. Killed poor Alice, then blew his own brains out. End of Story. The sick fuck.

'What about the girl?' he asked Pepper as they started their walk, retracing the route they had come with the Captain. She caught the whisper and looked over, managing a weak smile in the torchlight. He winked.

Pepper ignored him, adjusted the flashlight to wide beam, and motioned them on. From above Hilton could hear the rumble of trucks. The real, genuine world was only fifteen, twenty feet above them. He wished he could just grab the girl and levitate right on out of there. Wouldn't even mind doing the time at this point. He was sure he could skip the death penalty. It was an accident. Almost self-defence. Maybe the video tape in the store would back him up. Thought he was going to get his head smashed in. How was he to know it was only a plastic bottle? How was he to know he was going to end up getting the daughter capped, too?

He reached out and took Ali's hand. He wondered where death figured in her overview of life. Probably nowhere until tonight. Well, he had changed all that – that egg was seriously laid.

The ground started to descend, and Hilton could see the twisted stumps on the exposed metal reinforcements that protruded from one of the collapsed sections. He knew where they were now. Sure enough the smell, the odour of ancient decay started.

'Smoke?' he asked.

'No thanks,' said Pepper.

'No—' He bit on the words: 'you dumbfuck'. 'Can I have one? Just two blasts to fill the lungs. In the absence of a hearty breakfast, if you get my drift.'

Pepper nodded and Pig took out a pack of Winston Lites and shook one free.

'Lites? Hey – you frightened a full-strength one gonna damage my health?'

Pepper laughed. He kind of liked the guy.

'I got some in my coat—' He pointed at Alice.

Pig searched the pockets and came up with a battered, flattened pack. It had been through a lot, one way or another. Hilton took a tube that was less crushed than the others and with exaggerated care he pulled out his lighter. Still didn't work. Pig put him out of his misery with a match. 'Jes' keep walkin'. You can smoke and walk at the same time, can't you?'

The smell got stronger, and the two escorts made unappreciative grunting sounds. Pig pulled his sweater up over his mouth and nose. 'Man, that is fuckin' ripe.'

Pepper flashed the light ahead. 'Just up to that ramp at the far end, then three, four hundred yards, we part company.'

Hilton got another big lungful of smoke as they drew level with old Sam Napoleon Wilson's burnt-out nest. As unobtrusively as possible he scanned his head from side to side, as if trying to relieve a stiff neck. Was it here? He couldn't recall the sequence exactly. Had to be here.

The shaft of light ripped down from above like a finger of God, framing Pepper perfectly. Everyone froze. He looked as if he was about to be beamed up. Great, thought Hilton, rescued by alien abductors. Another one snapped on, and they gaped open-mouthed as the columns burnt through into the underworld. Squeals of pain came from the odd rat caught in the glare, and Hilton could see the shapes scurrying for cover. Again, like a laser beam, another thin column of pure, luminous light seared down. Then another, each spotlighting the garbage and the shit and the dust and the grime, bringing the first real illumination for years and years.

And as he followed one he saw it, a perfectly framed black 'O': the entrance to Lake Shiticaca.

It all seemed agonisingly slow. He sucked on the filter and watched the tip glow bright red, then flicked it towards the hole, at the same time grabbing Ali and leaping for the burnt-out nest. Pig and Pepper, still trying to take in what was happening up above, watched in half-amusement, knowing the Ingram could cut him in half in a second.

Hilton reached the slimy, charred remains of the mattress, flung Ali down on it and dived, yanking the whole rotten confection over on top of them, and scything the sentry-box structure like a falling ten-pin.

He waited, panting, clutching Ali hard to his right armpit, hoping he didn't smell too bad, then realising that his armpits at their worst couldn't compete with the assault from the mattress. He found he was praying. Yeah, do you believe in an interventionist God? Duck had asked him that once. He didn't know Duck knew words that long, let alone what they meant. Turns out he got the line from a song. Well, did he? Now seemed as good a test as any.

In his mind he could see the cigarette arcing through the darkness. He knew he would have made the hole

OK. He never missed. Not with all that practice flicking butts at Duck every time he screwed up. But then he could also see it hitting the vile sludge below them, bobbing on the thick surface, and slowly hissing out.

Pepper cocked the Ingram and walked over to the manhole cover and looked down. The stench knocked him back. Whatever the guy had hoped for wasn't going to happen. He turned and said, 'You got five seconds to come out.' No way was he going to dig through that garbage to get them himself. He threw the .45 to Pig and made a few hand signals to indicate he would flush them out and Pig was to shoot them.

More lights flicked on two hundred yards away. It was probably too late for Annie's plan. Whoever was switching on the power down here, they would hear the Ingram. Couldn't be helped. But it meant the game was up. Best to abandon ship. He'd have a word with Annie, he was sure they could come up with another scam. One that didn't involve Ricky. Just him and Annie. 'Two.'

Yes, get Annie, abandon the dope – it was all Ricky's cash involved anyway – and see what happens. 'One.'

Of course, he *could* let them go now. But hell, it was their fault they were losing it all. Pepper felt the M-11 kick as he squeezed the trigger, and he pushed to counteract the juddering that would otherwise force the gun up towards his shoulder. The floor next to the mattress exploded into a flurry of dancing dust and splinters. He moved the stream to the left, and watched the mattress heave and convulse under the impact. Finish it now and get moving.

FORTY-FOUR

The Ready-Park 24-Hour Lot, Fourth Avenue and Virginia, Seattle. 3.10 am

After checking that all was well back in Spokane, Major Milliner inspected the opening his home team had made by taking up the steel cover set in the floor of the parking lot on Fourth Avenue. He knew this place. He often had breakfast in Steve's Broiler across the street, or dined on the fusion food at the Dahlia Lounge, its neon fish sign still jerkily flipping its tail even at this time of the morning, had even misguidedly caught some of the experimental theatre at the Annex. And when he first came to the city he had put up at the determinedly old-fashioned Claremont behind him. And all the time, the diners and guests and monorail riders never suspected what was under their feet.

He looked over the lip, where the last of the surface water was draining into long, slow drips, the compounds they picked up from the tarmac making them viscous, like strings of saliva, reluctant to let go. They had a journey of twelve feet before they plopped onto the earth again, a trip through what would normally have been almost total blackness, but was now lit with a soft glow, thanks to the lighting system on the sidewalks. The old smell wafted up, the odour of filth and decay and rat shit familiar from hours in these tunnels clearing out all the vagrants and the misfits. *Almost* all, he reminded himself.

His throat was dry. Unlike the others, he knew what was down there, a kind of negative of the city, dark where it was bright, cold where it was warm, still holding the memory of old corruptions and deceit, the last will and testament of the original carpetbaggers, freeloaders, robbers, deviants and perverts who built this city.

He glanced back along Fourth Avenue, now ablaze like some long, linear movie set. A small crowd was gathering – disturbed residents, night workers, the homeless – and he testily ordered some troopers to push them back. He looked up at the windows of the Claremont, where a few residents were wondering what all the noise was. Someone was bound to hit 911 to complain. And the K5 news crews would be here soon, no doubt. Had to get moving. If anything went wrong here, he didn't want his naked ass on prime time again.

He had sent Marzo around to Henry to get a copy of the underground plans – for what they were worth – from the cops, who, he reported back, were fannying about in total inaction, apart from having sent two men down, to be followed by a couple of S&R firefighters. S&R my ass, he thought.

The plans were laid out on the bonnet of the Transaif. An X marked where the guy and his captive had fallen through into the Underworld. 'How long ago did you say?'

'Two, maybe even three, sir.'

He nodded. Over two hours wasted. How far could he have got in that time? Well, not that far, because certain physical blocks – such as new basements and tunnels – tended to confine the area that they could move around in.

Marzo said hesitantly: 'Of course, he could be up by now, sir. There must be any number of ways of getting out. He might be long gone.'

'Hmm. But my waters tell me he is still down there.' He felt a twinge at the back of his neck as if to confirm he was right. Those old antennae never let him down. 'And you would be surprised at just how few entrances and exits there are these days. Look – he can't have gone this way, because that new mall has a ten-level underground car park, so that cuts him off from the Pioneer Square section. The tunnels run here, here and here, there is a wall here. And lifting these metal plates in the sidewalk, always assuming you can reach them, is no stroll in the park. No, he's down there. And he is within here.' He circled a finger over an area. 'Are we ready?'

Marzo caught the eye of a corporal who gave him the circled finger. 'Ladder in place, sir.'

'OK, we will head this way, to the bootleggers' wall. If he does what I think he will do . . . if he is where I think he will be, that should flush him out. Either way, he will be the filling between us and the S&R they are sending in from Henry. Sergeant Robertson will be surface coordinator and control. Clear?'

If any of his men were wondering about the wisdom of the unit's leader – the unit's ageing leader, he had to be honest – taking a prime role rather than acting as control, they had the good sense to shut up. But just in case, Milliner made a great show of going down first, scurrying down the rubber-coated aluminium ladder – no easy task in a fully packed armoured vest – and catching the MFT as it was dropped down to him. He adjusted the straps and slipped it on over his vest, now making him very bulky indeed, but it didn't matter. He wasn't going to have to run anywhere.

As the others joined him he looked down the long-buried street ahead of them. The lights above had taken the edge off the blackness, but they left many deep pools of dark untouched. Milliner switched on his Sure Fire light and played the beam around, occasionally consulting the tightly folded plans using his less dazzling helmet light.

The Sure Fire was picking up piles of garbage testifying to a human presence down here. Some old, liquefied, others wrapped in black plastic sacks – more recent, although, given the way rodent teeth had slashed and ripped and rummaged through the contents, it was impossible to tell whether they were months or even years old.

He bent down and picked up a newspaper, shaking it to let the dirt slide off. It was like parchment – obviously this section of the tunnels must have remained relatively dry – and he looked at the date. October 14, 1982. The headlines outlined the ambitious plans to drive bus tunnels under the city to relieve downtown congestion, using the old buried Third Avenue.

Every part of the Underworld had its own history, and he was well aware of what had happened in this section. About a thousand yards down this sub-street ahead the entire road and sidewalk had collapsed into the basement. It was one of those sections that should have made good when they did the tunnels, but work on this section was abandoned – after it had been rendered safe and supported – when the other north-south arm of the Metro tunnels was shelved. The idea had been that this section would be concrete-clad and used as a ready-made bore to run the buses to the Space Needle, paralleling the monorail. But the monorail and the Seattle Center had objected to the competition, and the plan was dropped. However, the city never filled it in because they knew, one day, when the political clout changed, it would happen.

Then, beyond the collapsed section and the formidable concrete trusses, was the so-called bootleggers' wall, some big, empty rooms, and then the carapace of the Pine Street/Westlake bus tunnel. The fugitive was in this section somewhere, he could feel it. Somewhere ahead. All routes led to this street, everything else was sealed off in one way or another.

Marzo, Bayne, Liddon, Faussett, Samson and Collyns clustered around the base of the ladder while Milliner went quickly through the lay of the land, and mapped out the basic rules. He could see them making furtive glances beyond him while he talked. It was damned spooky, they seemed to be saying. They were right.

'We want the girl alive.' His voice echoed among the pillars and posts, but fuzzily, as if it was bouncing off felt. 'We don't care too much about him. We also want anyone else we find immobilised until we can scoop them up.' He unclipped a pouch from his webbing and issued each man with two pairs of the lightweight carbon-fibre hand restraints within. 'Clip the miscreants to a pipe or to each other or both.'

'Sir, how many we expecting?' asked Bayne.

'When I worked the tunnels, we had three dozen or more. I would reckon half of them are dead by now – no

Blue Cross down here. Anything from two to a dozen, I would say.'

Bayne bent down and picked up an empty wine bottle. National Wine Company. From the days when Seattle went dry on Sundays no doubt, thought Milliner, and this place was the Downtown Social Club. Times change, he thought: the Washington wineries that used to make such cheap hold-your-nose battery acid now shipped fancy-labelled varietals costing fifty bucks.

The team threaded the cuffs onto their belts, did a final weapon check and the seven beams of light started to cut through the partly lit gloom. They fell into formation. Into a wedge shape, with Marzo at the pinnacle, the paired-off troopers spreading out beyond him, with Milliner taking the rear right flank. The shape gave them a good field of view, something very restricted if they had to go to NVGs. Marzo had secured his respirator to his helmet and armed his monitor, which was now sucking in tiny pockets of the fetid air and analysing for noxious compounds. Anything life-threatening would trigger an audible howl from the unit.

The communication systems were on, and through his headset Milliner could pick up throat-clearings and the occasional exclamation as the helmet torches played on long forgotten shop fronts and signs. Liddon and Samson, the middle pair, giggled over the 'Enid Stevens' Ladies' Lodgings' sign, speculating that more than lodging probably went on so close to the waterfront. 'Keep it down there.' They were wrong. In the old days, this was about as far away from the waterfront as you could get and still be in Seattle.

They had barely gone a hundred yards when the

sound of machine-gun fire came sweeping through the sunken streets towards them. Milliner was about to order them to run when he heard Marzo shout: 'Holy shit – willya look the fuck at that.'

Harry held onto Lewis's coverall, bunched it in his hands. The darkness was total, lights out, like no blackness he had ever experienced before, as if his optic nerve had been cauterised. But he didn't feel panicked or spooked. Maybe he was picking up something from this guy. Even the blups and plops of falling water, and the occasional rustle of a living creature, failed to move him. Maybe it was the fact he had one hand on the switch of his flashlight, and the Glock under his armpit. It couldn't be because, despite everything, he felt reassured by Lewis. Could it?

Harry was only catching every third word when the guy mumbled. What the fuck was a Kit Carson when it was on the range? This guy's belt obviously didn't go through all the loops. 'Good to have a KC along. Just stay cool. Stay cool. If I say hit the floor, then hit it. That's where the oxygen will be. On the floor. Just suck air for now. Through your teeth if you have to. Suck air.' Lewis was letting it run now, letting it all come out. Don't fight it, revel in it. It felt warm, familiar, good. Cathartic.

Harry wondered about hitting the flashlight, but Lewis was making good progress. Whatever the contraption on his head was, it worked, and, amid the babblings, there was sound advice. 'Loose wood here. Watch the hole to your left. Duck – there is a beam coming up. You're clear. OK.' And anyway, if he switched on and that guy with the wobbly teeth saw it, that might be it for the girl. He was aware that Tenniel was convinced Hilton was the Pillsbury Dough Boy underneath, but he hadn't been face to face with him. Well, face to mask. Harry knew Hilton could shoot when he had to. Popped the old man and didn't seem too cut up about it. Might as well do the little girl. They can't hang you twice.

Then they hit the wall.

Harry felt him pull up sharp, and heard a hand scraping across a surface. Lewis was breathing hard. 'We got to turn around?'

'No. There is a crawl tunnel. You can risk the light. Hold on.' Lewis adjusted the goggle sensitivity so he wouldn't be blinded and said, 'Now.'

Harry got the picture through a series of rapid blinks and flicked off the beam before his eyes filled with moisture. He didn't believe this. It was like someone was taunting him. Throwing the most bizarre initiation they could think of. He hoped the communications wire didn't snag in there. He pressed 'send' and spoke into the handset.

'Sergeant?'

'Yeah, we're here.'

Harry hesitated. Was this the best time to tell him that Lewis appeared to be – what was the best analogy here? – a pit prop short of a mineshaft? Maybe not. 'We are going into a small crawl tunnel. Give us plenty of slack on the wire.'

'OK. Listen, we also have a couple of Search and Rescue guys come in from the Fire Department. Used to this kind of shit. Just finished picking up the pieces over on the freeway from one of the drive-bys. They know their stuff when it comes to getting in and out of tunnels. They'll stay well back until you need them. But don't get jumpy.'

'Copy that. We took the middle tunnel to the right, tell them. I will try and leave marks on each tunnel entrance. Three horizontal scratches. Just in case there is a choice.'

'Roger. Listen, we just got word from the docs. Looks like the kid's old man will pull through. Make sure you tell Hilton that. And make sure he believes you. OK?'

'Sure.'

'How's Lewis?'

Harry paused. 'Over and out, Lieutenant.' He'd get the message.

Lewis went in first, with Harry trailing in his wake, spluttering at the dust he kicked up. Lewis stopped and snapped back: 'Sshhh.'

They crawled and scraped in silence after that, Harry doing his best to stifle his coughs. He could feel the particles sticking to his skin. Already he wanted a shower. Then he felt Lewis pulling him upright.

'We are in some kind of chamber. Someone took a leak here recently. Smell it?'

All Harry could smell was the half-pound of cement dust stuck to his nose hair.

Lewis looked up. His goggles picked up the faintest of lights coming from the ceiling, as if it was struggling through layers of grime. 'OK,' started Lewis, 'this is how we play it—'

He stopped when something bleached out the goggles, burning his eyes in a supernova of painful light.

Rats. A sea of them. Or, rather, thought Milliner a river,

twenty, thirty deep, blocking their path, squirming and climbing over each other, giving the effect that they were boiling, bubbling, a brown mass, but flecked with red here and there, he could see it on some jaws and some paws. They had been feeding.

He felt the old horror tiptoe up his back, pinging the nerves as it went, pinching his heart. Disgusting.

'Stand back,' he muttered into his throat mike and brought down the protective eyeshield over his Orlite helmet. He pressed the charge button for the igniter crystal, waited the thirty seconds and hesitated.

Still they sat there, oblivious to him and his men, lost in their own thoughts, unaware of what was about to descend on them. Much like the guy who had the girl. Be down on him in a second, as soon as we toast these guys. He pressed the trigger and felt the liquid speed down the barrel and ignite with a whoosh, heard the first of the dying squeals, and the panicking shrieks as they tried to get clear. The piercing noise of panic and pain filled his ears. He swung an arc, watching the animals scrabble over each other, trying to make themselves small, then lying still.

There was another noise now. Not animal, but machine-made, urgent, strident. How long had that howl been going on? He felt a hand on his shoulder. He let go of the trigger and the flame stopped. Marzo was pointing at his BioChem detector, which was flashing red and emitting the piercing alarm. Milliner turned to look at the shrivelled, smouldering corpses and saw the little blue flames dancing among them, like little rat souls rising from the dead, heard the whoosh as they gathered together and sped towards the cracks in the ground.

* * *

The ancient stuffing in the mattress leapt into the air like a flurry of dirty grey snow. The line of shells started to move towards the centre, where Hilton and Ali lay. Why hadn't the cigarette worked, thought Hilton as he heard death inching towards him. The old man had said it was inflammable down there.

And then he heard it, a rolling thunder under the earth, and he knew something – maybe his cigarette butt, maybe something else – had ignited it. Lake Shiticaca was coming to town.

The gas had been sitting above the lake for years, slowly consolidating into a thick flammable blanket. As its messenger came from the surface it took the heat to itself with ardour, blossoming, letting it roll along the surface of the vast underground cesspit, exploring corners and tunnels and pipes, sometimes dying and choking where the oxygen was exhausted, in other places burning bright, turning from blue to yellow and leaping to the surface with joy. And then it found the old Seattle Steam and Light Company experimental gas main, long tapped off, but never fully bled, the thin, rusted walls of the six-inch pipe split and spilled and the two gases met and intertwined and the blue flame took its companion up and up to ignition point. Together they exploded skyward, seeking every weakness to blow a hole into the overworld.

Milliner felt the rumble and turned to look at his men. They were hurrying to fit the respirators to block out the stench of burnt rodent and protect against whatever Marzo's BioChem was howling about. All around them the surviving rats were scuttling for cover, some stopping to try and find flesh, but sinking their teeth ineffectually into assault boots. Milliner was puzzled. The earth was moving under their feet, rippling and dancing. He watch the motes and splinters and chips under his feet jiggle and bounce. 'Marzo—' was all he managed to say before the old roadway shattered and cracked and splintered, and he found himself falling into space, through a column of burning air.

Annie felt it too. Or rather heard it first. Eventually. She was too busy thinking about how many plants she had. After fifty, the Federal Mandatory Law kicks in. Big sentences. And they had a lot more than fifty. She flicked the next row of dimmers a quarter turn. Taking the lights down gently preserved filament life, but also made sure a sudden surge or drop didn't alert the Metro engineers down in the Exchange Building to a dramatic change in the electricity usage. That was why they were down here, after all – all the free juice they needed from the bus tunnels next door to run the lights and the air conditioning. It was a mere blip compared to the amount generated to run buses and lights, escalators and elevators, but it was worth a few thousand bucks to them.

She had got the halides down to half-strength when she finally noticed the new tinkling sound above the fans. Almost like someone playing a triangle. Slowly at first, then rising in pitch and speed, faster and more frenzied until it became a metallic screech. It was the lights rattling in their sockets and the feed pipes banging against their troughs. Then she realised the floor was moving as if something, some giant beast, was rolling over beneath her feet, like a dragon stirring from a long sleep.

She raced out of the control room and grabbed one of the lights, burning her hand. It was no good, they were swinging wildly. There was a dry rustle as the plants' leaves flapped – they waved frantically at her, like a plea for help, as if they were drowning or trying to pull themselves free of their clamps and walk.

The first bulb blew on the row next to her, and she squealed as hot glass and gasses streaked by. Then the next one went in a shower of sparks. Then the next. All over the two rooms the fragile bulbs began to disintegrate with loud pops. Annie knelt on the floor and sobbed. It wasn't fair. It just wasn't fair. The rumbling noise grew louder, the floor was flicking now like a rope, it whiplashed across to the control room, where the windows starred and shattered. There were a series of pings as wire supports snapped, and all around the control room and the access tunnel, the ceiling unpeeled like the skin of a fruit, crashing down onto the computer and glass-fronted booth.

Oh, fabulous, she thought. What next. Then the last of the lights flickered out.

Tenniel noticed it in the coffee cups first. Bowman had put down his Why Bother? and started to read off Hilton's 'want cards', both previous and pending. He stopped listening when he saw the surface of the liquid begin to shimmer, circles forming in the middle and spreading out. Then the cups themselves became blurred as they too picked up the resonance, and started a slow, steady migration towards the edge of the table.

'John?' said Bowman with a tremor in her voice. She could feel something in the soles of her feet.

The lights started to vibrate in their holders, sending out an uncomfortable whine. Tenniel went to the edge of the hole, and peered down, listening to the groans and detonations.

He glanced at the Man With The Plans. 'What the Jesus Christ is that?'

'I don't like to think.'

'Fucking Girdlestone,' he said out loud. He felt Bowman grip his arm tightly. He didn't move away this time.

It lasted no more than two minutes, and they sensed rather than heard the sound of distant detonations rumbling through the earth. A cloud of debris was leaking from the hole now, like some kind of smoke signal.

He turned to the two Search and Rescue operatives who had arrived from the Fire Department, fully rigged up with Scott Airpacks. They switched on their hat lights and walked gingerly towards the punctured floor.

Tenniel flicked the radio switch to receive and heard the small voice. 'Man down. Explosion. Medevac . . .' It didn't sound like Lewis, but it must have been. Medevac? He tried to raise him but got only static. The voice grew fainter and disappeared. Explosion?

Who was down? It didn't sound like either of them on the ROVER. Tenniel looked around for Dinah. He had to reassure her. It had been his dumb-ass idea after all to send her old man down.

He scanned the worried-looking faces for her. She was gone. Great, add that to the girl's mother – just another woman seriously pissed at him loose on the streets.

It was dark. Very dark. Must have been a booby trap that blew up. How come he had missed it? Always spot the booby traps, me. Famous for it. These tunnels were like a living thing to him, living and breathing, and he could read them. Who had been point, him or Willie? No, not Willie. That Viet. The Kit Carson. The last thing he remembered was choosing an entrance tunnel and telling the KC . . . where was he? He flicked on the IR light. Nothing happened. He reached up and touched the goggles. He could feel the big split across the centre. Broken. That's what had happened to his vision. What was the KC's name? Harry. Not a KC. Just small like one. He took off the goggles and there was light again, bleeding down from the grille at the top of the room. The light that had blinded, disoriented him. And then . . . what had happened?

'March? Harry? You OK?'

There was a groan and Lewis crawled over the rubble in the direction it came from. He could see him, at least his top half. Some kind of thick concrete beam seemed to have been dislodged by the vibration and was lying across Harry's lower body. The dust-filled light from above wasn't enough for him to see how much damage had been done. It took him several seconds to find the ordinary flashlight. He prayed hard and hit the switch. Nothing. He clicked it off and on again and shook it.

It came on and he snapped forward twenty-five years. Not Vietnam. Seattle. A little girl. Little girl. He yo-yoed back and forward for a while, remembering the taste and sounds and sights, the whirl of helicopters, the rattle of the Swedish K. He could feel this odd warm glow in his chest, even though he knew it was very cold down here. He could see his breath in the torchlight, streaming and rolling across the beam. Perhaps it was just the memory of a glow, kept and stored in his synapses for all these years, not the warmth itself. Jesus, he had to keep it together, he was losing control of it.

'Uh.'

He touched Harry and held up his hand. It was soaked in blood. He wiped it on his coveralls. He played the beam up and down the body, could see that the concrete had done damage. Crushed pelvis maybe. Ticket home for that man. Back to the world. 'Medic!' he felt like yelling. Weren't medics on their way? From Tenniel, yes, Tenniel. The scar on his left hand started to throb and he rubbed it hard. The pain helped focus his thoughts. He could hear the muffled squeals of sirens above. Seattle. Not 'Nam. Little girl. THIS ALWAYS FUCKING HAPPENS, his brain yelled. You always get so fucking mixed up. Pull yourself together.

He stood up and tried to lift the beam, but it wouldn't shift. After all that gym work. He moved his legs further apart and heaved, felt the capillary rip in his arm – that'll be black tomorrow, he thought distractedly – and felt the beam give. He pivoted it on one corner and dragged it free.

He ran the light over the freshly uncovered section of the body. As he had thought, it looked bad. 'Harry, listen, I can't move you. Tenniel is sending those two guys down, didn't he say? Can you hear me?'

The eyelids fluttered. 'Yeah.'

Lewis unclipped the handset from Harry's belt and tried to raise Tenniel. It was dented and twisted where the concrete truss had bounced off it. It was a long time since he had broken squelch, he realised. Then he saw the little lazy, dancing lights arc across his vision. Tracers. Always came to get you in slo-mo. How come they were travelling at hundreds of miles an hour, but looked as if they barely had the energy to arc up into the night sky? He remembered the slick pilot fighting the controls as they got hit on the way back to base once, the great stars in the Plexiglass, the blood splashed up it from the co-pilot, the rounds having punched straight through his chest protector. And he remembered being frightened at how little this meant to him. Not an Underdog down. Just another dead chopper pilot. Next, please. A little fizzing started behind his eyes.

He started to shout: 'Can you hear me? Mayday. Man down. Man down. Get me some Medevac.' He flicked to receive, but there was nothing. He got the sense the power was draining away from it. He pulled at the wire to make sure it was free. Shit, what he needed now was one of the old wind-up telephones. Not some garbage that ran on batteries.

Lewis shone onto Harry's face again. He was weak and he was pale. His eyelids were fluttering. He had to keep him conscious. Lewis took the gun from his belt and laid it down, moved himself to lie parallel with Harry and put an arm under his head. Harry was bleeding from several bad gashes. A few thin streams of grit were trickling from above. The last thing he needed now was for them to be buried under more rubble and metal. He shone the flashlight around the chamber. Most of it was intact. He flashed back at the ceiling. He could see where the concrete had torn away, could see pieces of metal, some four inches long, others approaching a foot, dangling like umbilicals. But only one piece of support had fallen down. And Harry had to be under it. It was just bad luck, was all. Bad karma.

Got to keep him talking. He was shivering.

'*Dau o cho nao?*' He said it before he realised.

It was a stupid question. Where does it hurt? Well, where I've had this big concrete beam lying across me crushing my bones. And it was in a foreign language.

'*Ngay cho nay,*' came the reply.

'You speak Vietnamese?'

Harry shook his head. 'Bits. If you are so surprised why did the fuck you ask me in Vietnamese?'

Lewis shrugged. 'Force of very old habit.'

'Which was?'

Lewis shook his head. Not now. 'How come you speak it?'

Harry grimaced as a stab of pain spread up from his hips. 'Girlfriend . . . Fiancée. She's . . .'

'Vietnamese?'

Another nod. His features relaxed as the pain receded. This was one wave he didn't want to catch again in a hurry. 'You did this shit in the war?'

'Now there,' said Lewis slowly, 'lies a story or two.' Several, in fact, so intertwined over the years he couldn't tell one from the other, lies from truth, fact from fantasy.

Harry felt the pull of the pit at his back, the darkness at the periphery of his vision growing. He blinked hard, sending it scurrying away. 'I ain't goin' nowhere.'

Lewis wasn't so sure.

* * *

Milliner was aware that his arms and legs were flailing as he spun round, felt the fire dive under his visor, smear over his face, taking his eyebrows and eyelashes. And then the freezing cold liquid closed over him. It was thick, and viscous and vile and lumpy, and it crept into his mouth and nostrils even as it sucked him down, down, down. He fought hard to suppress his vomit reflex. It's just organic matter now, he thought, a mulch, compost, don't think what it once was.

He thrashed wildly, trying to get a purchase, trying to kick to the surface, except he had no idea where the surface was. Gradually his speed diminished and he felt himself rising, slowly, painfully slowly through the gloop.

After all those hard landings, that it should come to this. Lost in the waste of the old city. As he came up he shot an arm into the air, clenching and unclenching his fist. And as he did so he hit metal, painfully bending his index finger back. Then it was gone, out of his grasp. It was the American Beauty. Light it may be, but the weight of the liquid was dragging him under, keeping him from reaching up.

He forced himself to open his encrusted eyes even as he was sinking back down, blinking hard to try and bring the gloom into focus. There was a partial grid pattern above his head. At one time there had obviously been a system of walkways over this giant cesspool. He let himself go down in the granular embrace of the slop once more, and struggled with the quick release straps. Quick release except when lubricated with fat and oil. One came. Then the other. With a tinge of regret even as his lungs were bursting he let the flame-thrower go, then kicked as hard as he could, beating the surface with one arm while lunging upwards. His arm caught on a raft of something ancient, old newspapers by the look of them, and they gave him the leverage.

Three fingers wrapped around the metal and he locked them this time, inching across the raw metal surface until he had a decent hold. He dangled there, coughing and hawking and spluttering, fighting that urge to vomit. He opened his encrusted eyes again, and blinked painfully. Above him he could see the torn and twisted surface they had fallen though. Something had been powerful enough to punch through two floors and pull them down. Some light from the street even reached this far down, and he could see the contorted shape of a metal pipe, burst open like a pea pod along its length. Gas explosion? The flame-thrower. My God, why now, why not when he used it all those years ago . . .?

What about the others? Not four feet away one trooper was floating on the surface face-down. Blond hair. Bayne. He had a huge gash across the base of his skull. He must have hit one of the metal crossbars above the surface of the shit on the way down.

Marzo, like Milliner, had found himself able to cling onto the ironwork. It must have been sturdily built – the explosion hardly seemed to have affected it. Liddon and Faussett were attempting to swim to the far walls, but it was like trying to make progress through porridge. Around them what looked like small islands were moving, slowly but confidently, making progress towards the sides. The rats, paddling past the cinders that were their burnt colleagues.

He suddenly realised there was no sign of Samson or

Collyns: they were either still up above, or had been claimed by the pool.

Milliner felt his grip weakening. Marzo tore off his respirator and spluttered: 'Handcuff yourself on. They'll get ropes to us soon.' Milliner managed to free a set of manacles from his belt and fasten himself to the steel pole that ran over his head. It wasn't quite what he had envisaged when he issued them, that he would have to use them on himself. He let his weight go and felt the ordure try to suck him in like a greedy animal. He was grateful they weren't metal restraints, but even so he felt as if his arm was going to come out of its socket. Maybe he was too old, after all.

If nothing else the pain took his mind off the taste in his mouth. He watched as the muck slowly took Bayne, creeping over his arms and legs and torso, his uniform gradually disappearing until all that was left was the word SWOPS on the flak jacket, and then that, too, was lost to the sludge.

The four remaining hung onto their perches, handcuffed, feeling their skin chafe and pull away, wondering when the other team would peer over the great gash above their heads.

The pool gave a belch and a pocket of gas rose with a weary plop from where Bayne's body had gone.

Milliner felt himself grow very, very angry.

The Sorrento, Dinah knew, was north of HWY-5, up on Madison, but that was one-way the wrong way, so she took Spring, heading east up the hill, barely slowing for each red light. Willie had told Carl he was there. She was praying they hadn't discovered the credit card he'd checked in with was borrowed and turfed him out. Or called the police . . .

She did a right on Boren, and then back down Madison, pulling into the crescent driveway and leaping out without bothering to slam the door behind her. Six paces across the thick lobby carpet and she saw him. It had to be him. Small and scruffy. How come they let him in? No wonder Lewis had been surprised when he called up and said where he was. He was slumped on a stool at the bar of the tastefully dim Hunt Club, muttering and cursing to himself.

The cause of the complaint became clear as she approached. The bar was closed, and Willie thought it should be reopened for him. He had on his shirt, which had come adrift from his pants, and scuffed loafers without socks. He looked as if he had dressed himself with baseball mitts on.

Dinah slapped her gold Amex on the wooden counter-top, and stared at the barman. 'I'd like to pay this man's bill.'

She could feel quizzical eyes running up and down her. No, she felt like saying, she wasn't a hooker.

'Whoa, baby,' said Willie.

'I'd like to settle it now. Room as well. He'll be coming with me.' She turned to the night manager who had silently shadowed her and hissed in her best don't-fuck-with-me voice: 'Now. Please.'

He padded across the now hushed and dimmed Fireside Lounge to swipe the card behind the reception desk and she leant close to Willie. The stale booze and a residual aroma from his rancid coat had merged into some kind of lethal cologne. She stepped back to try and get a whiff of the Sorrento's more familiar odour, of leather and polish. 'Go get dressed. Carl needs you. I need you.'

'Carl? Oh yeah . . . Carl. Yeah, we spoke, it's . . .'

'Dinah.' The night manager reappeared, relieved there was no query on the Amex. She signed the slip for the tab. Extras were nearly two hundred bucks – he had dialled New York several times and had made a dent on the room-service menu. 'Willie, are you coming or do I have to tie your dick to my bumper? I'll explain in the car.'

Willie clung onto the dash in terror as she hurtled down the hill of Madison, leaving the ground as she powered over the stretch where the cable cars once ran, and swung a violent right on First. She hoped he didn't claw out the airbag, but at least the fast ride with the open window was sobering him up fast. And blowing out some of the smell. She noticed he had tried a quick shave, but from the look of it he'd put those mitts on again before the attempt. Specks of blood glistened on his jawline. 'They sent Carl underground?'

'They did. I did. I . . . I thought it might be a good idea.'

'You— C'mon, lady, what amateur psychology crap you been reading? Last thing he needs is to go down some fuckin' tunnels.'

'Well, I can see that now. I didn't know until tonight he had ever been down any in the first place. Anyway, it's not as if he's that fucked up.'

'No?'

'Claustrophobic maybe.'

'Claus . . . ? Are you nuts?'

'Look, there is a little girl down there. And now there has been some kind of explosion, and I thought if you two were buddies you could go down—'

'I could go down? *I* could go down? Christ. You got a drink in here? A soda?'

'There's an eight-year-old held hostage down there. If she is still alive. Didn't you feel the earthquake or whatever?'

He shook his head. 'Little girl.'

They were nearly there. 'What's the problem?'

'The problem, Dinah, is Carl Lewis.'

She reached the junction with Henry and pulled to a stop outside Pike Place Market. 'Is there something you want to tell me?'

'No.' He shook his head to try and clear the fuzz. His mouth was dry. He eyed the drinks machine outside the market and sucked his dry tongue. Damn, he hated being awake while he sobered up. 'But there is something I think you should know.'

Hilton used Ali as a crutch for the last ten yards before he collapsed down. He had deliberately chosen a tunnel where the overhead street lights had not penetrated, one where he could sit in the dark and think.

'Stop,' he said quietly. He put his back to the wall and slid to the floor. He felt Ali crouch beside him. Neither had looked at the damage, but Hilton knew a large section of his side was probably missing. He couldn't feel it yet – some kind of tissue shock, but when he tried to probe he felt the end of bone, and that sent a hot wire shooting up his side and into his brain. How come it didn't get his arm? Because he was hugging Ali. Exposing his ribs to the bullets. Only the gas going up had saved them. Thank you, God.

'We should stay here. Wait for help.'

Hilton took quick, shallow breaths. 'Like from the last people we met?' When they emerged from the mattress they had seen Pig, lying on his back. He had been flung onto the exposed metal reinforcing rods, some of which had punched through his torso, and Hilton had no intention of peeling him off them to see if he was still breathing. He had simply uncurled the fingers that still gripped the AMT .45 and dragged Ali off to look for shelter. Pepper – and his Ingram – was nowhere to be seen. This way, at least the cops might find them before he did.

He started to shiver and then the pain came in a great wave, a towering, rolling breaker, building and building until it crashed down somewhere behind his eyes. For just a second he felt himself go, flash out of consciousness into somewhere dark and warm. It felt nice, but he hauled himself out.

He didn't want her to see him die.

'I think you ought to get going. Police, fire, they all be along soon.'

It was hard to speak.

'No, I'll stay.'

'No, you can say I let you go. It'll . . .' He gritted his teeth. 'It'll go better for me at the trial. I need all the help I can get kid. I'm . . . I'm a PF. Here.'

He held up the gun. She shook her head.

'Pepper's still out there. Maybe.'

'I couldn't fire that.'

He laughed and felt something snag and burst in his side. 'Fine convenience-store robber you turned out to be.'

'What's a PF?'

'Predic . . . predicate felon. It means I got caught once . . . won't be a sentence of . . . of months this time around. But y'know, if you say I let you g—'

The next wave came, and took him under for a little longer. As he came back, he felt something on his ear, rubbing and caressing. 'Whatcha doing?'

'Don't you like it?'

'Feels good.'

'It's the way I used to get my dad to sleep. He liked having his ears rubbed. But he was too ashamed to let me tell anyone. Said they'd think it was odd. It's OK isn't it? Rubbing ears?'

Fuck. Rubbing ears. Well, I suppose he didn't deserve to be blown away for that after all. And he must be dead by now. Must be. Hilton couldn't even claim to have done that right now. Shit, if there was a God – and nobody could argue that there wasn't a case for divine intervention in that explosion – his celestial scorecard must look pretty grim.

He felt the next wave coming, knew it was a giant. He reached out, tried to run a finger through her hair but it snagged and caught because of the film of blood across his palm and the grit that had lodged in her tresses. 'I want you to go. Just hole up somewhere until they all come. Be here soon. Please?' He managed to get the last word out in a gasp before the sizzling started in his brain, the short-circuits popping.

He felt her kiss him on the cheek. She knew. She was no dumb kid. 'Bye, Hilton.'

'About your dad—'

She put a hand on his head, as if it was some kind of absolution. Maybe that would count: they, God, the kid didn't bear me no grudge. But then, she didn't know, did she, some smartass angel would chime in. Didn't know what he had done to her old man. After all, he knew Tenniel had been lying. 'He's dead. I'm real sorry. I figure that I must have hit something important.' Like his heart.

'You lied?'

'I had t—'

'You LIED to me all this time?'

Hold on. Surely the lying wasn't the crime, here, surely it was making Dad a peek-a-boo. She just looked at him open-mouthed, real horror on her face, and started to back up.

'No, wait, Ali—' She was going the wrong way, back towards the light.

'Ali—' It was too late to say he was just preparing her, that they hadn't actually said he was gone.

'Liar.' It was hissed and vicious, and he could hear the tears coming, and knew she was just focusing on the deception to give her pain somewhere to go. He hoped that was it.

'Ali. Please. Come. Back.'

She was silhouetted for a few moments at the end of the alley and disappeared, leaving a little sob hanging in the air. Another first-rate job, Hilton.

He lay there for a minute or two, listening to the tortured sounds of his own breathing, the loose rattling of his body. He rode out a few more waves of pain before he addressed the matter. He had often wondered whether he would have the nerve. He had a loaded gun at his side with, what? Two or three rounds left. Two. He had half a ribcage gone from an Ingram machine pistol, and a couple of pints of blood splattered across the floor. He wasn't going to make it. So why not do it quickly? What would keep him hanging on until those waves turned into one big massive wall of agony and swept him away? Then his ear caught something.

There was a scrabbling in the other, dark, end of the tunnel, the opposite direction to the one Ali had taken. He fingered the safety of the Hardballer. Well that kind of settled it. Being on the menu as rat chow definitely tipped the scales.

FORTY-FIVE

Ben Moc FSB, Vietnam. 1970.

By the flickering light of the nut oil lamp, Tran carefully replaced the launcher in the wall of the tunnel and pulled the jute sacking over it, smoothing the sides to push them into the wall. It might survive a cursory glance, or it might not. If not, he would have to tolerate the loss – it would slow him down, manhandling both the RPG-7 and the MAT-49 machine gun through these hastily dug tunnels.

From above he heard a secondary chain of detonations – ammunition or fuel going up. He wondered if the team in the second tunnel had broken off yet. To stay much longer would be madness. He thought briefly of poor Nguyen, caught by the mad, aimless fire of the Americans. He was ten metres from the entrance, but Tran could not afford to drag him back down. What was he to do? Stand there and pour rice wine on the body until they came for him? He would have to explain to his brave little daughter how he died a hero. He hoped – forlornly he knew – that they treated the body with some respect. Another photograph on the shrine. Then he remembered Nguyen had been Catholic. Still, he wouldn't mind. Nguyen always did believe in covering every possibility.

He collapsed the MAT, sliding the wire stock home

and swinging the magazine housing up to nestle under the barrel. It made the captured French weapon – now nearly twenty years old – one of the easiest to crawl with.

He folded himself double and quickly played out the trip-wire – the Americans' own communication wire – and assembled the device. It was an old favourite. He wondered if the Americans saw the irony of their cans being exactly the right size to hold a fast-fuse grenade? With extreme care he pulled the pin from each metal sphere and dropped it into the can, where the lever expanded against the oiled sides. He buried one in each wall, and ran the thin wire strand between them. He patted dirt over the can openings. It wouldn't take much pressure for one of the grenades to slip out of its well-lubricated home.

Carefully he backed up before squeezing himself into a U-shape and turning round again. The earth cracked and crumbled as he did so, dropping into his eyes. He wasn't sure whether it was him or the thumps from above causing the falls. These tunnels had been dug far hastier than most, and with minimum supports. Still, one more trip through was all they were required to do for the moment. He would send someone else to locate the launcher at a later date, assuming that they didn't blow up the tunnels. But then he realised they probably would – it was unlikely that the Yankees would be stupid enough to try and follow him. No, they would do what they liked to do best – blast the country to smithereens.

He blew out the lamp and started crawling. There had been no time to construct a multi-level tunnel; this one headed straight for the forward command post, and beyond that connected to the greater tunnel system, as well as surfacing in the meagre cover of the woods. All they had managed to do in the time available was construct one water trap to seal off any gas.

He stopped as he felt a large section of ceiling come free and fall on his back. He shook it off and upped his speed. More props, he thought, he should have insisted on more props.

Ten, fifteen minutes later Tran could hear them following. Scraping and coughing and talking. He waited for the booby trap to fire, but no. He hadn't thought it through properly. He should have used snakes. Snakes always slowed them down. Or just blasted the entrance, and risked losing the other ear to concussion. Too late now.

He reached the water trap, a pool of liquid that led to a short submerged tunnel, surfacing on the other side at the same level. Its job was to seal off this section from the CS they sometimes pumped down with fans. He turned and peered into the darkness. No sign of their lights yet. Had the shaft been dead straight he could have risked opening up, but like all of them it undulated. Anyway, he would only hit the first one. Time had told him that simply gave the second one good solid cover from which to return fire.

He hated this bit. From a small niche in the wall he took out a PX plastic carrier bag and wrapped the MAT in it, before strapping it tightly across his back. It would leak a little, but the gun never seemed to mind a splash of moisture, as long as it wasn't fully submerged. Then he slid head-first into the cold and stagnant water, felt its sliminess close over his body.

He found the rope attached to the ring and pulled himself down the two feet until he reached the horizontal section and dug his nails into the opening to pull himself down. His head and shoulders went through, but he suddenly felt the MAT snag on something.

Don't panic. He let some air escape from his lungs, to see if it would let him fall to the bottom.

He tried twisting.

More air leaked out of his mouth.

He yanked hard on the rope to try and pull himself through, and felt it come free at the far end.

Losing an RPG and a MAT in the same day would mean trouble, was all he could think. He opened his eyes. A mere hint of light was coming from the other side, where he had left a lamp burning. And a Type 56 assault rifle.

Another burst of air. His lungs were nearly deflated now. He knew the next step would be a great mouthful of water.

Tran managed to wriggle one arm down to his belt and draw his knife. He slashed at the strap across his chest, and felt the MAT fall free. There was still three, four metres to go and his lungs were telling him to breathe, breathe. He felt his mouth open involuntarily, and the fluid trickle into his throat. NO.

He burst through on the far side with an almighty gasp, spluttering and coughing. He sucked as if he was going to pull an entire column of air out of the tunnels, as if his ribs were going to crack open, his heart burst. Eyes still shut, he pulled himself out and lay on the floor of the tunnel, feeling the water drain out of his sodden clothes. He should go back and get the gun. As soon as he got his breath back.

The touch of hands made him roll over in fright. It was Mae, Nguyen's daughter, holding out some rough sacking. Without being asked she started rubbing him, putting warmth back into his limbs. He sat up, and held out his arms for her to do those, bowed his head while she towelled his hair. He wondered if, not too many years down the line, his own daughter would be under here, drying the hair of some other liberation fighter. It saddened him to think so. He could smell the lingering traces of food being cooked, smell the smoke, but he couldn't tell whether it was on her clothes or in the tunnels. He realised he was hungry.

Mae looked at the water trap, as the ripples finally died away to leave the inky mirror-sheen. Nobody else was coming through. Nobody friendly, anyway. He shook his head. Mae nodded, and he felt like crying for her. How old was she? Twelve, thirteen and already inured to the death of friends, family, father.

'The Yankees are coming after me,' he said quietly. 'Go and warn the others to leave. They can seal the tunnel behind them.'

'I would like to stay.' She looked over at the assault rifle.

'No, Mae, not now. We can grieve and get our revenge later. You must warn the others.'

'What about you?'

'Set the trap. I will hide above. If I get a chance to kill them, I will. Then I can make my way to the surface. We can meet at Nhuan Duc. You know how the trap works?'

'Remove the flooring and replace with the mat?'

'Good girl. Now go. I will tell you about your father later.'

She scrambled off, and Tran followed her for a few metres, before twisting himself into a sitting position, back to the wall, and laying the rifle across his lap. He felt certain they would not risk the water trap. But he didn't want to meet them halfway trying to fish the MAT out. Let it lie for a while. He would recover it later. He blew out the little candle and closed his eyes, and let some of those smells play with his senses, pretend the food was on his tongue. Imagine it was his wife's excellent *pho bo tai* he could taste.

FORTY-SIX

Henry Street/First Avenue, Seattle. 3.35 am

Dinah felt her hands tighten on the wheel. Her throat was dry. How long had Willie been talking? Ten, fifteen minutes at most, with a short break to grab a Coke, yet her brain was a mass of whirling initials – NETTS, FNG, ASDIDs, NOD. And other things she wasn't quite ready to grasp just yet. She still managed to say: 'Go on.'

'You sure?'

She nodded.

'So we went down after this guy; the Thin Man, Lewis was calling him. Didn't miss a trick. I mean – guy must've known we'd come after him, but he stops and wires the tunnel. But Fix, Fix knew something was down there. He made the Major stop, and I tell you five more inches and he would have tripped it. A couple of grenades in C-ration cans. So that brought us all to our senses a little bit, if you know what I mean. We made them safe – you shove bits of wood, like wedges, into the sides to stop the things popping out and then taped them up. Then we reached this thing called a water trap. It's a flooded pit linking two tunnels. Acts a little like a U-bend, y'know? So we're pretty sure this dink is on the other side. I mean, where else could he be? And the Major, he's a bit big – bulky, I mean – to be first under. So who's the smallest? I am. So Fix had had this idea of wrapping the gun in a plastic bag . . . after Wayland complained about jamming. And fuck me there is a stash by the water trap. The VC used the idea as well. Because you can still hold a gun through the bag, no problem. I go down, find this other gun and bring it back up. Hey – the guy has got stuck and had to dump his MAT. Good news. Still, be cautious, I'm thinking, so I go down, along the tunnel, and find this ledge where you can stand up and clear the water. Gun in one hand, flash in the other. Like this. Now guess what? I stand up, gun outstretched, hit the light switch and he's only sitting there, isn't he? I guess he must have been asleep, 'cause otherwise he would have heard the ripples. So there we are, looking at each other and I go pop just as he lets off a burst. Now, I get time to aim, but he manages mostly to hit the roof. But anyway, I go back down, and sure enough he has to change a clip – they empty real fast those AKs. But when I come up, he's gone. So I tug on the cord I had tied to my leg. The all-clear signal. Then go look-see, and yeah I hit him. Blood splashed up the wall.'

Dinah shuddered at this matter-of-factness.

'Then the others came through, just about. Tight squeeze for them. It was that that did it I think. Coming through the water trap. All went fuckin' wrong from there on in. Went wrong for Lewis, too.'

It was a long silence. Dinah thought about what she had heard, and what must be happening down below her feet. She should get Willie down there to pull Lewis out. But she had to hear the end of this. Had to make Willie go on.

'After the water trap the tunnel dropped down to a lower level. No trapdoor or anything, just a crude ladder that took us to ten, twelve feet below. Older tunnels now, well shored-up, the floors worn smooth with use, some of them four, five feet high – so you could stoop rather than crawl. There were even a couple of junctions leading off, but there was always a smear of blood telling us where to go. Too clear, I thought. Like a fuckin' big arrow.

'So we came into this big room. Well, big by Charlie's standards. Had one of their cooking ranges, some rice sacks, two ventilation shafts in the ceiling, tables, chairs, and against one wall a desk stacked high with documents. Two other tunnels led off.

'So there are five of us in the room, breathing hard. We could see a blood-soaked bandage near one tunnel entrance, but, shit, too obvious. We had to think.

'It was then that Lewis noticed us, me and Fix. I mean, really noticed us. Puke on our clothes, God knows what our eyes were like. I remember he said: 'What the f-fuck is this – R-R-Rowan and Martin? What have you two been doing?' Well, Fix, Fix was . . . whatchacallit? . . . mortified. Scared. He just wanted to get out. I've seen that panic before. You get it at the deepest point in the tunnel, when you realise there is nothing but soil above and around you. I had it pretty much down . . . I don't think it was the pukin', I . . . I'd done it before, so I could sit on it, y'know what I mean? Fix, he musta still been sailing, y'know? I mean, it was real mellow stuff as I said, but . . . Jeez I don't really want to think about what he was seein'.

'So he was jumpy, primed, all his senses like full-on, and I don't think any of the rest of us heard it. It was barely a rustle. Must have been a shift of position. Fix heard it . . . probably sounded like elephants coming to him. So the next thing we know Fix has let rip with the Swedish K at the rice sacks. Fuckin' noise, screeching in the tunnels, and rice pouring out everywhere. Red rice, we suddenly noticed. She stood up at the end, but it was too late, she was full of holes. Must've been thirteen. No, I told you that already. 'Cause Fix, fuck, when he saw that gold bracelet . . .

'God, she looked . . . well Lewis knew what this would do to Fix, so he walked over and took the grenade from her hand. I mean, she wasn't some innocent kid hiding out there, she was a VC like the Thin Man, just as dangerous. He showed it to Fix, showed him he hadn't done anything any of us wouldn't have. But he wasn't seeing, he just sat down. Numb, I guess.

'It was me who noticed the wall. The K's bullets had punched holes in what looked like hardboard. It was a false partition, with clay all over it to hide it, make it blend in. Lewis was more interested in the desk with the documents – they loved a document did the VC, the amount of intelligence you could get was amazing – they recorded every man, every gram of supplies, worse than us for paperwork. But I stopped him and went over and pulled at this wall. Stupid really, could have been wired to fuck, but it wasn't. There were these ammunition boxes in there. Our ammunition boxes. US, I mean. So Hobbs and I pull them out, three of them, and we open them. It was gold. Gold for the ARVIN to buy arms. Fuckin' thousands, maybe millions, of dollars' worth. Like everything else, it left Tan Son Nhat airport and was never seen again. Everything was for sale, y'see, anything could be traded. Even US gold. Never got to the ARVIN, got to the VC instead.

'Christ, you should have heard the arguments. Jeesus – we were all shouting, trying to think of ways of getting it out. Too heavy to move, see. Weighed . . . well, Jesus it just *weighed*, know what I mean? Lewis wanted to bring a chopper in and I said, how many chopper pilots do you know who you can trust? That is when the penny dropped. Hobbs, Arnold and me, we saw it as Underdogs booty, y'know, finders keepers. The Major, he saw it as property of the US government. We said, no way, Major, we'll split it with Wayland and the others, but Uncle Sam has already written this off. That's when Lewis made his mistake. Fix didn't give a shit about gold at this point. He was looking at a little girl he'd just shot. I mean, we'd all seen worse than that, but not Fix. Lewis went over and tried to get the K off him, get some back-up. Big mistake.'

Tran knew he had miscalculated. He was losing blood faster than he had thought. He had had time to set the trap, to hide Mae behind the sacks – stubborn little girl wouldn't leave – to climb up here in the ventilation shaft, but he knew that he was too weak to swing down and finish them all off, even if they did fall for the bait. The sound of the submachine gun had startled him, almost made him lose his grip on the rope. He knew what it meant. Mae . . . poor Mae.

There were Yankee voices now, getting louder, arguing, although he couldn't follow it all. Gold, they had found the gold. He closed his eyes. He had to rest. No good sacrificing himself if he didn't even get to take one of them with him. He knew blood was dripping down. It could only be a matter of time before they saw it and came to investigate. Gingerly he changed his grip on the AK. Take one of their faces off if they looked up.

The argument got louder. Shrill. He could hear sounds of a scuffle, and then, suddenly, a figure came into view, arms flailing, feet scrabbling, the balance all gone, heading for the pit. Tran watched as the rush matting swallowed him up, as he fell backwards, as the hardened spikes slid effortlessly through the front of his uniform, great red blossoms spurting up above the stems.

The voices stopped. The punji pit had been designed to trap them as they walked to the desk to look at the displayed documents. Two, or three of them, pinned through their feet, so he could take them out from above. Kill the others in the confusion. Now just one man filled the pit, still alive, head up, as if examining in disbelief the stakes protruding from his chest. A drop of blood left Tran's leg and plinked onto the face. The eyes below him sought to focus in the gloom, to see where this final insult was coming from. Tran knew from the widening pupils that the man could see his shape hiding up here, in the roof shaft. The man tried to shout warning, but all that came out was a long, slow gargle.

Another figure stepped into view. It was a younger man, not like the Major who was lying in the pit. The gargling again, even as he was dying the Major was trying to tell them, alert them, but it must have just sounded like pure agony. Probably was, mostly. The younger man was crying. 'Sorry,' he was saying over and over and over again. He raised his strange gun and pointed it at the Major. He squeezed the trigger. There was a sound like a kiss being blown.

FORTY-SEVEN

Henry Street, Seattle. 3.45 am

Willie drained the last of the Coke, crumpled the can and licked his lips. Dinah was numb now. He was no great storyteller, but the flat, unemotional delivery lent the tale an even greater horror. She let it all sink in. A gun that sounded like a kiss. *That* gun. The surfer's gun. The one she had delivered a few hours earlier.

'You have to understand,' said Willie quietly. 'It was an accident. Lewis tried to grab the K off Fix, and Fix pushed him away. Harder than he realised. Didn't know his own strength I guess. But you also have to see . . . to realise, that it wasn't the Major he was seeing. He was freaked.'

'How . . . How did you get him off? The Major – Lewis – off . . . the things?'

'Hobbs and Arnold went down into the hole and pulled. I tell you, you never want to hear a sound like that. We was all cryin' and sobbin'. But we wanted to bury him.'

'Bury him? *Bury* him?'

'Fuck yes. OK, so we couldn't tell the whole truth, could we? We had a snit over some contraband gold and ended up fraggin' our officer. Accidentally, that is.'

It hit her like a hammer blow to the skull. She kept reaching and grasping to pull the strands together, but it was like trying to catch a pack of cards flicked up in the air. One by one they fell to earth.

'So Lewis—'

'Is dead.'

'And my Carl—?'

'Well, he was called Fix when I first knew him.'

'Why? For Chrissake you said it was an accident—'

'Yeah, but if we hadn't tried to get strung out that night. If we had put our hands up and said we can't go down—'

'Jesus, remind me not to call you for the defence.'

'I'm trying to make you understand what went though our heads. His head, that night.'

'So you got the body out?'

'Yeah, Hobbs found a way into the woods down one of the tunnels. We used shaped charges to blow a grave. A deep grave. We took two bars of gold each, all except Fix, and buried the rest . . .'

'And?'

'And laid the Major on top. Figured if anyone found the body they wouldn't dig much deeper. We took the co-ordinates anyways, but we scattered several pieces of metal around and above the body, so we could use a mine detector to find the site again. Which was a joke, because the whole area was full of shrapnel, but it was all we could think of. We just took a couple of bars each, as I said, to tide us over until we could get back – not Fix, wouldn't touch it. Then we went back and blew the tunnels to fuck.'

'And told everyone what?'

'That he'd been caught in a firefight. That we couldn't get to the Major's body. The VC used to like stealing the corpses – knew it screwed us up bad. Knew we liked body counts and real bodies to bring home. It wasn't like it didn't happen.'

'So . . . how did Fix begin impersonating Lewis?'

'Nah, you got it wrong. He didn't impersonate him. He sort of became him.'

She knew then she had to get him out. Had to persuade Willie to pull what would be left of him out of there. But he was still talking.

'It was almost dawn by the time we had finished and got back to the base, which was still smouldering. We was . . . well, tired isn't the word. Like husks, y'know? Not really human if you ask me. Not after that. So Chessyre went into the hut, Hobbs and Arnold and me crashed out in the GPs. I was just drifting away when I realised what he must be thinking. Fix, I mean. I got up and went to the room, and I was right.'

'What?'

'Fix was there with the gun in his mouth. You know, his gun. He's figured—'

'That he should have gone in the pit, not Lewis.'

'Correct-amundo.'

'So what did you do?'

'I had to think fast. One, I didn't want him killing himself, and two – I didn't want the bullet to come through the back of his skull and hit me. So I grabbed my K-bar – knife – and did the first thing that came into my head. I put the knife through his hand. Pinned it do the desk. That brought him round.'

'The scar . . . ?'

'Yup.' Willie put a hand on Dinah's shoulder. She was tense, rigid, afraid to let go unless she collapsed. Softly he added: 'You will have to ask him the rest. I know some of it . . .'

'Has . . . does he face up to all this now?'

'Face up to it? I don't know. I guess I didn't help turning up like that. Kind of threw him. I guess you didn't help suggesting he go play tunnel rats again. What he said to me was this: that Chessyre had to disappear. Had to die. He could either swallow the bullet, or rub him out.'

'So he isn't who I think he is at all? Not the man I live with. He's someone else altogether.'

'You kiddin'? He ain't Carl Lewis. I told you Carl Lewis was strak – always played it by the rules. Well, his own rules, anyhow. Except for that one time. True, this guy here ain't exactly the Fix Chessyre I knew, but then – are you the person you were twenty-five years ago?'

'I was six.'

'Well I rest my case. We all change. I guess he just changed more than most.'

'How did he become Carl Lewis?'

'I dunno. I just—' He hesitated, wondering about how valid his promise was now. 'He told me in the bar. He sort of doesn't stay being Lewis. He said, at the end, after a couple of beers, that it took about two years.'

'What did?'

'For the, uh, façade – façade, is that right? – yeah, for the façade to break down, was how he put it. For the old Fix to reappear. Only way to keep him down was to move on, re-establish Lewis somewhere else. He reckoned . . .' He snorted. 'Said it was called . . . some shrink told him . . .' He rubbed the bridge of his nose, trying to push away the dull throb lurking within. 'I think it was FDS.'

Dinah snorted. She knew it from her training in art therapy. 'DFS. Dissociative Fugue State. It's a piece of pop psychology. Big on the soaps. What it means is, you suppress something you don't want to remember. It's just an extreme version of what gets us all through the days.'

'Yeah, I tell you, I seen stranger things come out of 'Nam than this. You heard them all. But remember, three million Americans served in Vietnam in the sixties and seventies. So fuckin' what? you ask. So how many of those went nuts? I'll tell ya, far fewer than you think. OK, you hear about the ones that killed their wives in their sleep, or won't live near Orientals. But most came back and got on with life. But there are a few that didn't make it. And I'll bet a high percentage of those were tunnel rats. We thought we were supermen. What we was doin' was fuckin' ourselves up. So if you don't want to end up climbing the walls of some hospital, you gotta find a way to cope. Lewis, Fix, found his. Weirder than most, hard on him, too, but it kept him together. But then again, some of us walked away from worse than what he did. I guess he went in too fast. Like a climber. Didn't get used to it gradually, didn't . . . what's the word?'

'Acclimatise?'

'Yeah, acclimatise. And that was the Major's fault. Should've given him time. But the Major always thought time was running low.' He snorted. 'Well, I suppose it was for him.'

'What about you, Willie?'

'Me? Damn, by tunnel-rat standards, I'm Mr Well Balanced. Apart from the fact I'm stupid enough to think about going back.'

'To Vietnam?' He nodded. 'Is that wise? I mean, I thought it was a good idea for Lewis to confront . . . you know, I was tired of living with a man who wouldn't switch the light off and stuff, but look where making him face up to it got me. Can't you let it lie?'

'I ain't going for my mental health here. The old noggin is pretty clean, pretty reliable. OK, I like a drink, but, hey, as I said, you gotta cope with life one way or another.'

'Then why?'

'The gold. We never got to pick it up. Couldn't figure a way of getting it out of the country. It's still there, underneath poor old Major Lewis.'

Hilton's last breath was a long, drawn-out affair, it started as a quiet stream, became a low moan, and finished on a soft gurgling sound. The Captain closed his eyes. He had just been in time to stop Hilton blowing his own brains out, thinking the Captain was a rat come for supper. They would eventually, no doubt. Acting mighty strange, those rats. Used to be content to hole up in the theatre since the days of the burn-'em-out campaign. Now they were just wild, ever since old Ace here shot Whitey and left the other two for rat-snack.

The last of the air from Hilton's lungs came out, a final low moan, like a mixture of pain and relief. Maybe the Captain should have let him pull the trigger. He was going anyway. Perhaps he would bury him later. But now, at least he had an assignment.

This poor stiff was the only person he had told in years that he had never been a cop, not of any sort. Never had been. He was mock police through and through. Oh, had seen all the films, watched the TV shows when he was above ground – Hill Street Blues,

Law and Order – bought the manuals, the weapons, the uniform. But Seattle PD? 4F. Psychological profile too unstable to serve and protect. Too unstable? What did that make some of the guys they let in?

Every now and then they would clock him hanging around precinct houses and roust him. All right, so he posed as a detective a couple of times and did house-to-house interviews. Got into a few holding cells. Passed himself off as a traffic cop to a few damsels in distress. What did that make him? The Green River Killer? He let out a chuckle. They were just pissed 'cause he'd dented their security. So what did they do? Decided he was mad. Needed treatment to cure him of this police fixation. Lithium. Largactil. Whatever pills we got hanging around.

But now, this was a promise, a proper protect-and-survive mission. It was all over down here anyway. After all the detonations and tunnel falls, they were bound to come in and fill in the Underworld once and for all. Maybe they should have done it years ago. Either way, his time underground was at an end. Time to rejoin the real world again. He felt a chill ripple down his spine at the thought. Bet real cops don't get that, he thought.

There is the truth, thought Lewis, and then there is the truth with the bones taken out, like those mushy chickens they used to get in the C-rations. Boneless chickens. It sounded as if they bred them that way, specially floppy to be folded into army tins. He was drifting again, and Harry needed him. His lips were blue in the flashlight. But it wouldn't be long now. He could hear scraping and digging coming from the small crawl tunnel. Someone was coming through. He just hoped they had a stretcher. This guy's legs weren't going to be moving for some time. If ever.

'Then what happened?' asked Harry.

Ah yes, the truth. Then what happened was . . . well, he didn't see Lewis at that instant. His addled brain saw the girl's father, come to berate him, to kill him, to punish him, and he had . . . he had . . . what he had really done was push his commanding officer into a pit of stakes and shot him. No excuses, no it-must-have-been-the-acid . . . or the stress . . . or a trick of the light. But it meant they couldn't take him back to base because there were three rimless low-velocity .22 slugs that would be found and ID'ed as being from the Chess. And then there was the gold. Best ignore all that.

'The Major fell into a punji pit. You know what they were? Subsequent infection killed him. Without a CO, Underdogs were returned to unit to await further orders. I was flown back to Oakland.'

'And became an American citizen?'

'Yes.' Well, not immediately.

'You know . . . my soon-to-be father-in-law, he was in the war.'

'One of the ARVIN lucky enough to get out?'

Harry laughed. 'N-oooo, not exactly. He was with the other side. He was a VC. Funny, he doesn't look like he could even lift a gun, let alone fire it. He could have been trying to blow your head off for all I know.'

'He was down tunnels?' Incredulous now.

'Christ, who knows? He'll never talk to me about it. Never talks to me, period.' The numbness of shock seemed to be wearing off, because each chuckle sent little spasms across his face, and his eyes were starting to dart wildly. 'So I dunno what he did. Or how he got out. I heard some rumours though. That he got out with a shitload of money, lots of it in gold.'

As the little rancid worm of a thought burrowed into his cortex Lewis shook his head. No. Ridiculous. Stop that right now. He wondered if Harry had ever heard of Elder Sanchez and his synchronistic paintings. This was a frozen moment if ever there was one. It was all there, splashed across the canvas, an umbilical running across the world from Vietnam to Seattle. Had to be bullshit. Didn't it?

Harry gasped a little bit. 'Not that I'll ever see any of it. Even if I marry her . . . he's not going to let some surfer Yank get his hands on it.'

'You are a surfer?'

'Was. Was a surfer. Then someone took me aside and said, very nicely, that's it. You can carry on doing this for the next ten years, but you will never get any better. Not junior league exactly, but not majors, either. You? I mean, bein' Australian?'

Lewis could just – just – remember the beach and the boards, but it was . . . it was a long, long time ago. He looked at the barrel of the Chess, thought about the honeycomb and foam interior of the suppressor. 'Not really.'

There was a loud grunt as the first of the S&Rs pulled themselves through. 'I am glad to see you,' Lewis said, and hesitated. It had been a long time since he had used the words. The name. His name, damn it. *His* name. 'Chessyre. Felix Chessyre.' He tried not to catch Harry's eye.

FORTY-EIGHT

Underworld. Seattle.

Milliner examined the troopers crowding round him. He brushed off the medic who was trying to finish dressing his wrists and pointed at one of the men. 'You.' He read the name stripe. 'Cobb. Take off that uniform. I need your coveralls.' Cobb was about his build. The shit was already drying, like it was some sort of disgusting Plaster-of-Paris cast, and soon he wouldn't be able to bend his limbs in it. He stripped off the vest, the armour and pulled down the zip on his uniform.

It had taken twenty minutes to get them out, twenty minutes while he was convinced all that was going to be left by the time they reached him was a severed arm hanging onto a crossbar. Now they were trying to get them to go to the Mason Medical Center, fussing and pushing and cooing, as if he was damaged in some way. Marzo was going along with this. Marzo. He couldn't believe it. M&Ms: thought they went together like that. A team. Well, *he* wasn't finished here, he thought as he pulled on the embarrassed trooper's clothes. Not by a long shot.

Another trooper, white-faced from his fishing expedition, appeared. Milliner smiled when he saw what he was holding. 'Get it cleaned up,' he said. 'At least we know it isn't going to do that again.'

* * *

Sergeant John Tenniel looked at Harry, knew he was hurt badly. He knelt down beside the stretcher and brushed the dirt and filth from the parts of his face not covered by the oxygen mask. The eyes were shut. Bad call, John, very bad call. Time to tend the roses, see the wife, buy a second dog. There were a lot of conversations he had to have, none of them good. And a lot of them with himself, asking what possessed him? After a career following the book, what grabbed him that night and said: 'I've got an idea for a great wheeze here.'

Lewis's woman walked up and put a hand on his shoulder. He couldn't look at her, just squeezed back on the calf. He barely noticed the other set of legs in the scuffed shoes standing next to her. Two paramedics lifted the stretcher. 'He'll be OK, you know,' said one S&R guy. 'Banged up bad. Have to walk with a stick, maybe. But he's alive.'

'What about the other guy?' asked Bowman, looking at the hole, waiting for another figure to emerge.

'Oh, yeah. I forgot. He says he's not coming out. Got a kid to rescue. Truth is, I think he's a slug short of a full magazine, Sergeant. It ain't exactly safe where he's heading. Not after what happened.'

Bowman put her head close to his: 'I need some air,' she said gently. 'I'll be in the car.' Tenniel put his head in his hands and rubbed his face to try and put some circulation into his brain. Would this never end?

Pepper had lost his back. A great strip of clothing and skin had been torn off, leaving him looking like a raw, bloodied skunk. It was prime steak in places. Hurt like he'd been caught in a mincer and then flame-grilled. He felt like a human Whopper.

He had been blown well clear by the blast, which had channelled its way out through the open manhole cover in a straight-sided column of fire, like something biblical. At least he had made a soft landing in a pile of garbage. By the time he had recovered, the girl and the guy had gone. Pig was dead. Half the walls had come down. And he could hear voices. He pushed himself up. Where was the gun? It took him three minutes to find it. He changed the clip. And then very stiffly sat down to think.

He had to get Annie. He wondered if the garage entrance was intact, whether the plants had survived. A slow, creeping feeling of listlessness came over him. Maybe he should just sit here and wait. It was the pain stopping him moving, the dull throbbing from his back, ennervating him completely. He was crouching there, thinking about what the cops could do to him, and whether they had first aid, when he heard the small footsteps coming his way.

Fix had gone a hundred yards, just crossed an open water main, when he heard the scrabbling behind him, and saw the light. He flashed his own beam back and caught the face of Willie in it. Willie. Did that mean Hobbs was far behind? Hobbs was always the best anchor man.

'Hey, Mr Dodo, wait up.' Willie reached him, gave him the once-over in his flash beam. He looked OK. Dusty. Lot of blood, but that was probably the cop's. 'Dinah sent me.' Ain't that the truth, he thought. Damned near ordered him down in the end. 'And the

Sergeant up there. Show's over, Lewis. Coupla tunnel cops right up my ass.' He flicked around. There was no sign. 'Unless that porky one got stuck in the tube back there.'

'Fix. Let's cut the bullshit. It's Fix. You know it's Fix. I know.'

And so does your old lady, he thought – but I ain't gonna be the one to tell. 'Well, I tell you, that's a relief. But the show's over whatever you fuckin' callin' yourself.' Willie grabbed his arm and got to look down the barrel of the Chessyre Close Combat Pistol, to give it its full name. Fuck, he even had his crazy gun with him.

'You stopped me once, when I should've done something, Willie. Now I've got something else to do. Little girl. Twelve, thirteen.'

'Way I heard it, she's eight and blonde and definitely not Vietnamese.'

'I know that. I know that.' He shook his head hard. It was confusing. It normally took more than one night. A week, a month sometimes before it all leaked out and he was back facing everything he had done again. And every time he made the same decision. He couldn't live with Fix, not that stupid, gauche kid – it was the Major who deserved to survive. Time to move on. Bury it again. All over again. Feel the stakes puncture the skin, hear the artery snick, watch the blood froth out, staining the sharpened stakes. Die in his place. Well, maybe not this time. But shit it was hard to tell the truth from all the lies right now.

'Look, this ain't some cheque and balance thing,' insisted Willie, putting on his best TV salesman voice: '*One intact eight-year-old pays off previously incurred debt. You may lose your soul if you don't keep up payments on the Good Guy account*. Don't work like that. Just like keeping Lewis's name alive probably doesn't really help old Carl, does it? You ain't doing it for him. Carl is a bag of bones on top of some very expensive real estate. C'mon, Fix. Tell me a fuckin' joke.'

Fix looked at him. A joke? The whole story was one long joke. Should he blame Willie for giving him that acid? Probably not. Jesus, Willie thought he was doing him a favour. 'How's Del Cielo?'

Willie patted the little wooden rooster on his chest. 'Still workin', I guess.' And it was true, Willie looked more solid, less ethereal under here. He, too, had grown real at last. Those days, they'd been Willie's prime, his prize fight, his Rumble in the Jungle. Downhill ever since.

'You coming?'

'If you going, I suppose.'

'And Harry?'

Willie remembered the calm, waxy face. Close, but he won't be buying any farms. Won't be running any marathons, either. 'OK. He'll be OK. Shall we go and lay this egg once and for all?'

'Put the moose on the table?'

'Yeah, put the fuckin' moose on the goddamn table.' Willie knew what the ARVIN used to say when they saw them going down. Didn't think they could understand. *Dien. Ngu.* Crazy. Stupid. He was glad they weren't here now to see just how *dien* two Yankees had become.

'I'll tell you one thing,' said Fix, smacking his dry, dusty lips, remembering.

'What?'

'I could murder a cup of tea.'

In latteland? Now that *was* crazy, thought Willie.

Pepper found Annie outside the dope sheds, dazed and confused. Like him, she had slumped down, and now sat under a shaft of light from the road above, illuminated like some exhibit in what was turning into a freak show. She looked beat up, but apart from a dusting of glass shards down one side of her face, was pretty much intact. Better than him.

'Annie,' he said.

She looked up with the closest she could manage to joy, but the hint of gladness faded into something more twisted when she saw what he was holding.

'Look what I found.'

Annie leapt up, pulled her arm as far back as it would go, like a pitcher winding up for a curve ball, and slapped Ali as hard as she could. The scream got lost in the dust and space around them. Annie remembered her Para-Ord was somewhere under a pile of debris, and leapt to wrest the Ingram from Pepper, while he held onto the girl's collar and tried to fend her off.

'Annie, Annie, babe, hold up. We got us a passport here. Worked for the Hilton guy. Work for us.'

'Where is he now?' she said suddenly, panting. She poked the girl, hard, and she squealed. 'Where is he?'

'He's . . . he's dead.'

She turned to Pepper. 'Worked for him, did it?'

'Annie, that man fucked up by looking for help from us. Could've been home free. And I ain't spendin' ten years inside with Ricky, listening to his stories about what a great lay you are all over again.' She looked at him, shocked. That big mouthed, small-dicked . . . 'Shit,' he grinned, 'intend to find out for m'self. Now here – He handed over Pig's .38. 'Don't you go capping this little girl until I say so.'

As he turned she saw his back, and she reached out to touch him, but he shrugged her off. Hurt enough already. 'Now, can we get to the garage?'

Annie shook her head. 'Not unless you got an earth-mover in your pocket.'

'Wall on the other side – it look like this?' He pointed to the collapsed sections.

'Probably. A lot of masonry came down. I heard it.'

''Cause me and Ricky, we found a way out over there.'

'To up top?'

'Yeah – we gonna catch us a bus.'

Willie and Fix made good time. They found Hilton real fast, one side of him soaked in congealing blood. They shooed away the rat that had come out to sniff the entrée, and Willie turned his head to the torch beam. The face was ridiculous. Two front teeth had dropped down, making him look like a gormless rabbit. Willie pushed them back in and closed the jaw. He always hoped in the tunnels that, if he got it, someone would at least tidy him up a little. 'This the guy?'

Fix nodded. 'High body count here, Willie.'

'Yeah, well let's not donate ours to the grand total. What was the girl's name?'

'Ali. Alice.'

They emerged out of the tunnel into the spooky grey gleam cast by the over-lights and turned right. Some distance over their shoulder there was a mass of flash beams coming their way. 'The cavalry?' asked Willie.

'Well, they're late enough to be.'

Now that Hilton was dead, thought Willie, all they had to do was scoop up Ali, and it would all be over and they could worry about piecing Fix's brain together at leisure. Then they heard the scream of the girl, a shriek of real pain, come tumbling past them.

They ran as best they could, jumping the erratics of concrete that had been scattered by the explosion, dodging round the concrete supports, one or two of them now sporting fresh cracks.

They almost fell across Pig as they went down the collapsed section and up the other side. Willie barely glanced at the crucified form, but Fix stopped frozen, his jaw agape. It was happening again.

It was a few moments before Willie clicked in. The body with the metal reinforcing rods pushed through it. The blood and the gristle clinging to the ends, as if gruesome party poppers had exploded through the torso. Reversed now, like time running backwards. Back then, the girl went first. Then Lewis got his lights punched by the punji stakes. And in this weird half-light, this crazy fucking half-light pouring down from the heavens, lying there with patches of blood like macabre crop circles, it was like looking at Lewis all over again.

Willie grabbed Fix by the arm. The figures behind were getting closer. Someone shouted to halt. 'Hey, we're with you, buttwipe,' shouted Willie. And, in a moment of inspiration. 'Seattle PD Special Deployment.'

That almost stopped them in their tracks. He could imagine them thinking: No, hold on, *we're* the Special Forces.

Fix and Willie made it to the dope room first, and stood on what was left of the wall and surveyed the carnage. Even in the dimness, lit only by flashlights, the sight of the machinery and the plants, many now broken and drooping, was staggering. Willie sniffed. The air was full of an ammoniacal tang. He could hear the sound of running water or fluid, as if something was leaking. And underneath the sharpness, he could smell the plants themselves. He knew what was going on here. He examined the ceiling. The section to the left had peeled down like a piece of banana skin, crushing everything beneath it. Had to go to the right then.

They must have made a perfect target standing there on the low wall, waving their lights around. From the far side of the cavernous rooms Willie heard the warning cry a micro-second before he saw the muzzle flash, heard the ping of shells ricocheting off steel, and pushed Fix inside, rolling after him. Whatever firepower they had, it didn't have the range. But who the fuck was this? Well, whoever had been growing the plants he presumed, getting high by going low. Full marks for enterprise. He looked behind him. The SWATs or whatever they were had slowed down too; he could pick out the individual helmet lights now as they inched forward, that odd counter-terrorism shuffle, the assault rifles held high, the muzzle scanning left and right.

Well, this was a bad day for Seattle's dopers and smokers, a dip in the supply was on the cards – his money was on the SWATs here. But the growers were likely to be pissed, too. Pissed enough to try to blow the head off anyone they could.

He flicked off his own light, reached over and did

Fix's for him, took his hand and pulled him to the side, and started working his way through the debris towards where the flashes had come from. He was wheezing now, and the residual hangover was pounding his temples. He was getting too old for this. Then again, someone should tell his adrenalin glands. They, at least, seemed to be having a good time.

Pepper raised the M11 to let rip with a burst at the shapes he could see at the far side of the growing rooms, more a token than anything else. He reckoned most of it would hit the floor. Even as he hoisted the weapon he heard the girl cry, '*Look out*,' and the grunt as Annie smacked her across the head again. He fired anyway, and the nearest plants jerked and danced like speed-crazed punks as the bullets tore through them. There were pings as stray rounds punctured the feed troughs, and there was the sound of more fluid pissing onto the floor. Damn shame, he thought, all that dope dying before their eyes.

They had a hundred dark yards to cover to the first door – the overhead lights had not been deployed over this section. But it was relatively straightforward, and, if he remembered properly, there was an access door that would get them into the bus tunnels and to the surface. He could easily bust into any one of the stores in the Westlake Center and get them out that way before the cops realised what was going on.

The girl, still shocked from the force of Annie's second blow, was dragging her feet, and in the end he picked her up and put her under his arm. Annie was walking backwards, stumbling. 'It's OK, babe, that'll keep their heads down.' He flashed on the MagLite for a few seconds at a time, just enough for them to check the terrain.

They hit the wall of the Metro tunnel, smooth and new compared to everything around them. Thick trunks of electrical cable snaked above their head. He could see the frame of the door, but no handle. They'd taken the handle off this side. He fought back a flash of panic. It wasn't here, was it? It was the other side. The door with the handle was on the other side, the east side of the underground bores. They'd checked it out when they had thought of setting up underneath Pike. He'd mixed up the orientation of the bus tunnels.

But this door had to lead somewhere. He handed the girl over to Annie, who squeezed her arm in a tighter grip than necessary. She held the .38 in front of Ali's face. 'One word, you snotty little bitch, and I'll shoot you, just like I should have shot your pal.'

Pepper shone round the frame. Steel door. No hinges. It was an access panel to check this electrical conduit behind here. So it probably opened outwards so nothing could block it from this side. Aware of how little was left in the clip, Pepper lined up at where the catch should be and signalled them back.

He felt hot metal fly past his ear and stopped. His ears buzzed with the noise. Annie said something to him, but he couldn't hear. He changed the clip and gave a shorter burst. Still nothing. Angrily he stepped up and put the full force of his right foot against the panel. It creaked. He launched himself at it again and it gave and flew open, and Pepper found himself clawing the air of the tunnel, fifteen feet above the platform. He windmilled his arms as if trying to fly, but to no avail. He plummeted through space clawing and reaching for a hold on one of the big Deco lamps that festooned the station, but the side panel came off in his hands. He crashed into the deluge pipe, designed to flood the tunnel in case of fire, and spun into the wall, where his skull smacked onto the Fay Jones shopping mural, adding his blood to the abstraction until he bounced off one of the benches below, designed to stop loiterers. Pepper managed to crawl three feet, before he let out a long sigh and lay immobile in the centre of the platform.

Willie relieved Fix of the gun and ran ahead. He could hear him behind, shuffling, trying to keep up now. Ignore Fix. It was up to him now. All the old excitement was there, only purer. No strange and foreign land, just a little girl to be pulled out. Maybe he had been flirting with the wrong side of the law all these years. It felt good to be at least partly in the right at last. But then, he thought he'd been with the good guys in 'Nam. Then they tell him, Oops bad call. Go figure.

The oblong of light hurt his eyes it was so bright. What the hell was beyond there? He strode up to the edge and looked down, shading his eyes. The black guy looked pretty messed up. He was face-down in a pool of glass slivers torn from the light, blood slowly leaking out. His back was crusted with dried gore, and one of his legs was twisted at a crazy angle. A machine pistol of some kind had skidded into the middle of the bus lane. This must be the dope grower.

There was a woman, probably an early passenger, kneeling over him. She seemed to be cuddling a little girl. That was it then. All over. When he glanced back he could see the helmet beams of the SWOPS. A mechanical, disembodied voice was filling the station below: 'Stay where you are. Help will be on its way soon. Stay where you are . . .' The controller's tone was shaky, and Willie guessed the things that looked like disco glitterballs were his cameras and he'd viewed all this – powerless to help – from his control desk downtown somewhere.

About a hundred metres away from the dead or dying doper, down at the far end of the platform, was one of the dual-power buses that ran through the tunnels. No sign of the driver. He had probably seen the flying act by the black guy and made a sprint for it. Midway between the woman and girl and the bus was a slumped form on the bench, someone sleeping it off by the look of it. Had to have been – the benches were humped to make them as uncomfortable as possible for loiterers. So, as he had thought – pick up the little girl, put Lewis/Fix back together again, and case closed.

The first shot hit the door frame, and Willie's old reactions let him down. He should have dived forward, but instead he twisted to see where the fire was coming from. Even as he did it he remembered. You don't do that. You dive, and then you look. Stupid. Stupid old man. The .38 caught him low in the back and his legs buckled.

As he was thrown forward by the impact Fix instinctively caught him and lowered him to the ground. Willie blew air out with bloated cheeks, his Dizzy Gillespie trick, trying to keep the pain at bay.

'Willie, fuck, Willie, No. Willie. Bad karma, man, bad

karma.' He was speaking so fast he was dribbling in Willie's face, the saliva being pushed out with the torrent of words. The smell of cordite, the thick aroma of dying dope plants, Willie could feel the man's senses working overtime. He had to bring him back. It wasn't over. None of it was.

'Still got the girl . . . down there, Fix.'

'Drop your weapon. DROP YOUR WEAPON.' The night controller had turned strident, bellowing into the mike from his desk nine blocks away, obviously feeling impotent.

'Willie. Oh, fuck, no man. Medic. MEDIC!'

He tried again. 'Lewis – save the girl.'

Willie looked into the face, harshly bleached by the light from the bus tunnel. The controller had turned the illumination up full to give him a better CCTV image. The glare was hurting both their eyes. But, even though he was squinting, Willie could see Fix's eyes were all over the place. Darting, confused. He did this to him. He made him drop acid. And it was the acid that had made him push Lewis, had turned a friendly face into some foreign fiend for one second. Just enough to cost the man his life. Turn on a friend to the good life. Yeah. It was down to him after all. Him and Lewis between them. But this wasn't the time to go over that. Just like it wasn't time to eat the barrel of the gun all those years ago. Bring him back, he thought, bring him back.

Willie carefully took Fix's left hand, and stroked it, feeling the old knife scar. He raised the .22 and pressed it against the palm. Fix didn't fight. Willie pulled the trigger. There was puff of air and a plop as flesh flew across and landed on the wall. Fix let out a long, low moan and grabbed his hand.

'The woman down there. With the girl. I think she shot me.'

Fix felt the vertigo come on, spinning the faces, watching Willie blur in and out of focus, one second early twenties, next a dying man of fifty. Dying? No . . . not dying. There had been enough killing. More than enough.

He stood up and took the Chess out of Willie's grip, and walked to the door, half-expecting to feel the shot tear into his flesh. The woman had an arm around the girl's throat and was backing up, towards the stationary bus. She waggled the gun in his direction, but he was fairly certain that had been a lucky shot with the snub-nosed .38. Not unless she was very good. Even better than he had been. And that was unlikely. Impossible, even. He jumped.

It was a long way. He felt the air pull at his face, billowing his hair, his clothes, felt light, light as a feather, as if he would never reach the bottom. Knew something was happening here that had been a long, long time coming. Time to meet Fix full-on after all these years.

The landing was hard, so he rolled to break the fall, taking in the glaring world of murals and shop windows and escalators. He stopped when he careered into the prostrate form of Pepper, which probably saved his life. He felt the dead man's body jerk as the .38s slammed into lifeless meat.

Fix lay where he fell for a moment and risked a look. The public address system had gone quiet. The controller was probably too stunned to continue, content to watch the bizarre scenes unfold on camera.

The woman was halfway to the bus and had picked up the machine pistol. Big firepower. Upper hand. Thirty, thirty-two rounds, empty in less than a minute. And with the other hand she had the .38 shoved in the girl's ear, hammer back, trigger pulled, just a thumb slip away from detonation.

'Fire when you have a clear sighting.'

Fix looked up. There were two snipers in the doorway, and above them a grizzled figure he assumed was their commanding officer, pointing wildly. 'Go for a head shot.'

'NO,' said Fix, waving them back. 'No. She gets hit she drops the hammer, the kid get's it. I got her covered. Stay cool.'

OK, so she had the girl covered – the second time this had happened to the youngster in a few hours, he thought sadly, but this time at least we know for sure there is a slug under the hammer – but the woman still had to get up the steps and drive the bus, all without getting plugged. She would only have to give those sniper guys one half of an opportunity and she was dead. How *did* she hope to get out of this? thought Fix.

The Captain shifted position on the bench and waited until she was level with him. Annie's body was turned so that the girl blocked any shot likely to come from the doorway above, so he could shoot her in the back, real easy, but that wasn't Police Code at all. No, he had to do this by the book, particularly with superior officers in the vicinity. He could see the SWAT team, and he wanted it to be his call; he had to give them confidence, let them know he was one of them.

He had promised Hilton and he was here. Look after the girl. Serve and Protect. Get the girl out alive. So he had shadowed them, watched them try to break into the tunnel. But he knew another way in, next level down, through what had once been the lake, now a harmless brown sludge beneath twisted metal, a route that surfaced where you were only briefly in view of the cameras. He wondered what was happening in that room where they monitored all the stations. Lights, bells and whistles, all going wild, he figured.

She was about fifteen metres away when he stood up and the coat slid off his shoulders to reveal the caked and stained uniform underneath. He pulled the big .45 Hilton had given him and he held it rock-steady, just like he always knew he would when he saw action. 'Armed police officer,' he said, relishing the phrase. 'Put her down. Drop your weapon and move away.'

Annie swivelled so hard she thought her head was going to come off, stared hard at the gun, then at the man. He was a filthy bum, there were almost cobwebs on him. And what did he have on? Jesus, the guy was a cop after all. Talk about undercover. No, no he wasn't, he was holding that big old shiny pistol all wrong, too tentatively. Recoil will break his fingers. Yeah, but it might just hit her beforehand though. She glanced to the front at the man who had jumped after her. He had cop coveralls on. But he looked like the genuine article. Blood appeared to be splashing from one hand, but he was ignoring it. She moved the gun from bum to cop, cop to the bum. Which one of them wouldn't have the nerve to shoot a woman. Which one? And who was going to risk hitting the girl?

'I'm OK,' said Ali, quietly, calmly, directly to the bum. 'Shoot her. I know you can do it, Captain. Shoot her.'

Annie slapped the side of her head with the butt of the Ingram and she could see the old man tense. Soon.

Milliner watched the old man in horror, checked the travesty of a uniform, saw him pull the gun, got a good look when the gnarled face turned to check out the party with the silenced weapon. He took in the cheekbones, the eyes, the eyebrows, the beard . . . he knew that face from a thousand replayed videos, grainy and fuzzy then, like some distant dream of a dissolute God, but even from this distance he could see it was the same man. Mad Milliner. It was a long way down, but he didn't hesitate. Nobody had time to stop him. He tightened the straps on the flame-thrower and jumped.

Fix kept pace with her, slightly side on to reduce the target area, remembering Willie and those smooth dancing movements. Keep the centre of gravity low. Don't hop. No dancing dodo. Smooth, smooth. No, Mr Dodo, like this. He crossed his right leg over the back of his left, then brought them together. Stepped again in the same way. Almost like being on rails. The front sight welded onto the big bulbous suppressor was bang on the woman's head. Ignore the pain in that hand. It'll pass. Did last time.

He heard the thud of a body hitting the ground behind him and half-turned. The figure approaching made him do a double-take. He had a helmet with faceguard on, but no black hood, and behind the Plexiglass shield his skin looked to have been pumiced raw. The eyes were two hideous circles, as if a red-hot branding iron had been laid over them. He had no eyebrows or eyelashes, and his hair was frazzled to steel wool. Both hands were swathed in bandages. There was an overpowering odour of decay. He was like a cross between the Toxic Avenger and the Creature from the Black Lagoon, giving off the odour of . . . he knew that stench. In his mind he flashed on the flaming oil barrels fired up to greet the morning sun, spewing their noxious odour across the bases of Vietnam. The man smelt of burnt shit.

Milliner took position behind Fix, and it took a moment for him to realise the man had tanks on his back. He had a flame-thrower. A flame-fucking-thrower? No wonder there had been an explosion. The nozzle of the weapon was describing an erratic arc, like a compass needle, from woman to hobo, hobo to woman, until it came to settle on . . . the hobo.

This was madness. A flame-thrower was hardly an appropriate weapon down here. The man must be mad, stark-raving mad. Fix carried on tracking the woman, one step after another, but he could feel the air growing viscous, slowing him down, as if it were Jell-o. This was it. A frozen moment, cryogenically inhibited until all activity was suppressed, every step taking an hour, two hours, all the time in the world to remember how he had come to this.

FORTY-NINE

Ben Moc FSB, Vietnam. 1970.

There was only one thought going through Fix's head that morning after they had got out of the tunnels: how did it go so wrong? It should've been me. Should've been me. I wasn't meant to come out of this. He could see that now. But somehow the gods had got confused, and Lewis went into the pit instead. Where was the justice in that? It was him who had killed the girl. Him who had thought the Major was some avenging Vietnamese. He was the one who deserved to die here. Not Lewis. No matter how he had let him down.

He sat at his desk and looked at the CCCP .22. The Chess .22. The Chessyre .22, the two pounds of pure ego that had brought him to this. He bounced it in his hand for a moment, fastened his fingers round the grip, flipped off the safety – whoever had designed that extra had done a good ergonomic job he noted with detachment, and put the suppressor in his mouth, tasted the bitter mix of metal and cordite. It would be just like being kissed goodnight. Better than Lewis got.

The pain was sudden and excruciating, so much so that he dropped the gun. He gasped in shock and looked down as he saw his left hand pinned to the desk by a K-bar, rivulets of red running down to stain the papers underneath. He thought he was going to faint, but Willie grabbed his head and jerked it around, pulling the tendons and clicking the vertebrae as he did so.

'Hey – is that going to bring you to your fuckin' senses? We already lost a man last night. One of our officers. How do you think if we lose them both? I'm being selfish here – we don't want a court-martial for fragging both of youse. We need a witness with a bit of brass on him. *Comprende*?'

He yanked the knife free and Fix winced as it scraped on the bones. Willie handed him a handkerchief. 'Got it in the fight with the VC. Probably get you a Purple Heart by the time we're finished.' He picked up the .22. 'I'll take this. You want to saw your wrists open, I suppose I can't stop you. But think about the rest of us here, huh?'

The door slammed. Fix felt his resolve ebbing away. Chemicals. They were confusing him. The handkerchief was soon soaked crimson and on shaky legs he went in search of the kitchen first-aid kit and managed to make a reasonable fist of a dressing. The door to Lewis's room was open, where the Major had hastily rushed out after the explosion. Fix pushed it and stepped inside, feeling those sad, betrayed eyes from the photographs on the wall boring into him. Lewis, Willie, The Bat – younger, fresher-faced. He tried not to meet their gaze.

On the bed was another LWL box, this one with the Smith & Wesson version of the Chess. Colt, Remington, they had all made prototypes. Next to that was the attaché case which Lewis normally kept chained to his wrist. It had combination locks, so Fix knew he was wasting his time when he reached out and flicked the slider. The catch released. He tried the other side. It clicked open. Lewis hadn't spun the tumblers after the last closing.

Several minutes passed before Fix summoned the nerve to lift the lid. It also crossed his mind that it might just be booby-trapped. He ran his fingers around the inside of the frame before pushing the top full open.

He picked up the Leica camera and weighed it in his hands, looked at the pictures on the wall. After a moment's hesitation he slid it into his breast pocket. Also in the case was a photograph of a Vietnamese woman standing next to the river in Saigon, in a big floral print dress, incongruously western, swamping her delicate figure. And another woman, this one blonde and full-faced, who wore the same sort of clothes with much less self-conciousness. And a quartet of kids, three institutional photographs from schools, and one snapshot. The one in the latter was obviously half-Vietnamese. He placed those back in the case.

He opened the brown envelopes and a stack of passports came out. Lewis as a Canadian citizen. Lewis as an Irish citizen. And blank ones. It explained how Lewis got things done. The best bribe in the world in Vietnam – a new identity for anyone who needed it.

Well, he needed one now. He carefully pocketed two of the unused US passports and closed the case. He waited a second and then scooped up the LWL case and headed for the door. He had an idea of what he had to do.

Hugo had been the key. The French spook, the man who had said the best trade in Saigon was in grandmothers – everyone was selling their grandmother's passports. If they were something other than Vietnamese.

There had been few formalities to stop him finding the man. The story about Lewis had been accepted at face value from the AAR – he wasn't the first man to disappear in the tunnels – and the Underdogs disbanded. Willie and the others were returned to their original units, and most rotated out within weeks, all watching the country disappearing beneath them and wondering about the gold. Still, they all had enough to be going on with, enough to help them fuck up their lives for the time being.

Fix was told he could go back to complete his exchange programme at the Land Warfare Laboratory, Aberdeen Proving Grounds. But things had changed. Kent State had happened. The dominos were tumbling all right, but not the way anyone had expected three, four years ago. He didn't want to go back. Not to that place, not to that person.

In Saigon, he had found Hugo at Lucky's, the bar where he had met Grogan and the other Australians before his disastrous night on the town. He remembered the righteous anger in Lewis's voice when he found him in the whorehouse. Was it hypocrisy? Or was he just looking out for him?

It had been two months since Fix had been in Lucky's, just two months since the Underdogs had gone in country to turn the underground war around, but already it felt oddly anti-climactic, like the party, such as it was, was over. Even the girls and mama-san had gone. 'First rats off the sinking ship,' Hugo had said. The deal was easy. How much for a new identity? Hugo had shrugged. How much have you got? Five grand? Just enough to put the correct stamps on the passport, set up social security numbers, the whole thing. How convenient. How neat.

Fix still had the silent gun with him, from the S&W case he had taken from Lewis's room. Thought about greasing Hugo after the deal was done. But he knew that was a waste of time. The guy had the gen about heavier dudes than Fix. But Hugo must have seen it flit through his mind. 'Don't you worry about me. But I don't have to do this in his name. You can have any name you like.'

He shook his head. He didn't understand. Felix Chessyre should have died in that tunnel. Not Lewis. Not Chi Mae. Felix Chessyre had killed a girl – bad enough, but no big deal in this war – and killed his mentor, his senior officer. Maybe, under that stiffness – and that smattering of hypocrisy – his friend. At least, perhaps he could have been one day, if Chessyre had earned it. But no more days for Lewis. How could he live with that? Now Chessyre had to disappear, one way or another. This way was best.

Fix was rotated out to Oakland, and he headed east, through Nevada, Arizona, Texas, New Orleans, Virginia. Like a worn-out reptile skin, Chessyre was gradually sloughed off, ditched. Fix became tidy, austere, began taking photos – not as good as Lewis, but passable – even tried to like opera, like Lewis. Some things took, some didn't. But he was damaged goods. There were places he could never go. Particularly small, dark ones. Never. It wasn't claustrophobia. It was the smell. Every time the walls closed in or the lights dimmed it hit him, the stench of fresh blood and rotten rice. But that was the only real glitch. By the end of the decade Chessyre was dead. And Carl Lewis had a life, of sorts. Until Chessyre started to reappear, a bit at a time, short bursts, as if he was struggling to come back. To surface from where he had been buried, his cerebral grave.

Each time a different part of him came out. Sometimes the idiot joker. Then the slob. Then the guy who wanted everyone to like him, incapable of a decision to save his life. Once it was the Underdog, over-cocky and dangerous. Now and then he even thought about Lewis's two families – the US one and the Saigon version. The American model probably had a pension and a picture on the mantelpiece. What about the Viet version? Trying to prove who they were during the last, chaotic days at the gates of the US embassy . . . it was then when he wanted to scream loudest.

Sometimes he told people. Felt the need to talk. Not all of it, but sometimes what they heard sounded crazy enough to drive them away. More often they got scared by the switchback mood swings, the sudden jarring personality shifts. To get back on an even keel, calm and in control again, it was as if he had to metaphorically go away and adjust his dress, tidy himself up, splash cold water on his face. So he always did. Over the past twenty years he must have killed old Fix a dozen times or more. He had had more lives than Dracula. Maybe this time he was back to stay.

FIFTY

Seattle Metro Bus Tunnels. Westlake Station. 4.25 am

Fix pulled himself back to the present and knew it couldn't be him. He couldn't make that shot. The Chess .22s were soft-nosed. Maximum damage at close range. But even at this distance, he could trust them to stay true. In a Viet tunnel it was different. Now he probably could hit the woman. Then again, he just might hit the girl. Might miss both. Couldn't take the risk that it would cleave the girl's forehead open. And the bum, he was waving the gun around, holding it like everything he learned was from the movies, all show. You had to squeeze hard on those .45s to engage the safety grip. Wouldn't fire otherwise. Did he know that? More to the point, would the babe with the machine pistol know that?

Annie looked outside again and in the corner of her vision saw the sad, twisted shape of Pepper. The other guy was still there, lined up on her. And behind him some, some gila monster, fresh fried and crispy, with a strange contraption in his hand, swinging back and forward, but more on the bum than her. Time to tot up the odds. Forget the Special Forces, they must have realised dropping her meant her finger came off the hammer. The old man here and the two guys to the left? No. Too many. Just the guys to the left? Yes. She looked again. The pool of blood next to Pepper had grown bigger. Would he bleed like that if he was dead? Had she hit him when she fired at the first jumper? Perhaps he'd been OK until then. Maybe he still was. And if a medic could get to him soon . . .

It was Ali who saw them first. All eyes were on her and Annie, the interlocked pair slowly backing towards the bus, nobody was looking in the other direction, at the two figures creeping along the tunnel wall, sprinting from meagre shadow to meagre shadow. But she could see them, and she would know those huge breasts anywhere, and that black, scraped-back hair, and the hideous scars of the other one. Not to mention the calf-skull-on-a-stick. It wasn't a dream after all. Well, it was always too strange to have been. And here they were again, weird and pissed off by the looks of it.

She opened her mouth to yell but Annie moved the barrel of the pistol under her jaw and it snapped shut. She grunted but the pressure increased, squeezing onto her windpipe. Too late, they were running now, heading for the Captain. She could see they were covered with what looked like scabs, dozens, hundreds of little wounds as if they had been slashed by . . . sharp teeth. They had had to fight off the rats. And now it was the Captain they wanted. They must have wanted him real bad to come up here, into the light, to show themselves as the freaks they were.

Ali twisted to one side, felt the metal of the barrel score her skin and yelled, '*CAPTAIN!*'

He half-turned just as the skull staff's arc caught him on the side of the head, sending him careering against the wall. The calf's head severed off its mounting and skittered across the tunnel roadway towards Ali.

Milliner was rooted to the spot. A huge, badly scratched woman in ripped Mariner clothes, battling with a down-and-out cop. His tormentor. The man he wanted. But he couldn't move, because he was transfixed by the other one, the one with the red face covered in a tracery of what looked like white veins. The one who was looking at him, staring at him, screaming at him, coming at him.

The man was sprinting now, his eyes wide, his mouth twisted in hate. Milliner took a step back, raised the Beauty and let him have a blast. The screaming became louder, changing to a shriek of agony as the fireball bloomed out from his chest, running across his arms, his back, flowing down his legs, crisping the skull, lifting it to reveal the ignited fat underneath, turning him into a human torch, and still he came on. Milliner dropped the thrower nozzle and reached for the sidearm strapped to his thigh, but it was too late; he felt the terrifying heat as the man reached him, standing inches away, his flesh boiling and blistering beneath the overcoat of flame. Then he reached out and clasped Milliner to his chest, holding him in a fiery embrace.

Annie watched the freak show with mounting disbelief. The flaming duo fell to the ground writhing, the SWAT team desperately trying to get a bead on the man who was engulfing their fellow trooper. The old man and the woman were still wrestling, and she had the upper hand, straddling the bum/cop, hands around his throat, yelling and spitting into his face. The guy with the bleeding hand had a bead on her, but obviously wasn't sure whether he could shoot a woman. If he should shoot a woman. Now was the time. This was the window of opportunity; it was small, but it was the best hope she had of wriggling on out.

Annie raised the Ingram and let off a burst at the doorway where the troopers were crouching, sending them scurrying back. At the same time she pushed the girl away, sprawling onto the roadway. Still loosing off quick bursts at the doorway she started to sprint towards the bus, fifteen metres away, maybe a bit more. Another burst. She was going to make it. Another. These were the dangerous guys. Keep their heads down. Another.

Ali raised herself up on her elbows and looked at her scraped hands, white, torn skin flecked with blood. She rolled over and sprung onto her feet, just like when she had been fouled at soccer. No play acting, Mr King always said, just straight back up and into the game. Sporadic bursts of gunfire were flying over her head, and she tried to ignore the screams that were filling the tunnel from behind her. Something else had caught her attention.

The skull was four feet away, still gently rotating where it had come to a stop. Ali thought about all those corners she had practised, all that video footage she had watched from France '98, goalkeeper after goalkeeper, Chilavert, Van der Sar and her hero Kasey Keller, and especially those long, long, impossible throws by Schmeichel that shrunk the pitch, placing the ball way down in the other half. That's the way to do it Mr King always said, even though her own throws seemed pathetic in comparison. But accurate he said, one thing you have Ali, is accuracy. She stepped forward and turned her right arm into the scoop Mr King always badgered her into imagining. Her small hand passed into the cavities of the skull, but she managed to get a purchase as she windmilled it around, past her body and behind her head and felt the muscles pull slightly in her chest as she stretched high and released the head into its journey.

Ali watched the white shape lift, spin eccentrically through the air, wobbling through its trajectory. Impossible to be accurate, she thought, as she saw the skull lose momentum and height, grinning bizarrely, wildly, in the tunnel lights, as if happy to be free at last. Even Peter Schmeichel couldn't be accurate with a pile of cow bones, she tried to console herself.

There was a loud crack as the skeletal projectile landed squarely on the back of the woman's head, shattering as the jawbone tore off and the cranial plates parted in a shower of ancient bone. Ali watched Annie stumble, just like she had, arms splayed, running, trying to keep her balance before she nose-dived into the asphalt and the gun burst from her grip.

Fix raised the pistol, flicked it onto semi-auto. This would be the last time he ever fired it, the last time he ever wanted to see it. He blocked out all the activity around the Major, the sound of the fire being put out, the four shots as they finished off his assailant, the yells as they were prized apart. Nobody was worried about the cop/bum here, they were too busy with their fallen hero.

The big woman was on top of him, her massive breasts jiggling as she throttled him. Fix moved the foresight across her body, down to her thigh. It'll make a mess, he thought, but it was a nice, beefy target. He pulled the trigger, and felt a tear squeeze out of his eye as he heard that soft sound once more.

The tunnel was a mass of flashing lights, blue and orange bouncing off every surface like some crazed subterranean aurora borealis. Police, ambulance, SWOPS, fire, SDS, tunnel maintenance, tunnel security, all brought their own rotating light to the party.

The scene looked flat, two-dimensional, cold to Fix. It was like the biggest drug come-down in the world, he thought, when you realise the world you had was only temporary, and real, boring life sucks you back in. Well, maybe it was. A twenty-five-year come-down. He thought of Dinah. And his father. Was he still alive? He'd be, what? Eighty. Could be. Hell to pay either way.

But one part of him was gone forever. After firing off the shot that incapacitated the she-man, he had taken the pistol and flung it hard, as hard as he could, and he watched it spark and slither into the mouth of the tunnel, swallowed by the darkness where it belonged.

Fix leaned over Willie, who was being stretchered into the ambulance. He looked strained, pale, but the .38 had passed straight through flesh. 'Who needs two kidneys anyway?' he shouted, and beckoned Fix closer. 'When I get out . . . what the fuck do I call you now?'

'Anything but Mr Dodo. Fix. No, Felix.' He tried to say it like a real grown up, but there was jelly inside.

'When I get out –' Willie lowered his voice to a conspiratorial level – 'we'll go and get it, eh? Finish this shit once and for all. Final chapter. Roll credits. We retire rich. I got it figured. Met a guy, knows everything about shipping back MIAs when they turn up. He's in for peanuts. Ten grand.' He laughed. 'We let Uncle Sam bring it back for us. What do you think?'

Fix squeezed his arm. 'Sure thing. One last pop for the Underdogs.'

'Yeah. You did OK in the end.'

'In the end.'

There was a pause and Felix said: 'Hey, you think this suit is bad? I told my wife to get a seersucker suit from Cox's . . . so she goes to Sears and gets a . . .' He let it hang in the air.

'Fuck it, man,' gasped Willie with a pained grimace. 'They haven't got any better, have they?'

The last to arrive were Tenniel, and Bowman with Dinah and Ali's mother in the squad car. Tenniel took in the scene with his usual snap-shot images. Except this time it looked like the cast of The Munsters were being tended to. Two body bags; the stretchered form of a woman, thigh tightly bandaged, emergency drip in her arm. Cuffed to the stretcher, he noticed. A female prisoner was also secured, this time to an officer, awaiting transfer downtown by the look of it, red-eyed and bedraggled, she had been crying. He took a second look. It was Annie Haart, Tricky Ricky's squeeze. He had known when Ricky went down that she had more on her plate than nail extensions. Well, there would be an interesting story there all right.

Against one wall, an old bum and the young girl were on the bench, both looking phased, twitchy, keen to be elsewhere. He did a double-take and realised the bum had on what had once been a police uniform. A couple of medics were attending to their cuts and bruises, so he decided the obvious question could wait a minute or two.

SWOPS soldiers milled around, smoking, vaguely disgruntled, cheated. One of them was sitting down having the final touches done to a balaclava of gauze. His hands were blistered and burnt, the Nomex overalls charred black – it looked like they saved him from something pretty fierce. Then Tenniel clocked the name badge. Milliner. Jesus, Milliner, it just wasn't his night.

He watched Dinah move towards Lewis, circling, waiting for him to finish with Willie. She was unsure, he could tell; she kept saying in the car she wouldn't even know what to call him now. One of the uniforms tried to explain what had happened here, but he wasn't fully listening, because Milliner slowly got up and walked over towards him, the blistered lips moving in the hole they had cut for the mouth, like a couple of fried earthworms trying to mate. 'What the hell were you thinking about? Sending two rank amateurs—'

Tenniel looked at him, scarred and burnt and angry, skin flaking off his lips as he spoke. Some kind of trauma, most likely. Go easy. More shocks to come. 'One of whom had experience of tunnel combat.'

Milliner rose up to look Tenniel full in the face. 'He was a civilian. Who could have been killed. I heard you lost one man—'

'In an accident. Same one as you. The explosion. Hurt, not dead.' Tenniel hated himself, but he knew he was rehearsing his lines for the board of enquiry. He could worry about Harry later. 'And let's not forget this – we got the girl out safe. And the father is alive. For the moment. So it isn't a bad score.' But the score would have been better with proper back-up, he thought.

'And how much do you think the bill will be to repair the damage after that explosion?'

'Probably a lot more than if someone had taken the care to build the city properly in the first place. Anyway, it's been a bad day for us all, Major.' He glanced over as Dinah and Lewis walked towards each other. He didn't want to hear what was going to be said there. She had told him some very strange story in the car. Very strange.

'Meaning?'

'Meaning we just got a call from Spokane. There was a gas attack through the sewers. Bombs wired to gas canisters under the manhole covers, all simultaneously detonated. They wanted you to go back—' He waved at the Major's face. 'But now your inj—'

'Go back to what? What are you talking about? We offered our help. I'm not answerable to them.'

'Major, we are all answerable to someone. FBI, Secret Service.' He tried to put some reason into his voice. 'Right now, they're looking for someone to blame. And maybe your Bomb Squad guys screwed up. Maybe you were meant to look under the ground as well as on top. I don't know. But they'll want someone to blame. And you weren't there, were you?' Time to tell him straight. 'This time next month, my guess is we'll have the SERT back at full strength with the Seattle PD. Like Whidbey never happened. No SWOPS, no personal vendettas being waged. For better or worse, back to one Police Force. You got any hobbies, Major Milliner?'

Milliner clenched his jaw and winced. Let him be bitter. A sergeant at his age. Pathetic. One of the paramedics put an arm lightly on his shoulder, trying to direct him to an ambulance. Milliner shrugged it off and pointed over to where the old man and the girl were sitting.

'I want that man arrested,' demanded Milliner. 'Damned medics over there wouldn't let me put him in cuffs. Treating him like some kind of hero. I want him arrested.'

Tenniel followed the arm. The two paramedics were gently cleaning the dust and dirt off Ali's face. They hadn't touched the grubby cop. Some kind of acetylene torch would probably be needed to shift his accumulated grime. Tenniel felt a spasm in his throat as the girl stood up to embrace her mother and swallowed hard. He thought of his own daughter at that age, felt a sudden hit of affection, his eyes stinging a little. So what was a little body piercing?

The girl and the mother moved aside, four tracks of tears trickling down their faces. Tenniel walked slowly over to the hunched figure on the bench. He could hear the girl saying to her mother: 'He's alive? You sure? ALIVE?' And she burst out crying again. Relief, probably.

'Who, exactly, are you?' he asked the Captain.

The wrinkled, grimy face looked up at his, held his gaze. 'Me? I'm nobody. I just . . . I was just . . . caught in the crossfire.'

He remembered what the uniform had been telling him about the confrontation. 'I hear you done good.'

The man shrugged. 'It was a promise.'

'A promise?'

'To the . . . guy who was with her. I promised I'd save her if I could. Even if it meant coming up top.'

'What's your name?'

He hesitated. It was a long time since he had told anyone his real, given name. 'Everybody calls me the Cap . . . Allis. Christopher Allis. Chris, I think it was. But you won't find it on any records, Officer. No rap sheets. I ain't even got a social security number. Can I go?'

'A guy comes out of the ground with a police uniform on—' Tenniel suddenly remembered the Man With The Plans. Surely not? 'We got some questions.'

'Like what?'

'Like what you were up to between 1982 and 1984. Little things like that.'

'Can we cut a deal?'

'Well, that's down to the DA's office . . . but we would be looking for a full statement and confession. I'll read you your rights—'

'He was called Sammy Napoleon Wilson.'

'Who was?'

'The man I think you are talking about.'

'Napoleon?'

'I always asked him how he got that name. He told me he would tell me before he died. He didn't, though.'

'He died?' Tenniel was trying hard to follow this.

'He used to borrow my uniforms, sometimes, to go up top. Said it was easier to move around. And he was right. But once it came back covered in blood. He had tried to clean it up. Wouldn't talk about it. And then I read a report about the case in the Seattle Times . . . we are talking about the Green River guy?'

Tenniel nodded.

'I . . . I . . . well, he told me. Promised he would stop

doing it. You have to understand, there is a diff . . . it's different, there's a code. You mind your own business, you don't go up and snitch. I made him promise to stop. He did. But one day, when they was building the tunnels he came to me and asked if he could borrow a uniform again. So I said, sure, but have some coffee, and I put a sedative in. All kinds of stuff in my room, easy to knock him out. I . . . I took him to one of the shelters, pinned a note to him, saying check this guy out, I think he's bad news. I knew security would find him. It was breaking the code really but . . . all those women, you know?'

'And?'

'And they came along and torched the place. Old Red . . . the one over there –' he indicated one of the black body bags – 'tried to get him out, was badly burned. It was crazy. We knew who did it. Him.' His head motioned towards Milliner. 'I guess old Red flipped when he saw the flame-thrower. Maybe he even recognised the guy, even with his face like that. But Sammy . . . even if he was guilty as hell, he deserved a trial, didn't he? Didn't he?'

'I guess he did,' said Tenniel slowly. And maybe the guy just had a rich fantasy life. Seemed to go with the territory down there. 'You did the bus painting?'

'Had to. Man was crazy. Using a flame-thrower. Even before we knew about the gas, it was . . . inhuman. Mad as a hatter. Lucky we didn't all go up then, eh?'

Why did Tenniel believe him? Because of the way he came to save the girl? Or because his cop instincts told him this guy didn't kill women slowly to watch them die, to enjoy their struggles. But the GRK, he had to be clever, be convincing, didn't he? No, not like this. This old guy certainly smelt, but he didn't smell right as a serial killer.

'Sammy Napoleon Wilson?'

'Yup. Look him up. He had previous.'

'I will, I will. But do you have proof?'

The Captain shrugged. 'Look. Officer, I have people. I ain't that hard to find. You need me, I'll be there. But I got people, people who rely on me down there. You know that feeling, eh?'

No, he wasn't sure he did, wasn't certain Seattle needed him at all after tonight.

'How do you get from here back to wherever you came from?'

'There is another access hatch just over there.'

'Over there? At ground level?'

'Yeah.'

Tenniel didn't actually ask the next question, but the man nodded and said: 'Yeah' again.

Tenniel looked around to make sure nobody was paying them much attention, but even Milliner was distracted with the thought of having to return to Spokane. Well, might as well finish off the day with another dubious decision. Get himself a full suit of rotten cards to play at the inquiry. 'How about you go along and see if it works. I'll be right behind you.' And he turned his back before the Captain could say anything.

Bowman saw Tenniel break away from the conversation with the bum, dug in her pocket and came up with a piece of paper. 'Sorry. Forgot. Came in while I was in the car. From your wife. She said Buffalo had gone missing.'

Shit, what was that? Nineteen? Then it hit him. 'You spoke to her?'

'They patched her through. She seemed . . . very nice, John.' He searched her face for sarcasm, but couldn't detect any.

Tenniel nodded. Her speech betrayed how tired she was, like she didn't have the energy to form the links between the phrases. She still looked pretty good though. Or would when her hair grew out a tad. Best not think like that. He knew he had some explaining to do back at home as it was. 'You working tomorrow?'

'Uh-uh. Welcome to the weekend for me. Why, what have you got in mind?'

'Me? I'm flying up to the islands with Catherine. We got a boat to look at. You know, to lease. Maybe.'

'Oh. Well, that's . . . nice. Why did you ask?'

He held up the crumpled note. 'Buffalo. It's my dog. A Lab. Old Girdlestone and his missing dogs. It's earthquakes.' He explained that the last big rattle on June 23, 1997 – 4.9 on the Richter scale – had been predicted by a Californian who used the moon and tide tables, but mainly the number of missing dog ads in the local newspapers.

'Gimme a break, Tenniel. The dogs know when there is a quake coming?'

'I know, I know. But we got a lot more pooches on the lam than they had before the '97 one. Girdlestone says this guy has always been right on the money every other time. And if it is proportional, then it'll make this lot –' he swung an arm across the scene – 'look like *hors d'oevres*. And you don't want to be downtown when it hits.'

She knew what he meant. The laughingly named

Public Safety Building on Third where West Precinct were based was designed to 'umbrella' around the lift shaft, partially collapsing each floor. Which is why they kept a spare dispatch system in the fire station in North Precinct. Just in case the Big One ever came.

'Well, I wonder what Girdlestone is up to?' she asked provocatively.

'He'll be off somewhere, trust me. He believes it. And he's got leave due. Ask him for a ride. He isn't seeing that woman from Community Policing any more.' She could do worse than Girdlestone, as long as she got to like sports. He thought about her put-down of him earlier. 'Careful he doesn't try and read your bra label.'

'Yeah, well, it's so long since I had any kind of action like that mine says: It's too late to stop now.'

There was a sharp pang in his guts which he quickly suppressed. It was better this way. He had looked into the black hole and knew where it led. He should sign on that boat. Get his brushes out. Get busy. Catherine would like that. Maybe the kids might come for once. He wondered if he could join Knight and take the early retirement cheque?

Their conversation, already faltering, came to a halt when Felix shuffled over with Dinah. Her eyes, too, were leaking fluid, but she was fighting it back, trying to be in control. She flashed a look at the little girl. Truth was, Tenniel reckoned, right now, she wanted her mom too.

Felix looked grim-faced, tired, looked in fact like a man nearing the end of his fifth decade on the planet. There wasn't much to say. Felix tried the direct approach. 'I'm . . . I'm sorry about Harry. I let you down.'

Tenniel unwrapped a stick of gum and folded it into his mouth. He watched Isa climb into the car and throw her head back, staring at the roof lining. Just tired, he thought. She's just tired. He turned back to whatever-his-name was. Just goes to show, you never knew who you got to play racquetball with these days. 'Yes, you did, Carl. Yes, you did.'

The sun was climbing over the jagged profile of the Cascades when they reached the apartment. The shadows of downtown stretched across over the water of Elliott Bay, rippling in the breeze. The glow made it look like a city of sandstone, not harsh steel and concrete. A pink city. Even the Needle looked like it was a thousand years old, as if it had been weathered into its flying-saucer-on-a-stick form. To its left he could see the artfully crumpled form of the latest edition to the complex, Gehry's Music Experience Museum. Really a homage to Hendrix by Microsoft's Paul Allen. He hadn't listened to Hendrix in an age, not since . . . well, the Bat, he used to play it. Voodoo Chile. Machine Gun. How would he feel going in there, into that museum now?

They hadn't said much on the journey back. He had filled in the gaps that Willie had left or didn't know. She couldn't offer much. She thought she knew him, now she didn't. Just like when you find out the other one has been unfaithful. You go back and at first stub your toes on all the little deceits and lies, which build up and up until you finally crack your head on the great beam of the elaborate, continuous, cowardly deception.

And just like then, she wasn't sure whether they could pick up the pieces. Might know tomorrow, next week, next year. But for the moment, she couldn't say. All bets were off. She wanted to hear the full story from beginning to end from him first. And then an explanation as to why he felt he had to go through such a ridiculous charade.

She had already tried asking him the last bit. He had just shrugged. At the time it seemed the only choice – it was that or swallow the bullet. Now he knew he could have got over it. Now. But he didn't have anyone like her back then to let him know that.

They parked outside the apartment, and he watched their two shadows merge and separate as they walked across the frontage. Just like him and Lewis over the years, merged and separated. And now only one was left. Trouble is, he wasn't sure which one. After all these years, how much of Lewis's character had become a real part of him, and how much was still an artificial graft? They would have to work that out. At least, he would.

'Mel Gibson,' she said suddenly.

'What about him?'

'He's Australian, isn't he?'

He nodded, and she shrugged. 'Well, I like him.'

'It's a start, I suppose. Listen, I got to go away,' he blurted.

Her heart sank. He wasn't even going to try.

'Vancouver.'

'Who as this time?'

'As me. I'll be back.'

'Oh yeah?'

It was a ridiculous thought, but already he could feel the uncertainty eating into him. He had to know if what he felt down there had been true. But as the daylight got stronger, so his conviction ebbed and it seemed more and more unlikely. But he had to do this.

'I want to see Harry's father-in-law. Just to be sure.'

'Sure of what?'

'Sure it is worth Willie going back. I'll explain later, when I can think straight.' He laughed, a hollow, weak sound. 'Which will be a first in itself for a while.'

In the foyer Dinah instinctively went for the stairs to accompany him up. Dinah had her foot on the first step, looking at him. He was outside the steel doors, a hand raised. Just briefly it was one of those frozen moments, before time snapped free to normal speed again and a great weight of fatigue descended on them. He pressed the button. 'Fuck it, let's take the elevator.'

UNDERDOGS

Author's Note: I have played around with the geography of Seattle somewhat – there is no Henry Street between Pine and Pike, for instance, and at the time of writing the Kingdome still awaits demolition – but the destruction of the city by fire and its eventual rebuilding one storey up is true, although most of this happened to the east of where *Underdogs'* action takes place. The cesspit and the street paralleling the monorail is, I am afraid, all mine. Seattle, however, *is* prone to earthquakes, and there was one in June 1997, while Hillary Clinton was in town, although the First Lady claimed she did not feel the earth move.

I am indebted to Officer Christie-Lynne Bonner of the Seattle PD for explaining the organisation and mechanics of the Seattle PD. For those who want to see what the real Underworld looks like, there is a tour that leaves from Doc Maynard's pub in Pioneer Square. It, in fact, takes in a tiny percentage of what is under the old downtown, and is probably best avoided if you are sensitive to tales of corruption, sewage and whores or come from Tacoma.

For the genuine story of the tunnel rats there is no better book than *The Tunnels of Cu Chi* by Tom Mangold and John Penycate. The gold incident here was suggested by a true story told in that book. And if you really want to know what it is like to be shot at in the flying bag of bolts that is a Huey, try *Chickenhawk* by Robert Mason. Inspiration and procedural information was also drawn from Mark Baker's *Cops and Bad Guys*; Connie Fletcher's *Breaking and Entering* and Peter A Micheels' *The Detectives*, all riveting accounts of police life in the big city. The SWOPS were armed up thanks to *Weapons and Equipment of Counter-Terrorism*, by Michael Dewar, *Delta-America's Elite Counterterrorist Force* by Terry Griswold and D.M. Giangreco, *Twilight Warriors* by Martin C Arostegui and *Special Warfare, Special Weapons* by Kevin Dockery.

I am indebted to Rick Young, author of Combat Police, who served as an MP in Vietnam and is now a Senior Special Agent with the Federal government – a man who has walked the walk, talked the talk and can tell a Sig from a Glock at a hundred yards – for reading and being so enthusiastic about the book.

There is a whole cast of characters to thank for helping either me or the book, but the core, in order of appearance, is: Deborah Ryan, Jonathan Futrell, Dylan Jones, Martin Beiser, Christine Walker, Peter Howarth and Laurie Evans, with special mentions to David Miller and Bill Massey.

Rob Ryan